Wonder Cat Kyuu-chan 2

Story & Art by **Sasami Nitori**

Wonder Cat Kyuu-chan

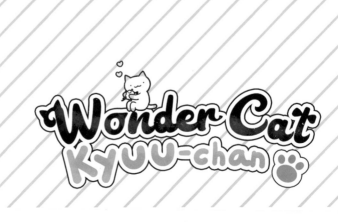

HERE

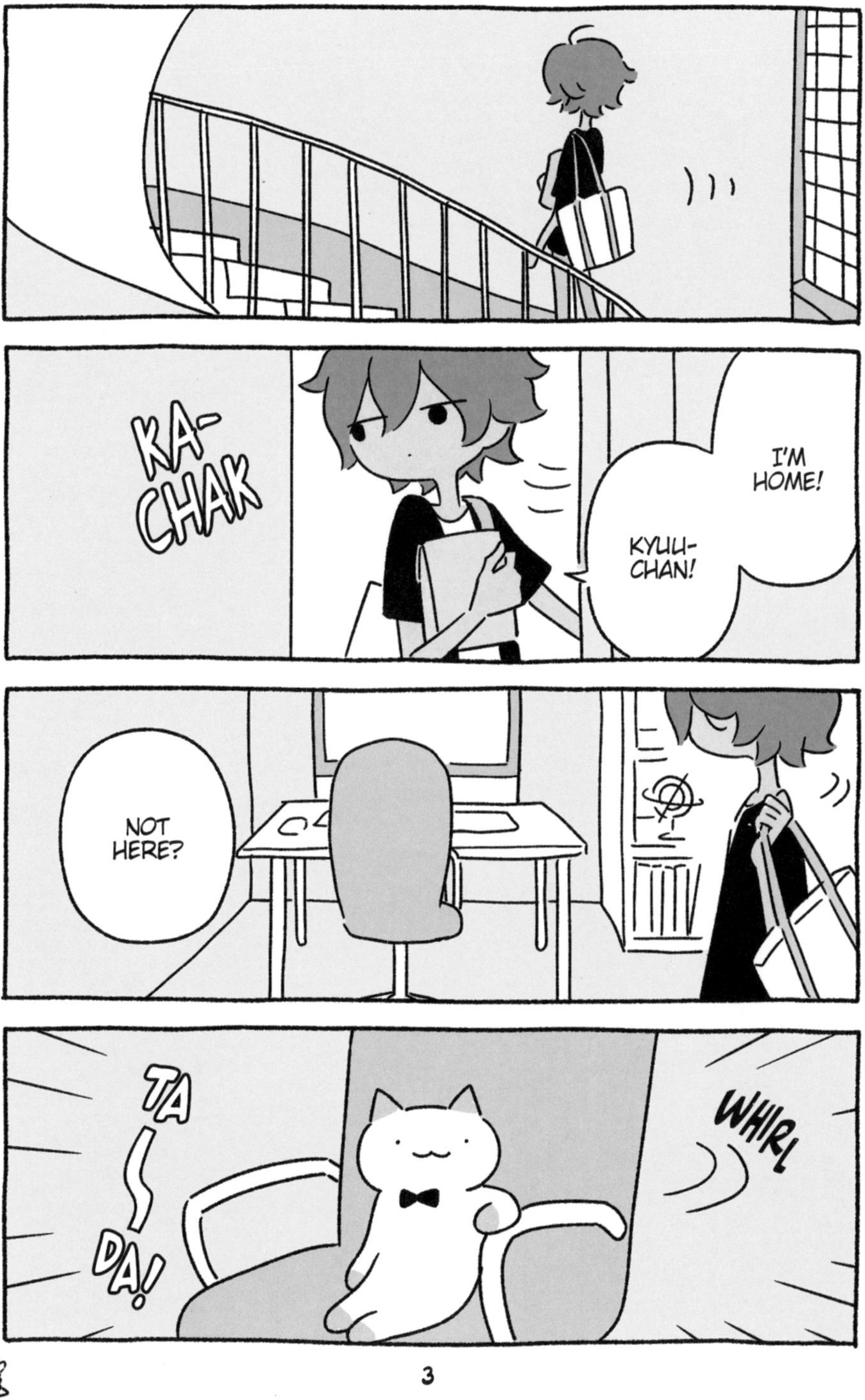

I'M HOME!
KYUU-CHAN!
KA-CHAK
NOT HERE?
WHIRL
TA~DA!

BAG

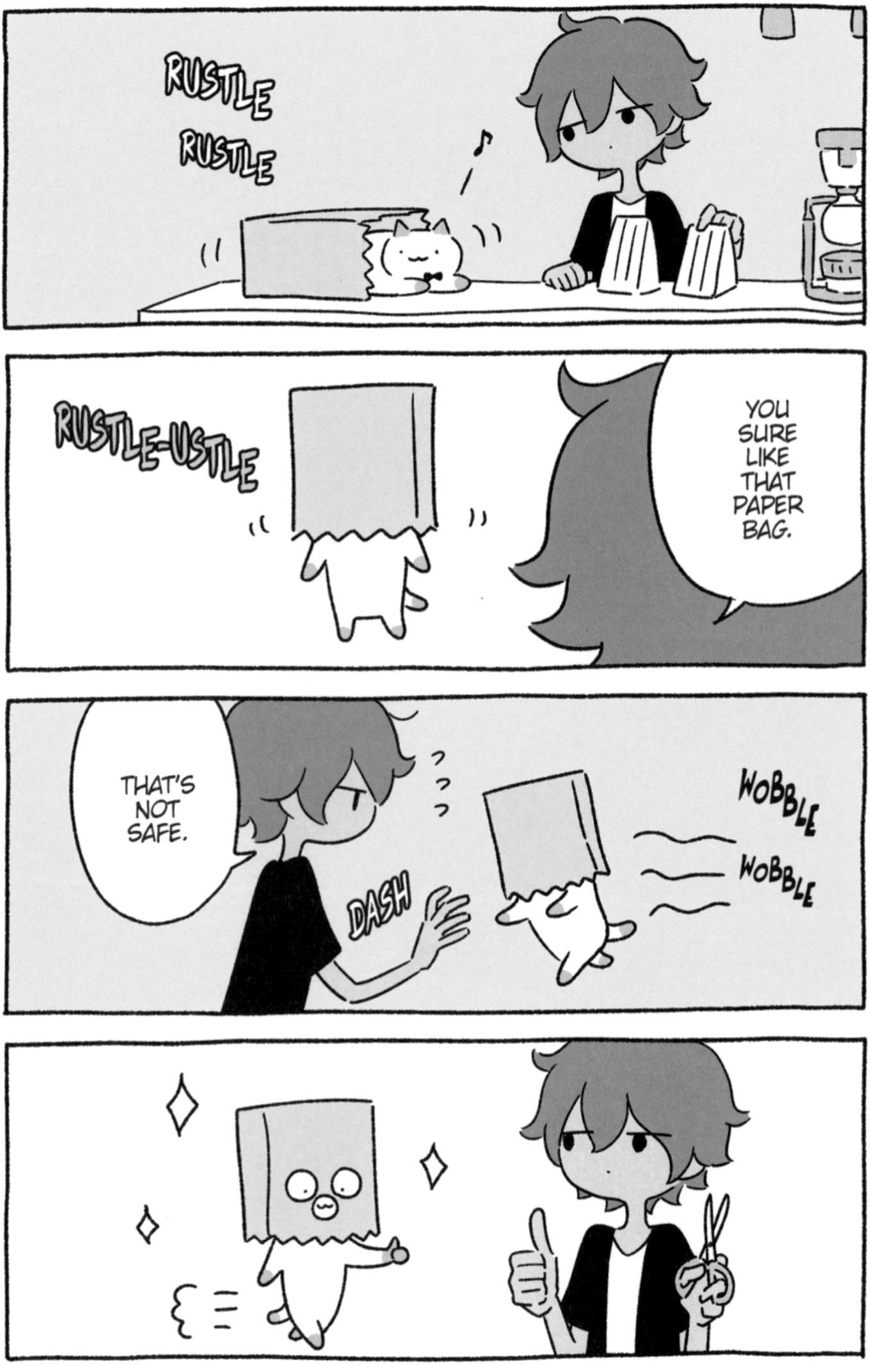
RUSTLE
RUSTLE
YOU SURE LIKE THAT PAPER BAG.
RUSTLE-USTLE
WOBBLE
WOBBLE
THAT'S NOT SAFE.
DASH

STICKERS ①

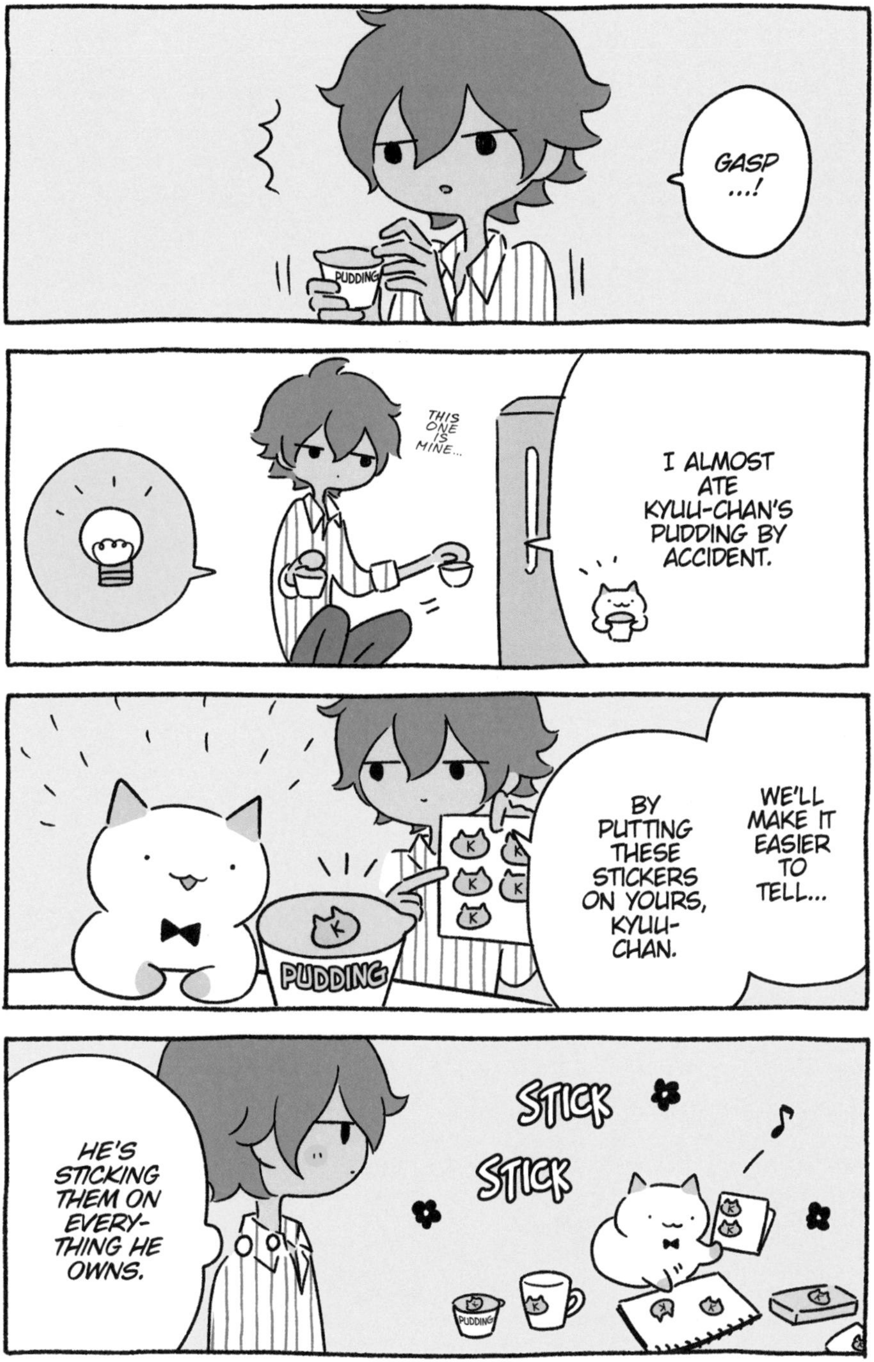
GASP ...!
PUDDING
I ALMOST ATE KYUU-CHAN'S PUDDING BY ACCIDENT.
THIS ONE IS MINE...
WE'LL MAKE IT EASIER TO TELL...
BY PUTTING THESE STICKERS ON YOURS, KYUU-CHAN.
PUDDING
STICK
STICK
HE'S STICKING THEM ON EVERY-THING HE OWNS.
PUDDING

STICKERS ②

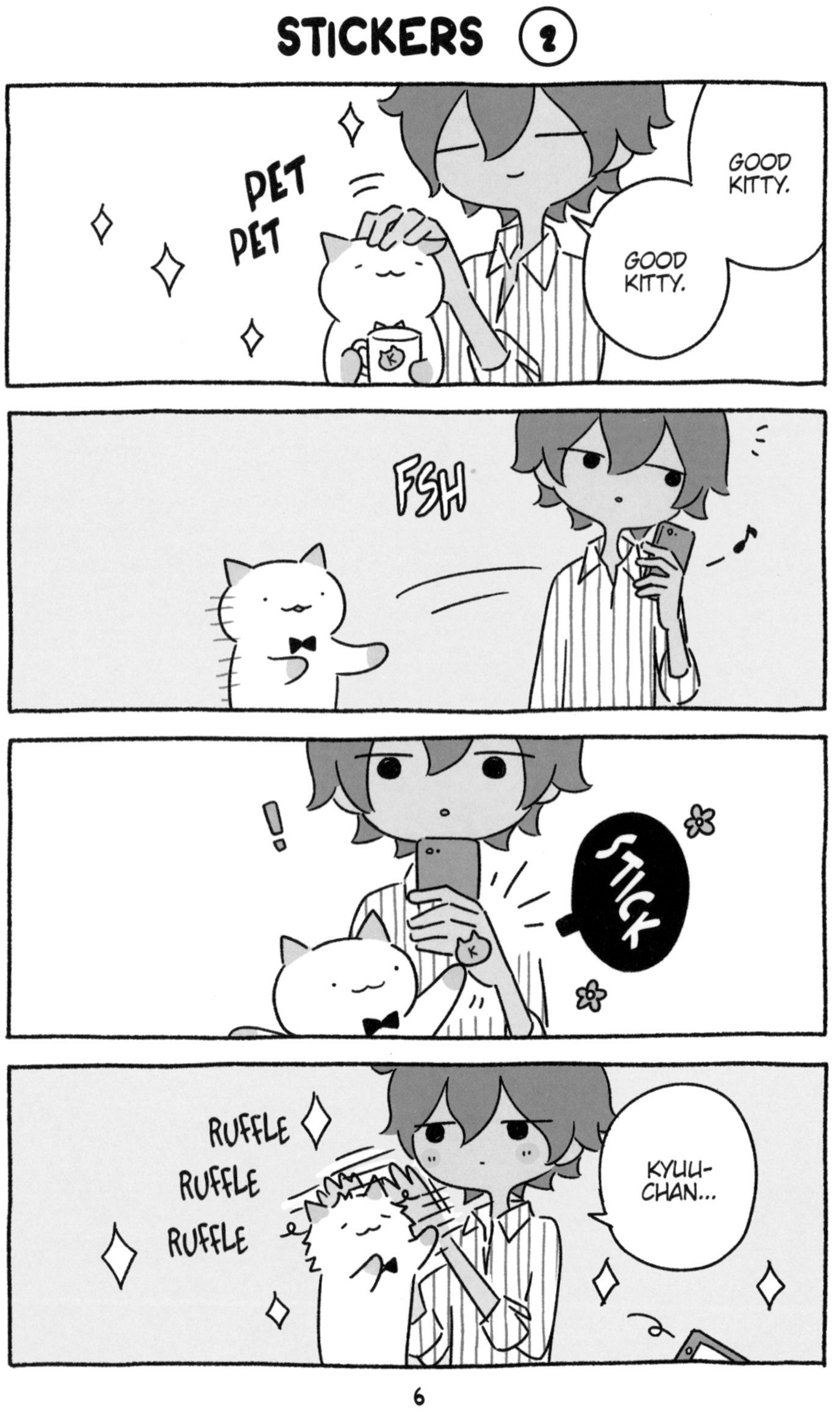
GOOD KITTY.
GOOD KITTY.
PET
PET
FSH
STICK
!
KYUU-CHAN...
RUFFLE
RUFFLE
RUFFLE

FASHION SHOW

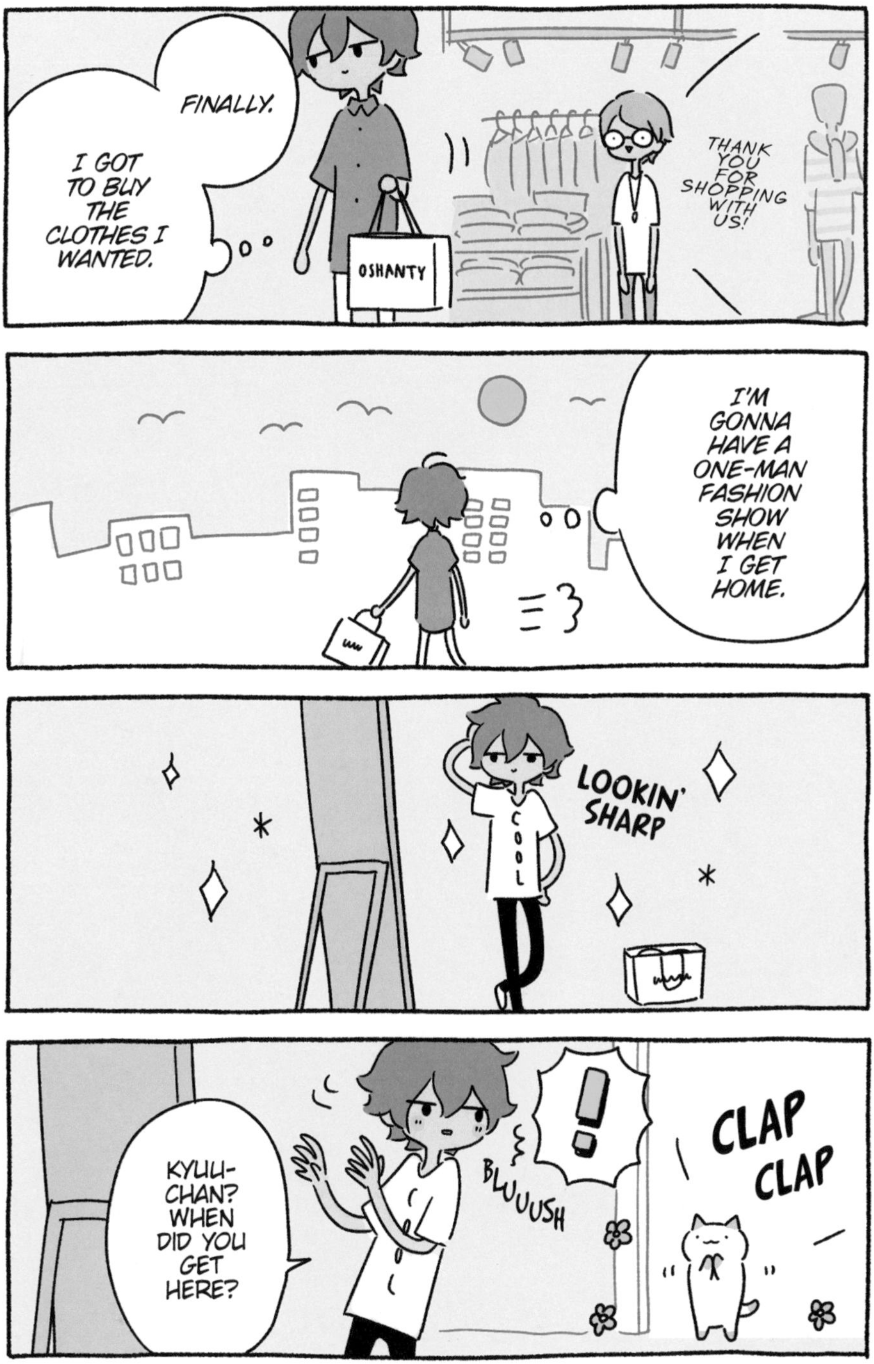
THANK YOU FOR SHOPPING WITH US!
OSHANTY
FINALLY.
I GOT TO BUY THE CLOTHES I WANTED.
I'M GONNA HAVE A ONE-MAN FASHION SHOW WHEN I GET HOME.
LOOKIN' SHARP
COOL
CLAP CLAP
!
BLUUUSH
KYUU-CHAN? WHEN DID YOU GET HERE?

I WANNA BE LIKE YOU

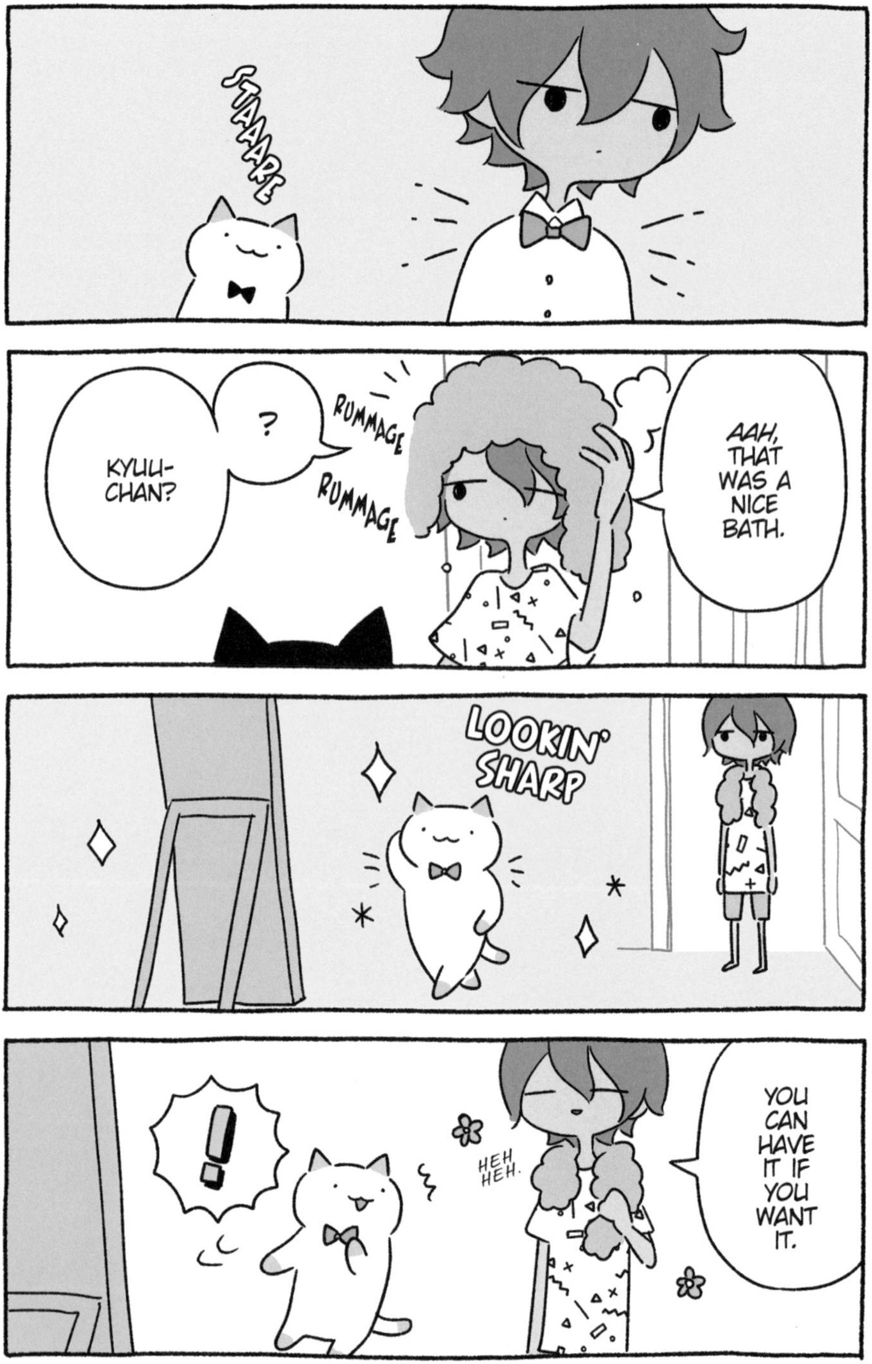
STAAARE
AAH, THAT WAS A NICE BATH.
RUMMAGE
?
RUMMAGE
KYUU-CHAN?
LOOKIN' SHARP
YOU CAN HAVE IT IF YOU WANT IT.
HEH HEH.
!

HAT

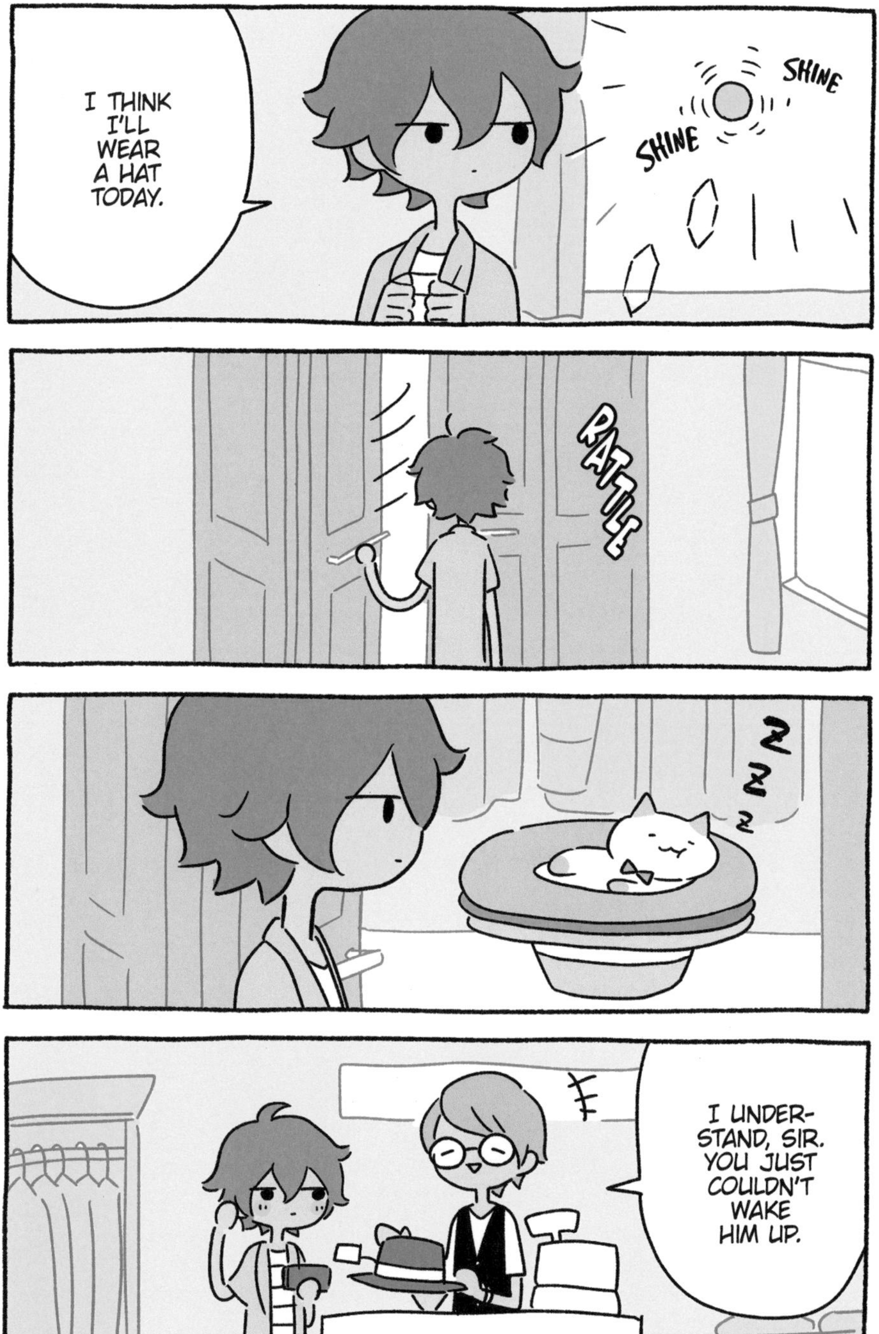
SHINE
SHINE
I THINK I'LL WEAR A HAT TODAY.
RATTLE
Z Z Z
I UNDER-STAND, SIR. YOU JUST COULDN'T WAKE HIM UP.

BEGGING FOR ATTENTION

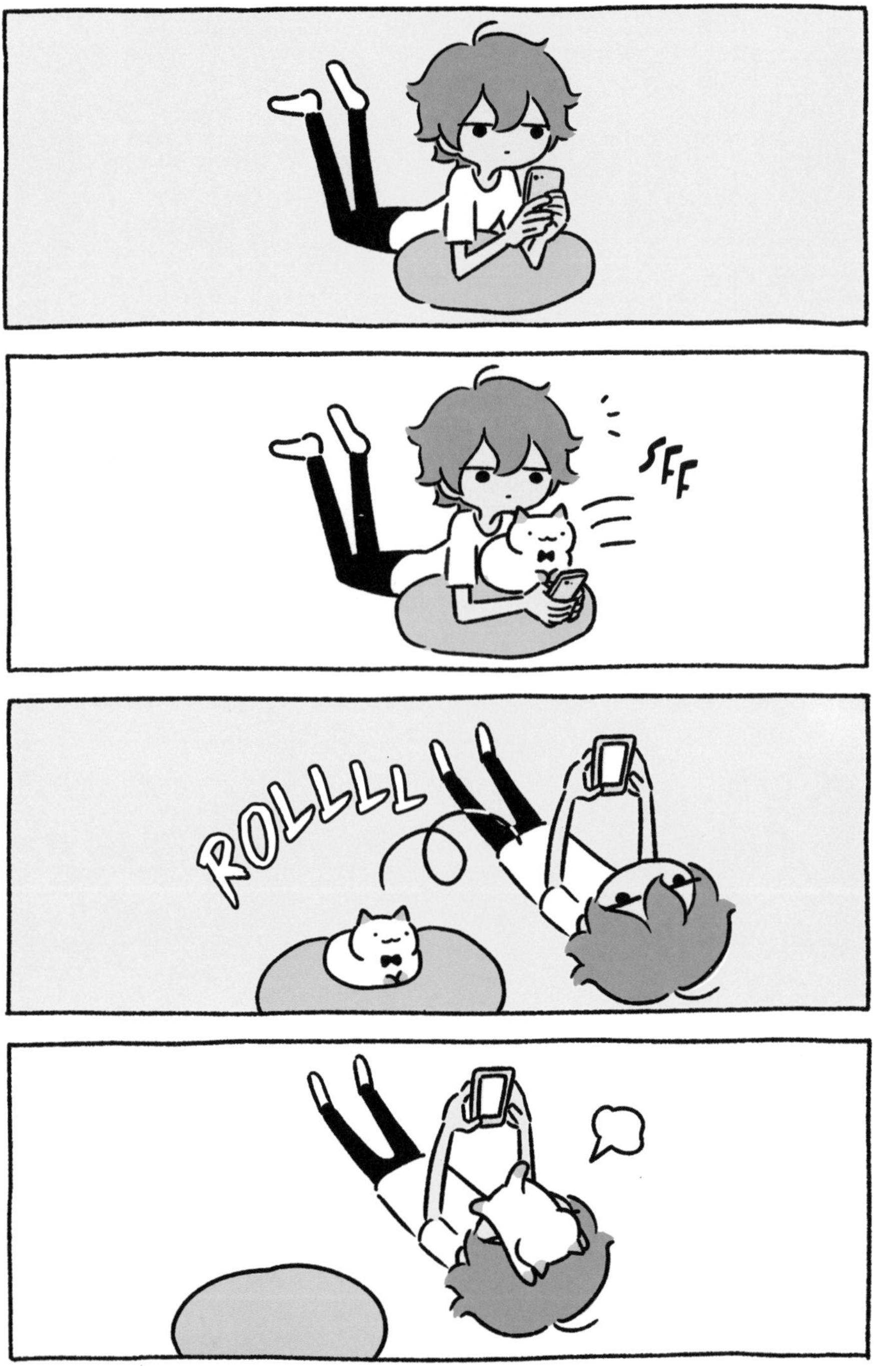
SFF
ROLLLL

E-MAIL

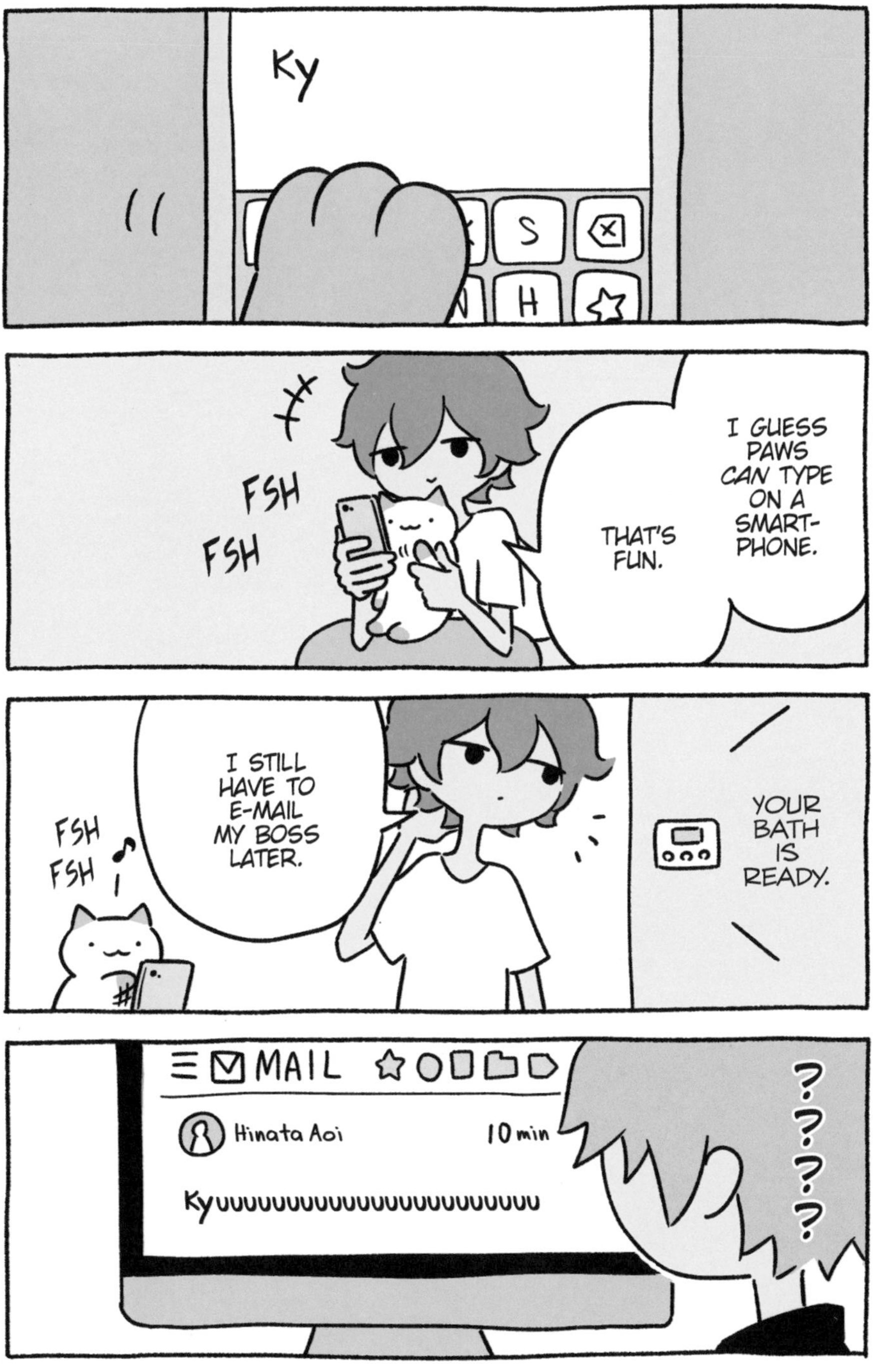

Ky
S
H
I GUESS PAWS CAN TYPE ON A SMARTPHONE.
THAT'S FUN.
FSH
FSH
YOUR BATH IS READY.
I STILL HAVE TO E-MAIL MY BOSS LATER.
FSH
FSH
MAIL
Hinata Aoi
10 min
Kyuuuuuuuuuuuuuuuuuu
??????

WAKING UP

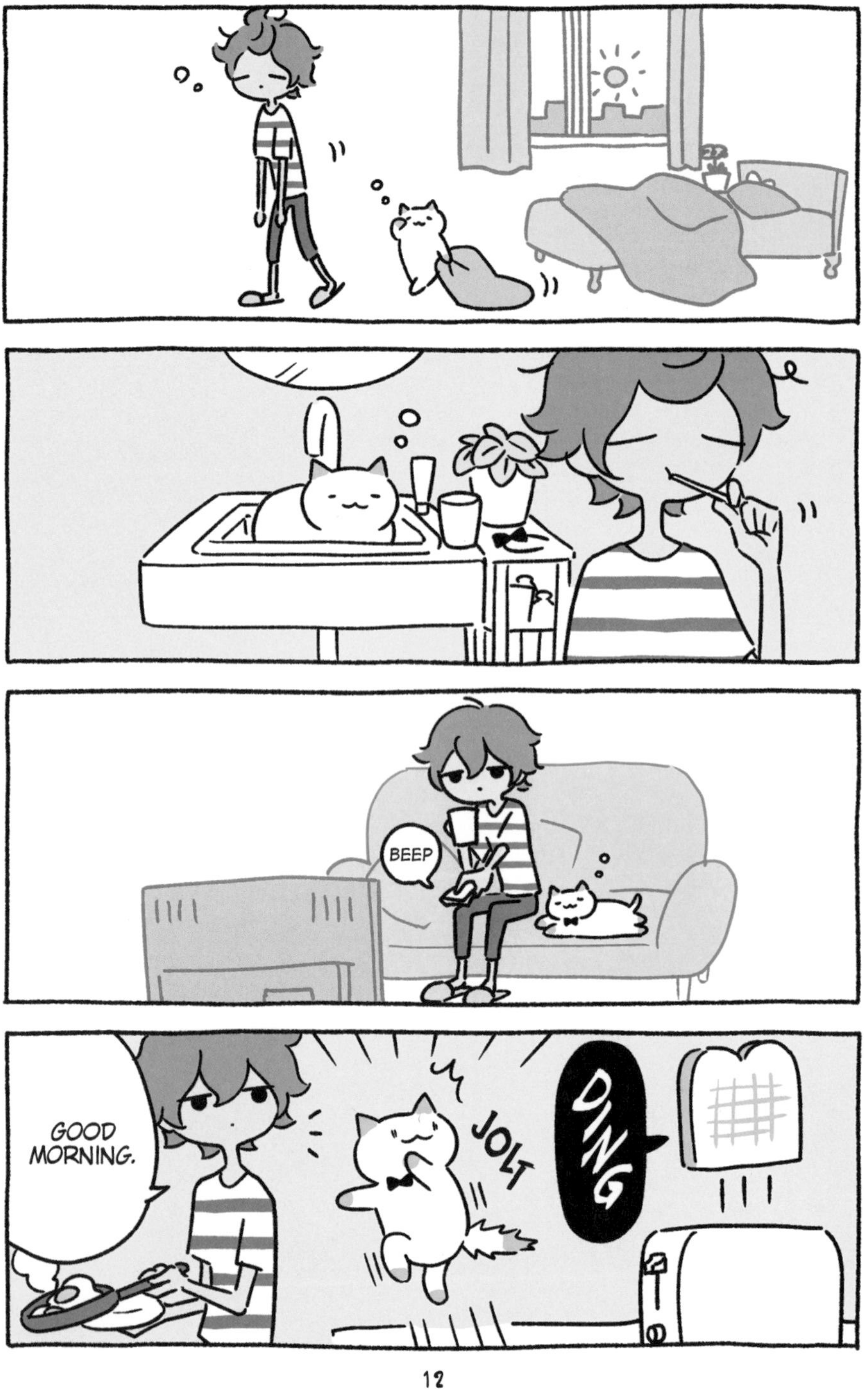
BEEP
DING
JOLT
GOOD MORNING.

CHOICES

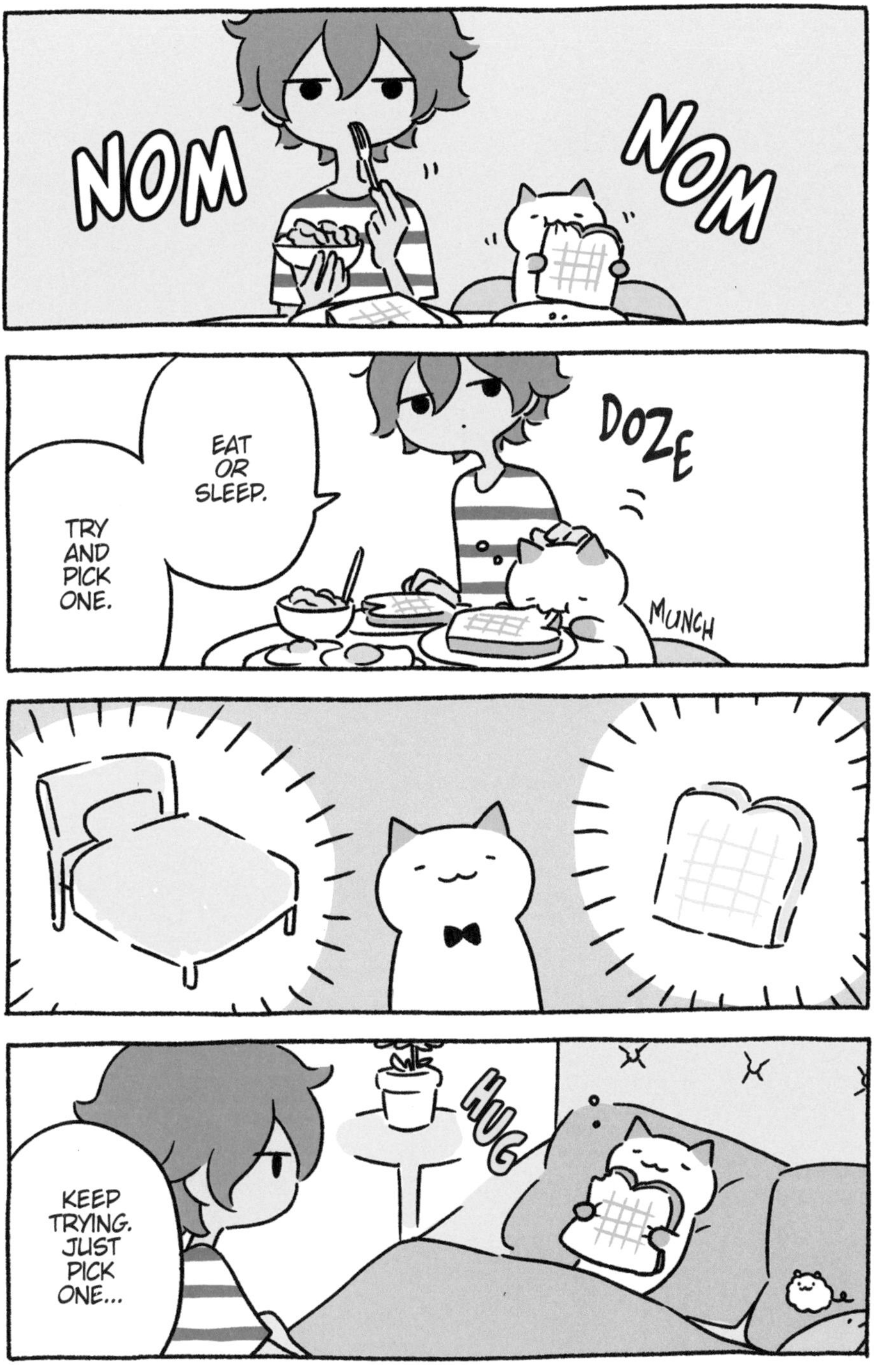
NOM
NOM
DOZE
MUNCH
EAT OR SLEEP.
TRY AND PICK ONE.
HUG
KEEP TRYING. JUST PICK ONE...

JAR LID

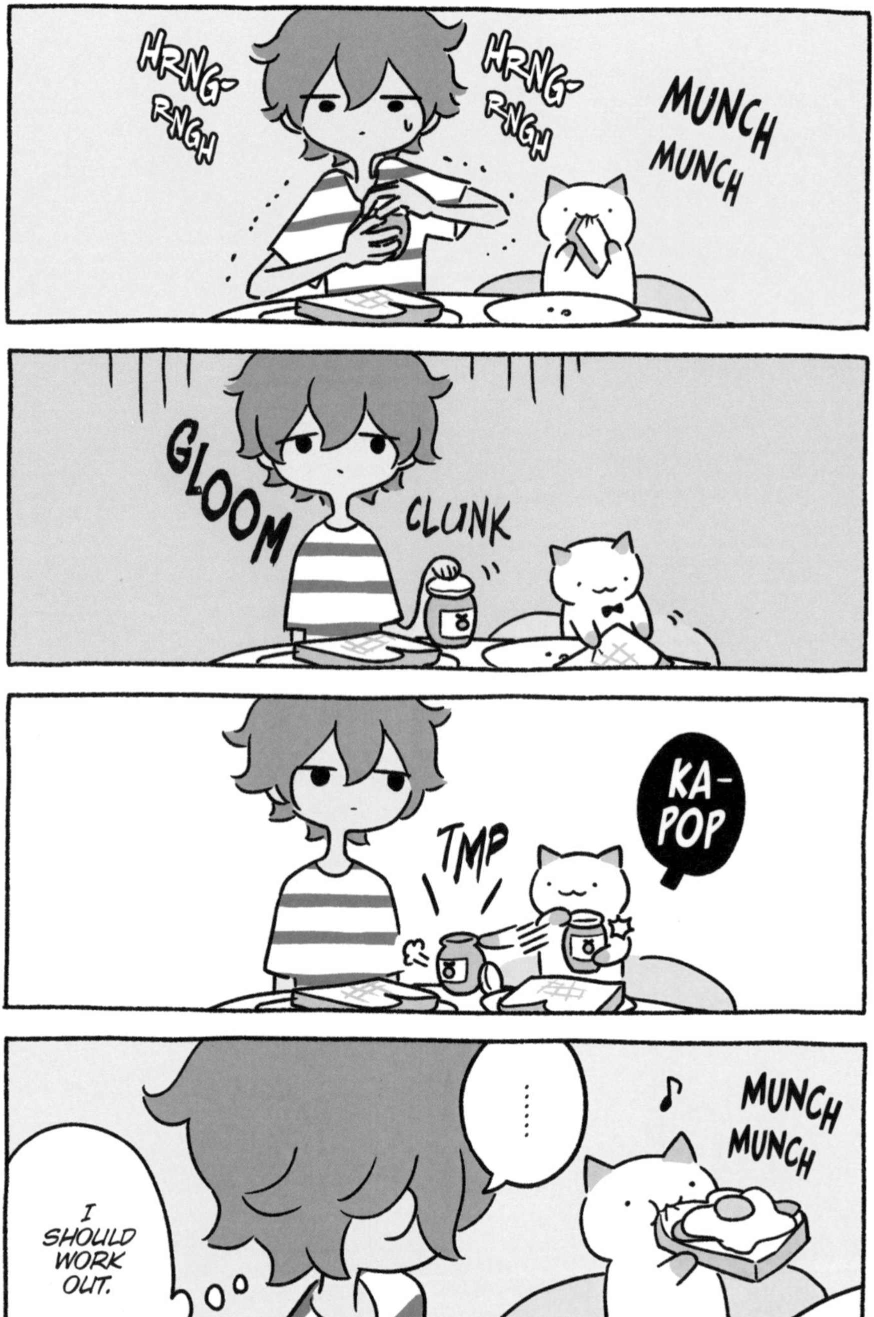
MUNCH MUNCH
HRNG-RNGH
HRNG-RNGH
CLUNK
GLOOM
KA-POP
TMP
MUNCH MUNCH
......
I SHOULD WORK OUT.

A-KYUUT ATTRACTION

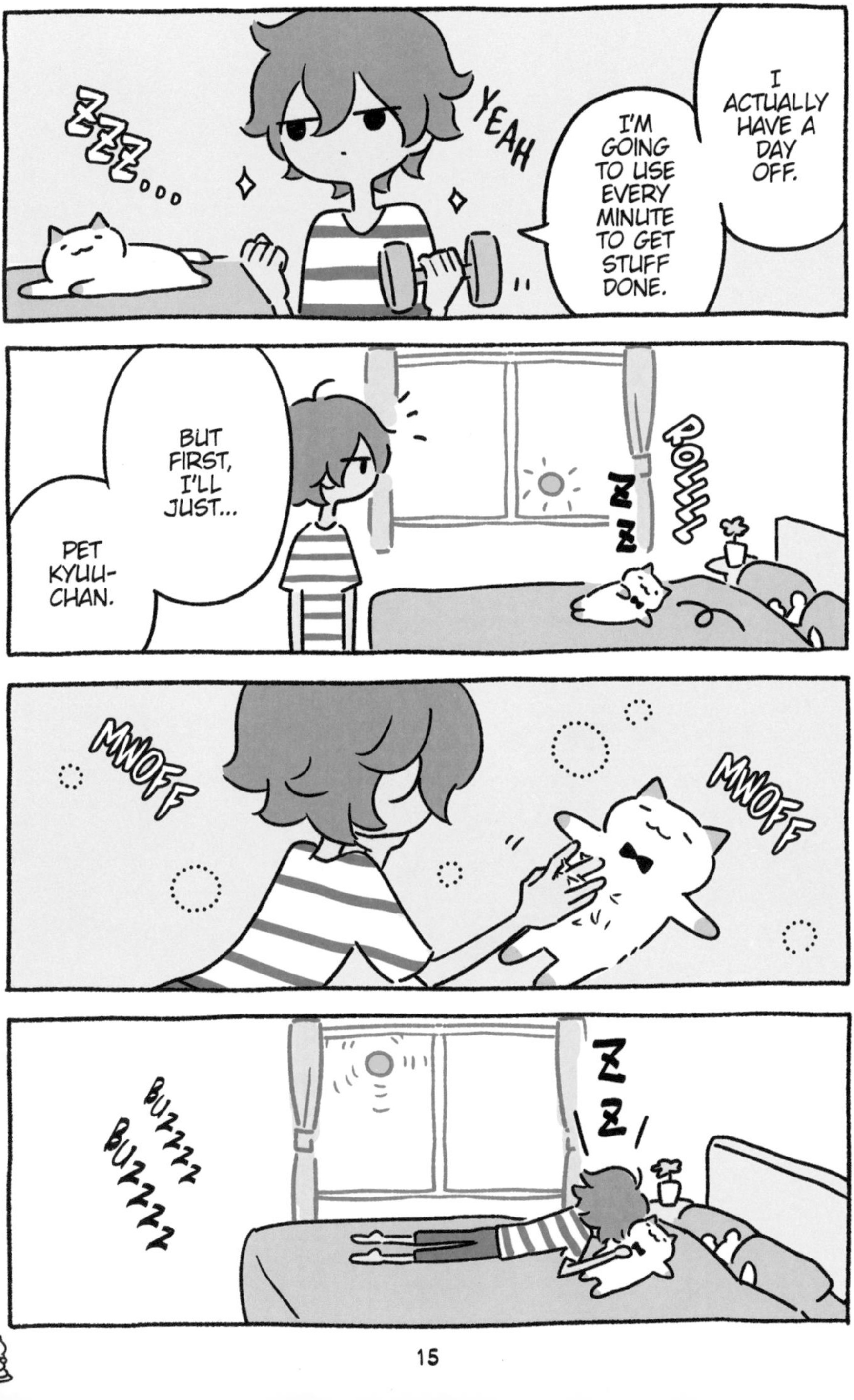
I ACTUALLY HAVE A DAY OFF.
I'M GOING TO USE EVERY MINUTE TO GET STUFF DONE.
YEAH
ZZZ...
ROLLL
ZZ
BUT FIRST, I'LL JUST...
PET KYUU-CHAN.
MWOFF
MWOFF
ZZ
BUZZZZ
BUZZZZ

ESCAPING THE HEAT

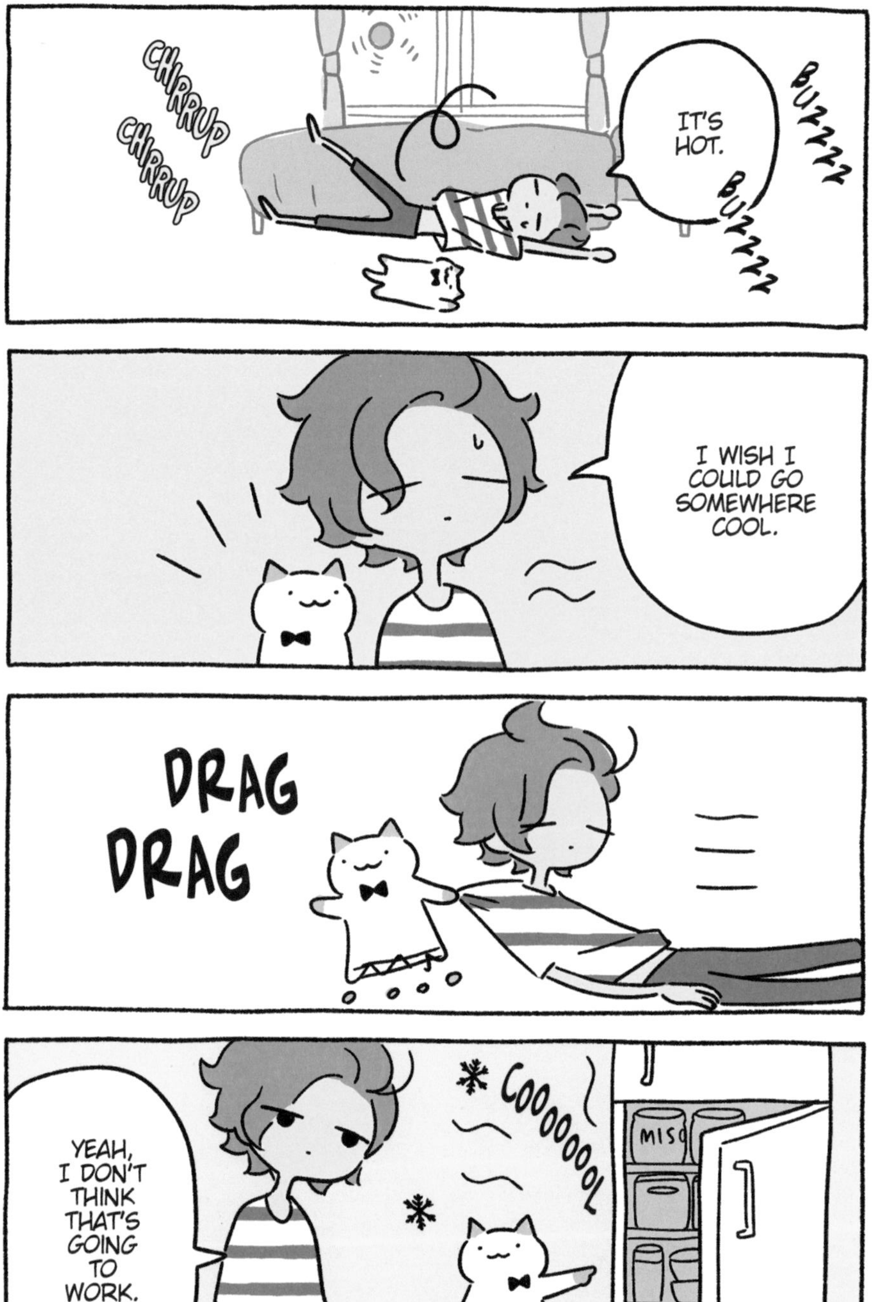
BUZZZZ
IT'S HOT.
BUZZZZZ
CHIRRUP
CHIRRUP
I WISH I COULD GO SOMEWHERE COOL.
DRAG DRAG
COOOOOOOL
MISO
YEAH, I DON'T THINK THAT'S GOING TO WORK.

GUIDE

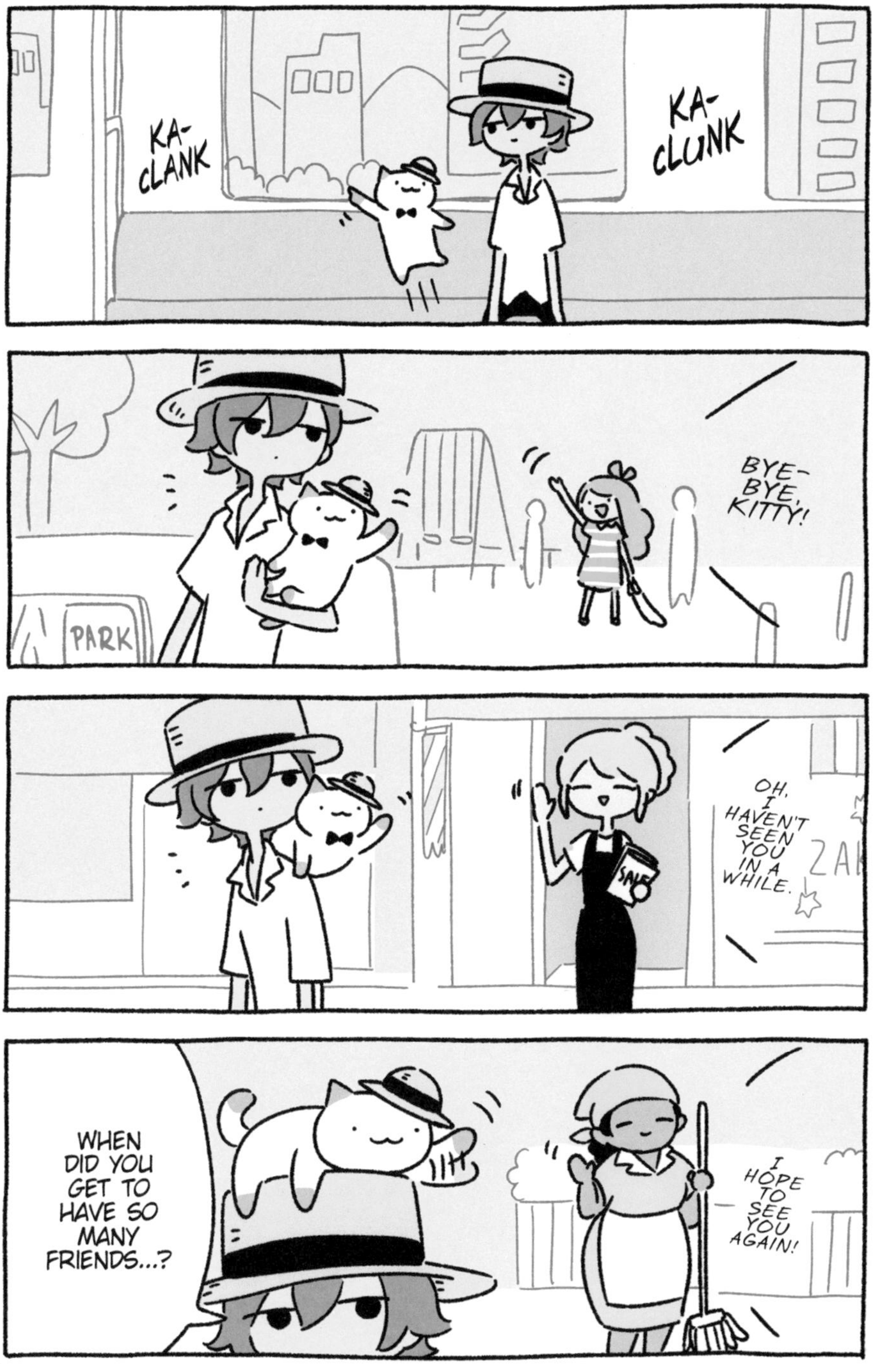
KA-CLUNK
KA-CLANK
BYE-BYE, KITTY!
PARK
OH, I HAVEN'T SEEN YOU IN A WHILE.
ZAK
SALE
I HOPE TO SEE YOU AGAIN!
WHEN DID YOU GET TO HAVE SO MANY FRIENDS...?

AVOIDING A FLAME WAR

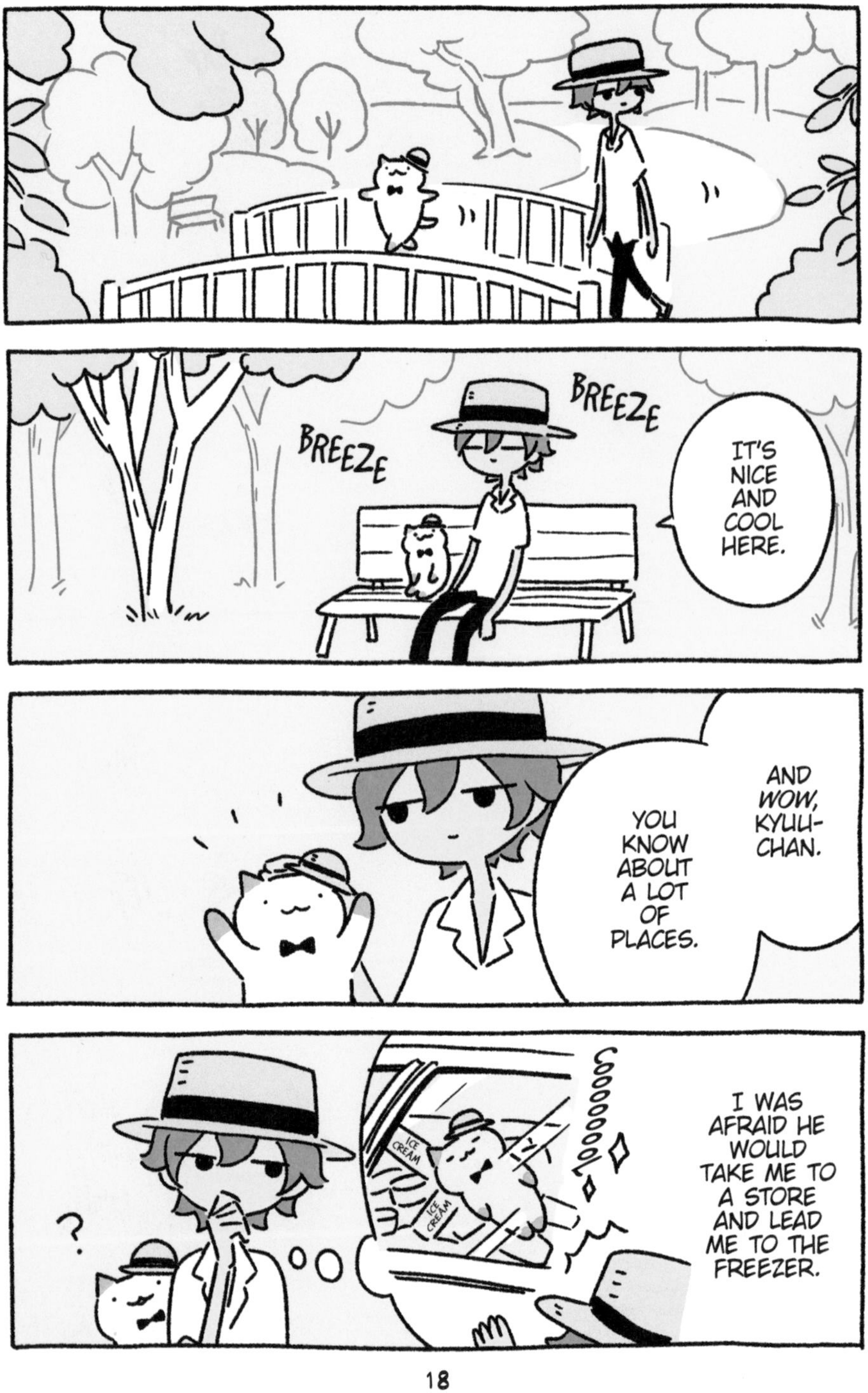
IT'S NICE AND COOL HERE.
BREEZE
BREEZE
AND WOW, KYUU-CHAN.
YOU KNOW ABOUT A LOT OF PLACES.
I WAS AFRAID HE WOULD TAKE ME TO A STORE AND LEAD ME TO THE FREEZER.
COOOOOOOL
ICE CREAM
ICE CREAM
?

COLLECTING

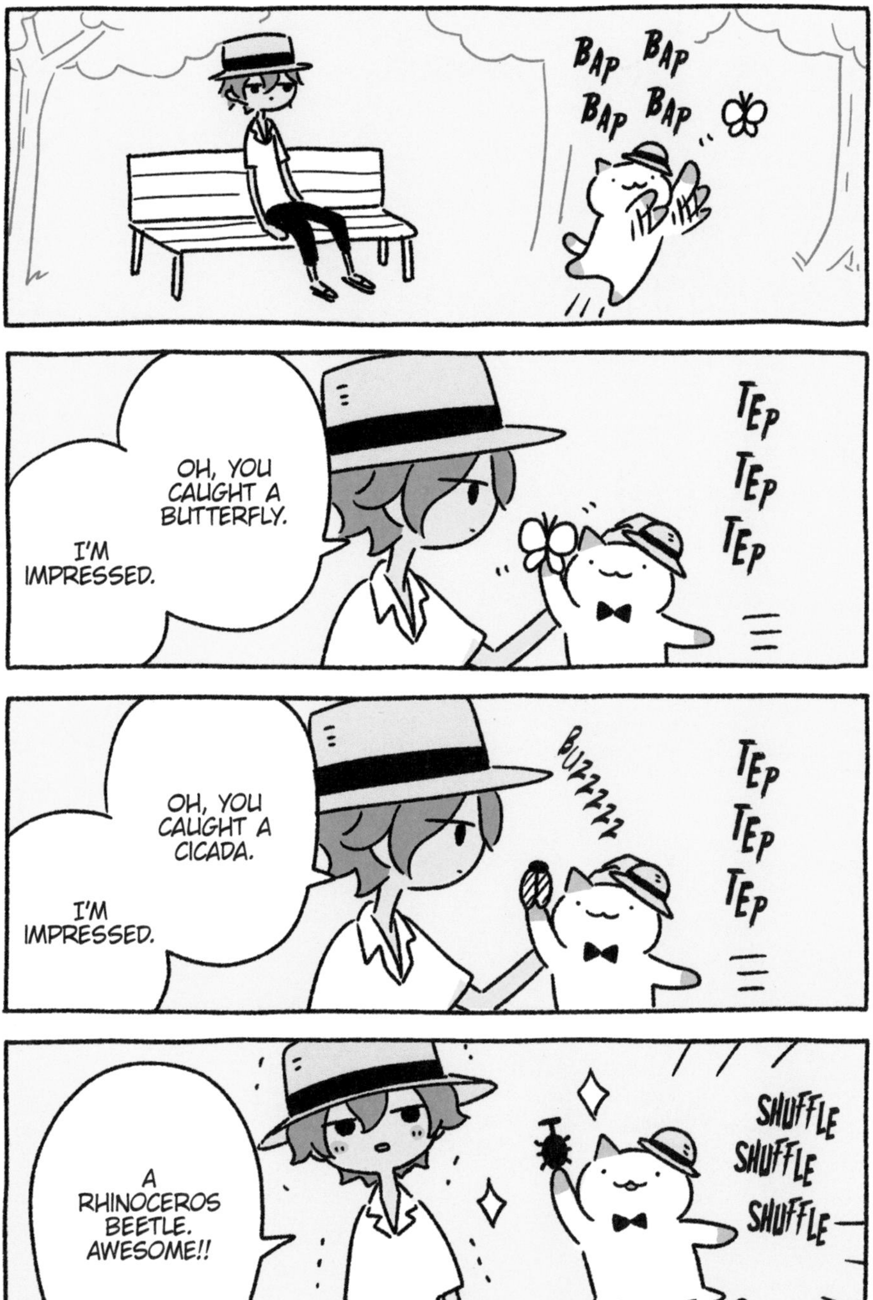
BAP BAP
BAP BAP
TEP
TEP
TEP
OH, YOU CAUGHT A BUTTERFLY.
I'M IMPRESSED.
TEP
TEP
TEP
BUZZZZZZ
OH, YOU CAUGHT A CICADA.
I'M IMPRESSED.
SHUFFLE
SHUFFLE
SHUFFLE
A RHINOCEROS BEETLE. AWESOME!!

HUNTER

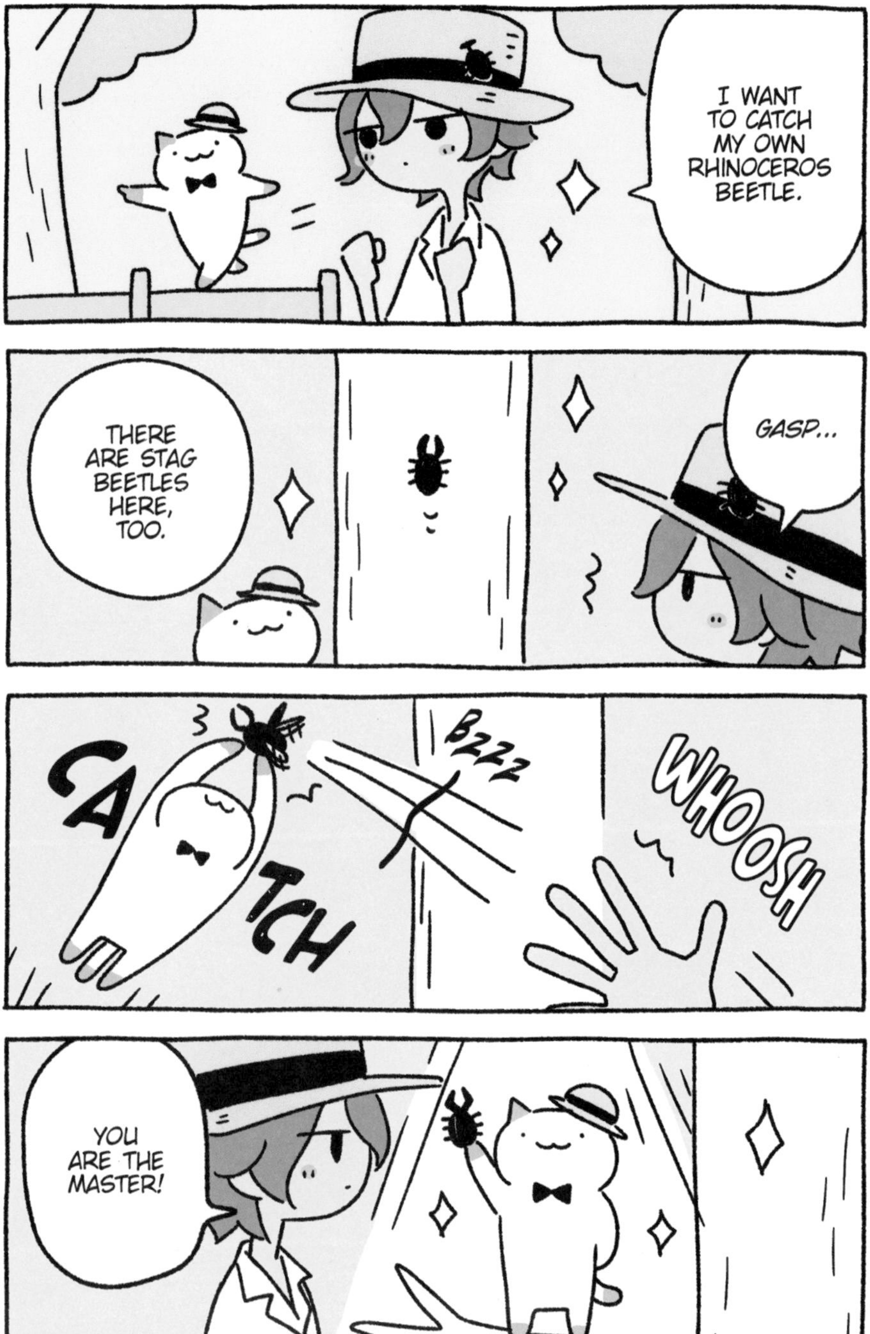

I WANT TO CATCH MY OWN RHINOCEROS BEETLE.
GASP...
THERE ARE STAG BEETLES HERE, TOO.
WHOOSH
BZZZ
CATCH
YOU ARE THE MASTER!

OBSERVATION

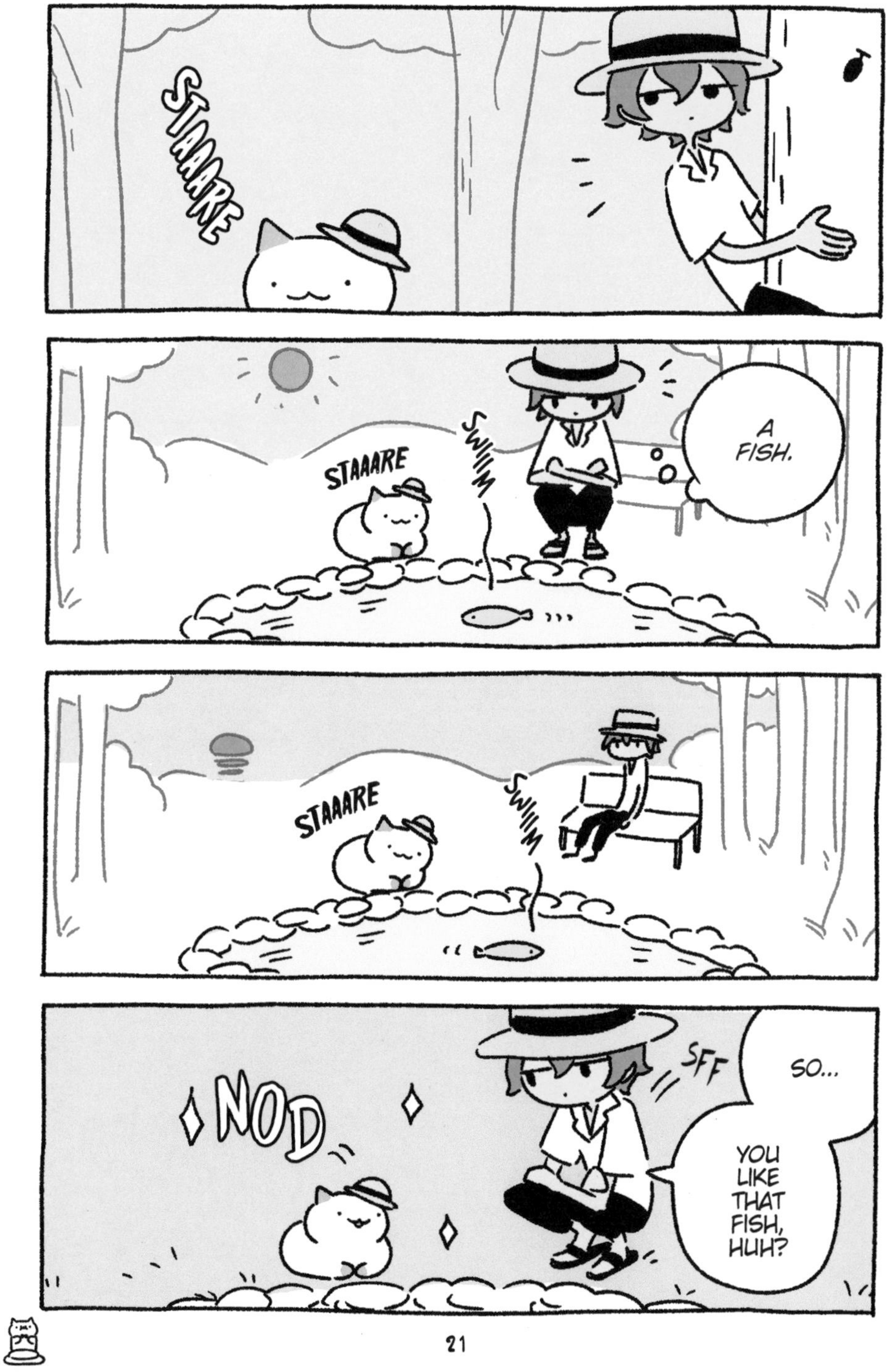

STAAARE
A FISH.
SWIIM
STAAARE
SWIIM
STAAARE
SO...
YOU LIKE THAT FISH, HUH?
SFF
NOD

BYE

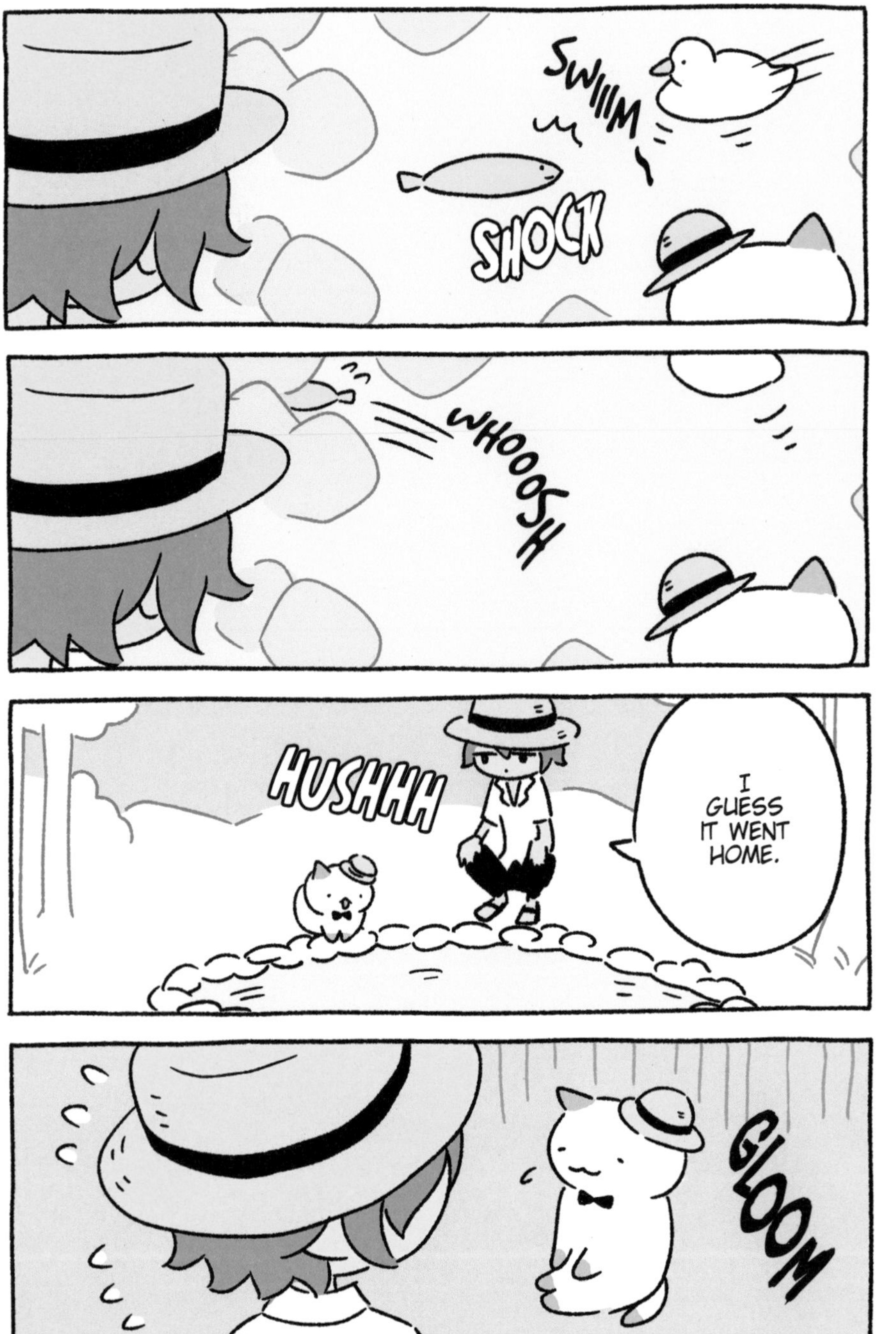
SWIIIM
SHOCK
WHOOOSH
I GUESS IT WENT HOME.
HUSHHH
GLOOM

CHEERING UP

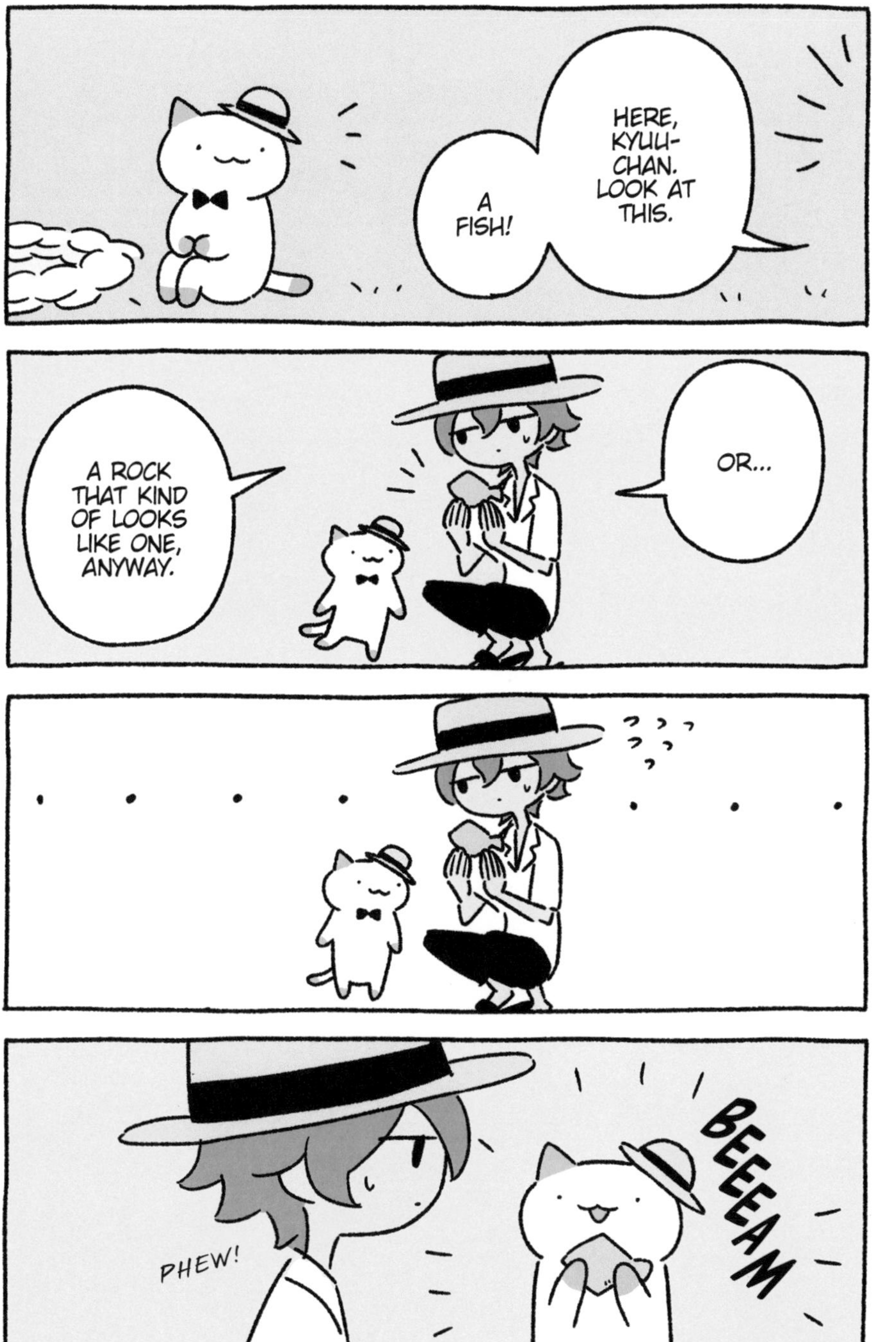
HERE, KYUU-CHAN. LOOK AT THIS.
A FISH!
OR...
A ROCK THAT KIND OF LOOKS LIKE ONE, ANYWAY.
BEEEAM
PHEW!

THE ROAD HOME

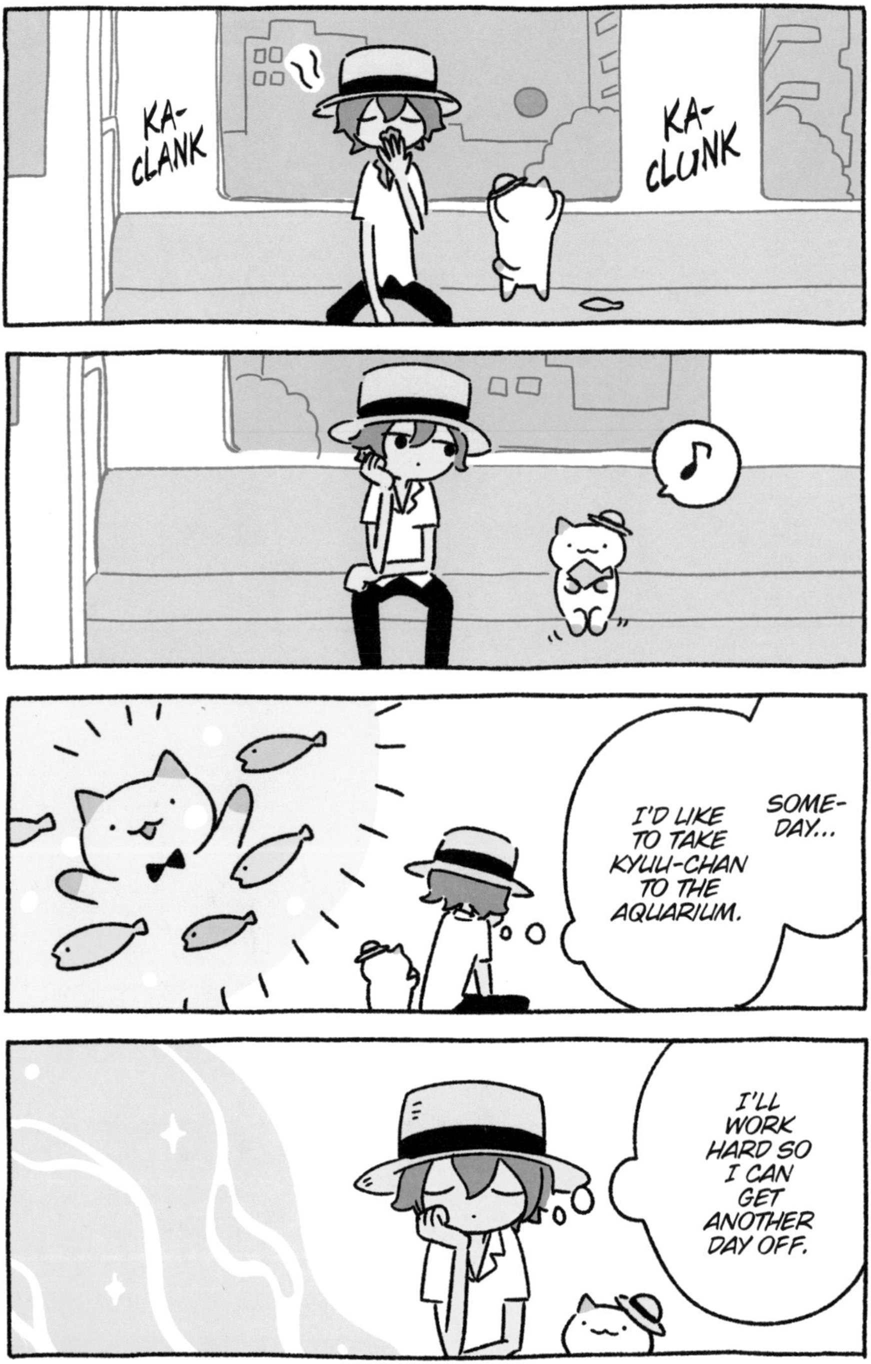
KA-CLUNK
KA-CLANK
SOME-DAY...
I'D LIKE TO TAKE KYUU-CHAN TO THE AQUARIUM.
I'LL WORK HARD SO I CAN GET ANOTHER DAY OFF.

THE AQUARIUM

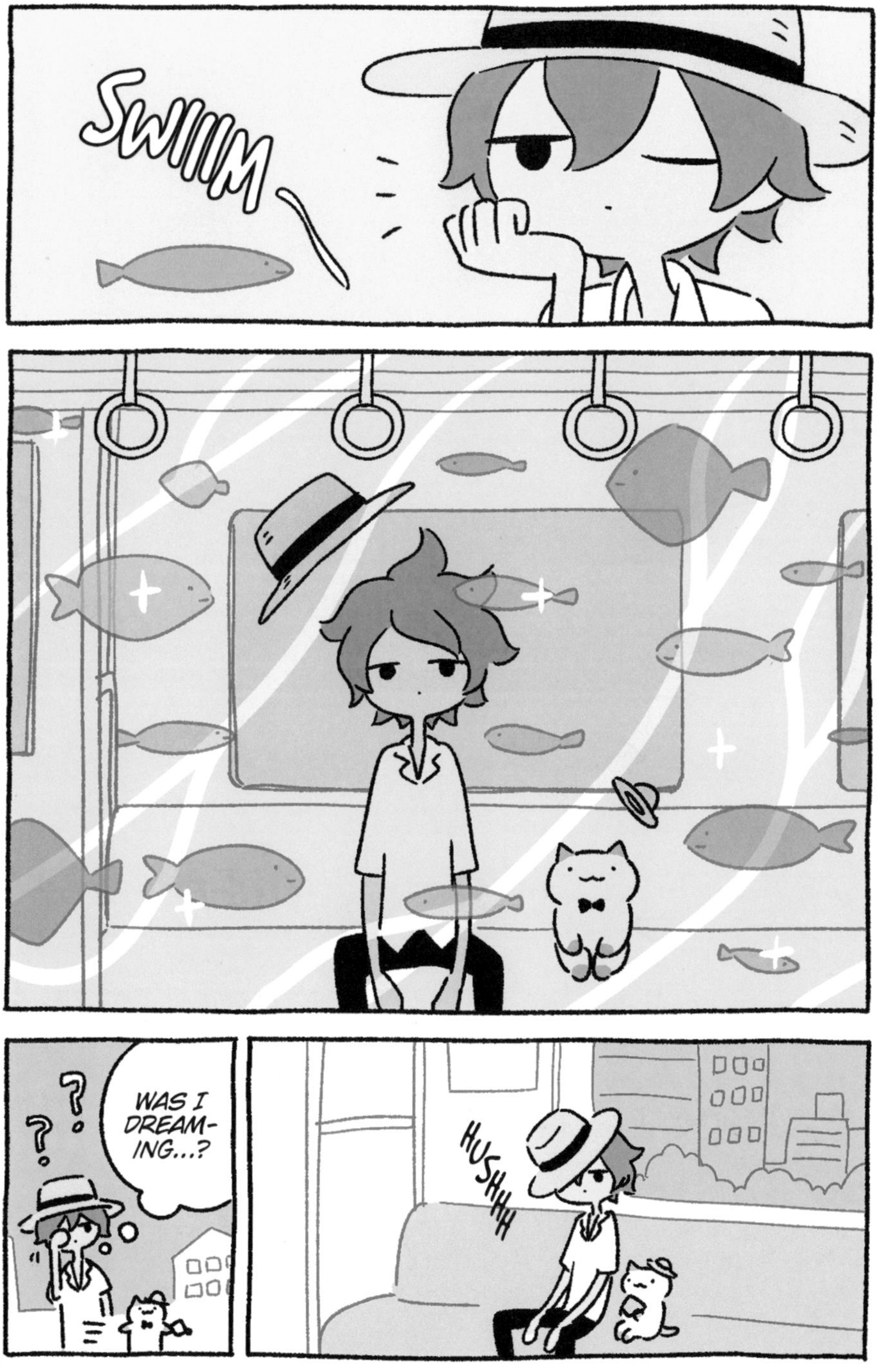
SWIIIM
HUSHHH
? ?
WAS I DREAMING...?

I WANNA BE LIKE YOU

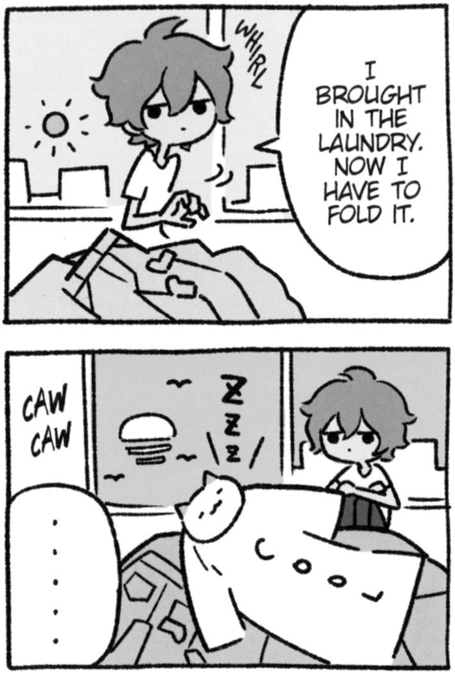
I BROUGHT IN THE LAUNDRY. NOW I HAVE TO FOLD IT.
WHIRL
CAW CAW
Z Z Z
. . . . .
C O O L

CHILLS

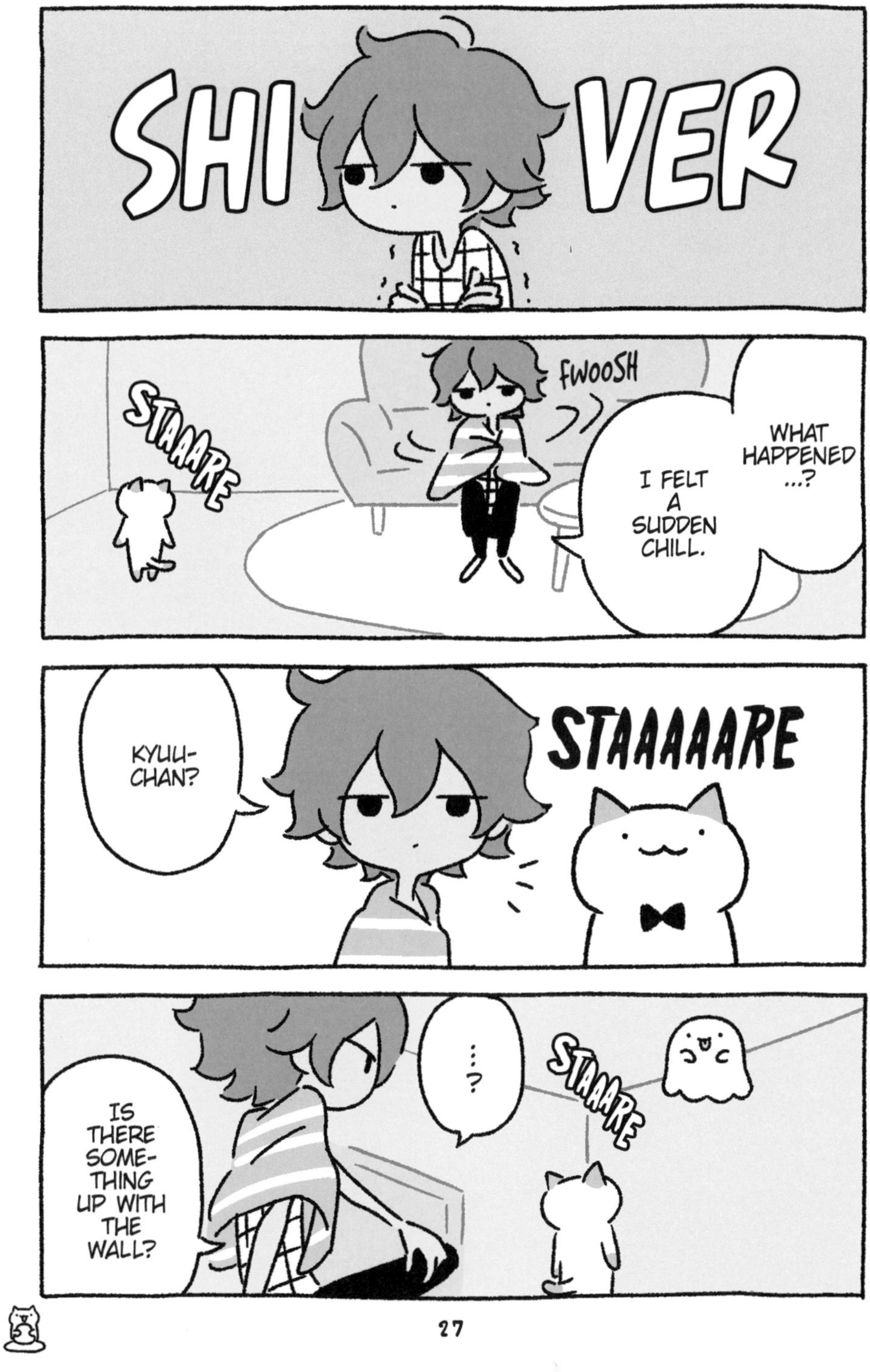

SHIVER
WHAT HAPPENED ...?
I FELT A SUDDEN CHILL.
FWOOSH
STAAARE
STAAAAARE
KYUU-CHAN?
STAAARE
...?
IS THERE SOMETHING UP WITH THE WALL?

SCARY

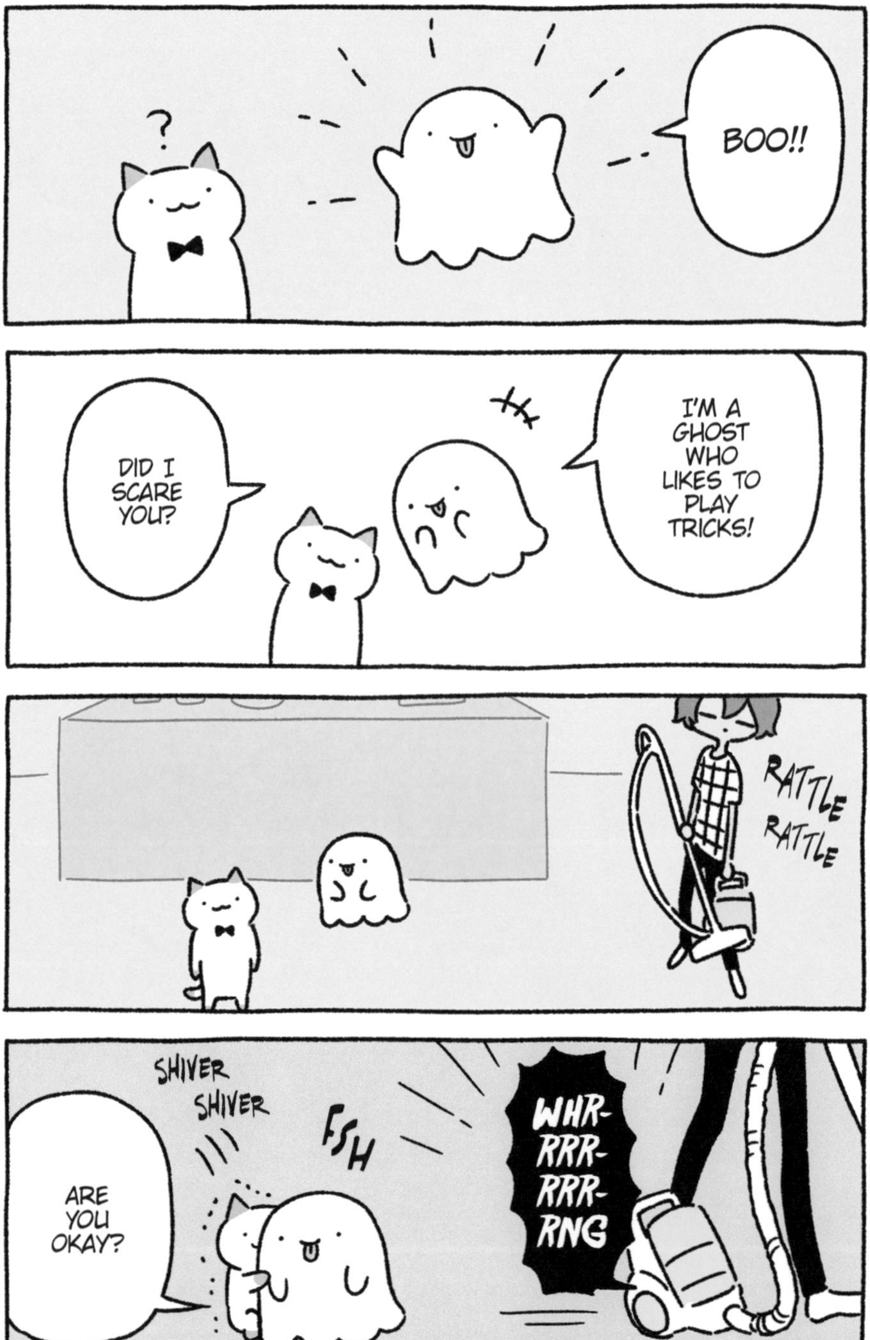
BOO!!
I'M A GHOST WHO LIKES TO PLAY TRICKS!
DID I SCARE YOU?
RATTLE RATTLE
WHR-RRR-RRR-RNG
FSH
SHIVER SHIVER
ARE YOU OKAY?

THE CHASE

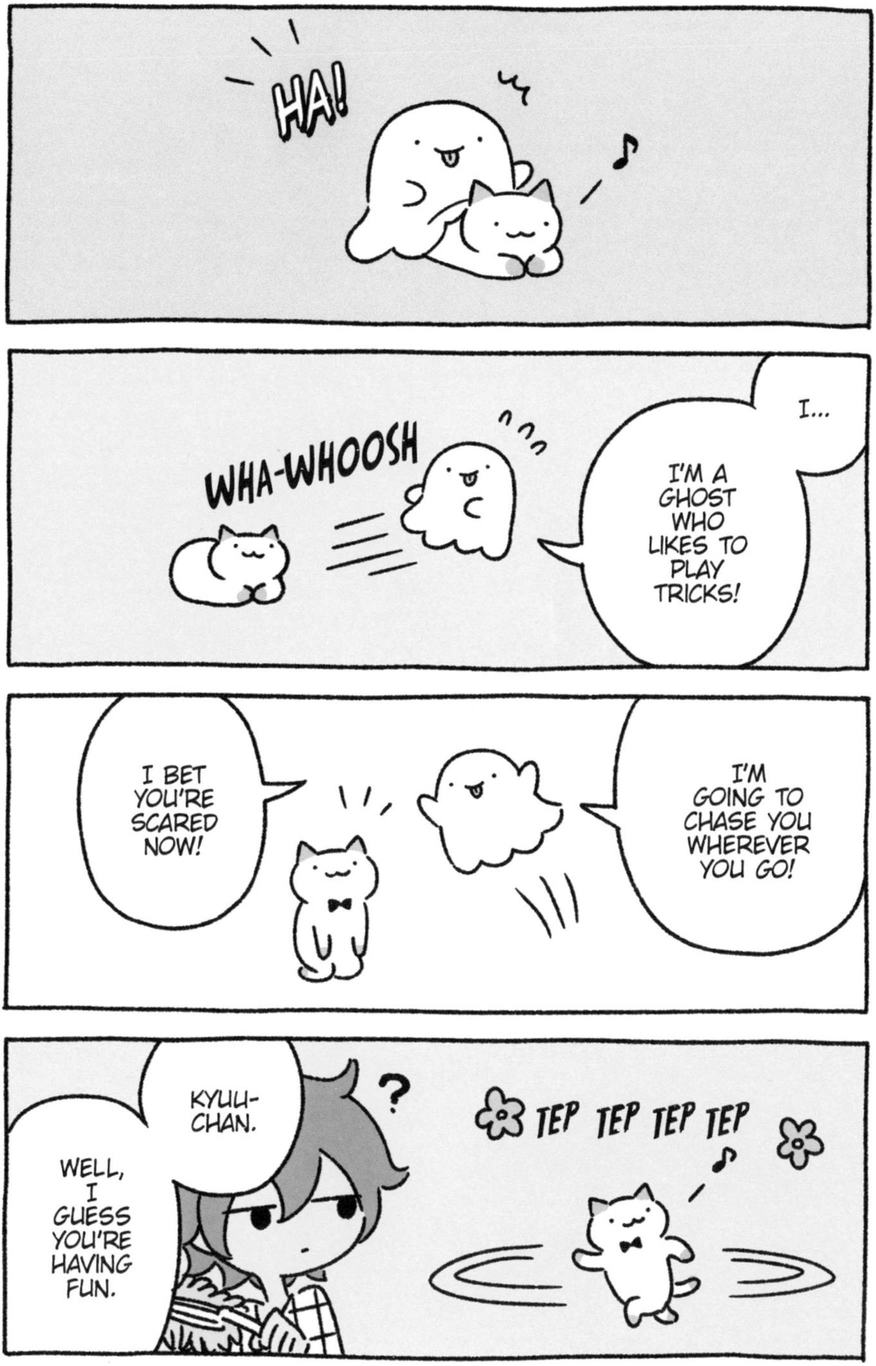

HA!
I... I'M A GHOST WHO LIKES TO PLAY TRICKS!
WHA-WHOOSH
I'M GOING TO CHASE YOU WHEREVER YOU GO!
I BET YOU'RE SCARED NOW!
TEP TEP TEP TEP
?
KYUU-CHAN.
WELL, I GUESS YOU'RE HAVING FUN.

SURPRISE

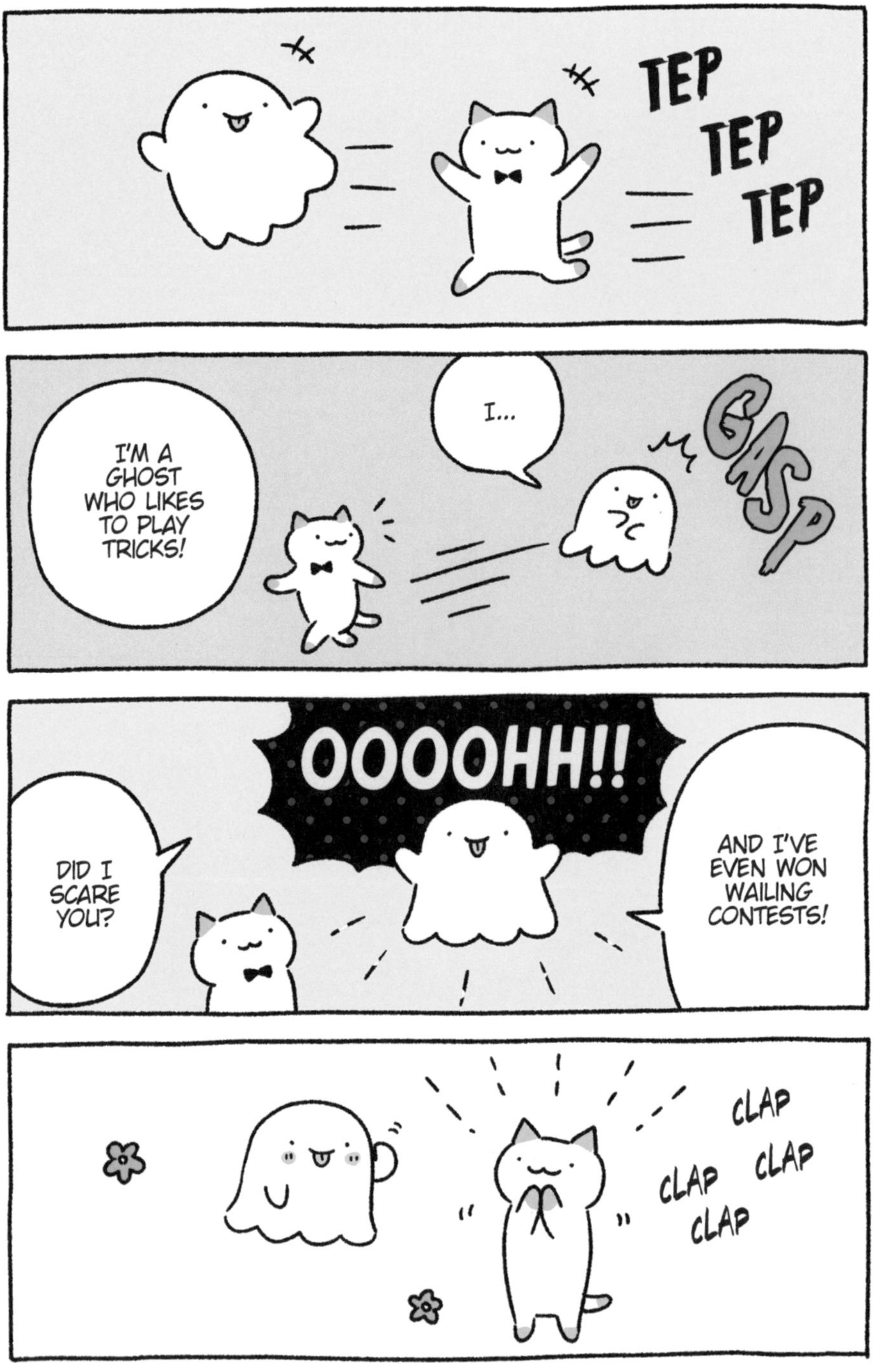
TEP
TEP
TEP
GASP
I...
I'M A GHOST WHO LIKES TO PLAY TRICKS!
AND I'VE EVEN WON WAILING CONTESTS!
OOOOHH!!
DID I SCARE YOU?
CLAP
CLAP
CLAP
CLAP

PARANORMAL ACTIVITY

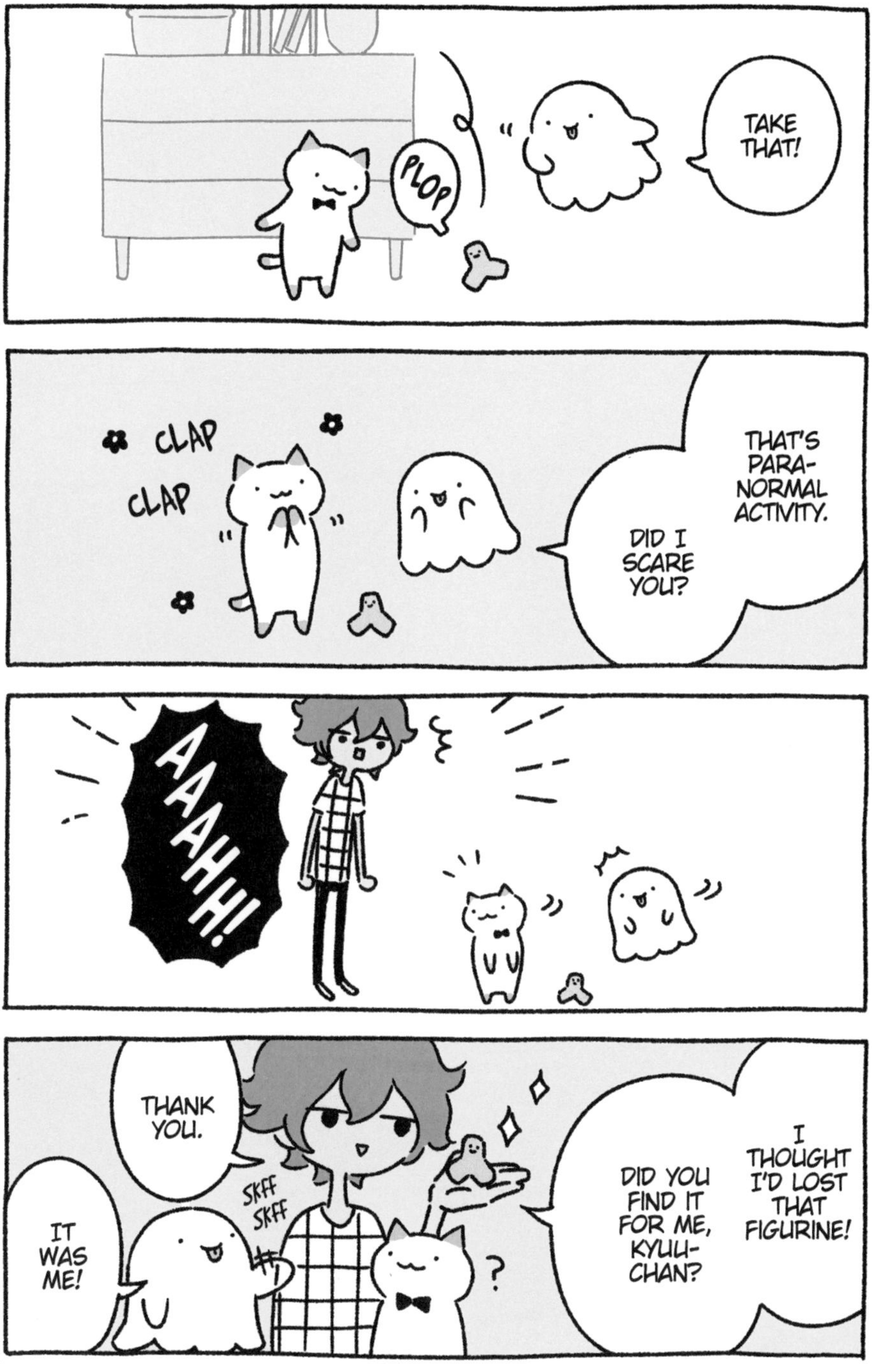
TAKE THAT!
PLOP
THAT'S PARA-NORMAL ACTIVITY.
DID I SCARE YOU?
CLAP
CLAP
AAAHH!
I THOUGHT I'D LOST THAT FIGURINE!
DID YOU FIND IT FOR ME, KYUU-CHAN?
THANK YOU.
SKFF SKFF
IT WAS ME!

LUCKY

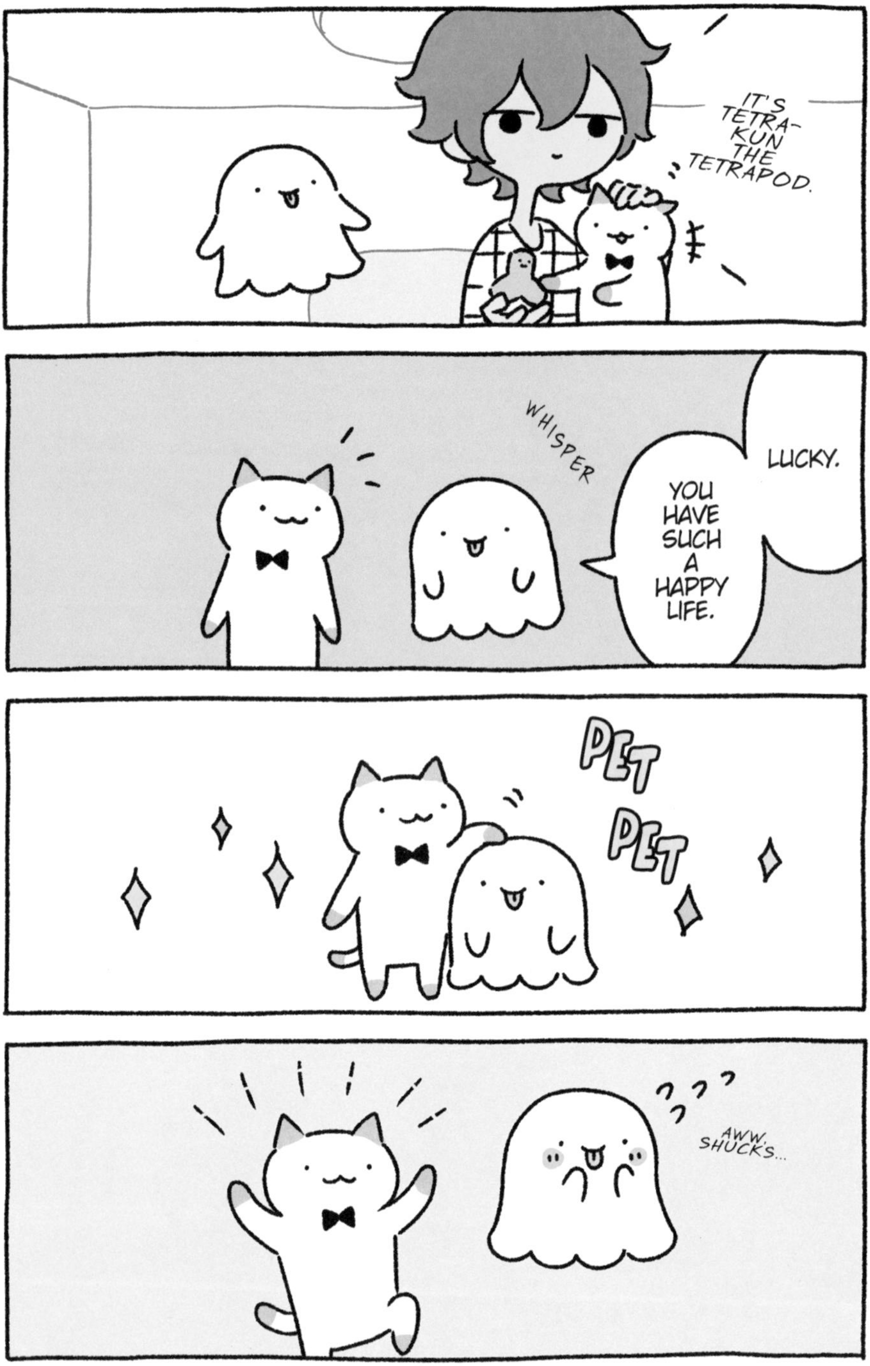
IT'S TETRA-KUN THE TETRAPOD.
WHISPER
LUCKY.
YOU HAVE SUCH A HAPPY LIFE.
PET PET
AWW, SHUCKS...

PROMISE

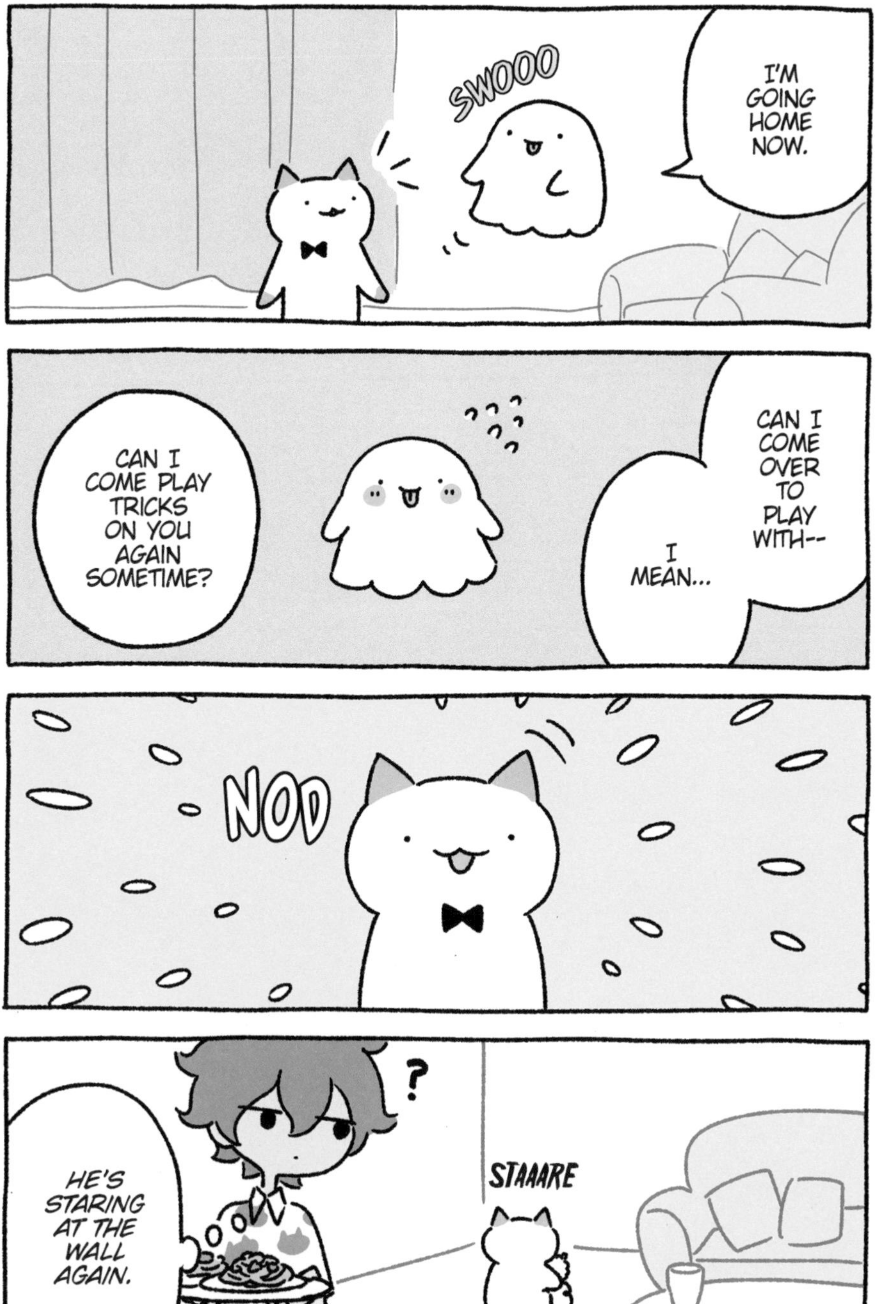
I'M GOING HOME NOW.
SWOOO
CAN I COME OVER TO PLAY WITH-- I MEAN...
CAN I COME PLAY TRICKS ON YOU AGAIN SOMETIME?
NOD
STAAARE
?
HE'S STARING AT THE WALL AGAIN.

CAT LOVER RETURNS

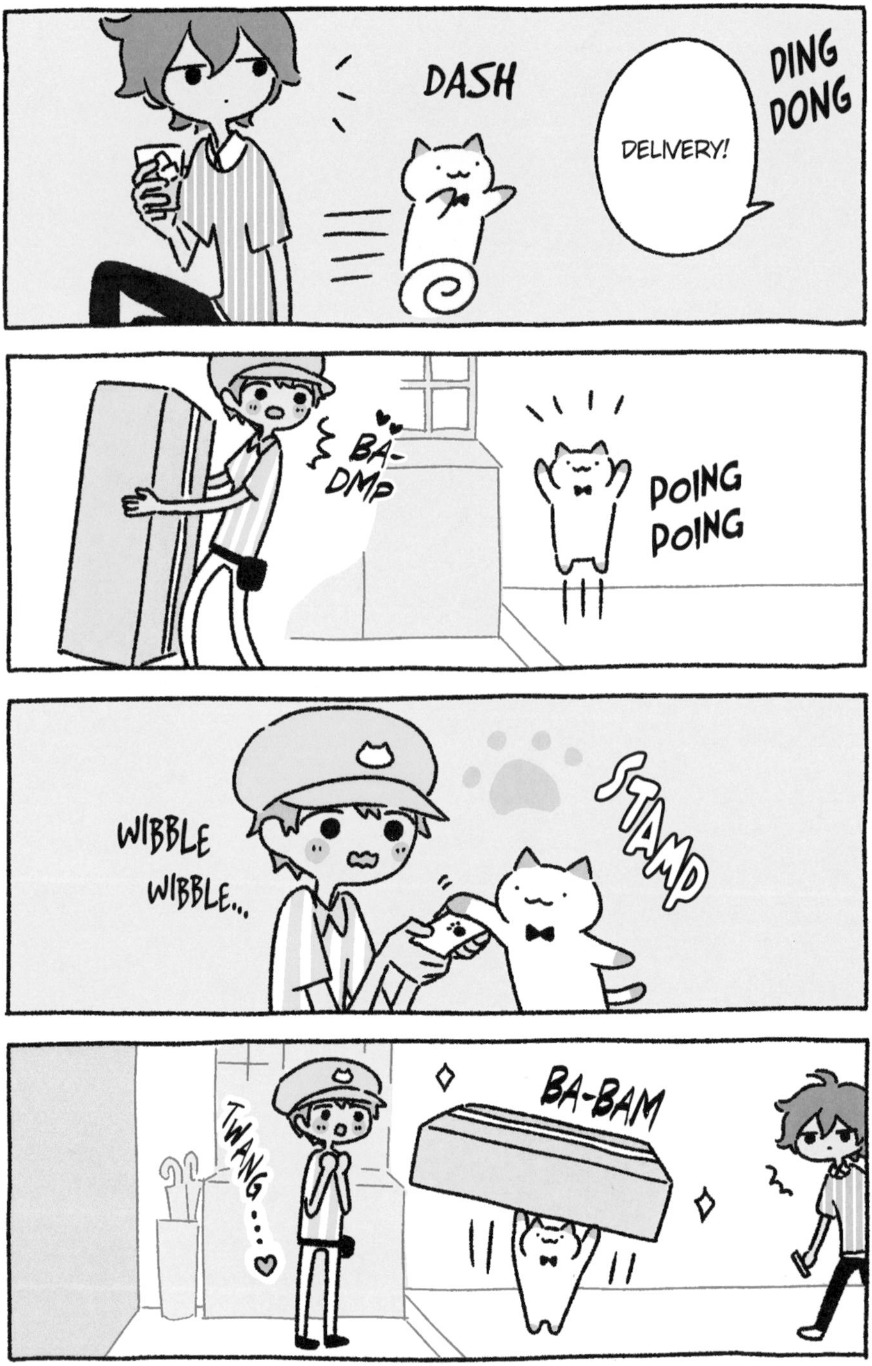
DING DONG
DELIVERY!
DASH
POING POING
BA-DMP
STAMP
WIBBLE WIBBLE...
BA-BAM
TWANG...

CAT TOWER

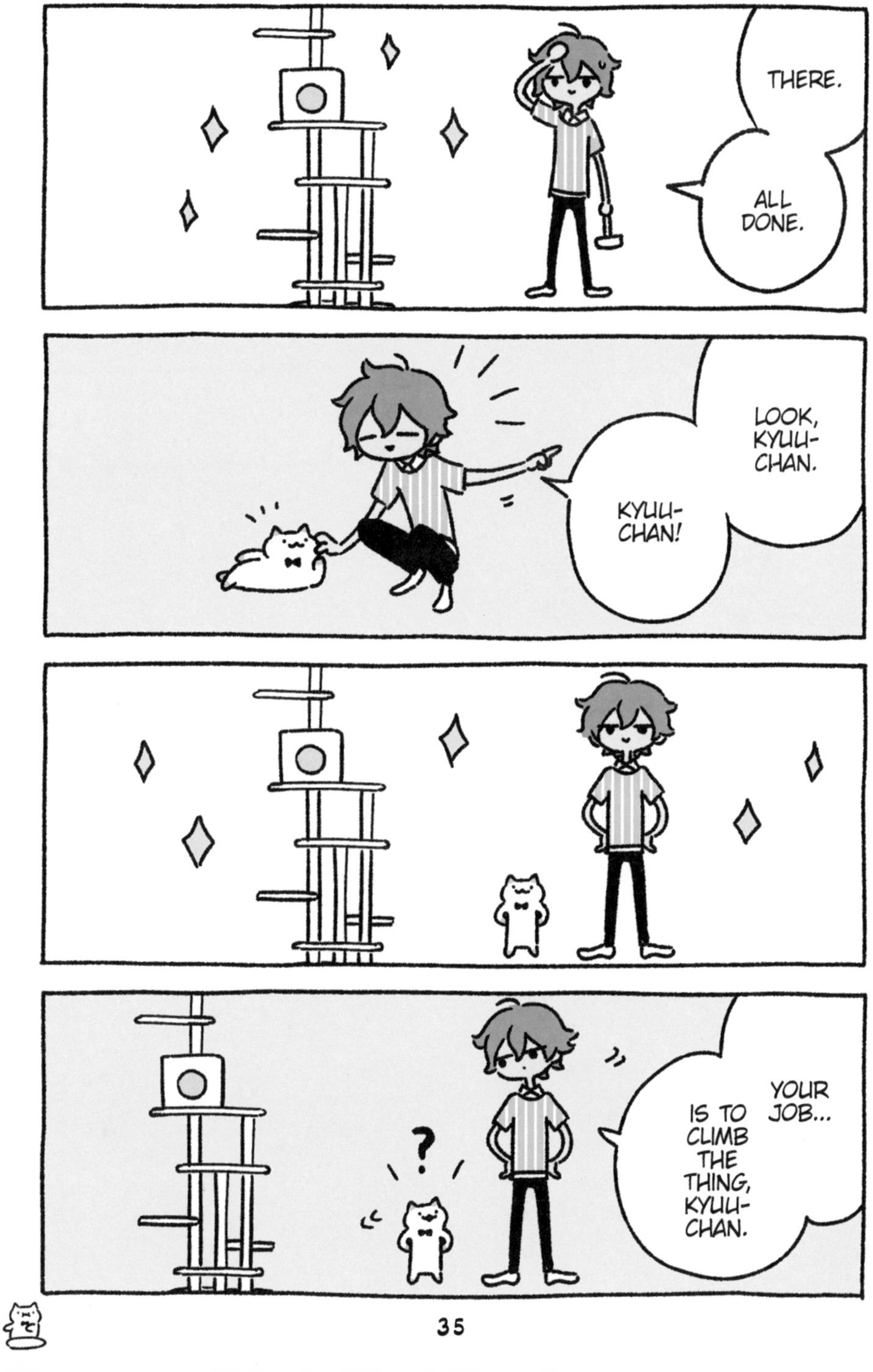
THERE.
ALL DONE.
LOOK, KYUU-CHAN.
KYUU-CHAN!
?
YOUR JOB...
IS TO CLIMB THE THING, KYUU-CHAN.

MAGMA

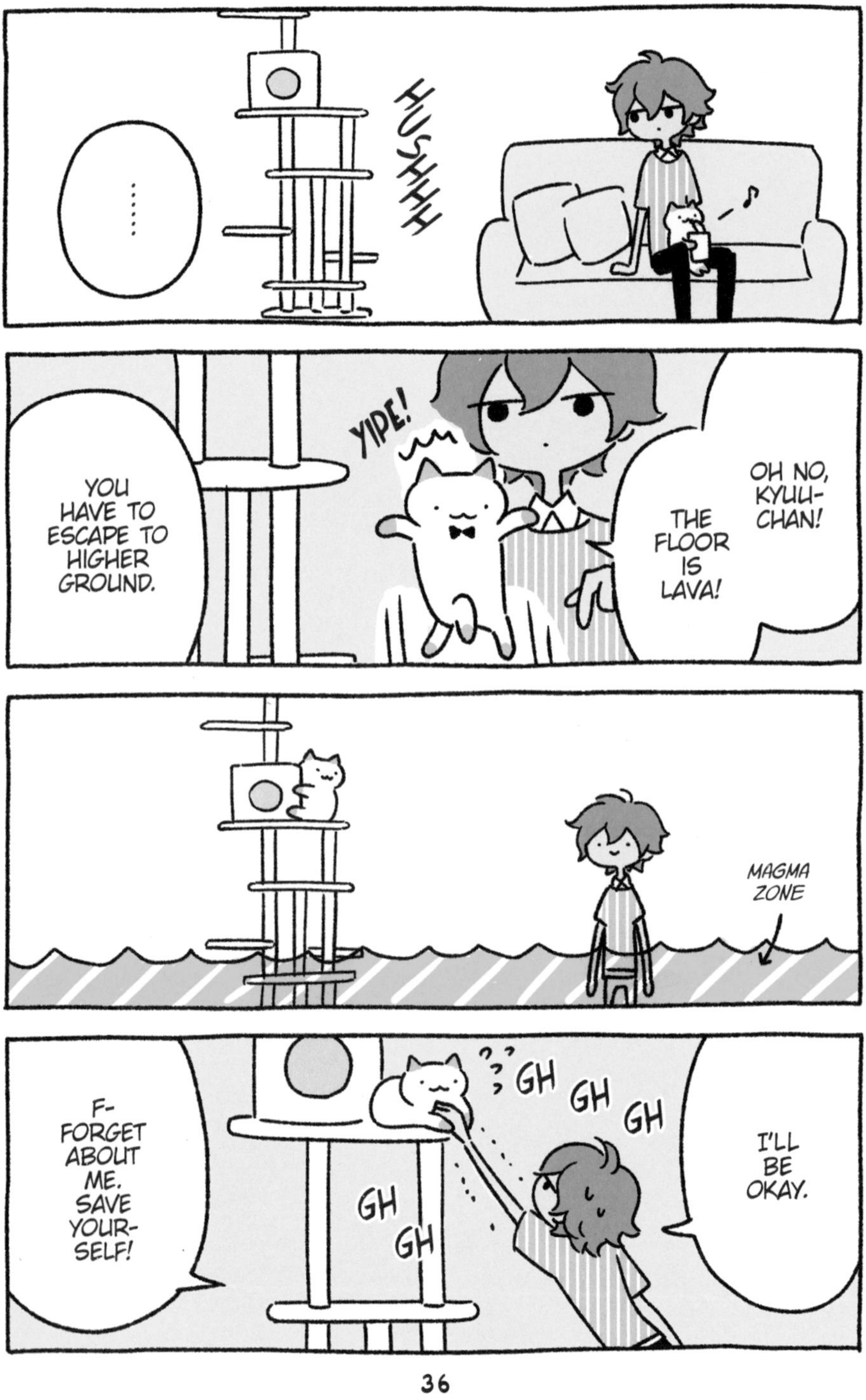
HUSHHH
......
OH NO, KYUU-CHAN!
THE FLOOR IS LAVA!
YIPE!
YOU HAVE TO ESCAPE TO HIGHER GROUND.
MAGMA ZONE
I'LL BE OKAY.
GH GH GH
GH GH
F-FORGET ABOUT ME. SAVE YOUR-SELF!

BEATING THE HEAT

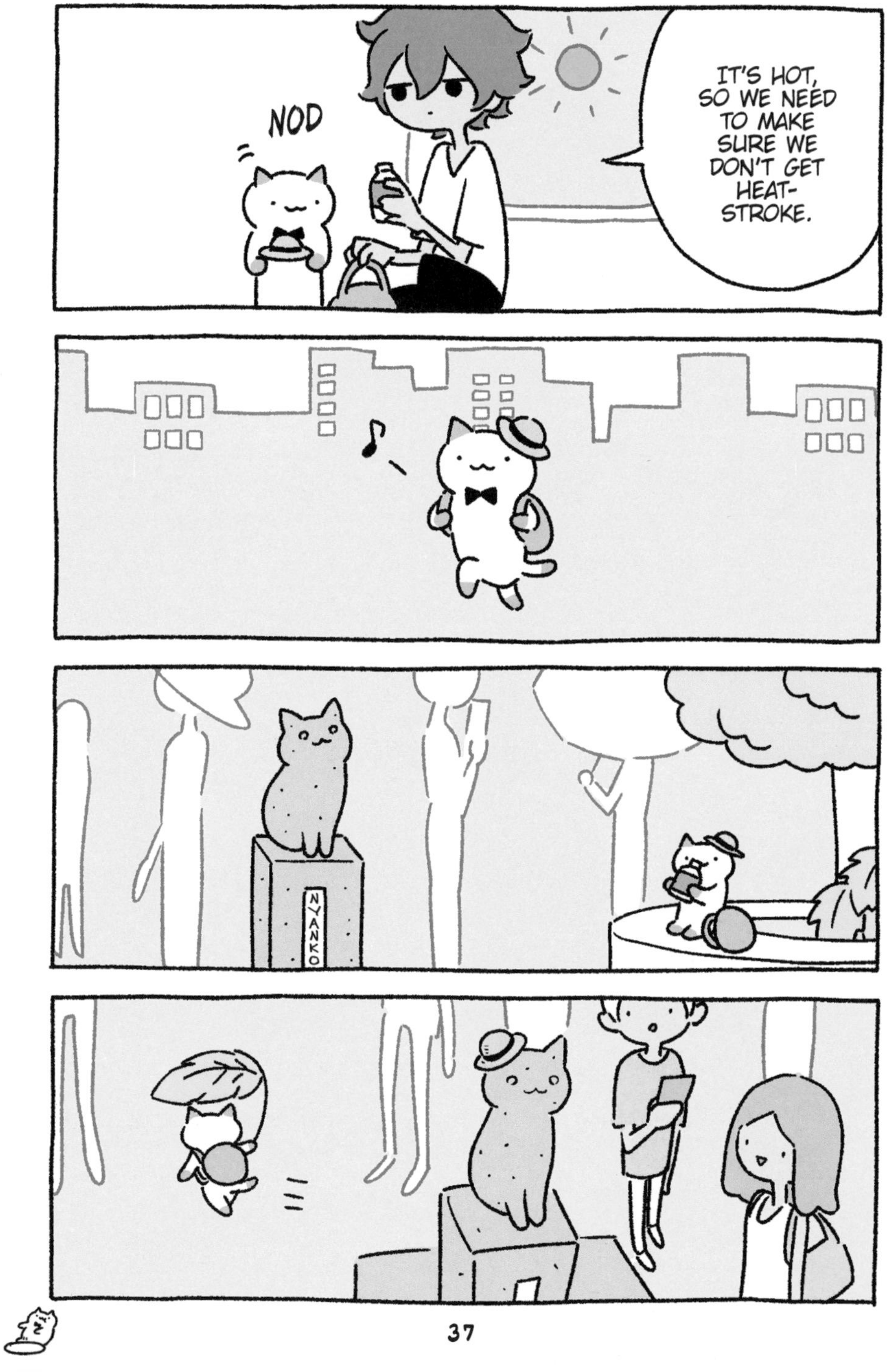
IT'S HOT, SO WE NEED TO MAKE SURE WE DON'T GET HEAT-STROKE.
NOD
NYANKO

DOUBLE

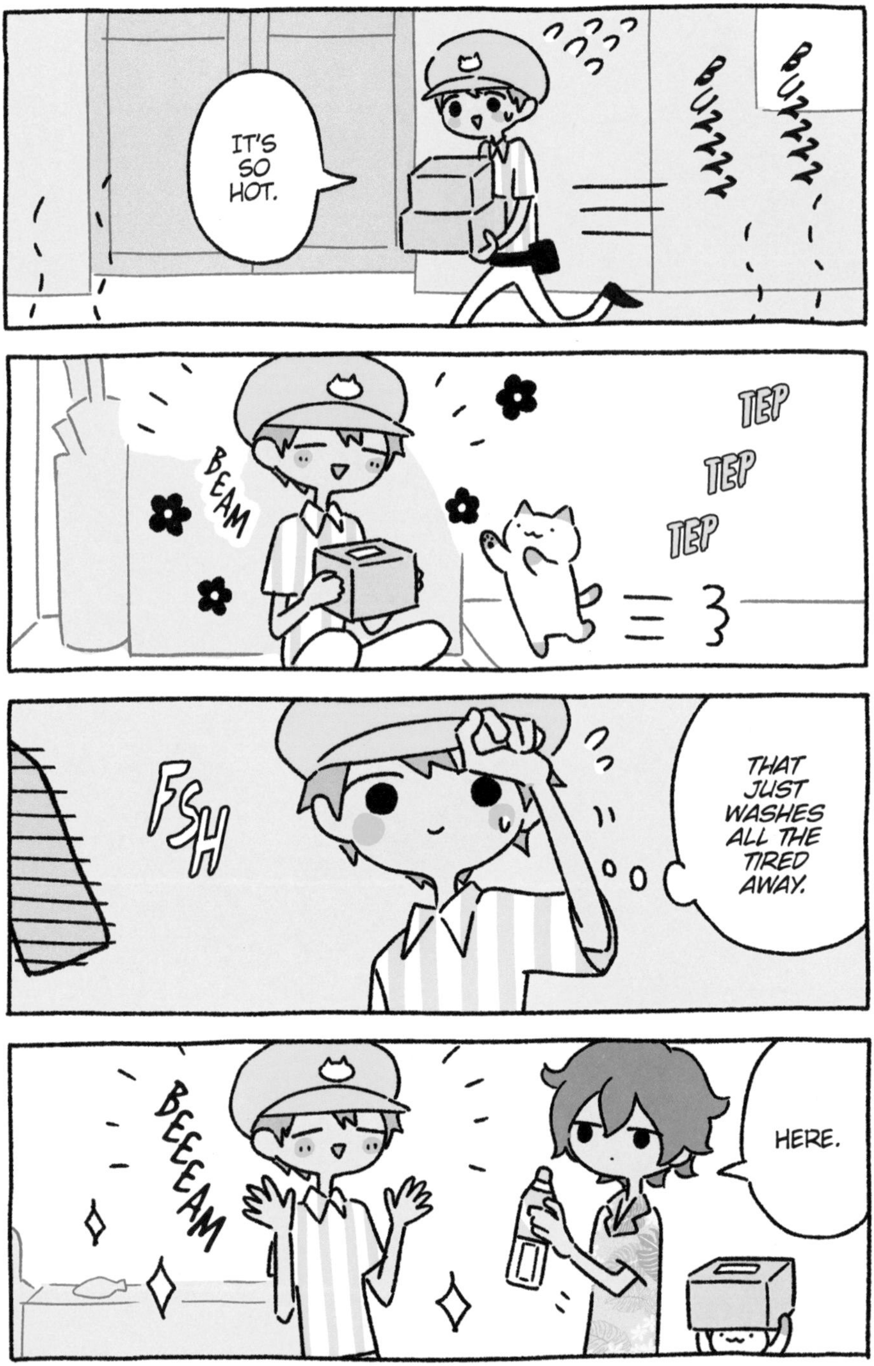
BUZZZZ
BUZZZZ
IT'S SO HOT.
TEP
TEP
TEP
BEAM
THAT JUST WASHES ALL THE TIRED AWAY.
FSH
HERE.
BEEEEAM

PET PET

MAY... MAY I PET...?
HE WANTS PET-TINGS...
KYUU-CHAN.
BA-DMP
BA-DMP
PET PET
WIBBLE WIBBLE...
NOT LIKE THAT, KYUU-CHAN.

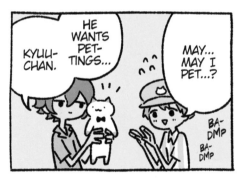

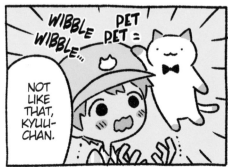

SEEDS

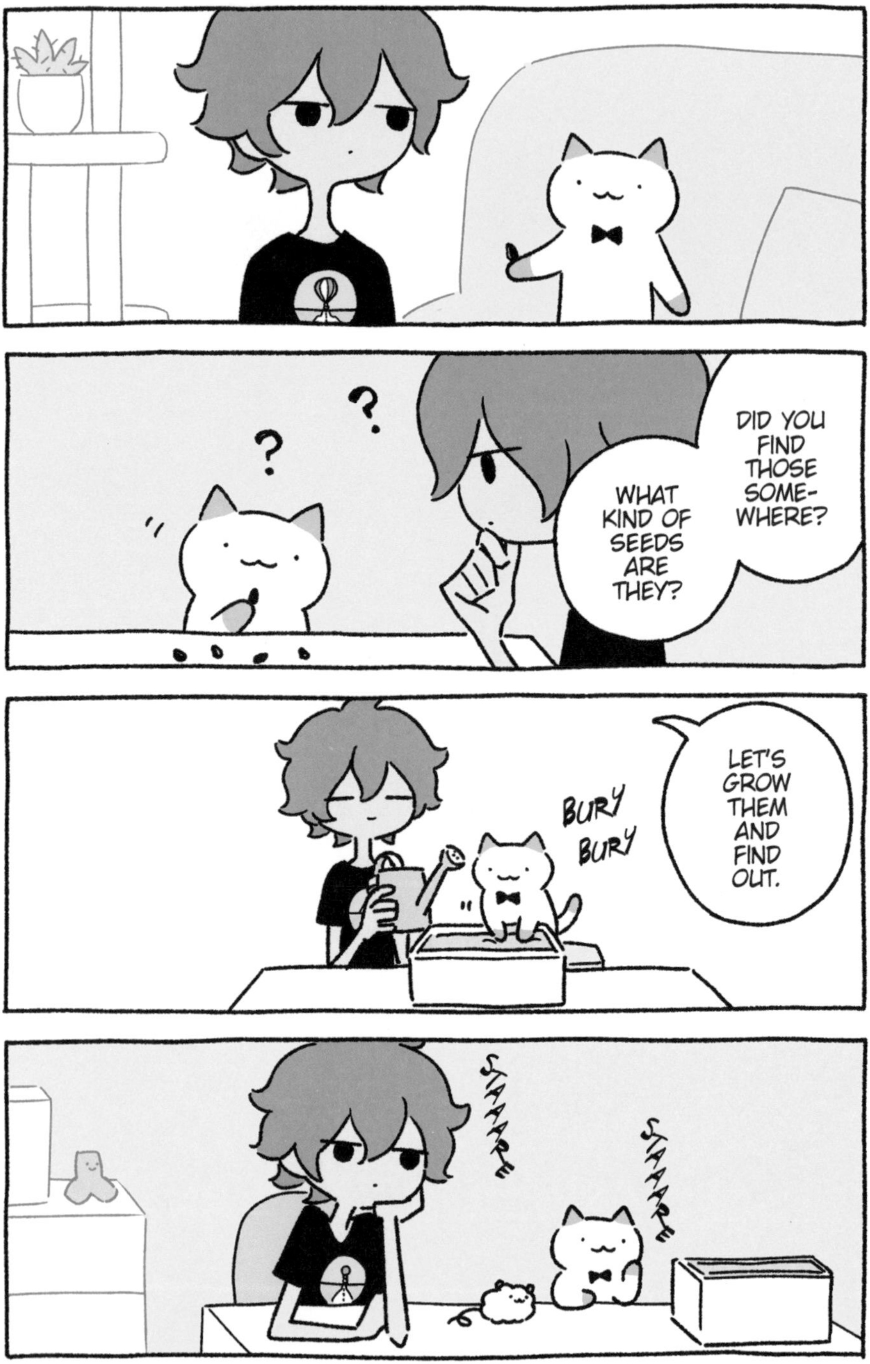
DID YOU FIND THOSE SOME- WHERE?
WHAT KIND OF SEEDS ARE THEY?
LET'S GROW THEM AND FIND OUT.
BURY BURY
STAAAARE
STAAARE

FIREWORKS

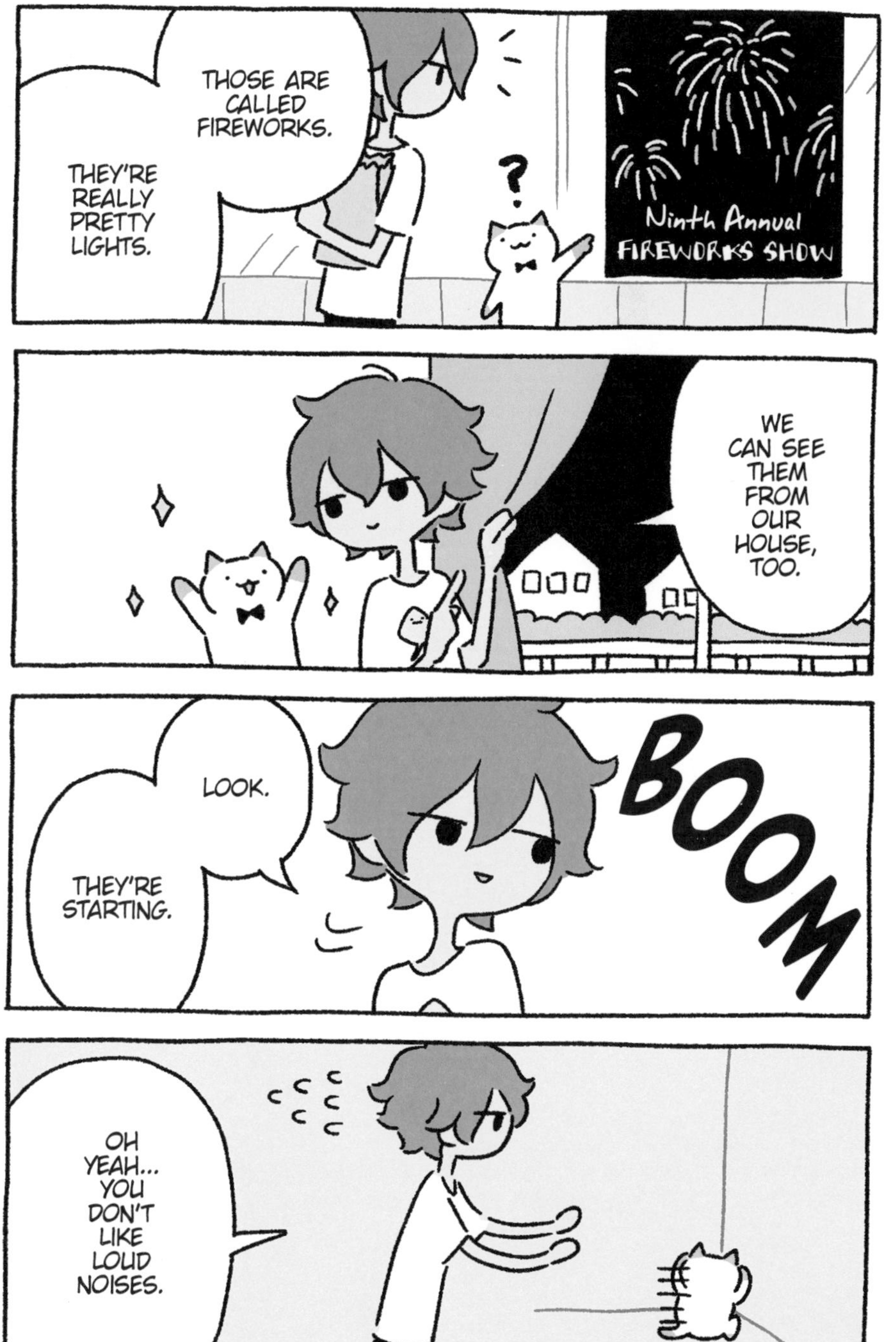
THOSE ARE CALLED FIREWORKS.
THEY'RE REALLY PRETTY LIGHTS.
?
Ninth Annual FIREWORKS SHOW
WE CAN SEE THEM FROM OUR HOUSE, TOO.
LOOK.
THEY'RE STARTING.
BOOM
OH YEAH... YOU DON'T LIKE LOUD NOISES.

SAD

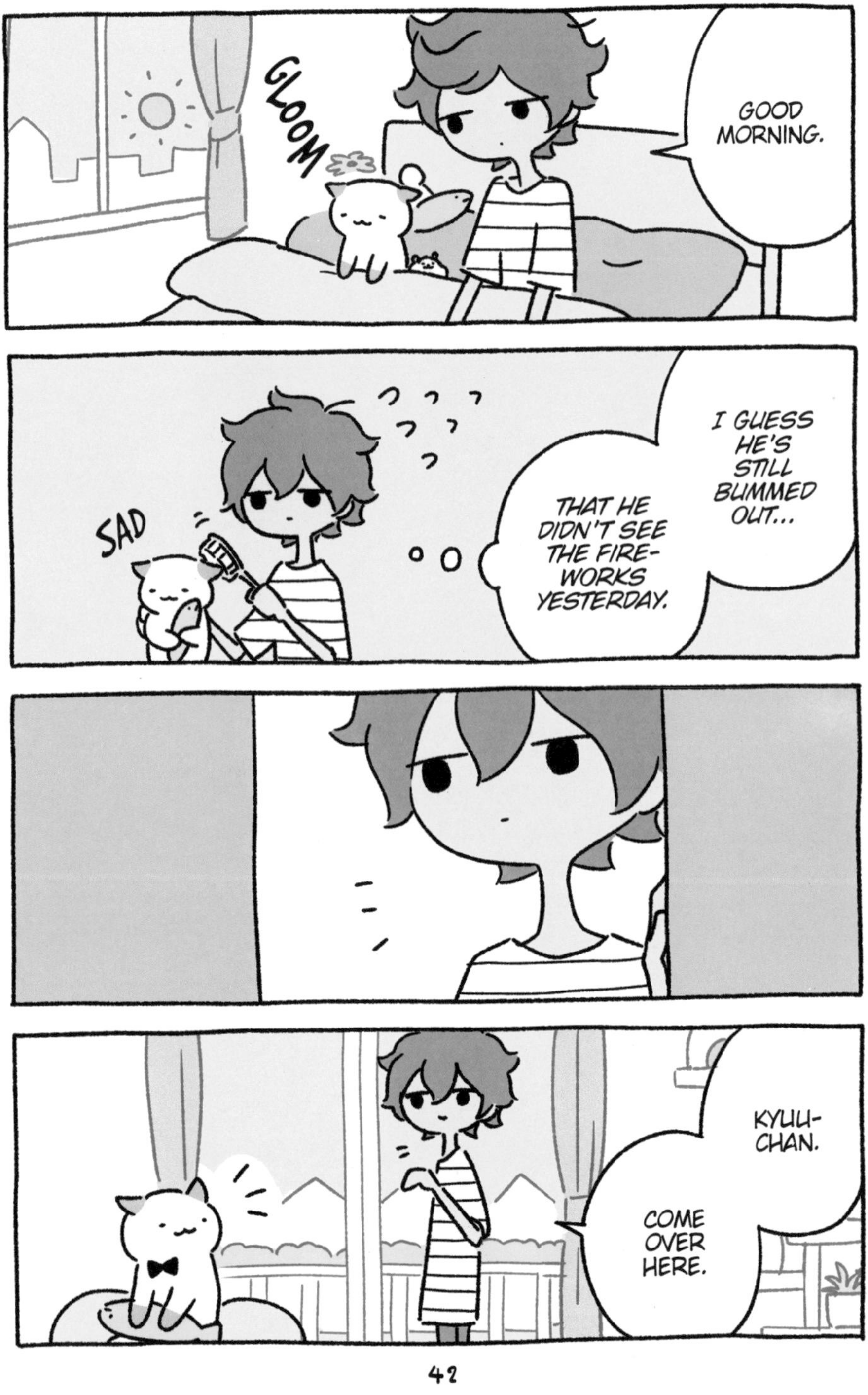

GOOD MORNING.
GLOOM
I GUESS HE'S STILL BUMMED OUT...
THAT HE DIDN'T SEE THE FIRE-WORKS YESTERDAY.
SAD
KYUU-CHAN.
COME OVER HERE.

BEAUTIFLEUR

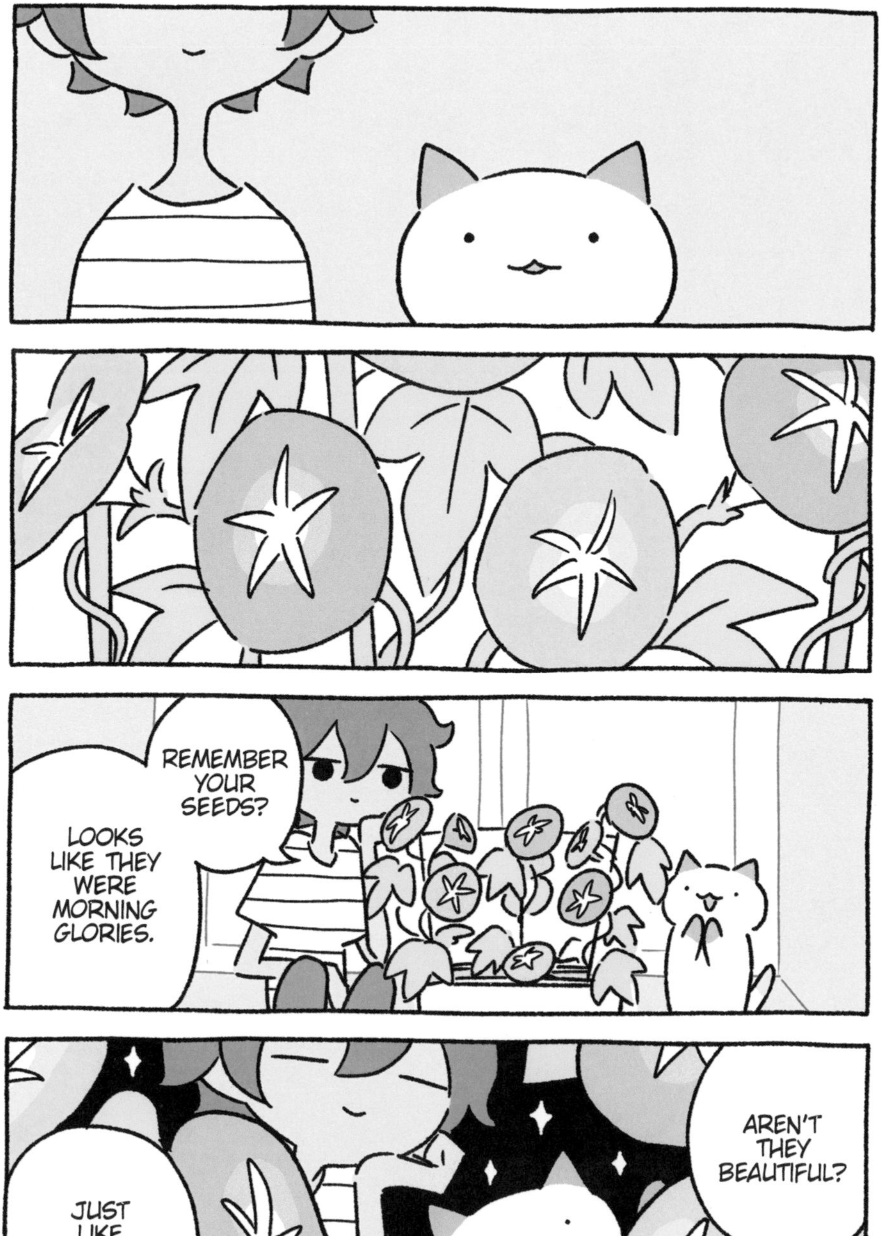
REMEMBER YOUR SEEDS?
LOOKS LIKE THEY WERE MORNING GLORIES.
AREN'T THEY BEAUTIFUL?
JUST LIKE FIRE-WORKS.

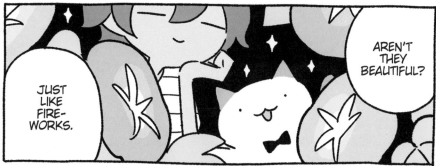

CAT AND DOG

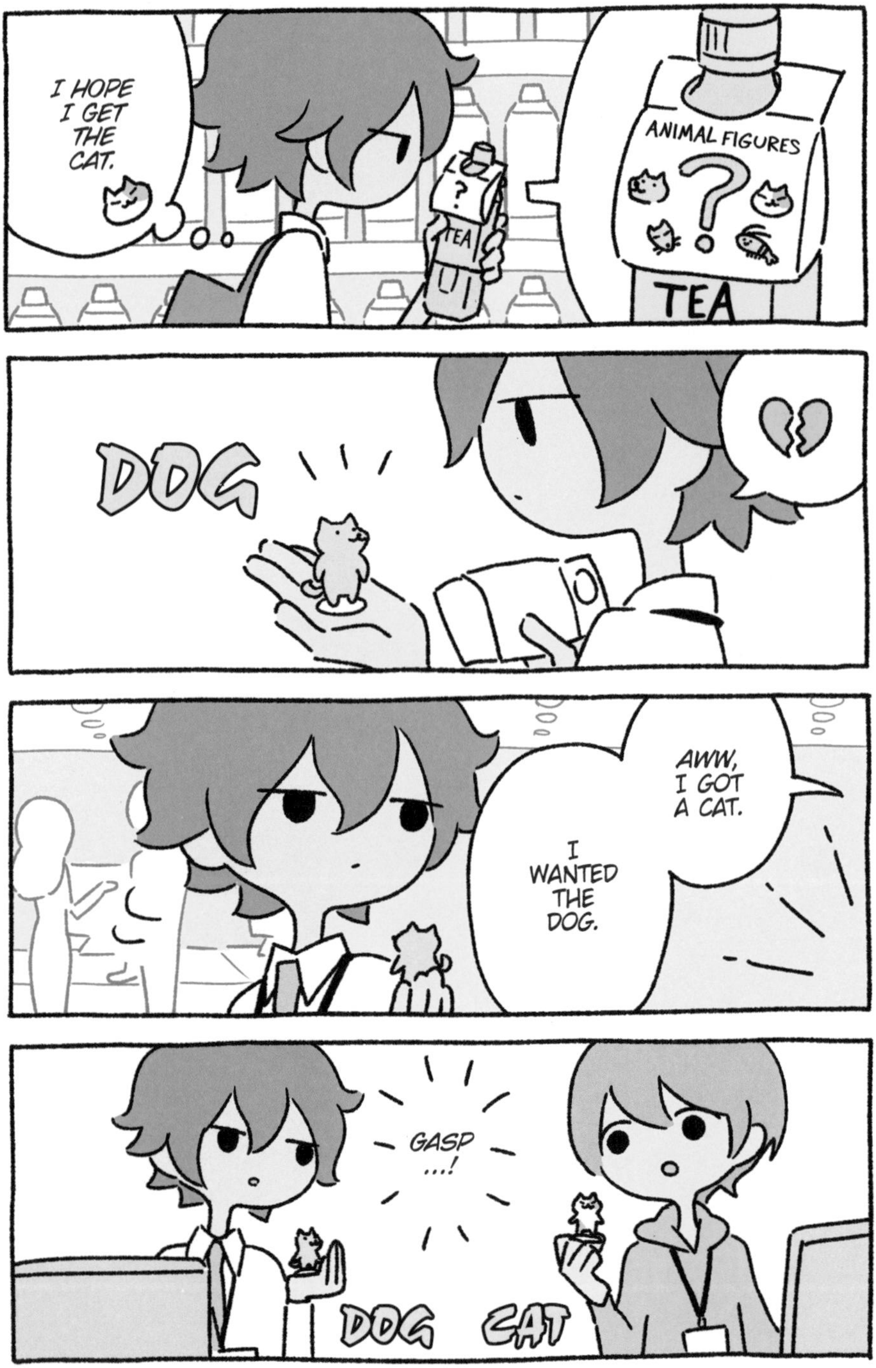
ANIMAL FIGURES
?
TEA
TEA
?
I HOPE I GET THE CAT.
DOG
AWW, I GOT A CAT.
I WANTED THE DOG.
GASP ...!
CAT
DOG

DOTING PARENTS

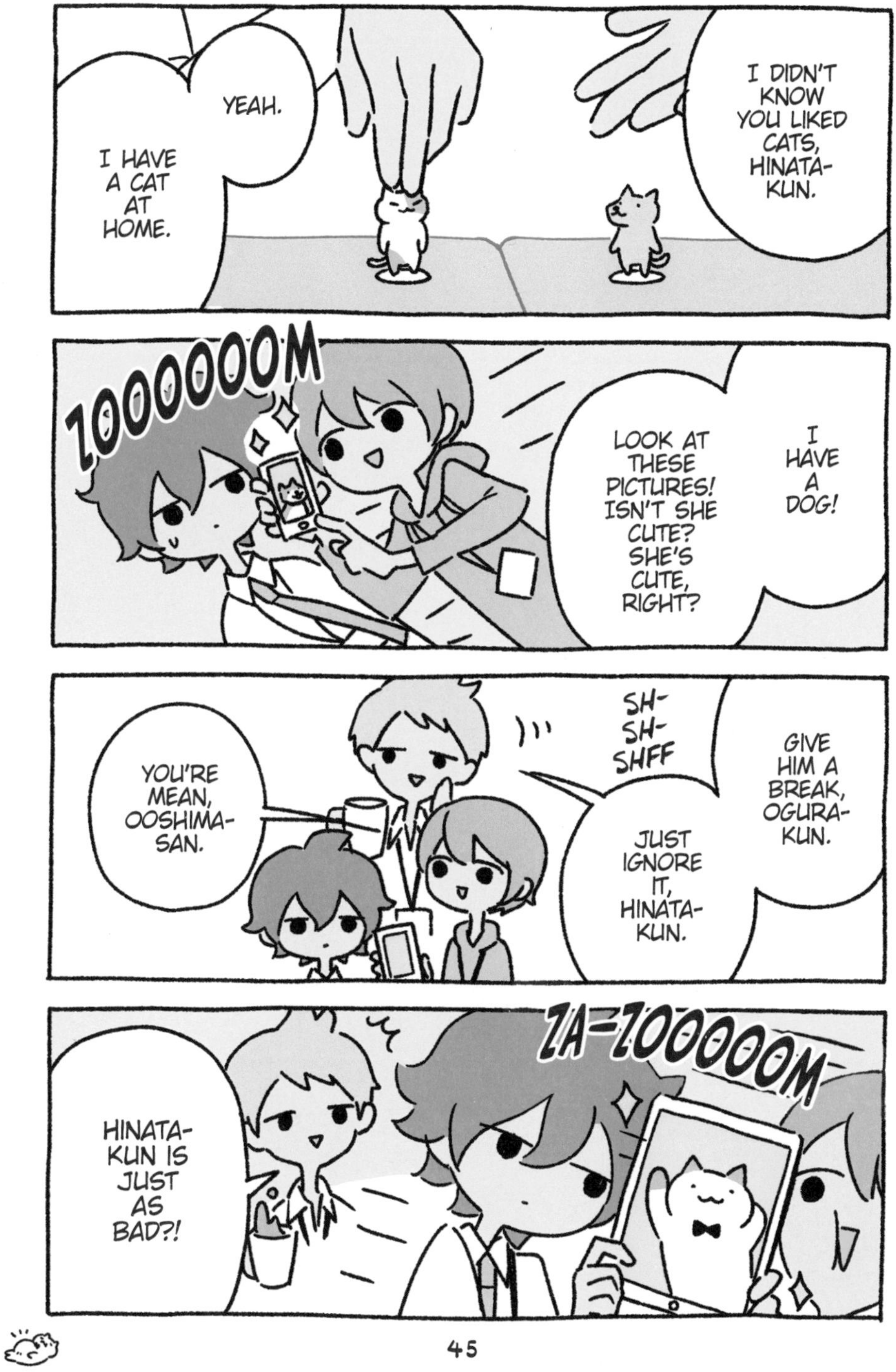
I DIDN'T KNOW YOU LIKED CATS, HINATA-KUN.
YEAH.
I HAVE A CAT AT HOME.
I HAVE A DOG!
LOOK AT THESE PICTURES! ISN'T SHE CUTE? SHE'S CUTE, RIGHT?
ZOOOOOOM
GIVE HIM A BREAK, OGURA-KUN.
SH-SH-SHFF
JUST IGNORE IT, HINATA-KUN.
YOU'RE MEAN, OOSHIMA-SAN.
ZA-ZOOOOOM
HINATA-KUN IS JUST AS BAD?!

CHARM

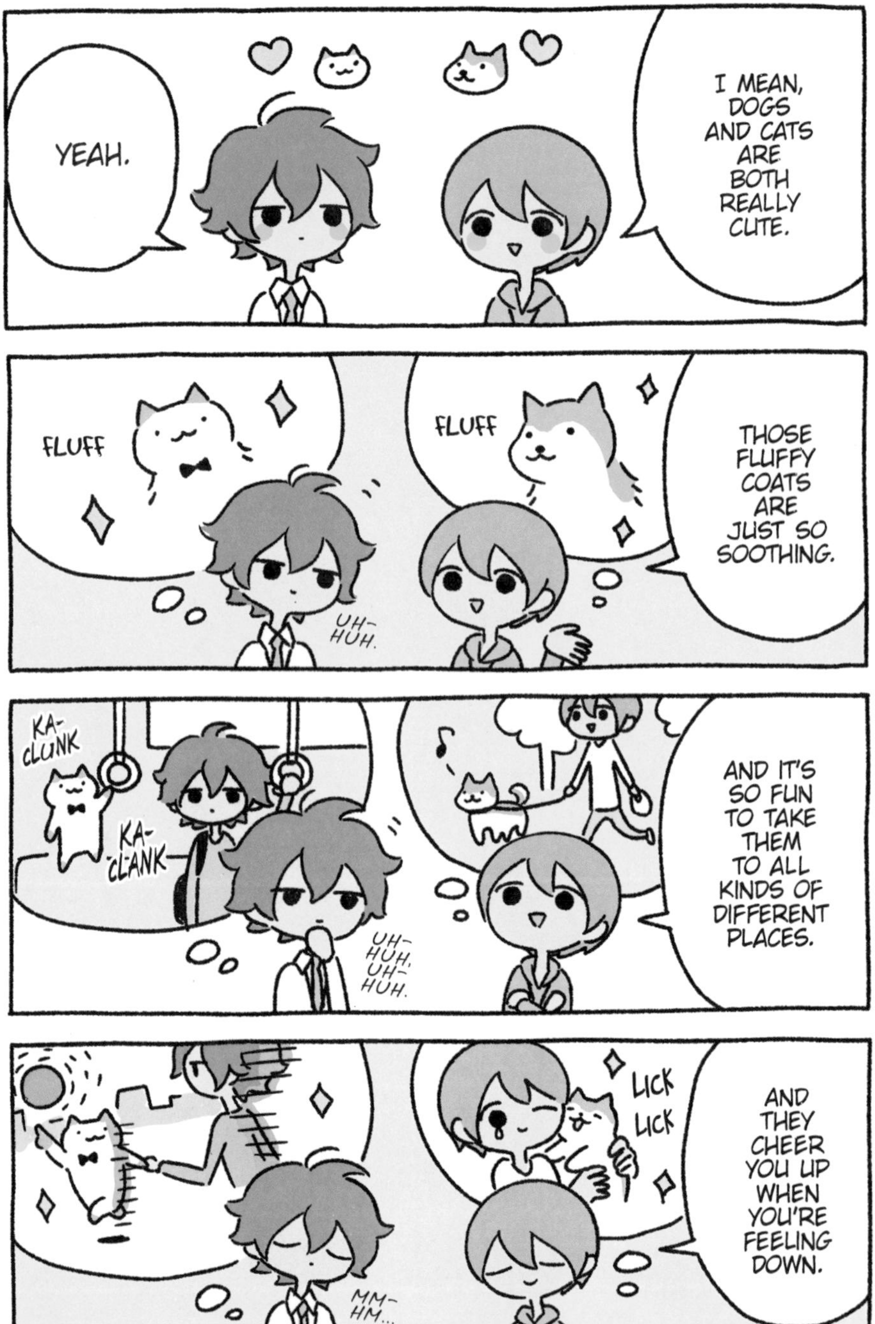
I MEAN, DOGS AND CATS ARE BOTH REALLY CUTE.
YEAH.
THOSE FLUFFY COATS ARE JUST SO SOOTHING.
FLUFF
FLUFF
UH-HUH.
AND IT'S SO FUN TO TAKE THEM TO ALL KINDS OF DIFFERENT PLACES.
KA-CLUNK
KA-CLANK
UH-HUH. UH-HUH.
AND THEY CHEER YOU UP WHEN YOU'RE FEELING DOWN.
LICK LICK
MM-HM...

CLAW SHARPENING

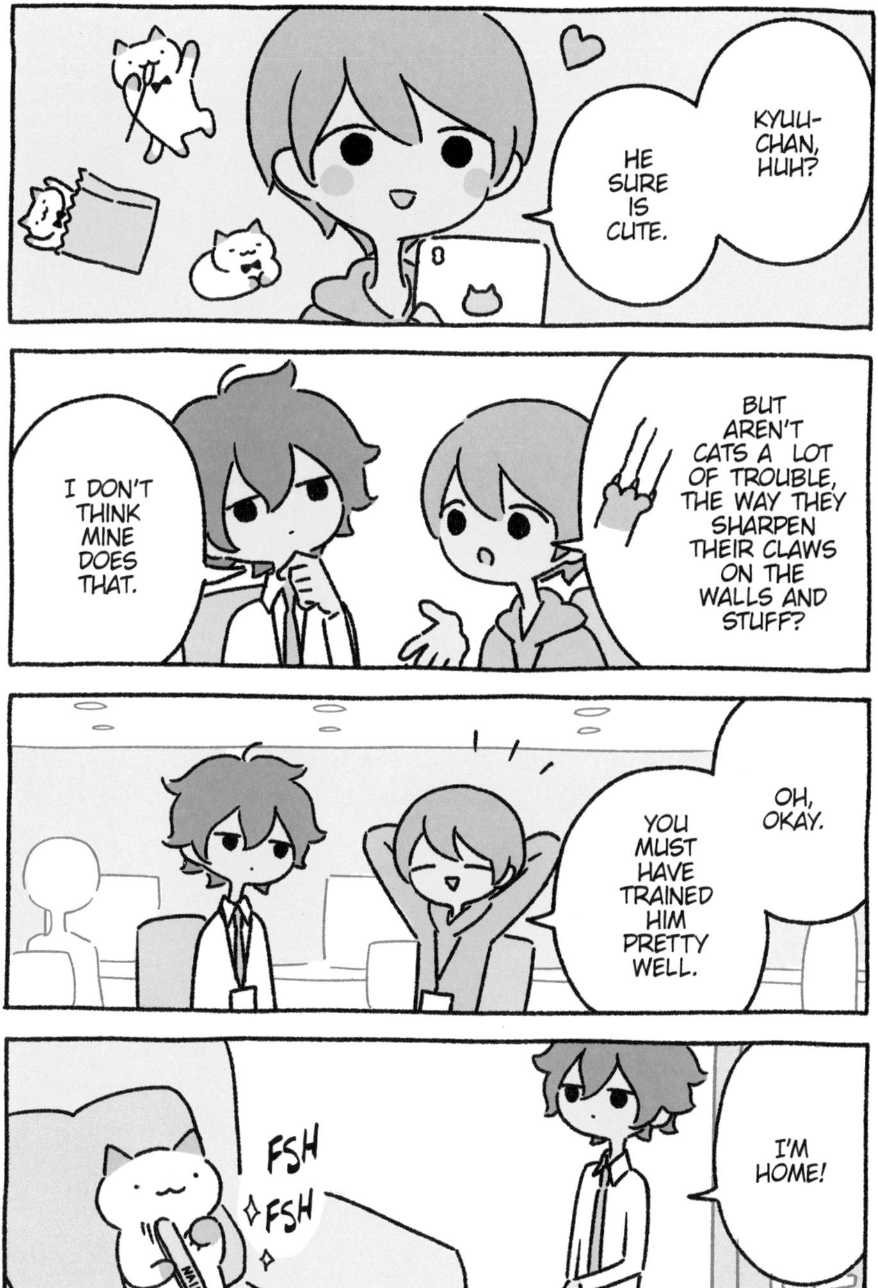
KYUU-CHAN, HUH?
HE SURE IS CUTE.
BUT AREN'T CATS A LOT OF TROUBLE, THE WAY THEY SHARPEN THEIR CLAWS ON THE WALLS AND STUFF?
I DON'T THINK MINE DOES THAT.
OH, OKAY.
YOU MUST HAVE TRAINED HIM PRETTY WELL.
I'M HOME!
FSH
FSH
NAIL

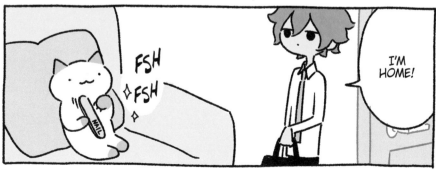

BIRDS OF A FEATHER

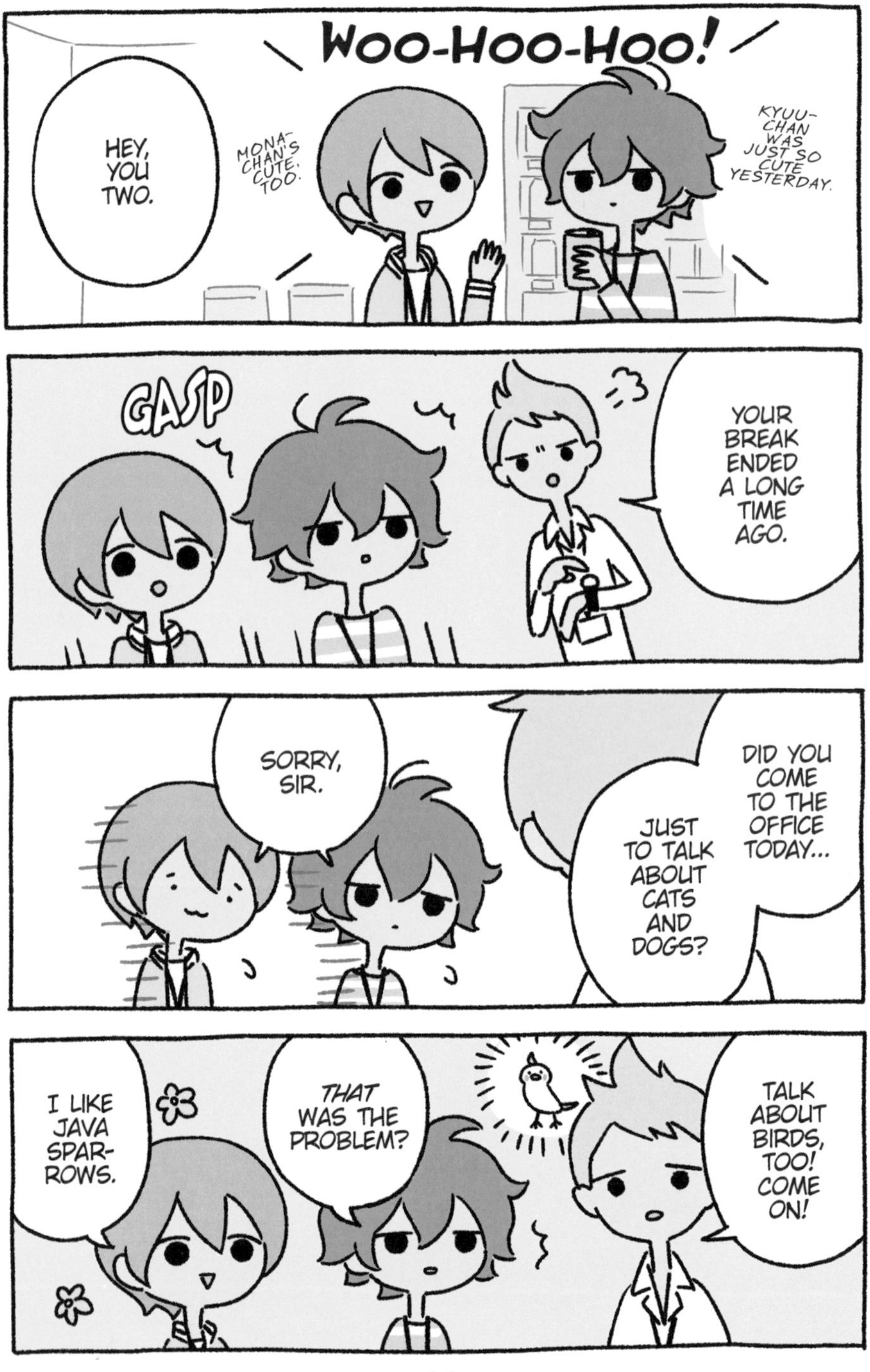
WOO-HOO-HOO!
KYUU-CHAN WAS JUST SO CUTE YESTERDAY.
MONA-CHAN'S CUTE, TOO.
HEY, YOU TWO.
YOUR BREAK ENDED A LONG TIME AGO.
GASP
DID YOU COME TO THE OFFICE TODAY...
JUST TO TALK ABOUT CATS AND DOGS?
SORRY, SIR.
TALK ABOUT BIRDS, TOO! COME ON!
THAT WAS THE PROBLEM?
I LIKE JAVA SPARROWS.

SLEEPING LATE

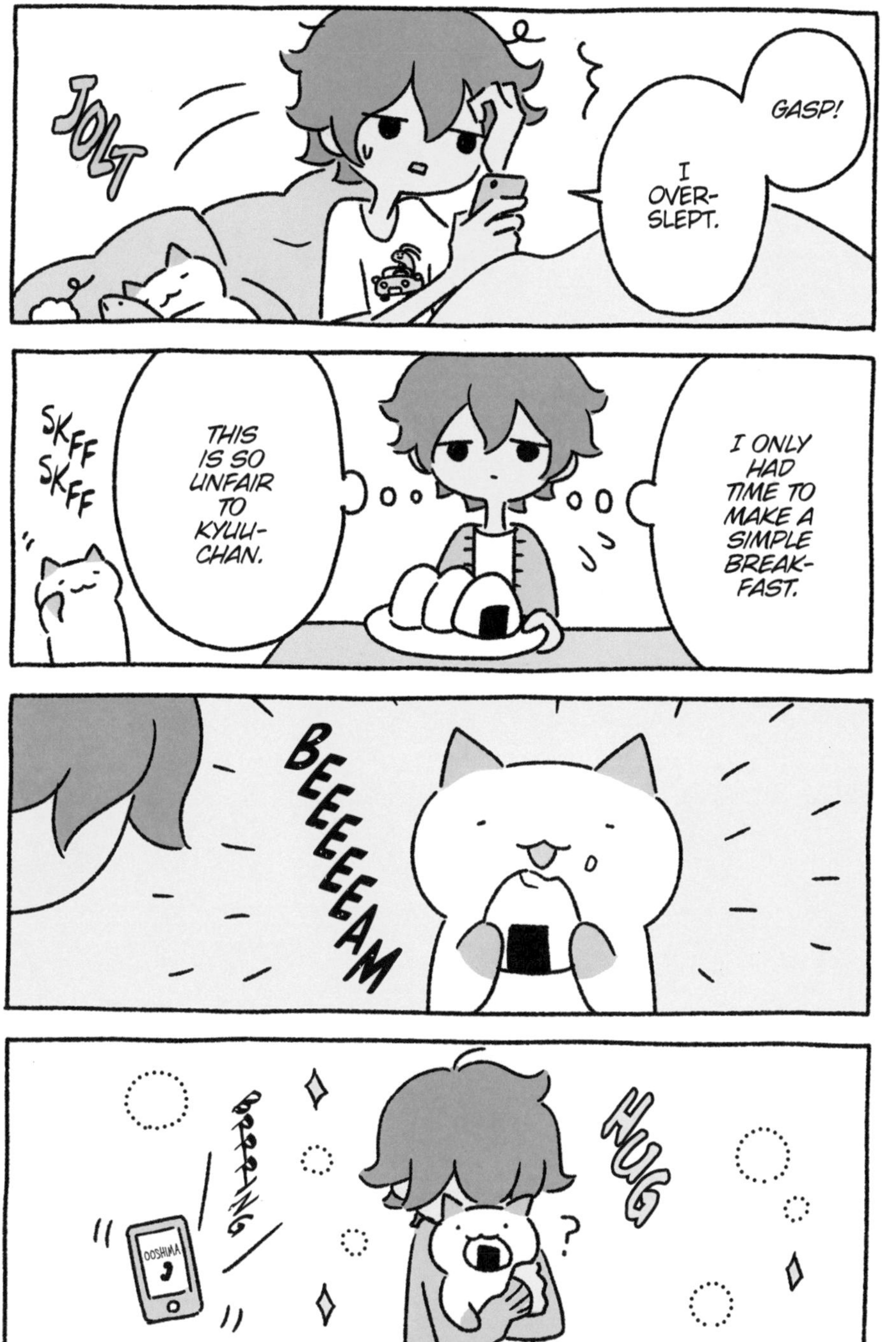
JOLT
GASP!
I OVERSLEPT.
SKFF SKFF
THIS IS SO UNFAIR TO KYUU-CHAN.
I ONLY HAD TIME TO MAKE A SIMPLE BREAKFAST.
BEEEEEAM
BRRRING
OOSHIMA
HUG
?

EAT UP

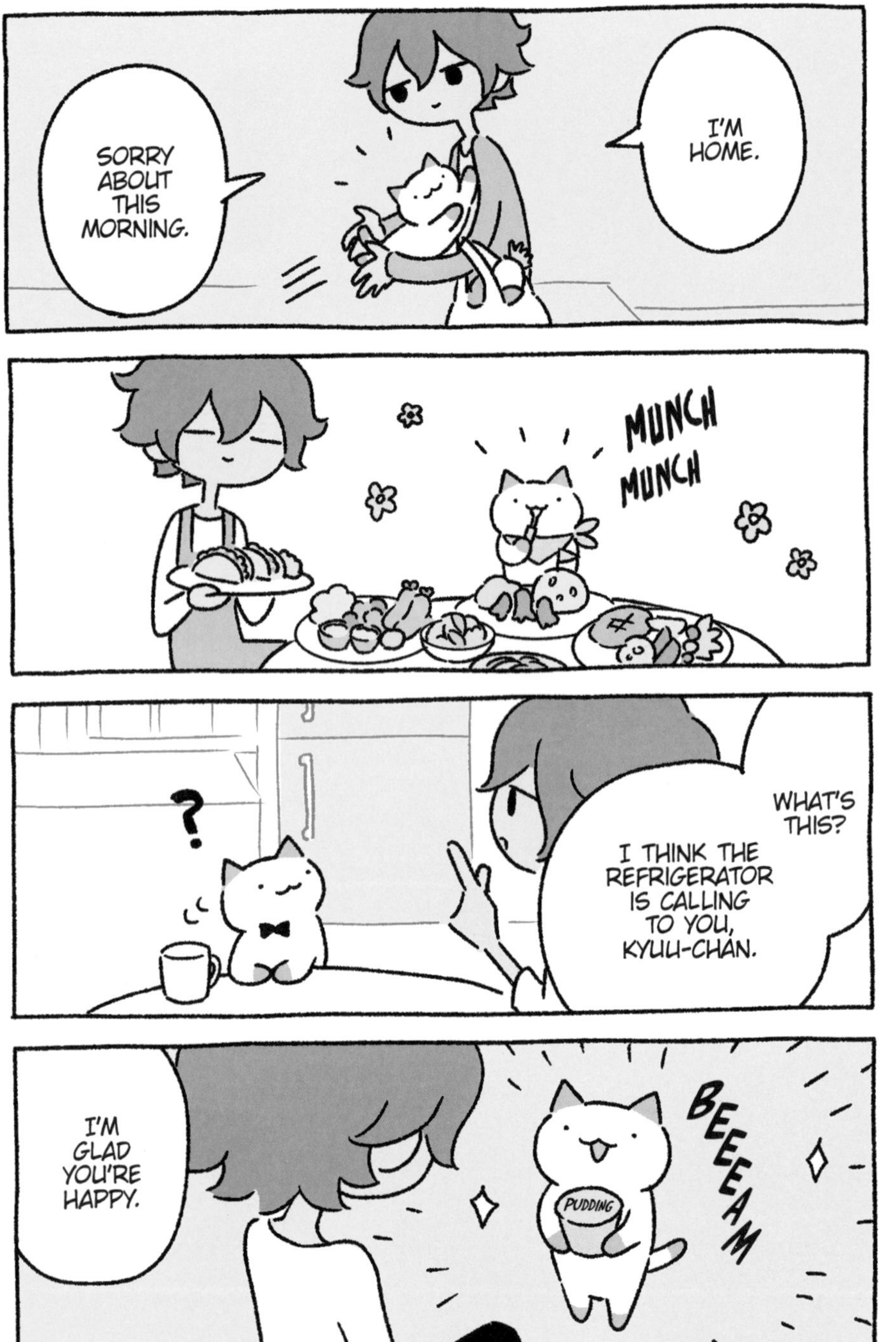

I'M HOME.
SORRY ABOUT THIS MORNING.
MUNCH MUNCH
WHAT'S THIS?
I THINK THE REFRIGERATOR IS CALLING TO YOU, KYUU-CHAN.
BEEEAM
PUDDING
I'M GLAD YOU'RE HAPPY.

I'D RATHER BE WITH YOU

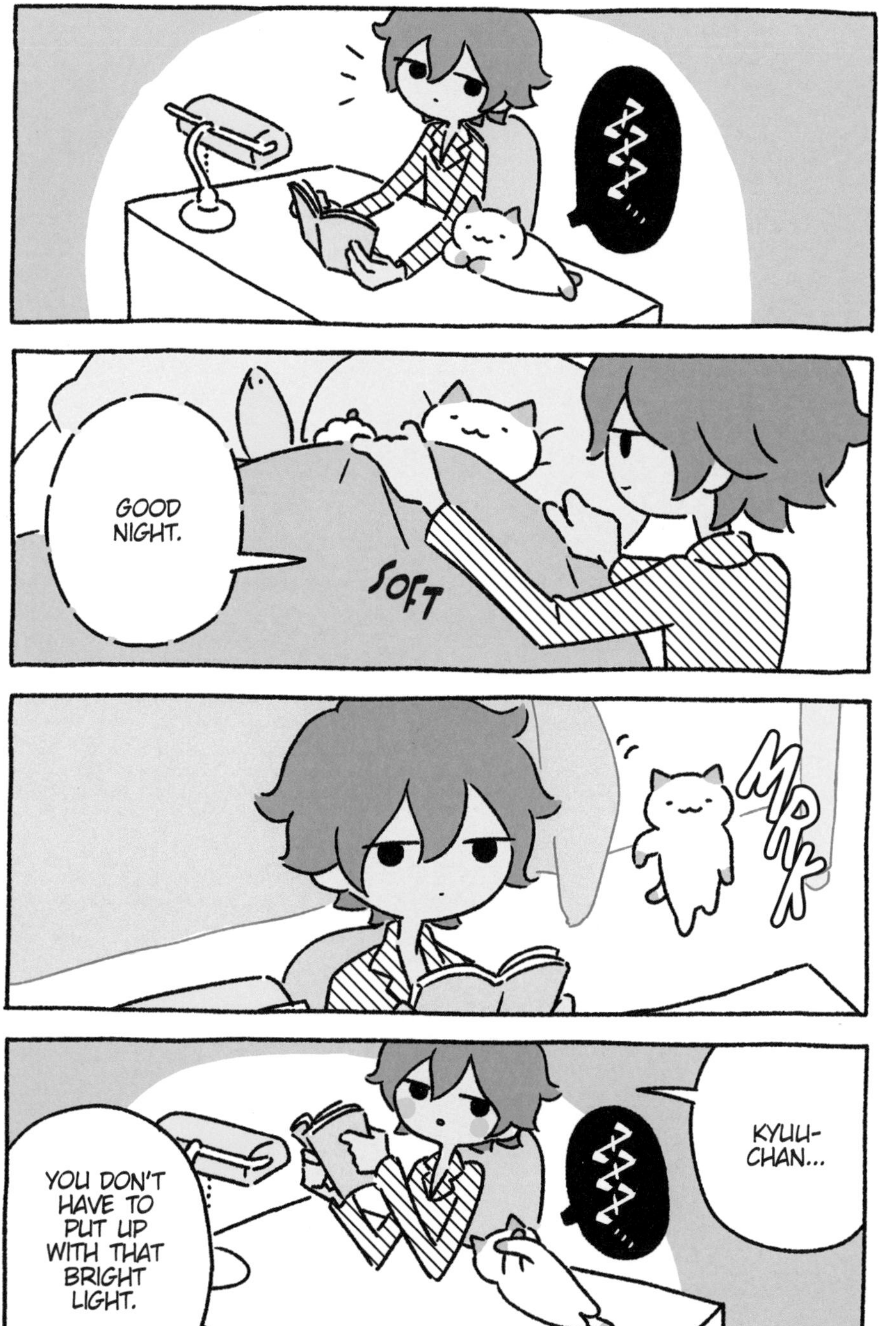
ZZZ...
GOOD NIGHT.
SOFT
MRRK
KYUU-CHAN...
YOU DON'T HAVE TO PUT UP WITH THAT BRIGHT LIGHT.
ZZZ...

CUCUMBER ①

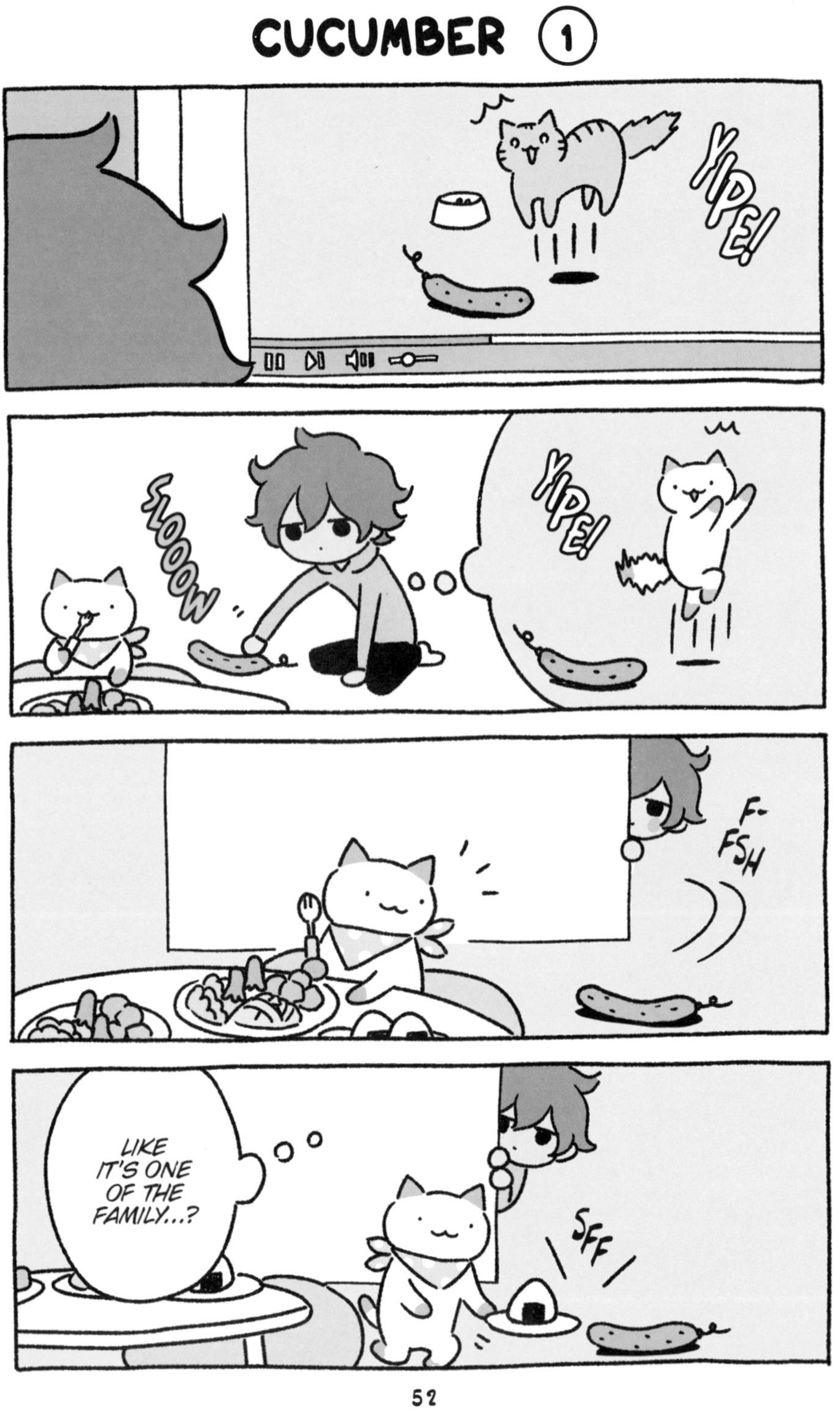
YIPE!
YIPE!
SLOOOW
F-FSH
SFF
LIKE IT'S ONE OF THE FAMILY...?

CUCUMBER ②

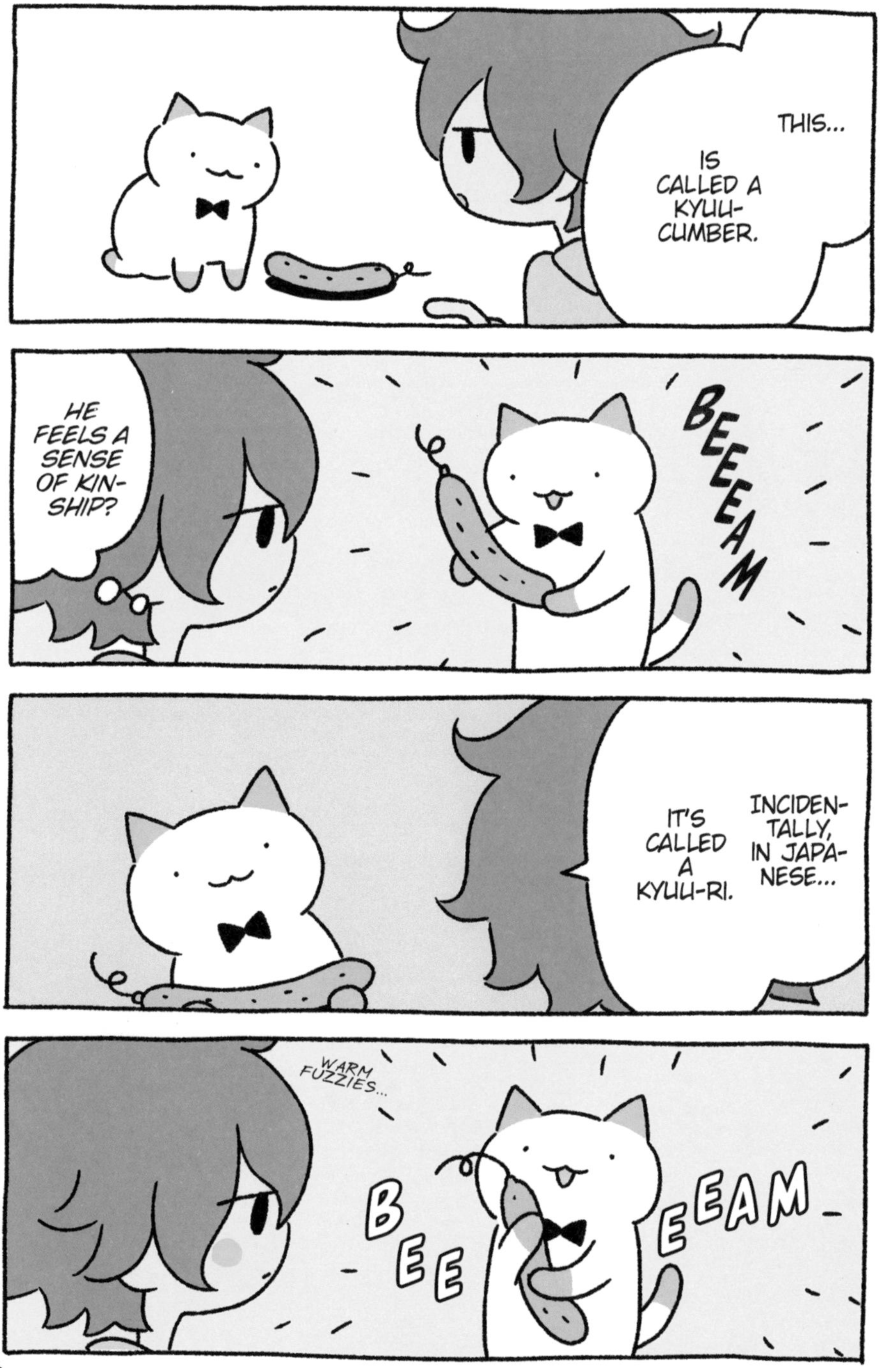
THIS...
IS CALLED A KYUU-CUMBER.
BEEEEAM
HE FEELS A SENSE OF KIN-SHIP?
INCIDEN-TALLY, IN JAPA-NESE...
IT'S CALLED A KYUU-RI.
BEEEEAM
WARM FUZZIES...

CLEANING DAY

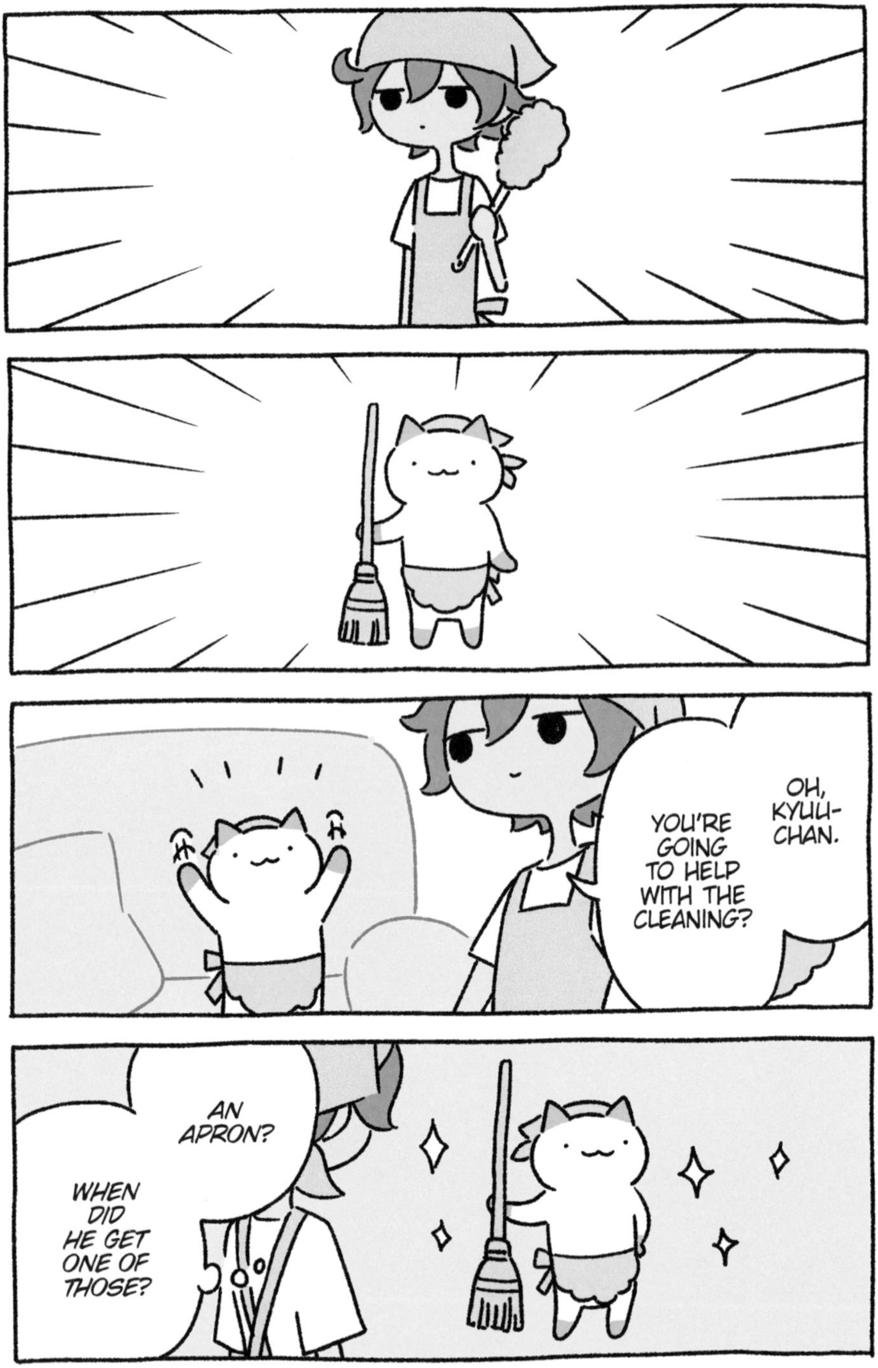
OH, KYUU-CHAN.
YOU'RE GOING TO HELP WITH THE CLEANING?
AN APRON?
WHEN DID HE GET ONE OF THOSE?

CAPTURE

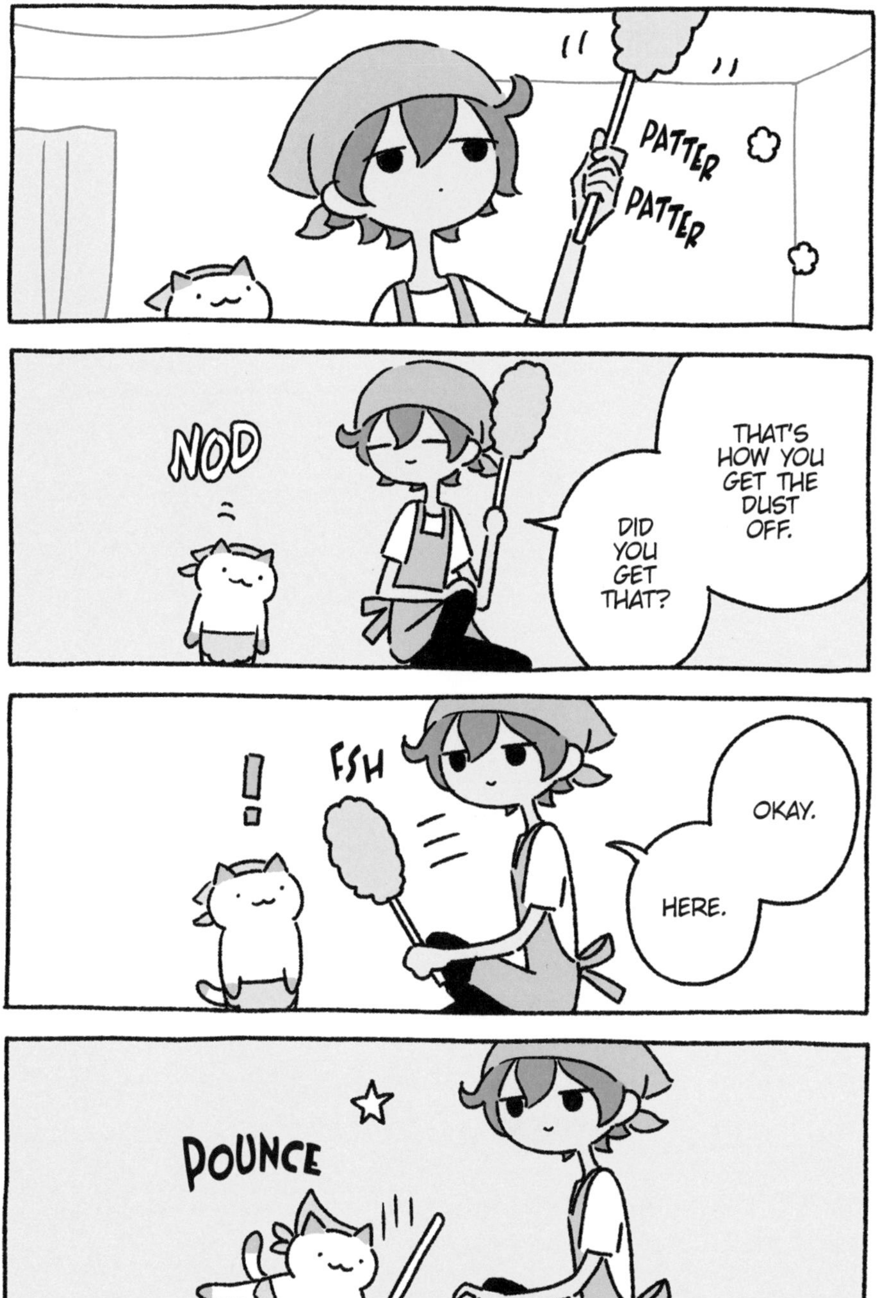
PATTER
PATTER
NOD
THAT'S HOW YOU GET THE DUST OFF.
DID YOU GET THAT?
!
FSH
OKAY.
HERE.
POUNCE

ENTHUSIASM

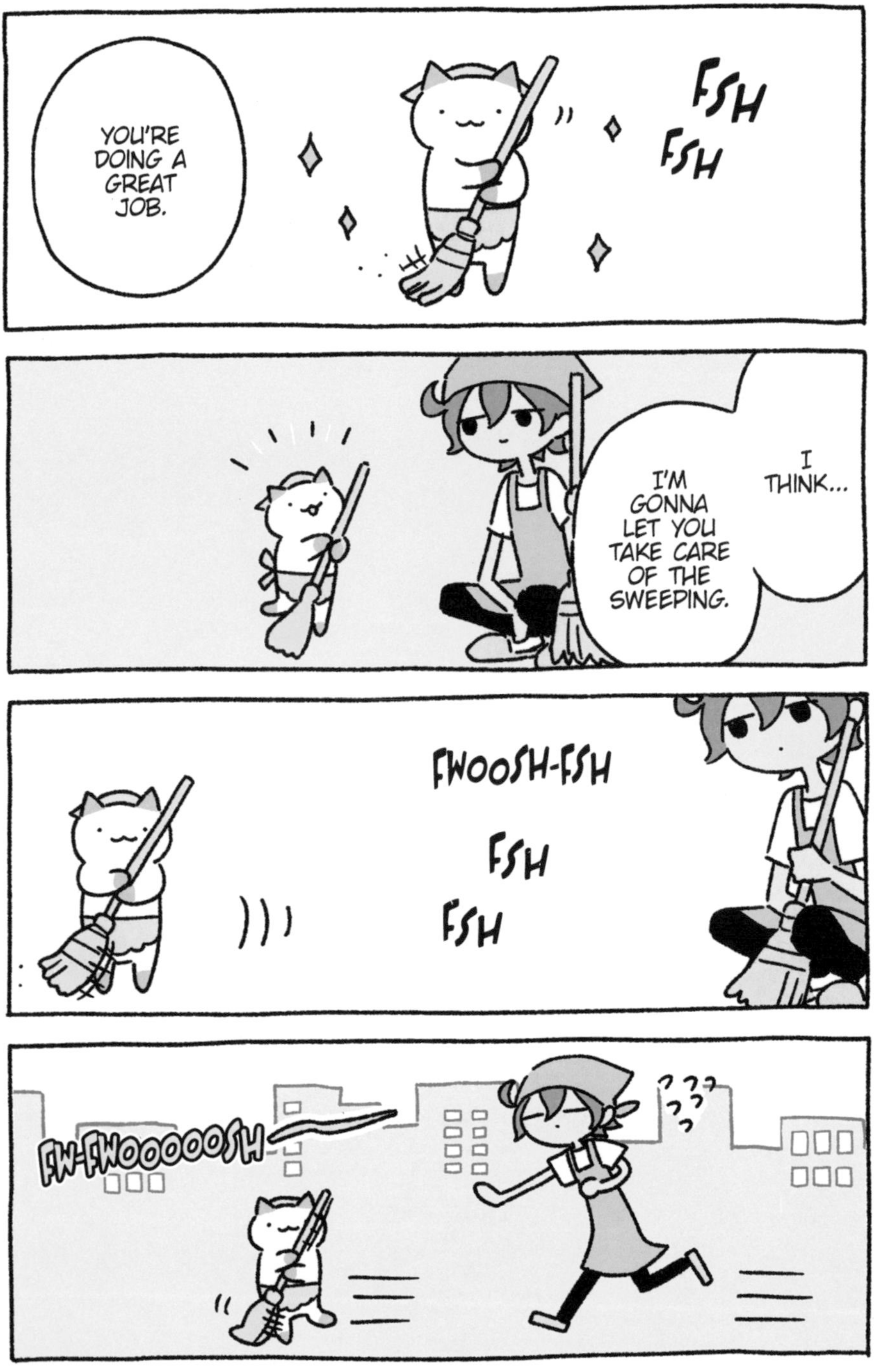

FSH
FSH
YOU'RE DOING A GREAT JOB.
I THINK...
I'M GONNA LET YOU TAKE CARE OF THE SWEEPING.
FWOOSH-FSH
FSH
FSH
FW-FWOOOOOOSH

DISTRACTIONS

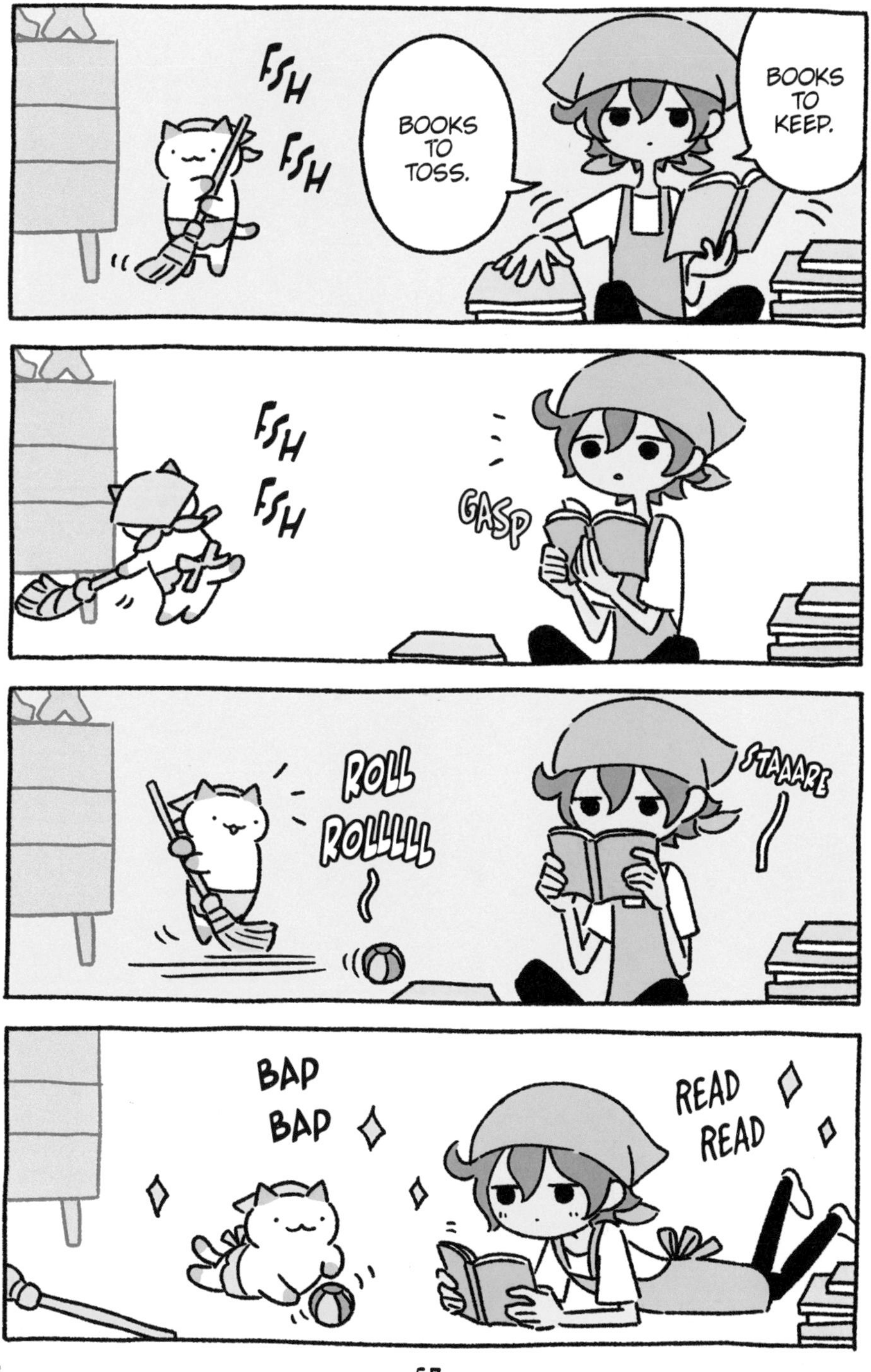
BOOKS TO KEEP.
BOOKS TO TOSS.
FSH
FSH
GASP
FSH
FSH
STAAARE
ROLL
ROLLLLL
READ
READ
BAP
BAP

MONKEY SEE, MONKEY DO

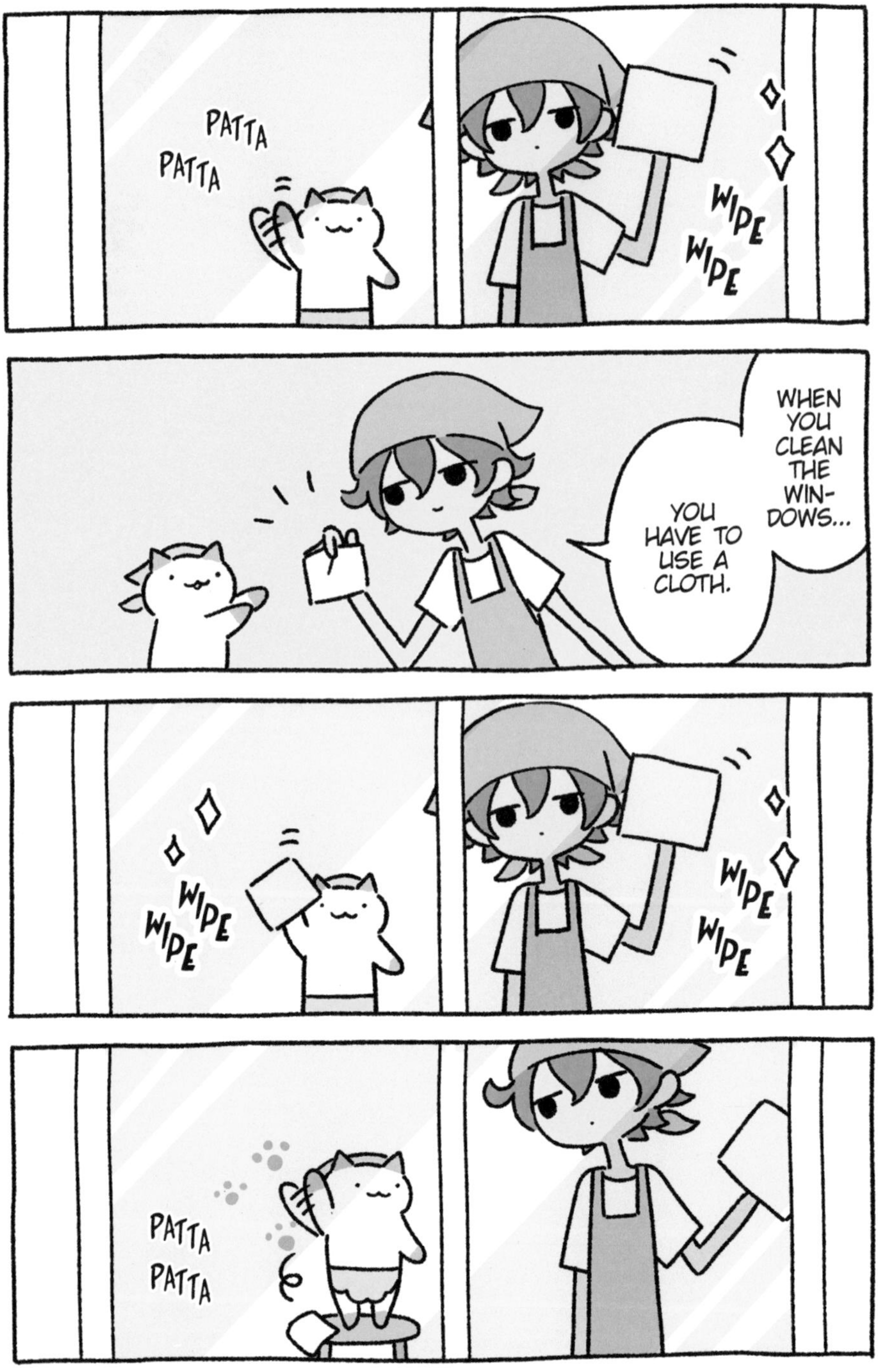
WIPE
WIPE
PATTA
PATTA
WHEN YOU CLEAN THE WIN-DOWS...
YOU HAVE TO USE A CLOTH.
WIPE
WIPE
WIPE
WIPE
PATTA
PATTA

FINISHING UP

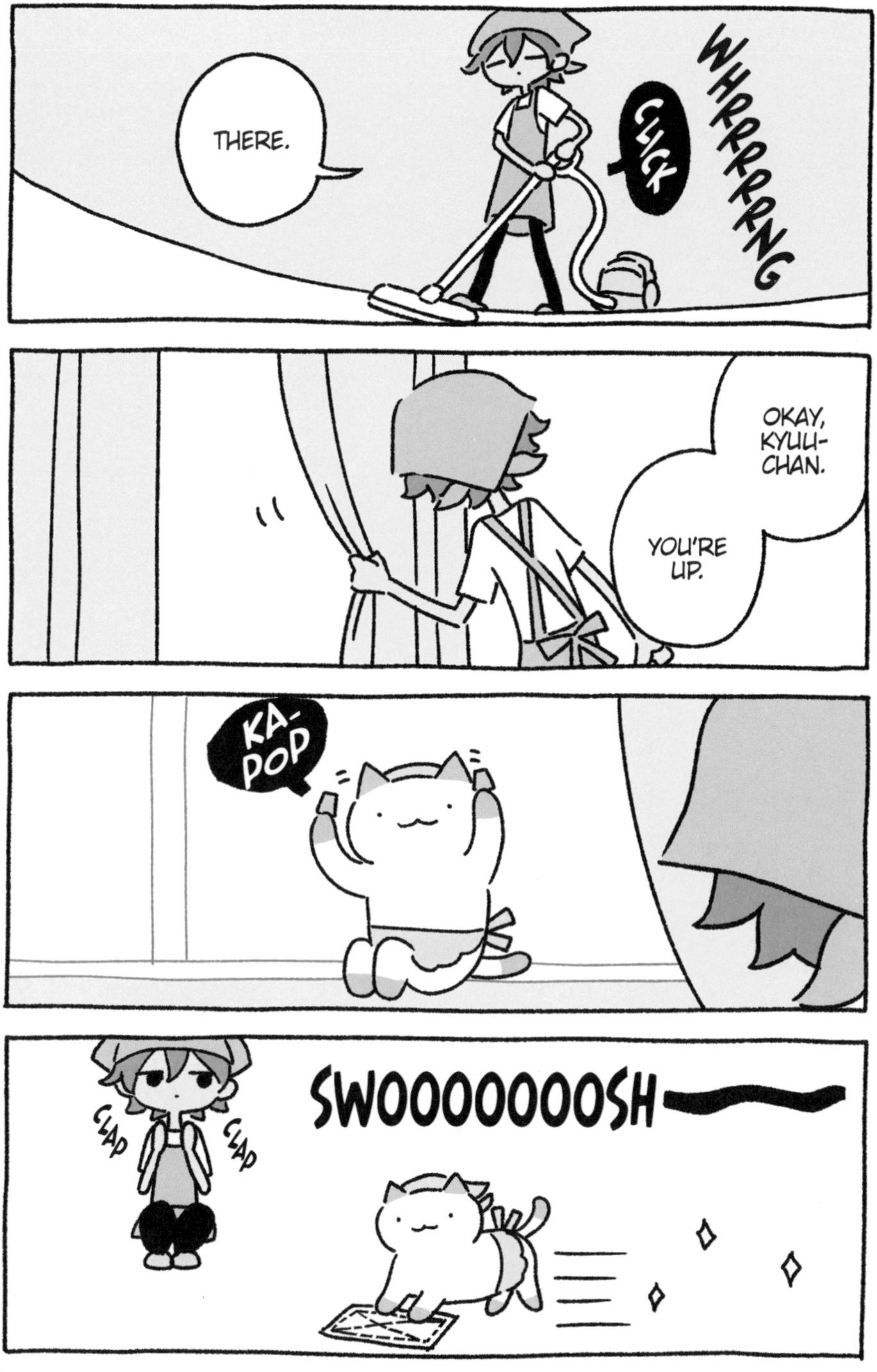

WHRRRRNG
CLICK
THERE.
OKAY, KYUU-CHAN.
YOU'RE UP.
KA-POP
SWOOOOOOOSH
CLAP
CLAP

A JOB WELL DONE

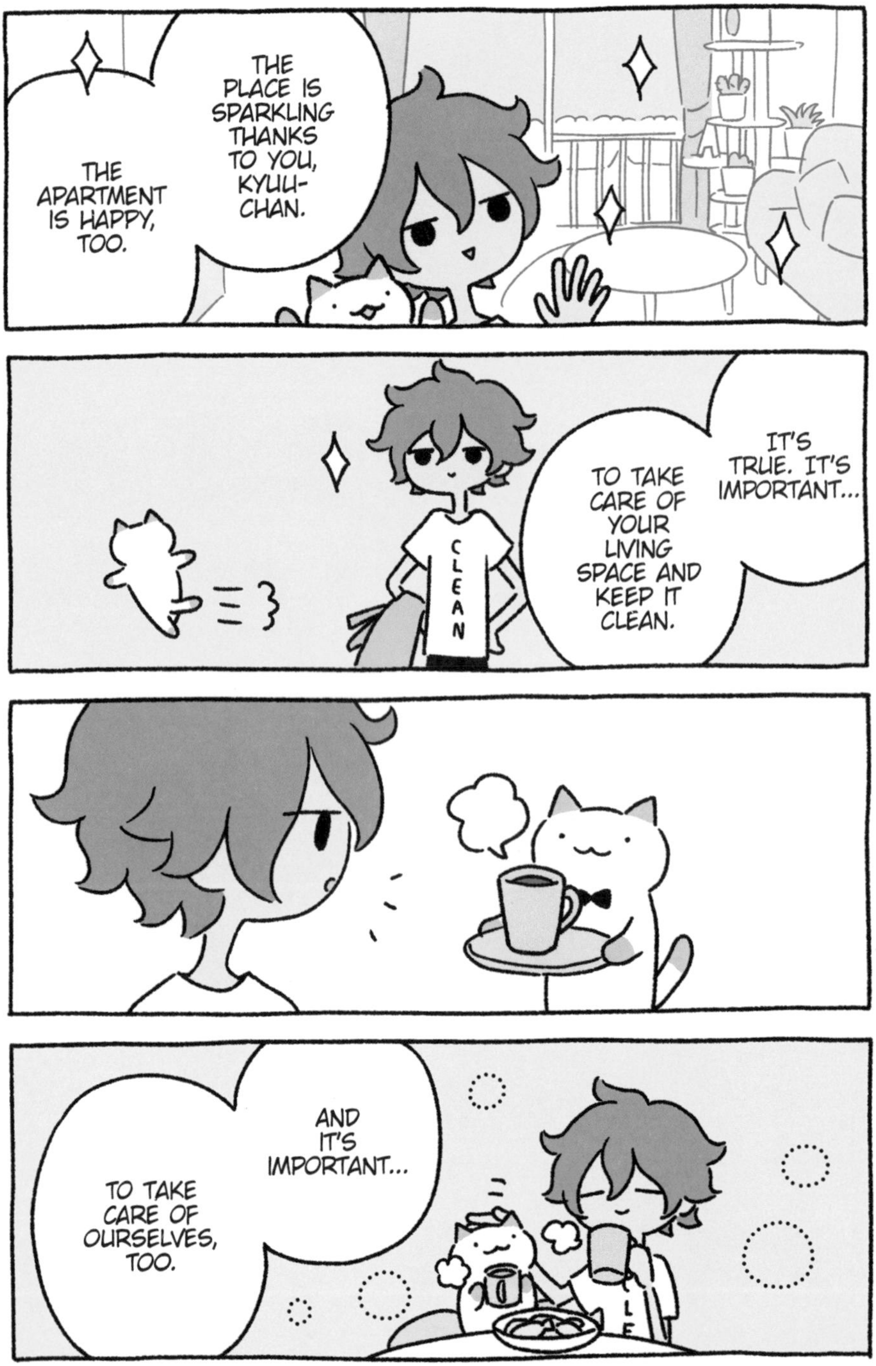
THE PLACE IS SPARKLING THANKS TO YOU, KYUU-CHAN.
THE APARTMENT IS HAPPY, TOO.
IT'S TRUE. IT'S IMPORTANT...
TO TAKE CARE OF YOUR LIVING SPACE AND KEEP IT CLEAN.
CLEAN
AND IT'S IMPORTANT...
TO TAKE CARE OF OURSELVES, TOO.

JUST FOR FUN

COULD YOU SORT THE PAPER TRASH?
NOD
TRASH
CHIP
WHAT HAP-PENED ...?
?
CHIPS

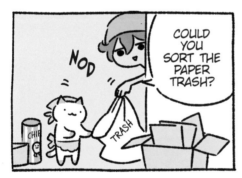

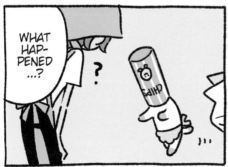

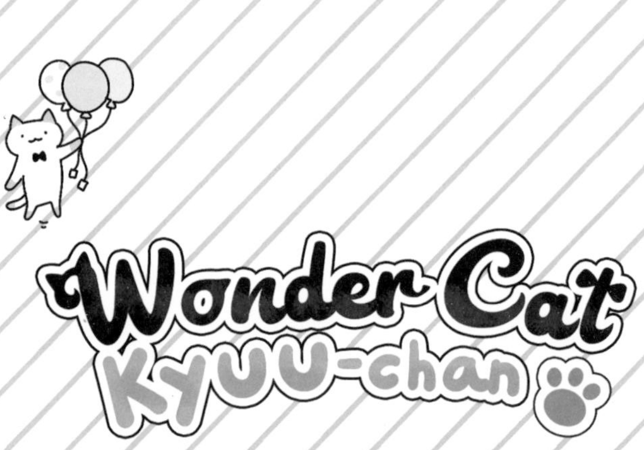

Wonder Cat Kyuu-chan

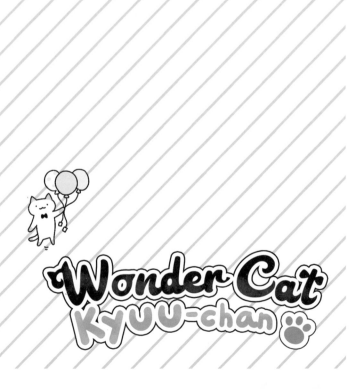

MORNING

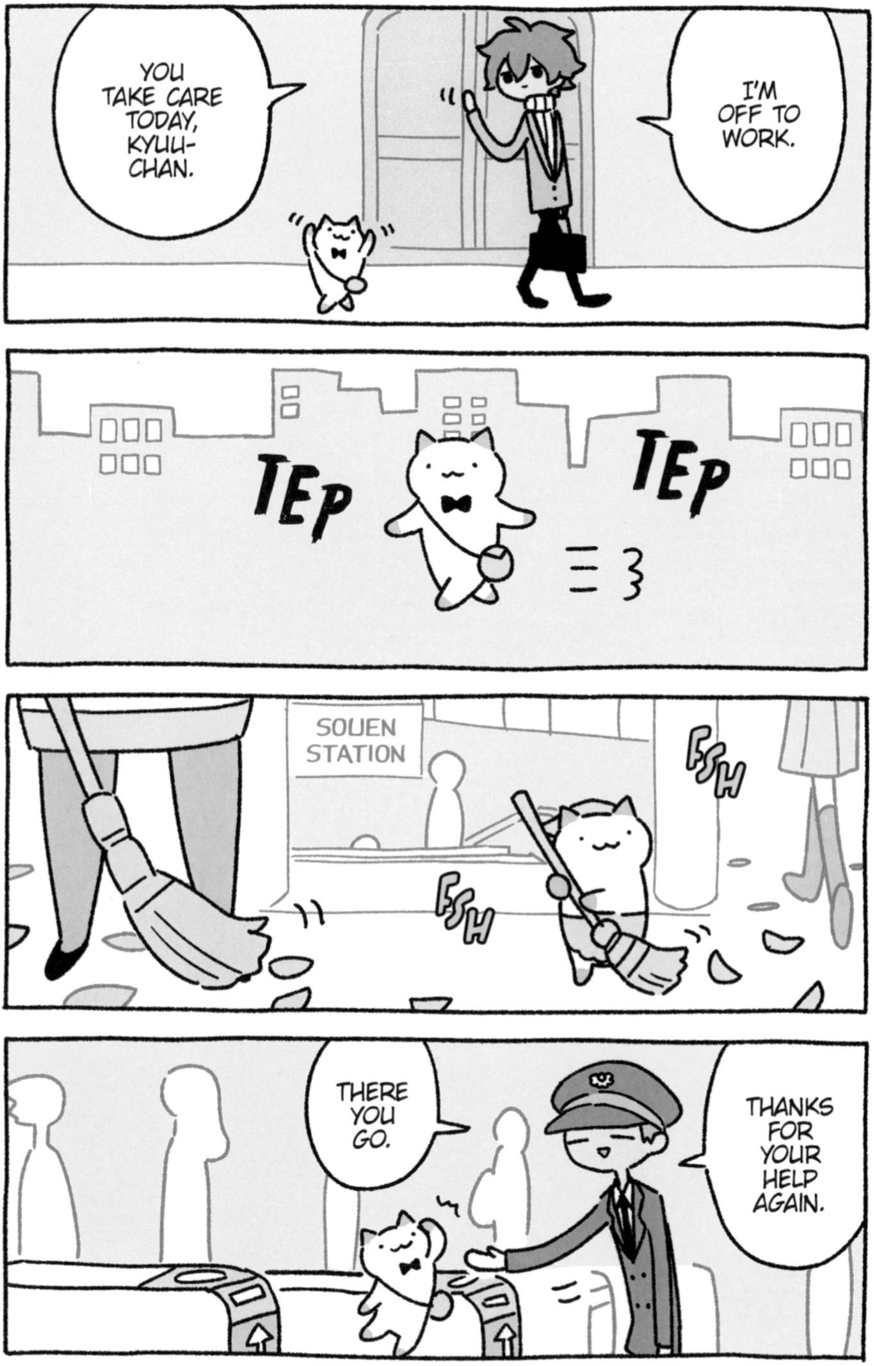
I'M OFF TO WORK.
YOU TAKE CARE TODAY, KYUU-CHAN.
TEP
TEP
FSH
SOUEN STATION
FSH
THANKS FOR YOUR HELP AGAIN.
THERE YOU GO.

HELP

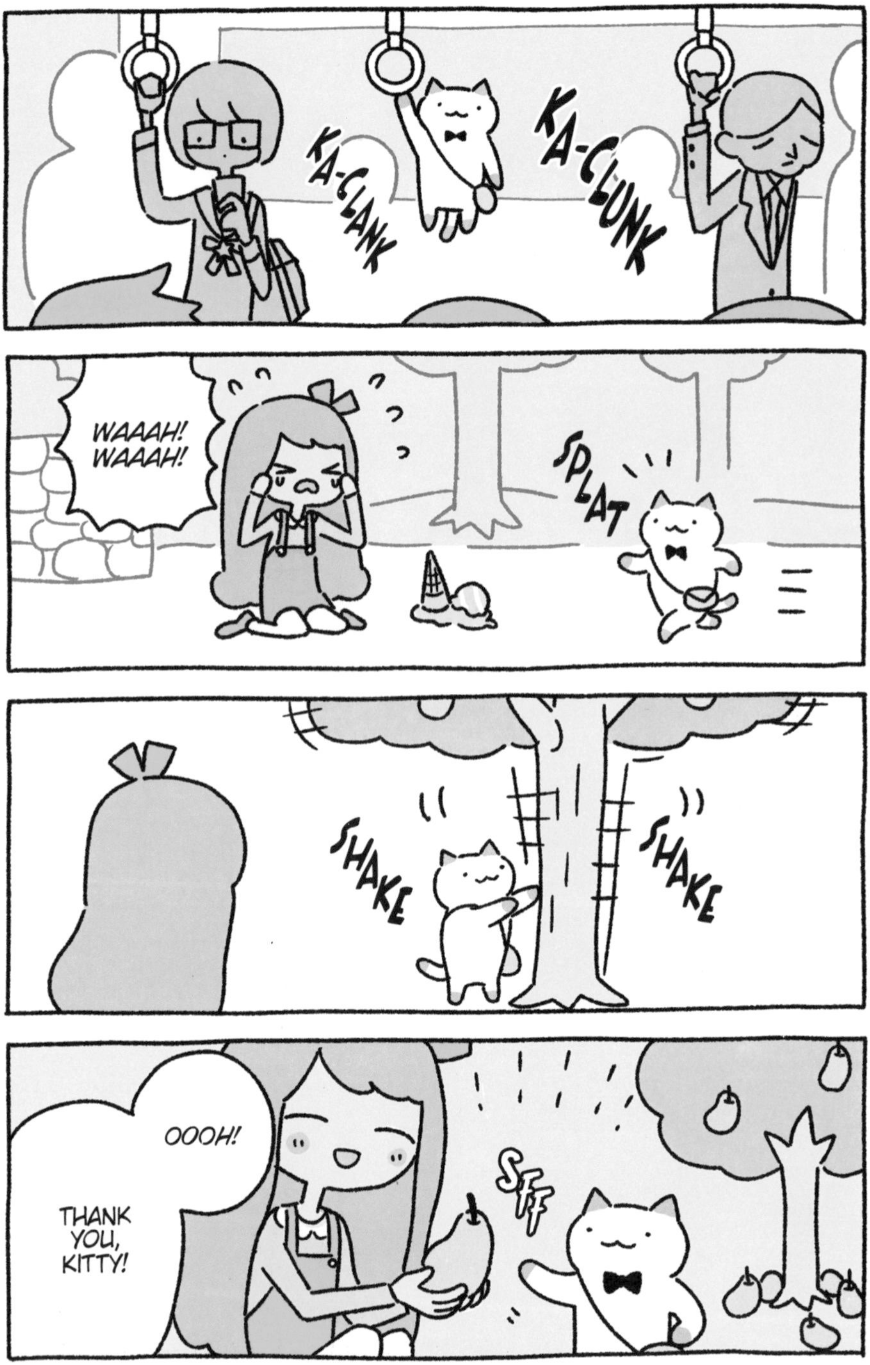
KA-CLUNK
KA-CLANK
SPLAT
WAAAH! WAAAH!
SHAKE
SHAKE
SFF
OOOH!
THANK YOU, KITTY!

GENERAL STORE

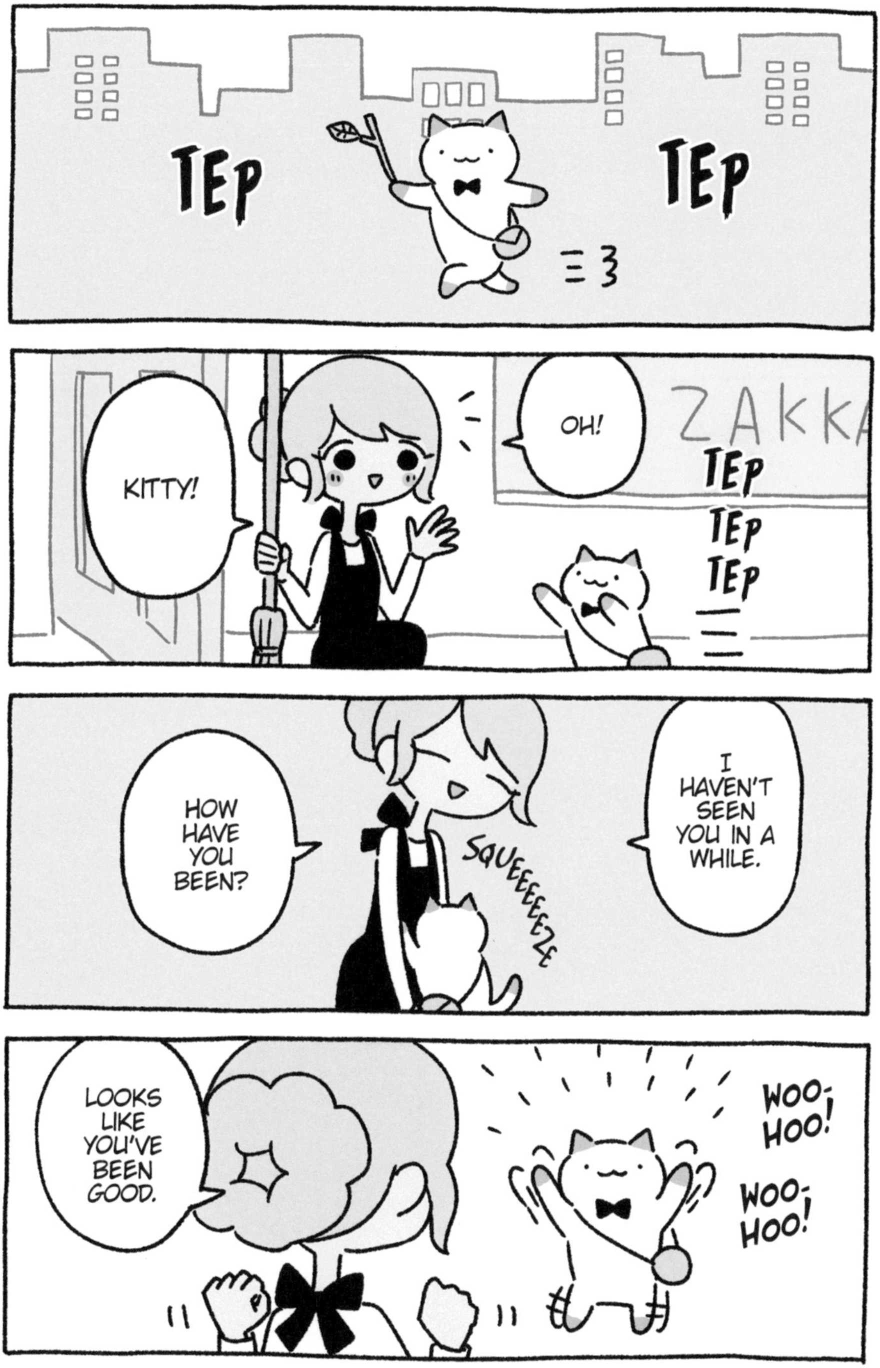
TEP
TEP
ZAKKA
OH!
KITTY!
TEP
TEP
TEP
I HAVEN'T SEEN YOU IN A WHILE.
SQUEEEEEEEZE
HOW HAVE YOU BEEN?
WOO-HOO!
WOO-HOO!
LOOKS LIKE YOU'VE BEEN GOOD.

JOB SHADOWING

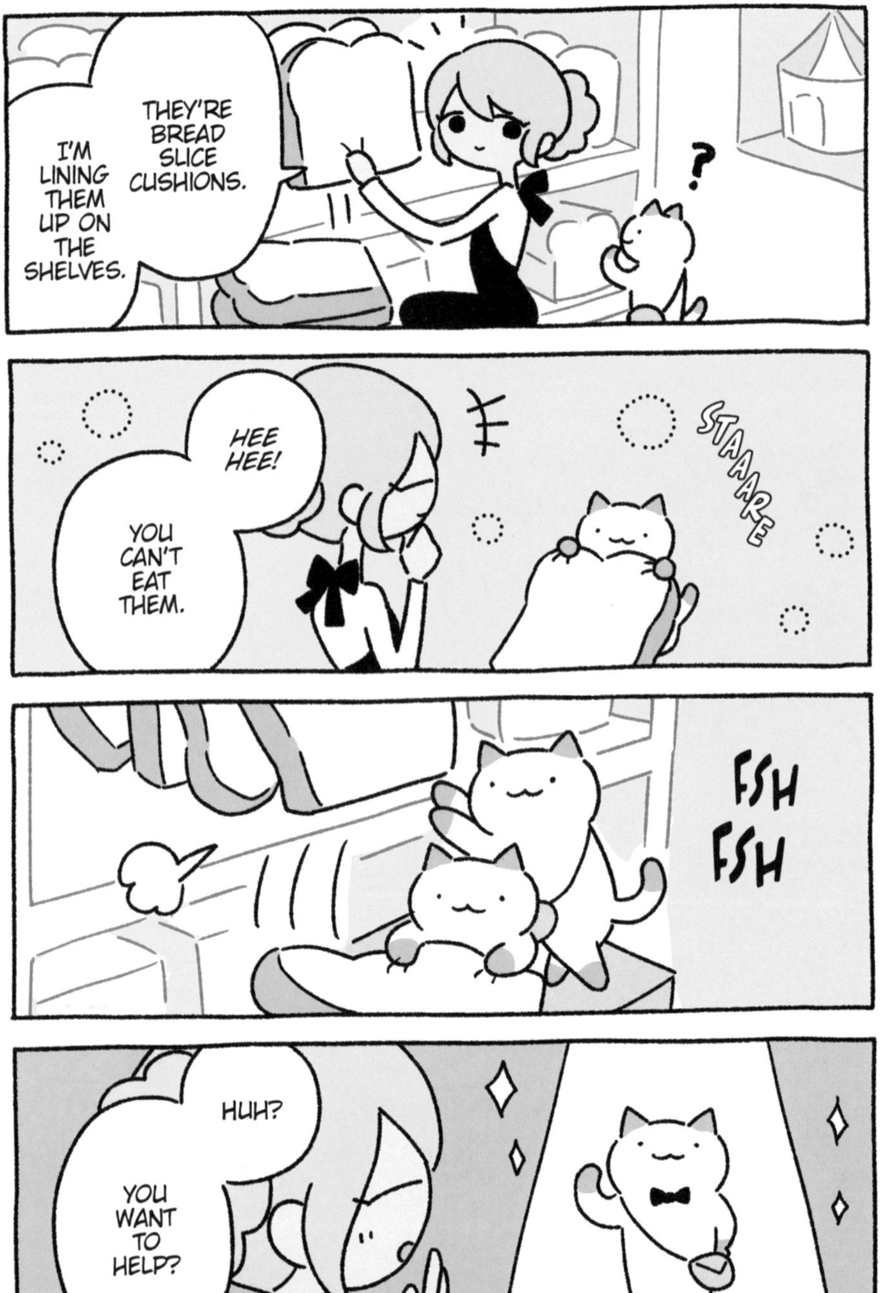
THEY'RE BREAD SLICE CUSHIONS.
I'M LINING THEM UP ON THE SHELVES.
?
STAAARE
HEE HEE!
YOU CAN'T EAT THEM.
FSH FSH
HUH?
YOU WANT TO HELP?

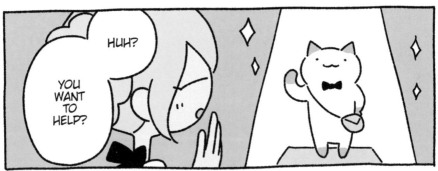

ASSISTANT

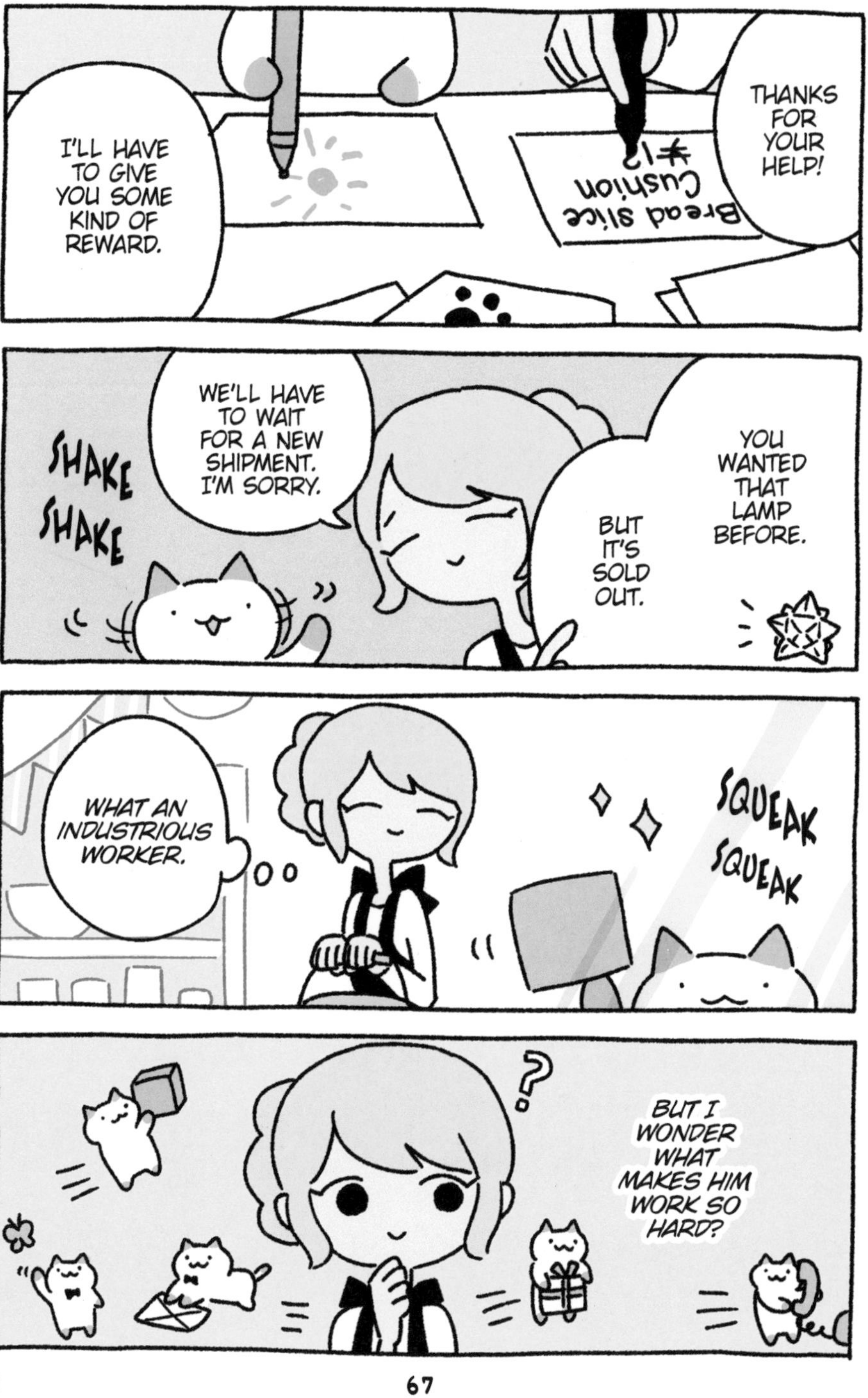
THANKS FOR YOUR HELP!
Bread slice Cushion
I'LL HAVE TO GIVE YOU SOME KIND OF REWARD.
YOU WANTED THAT LAMP BEFORE.
BUT IT'S SOLD OUT.
WE'LL HAVE TO WAIT FOR A NEW SHIPMENT. I'M SORRY.
SHAKE SHAKE
SQUEAK SQUEAK
WHAT AN INDUSTRIOUS WORKER.
BUT I WONDER WHAT MAKES HIM WORK SO HARD?

WELCOME HOME

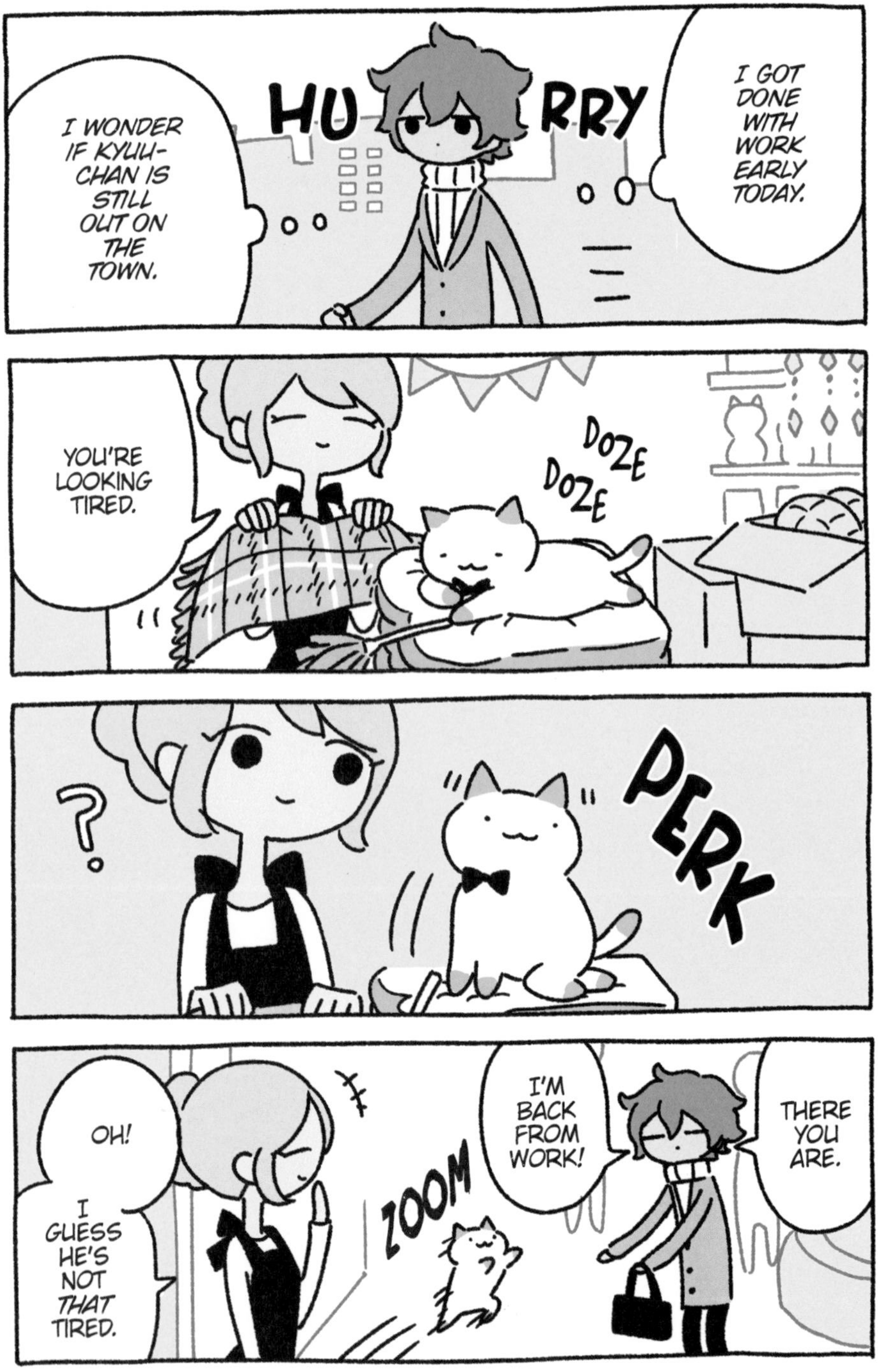

I GOT DONE WITH WORK EARLY TODAY.
HURRY
I WONDER IF KYUU-CHAN IS STILL OUT ON THE TOWN.
DOZE DOZE
YOU'RE LOOKING TIRED.
PERK
?
THERE YOU ARE.
I'M BACK FROM WORK!
ZOOM
OH!
I GUESS HE'S NOT THAT TIRED.

SOUVENIR

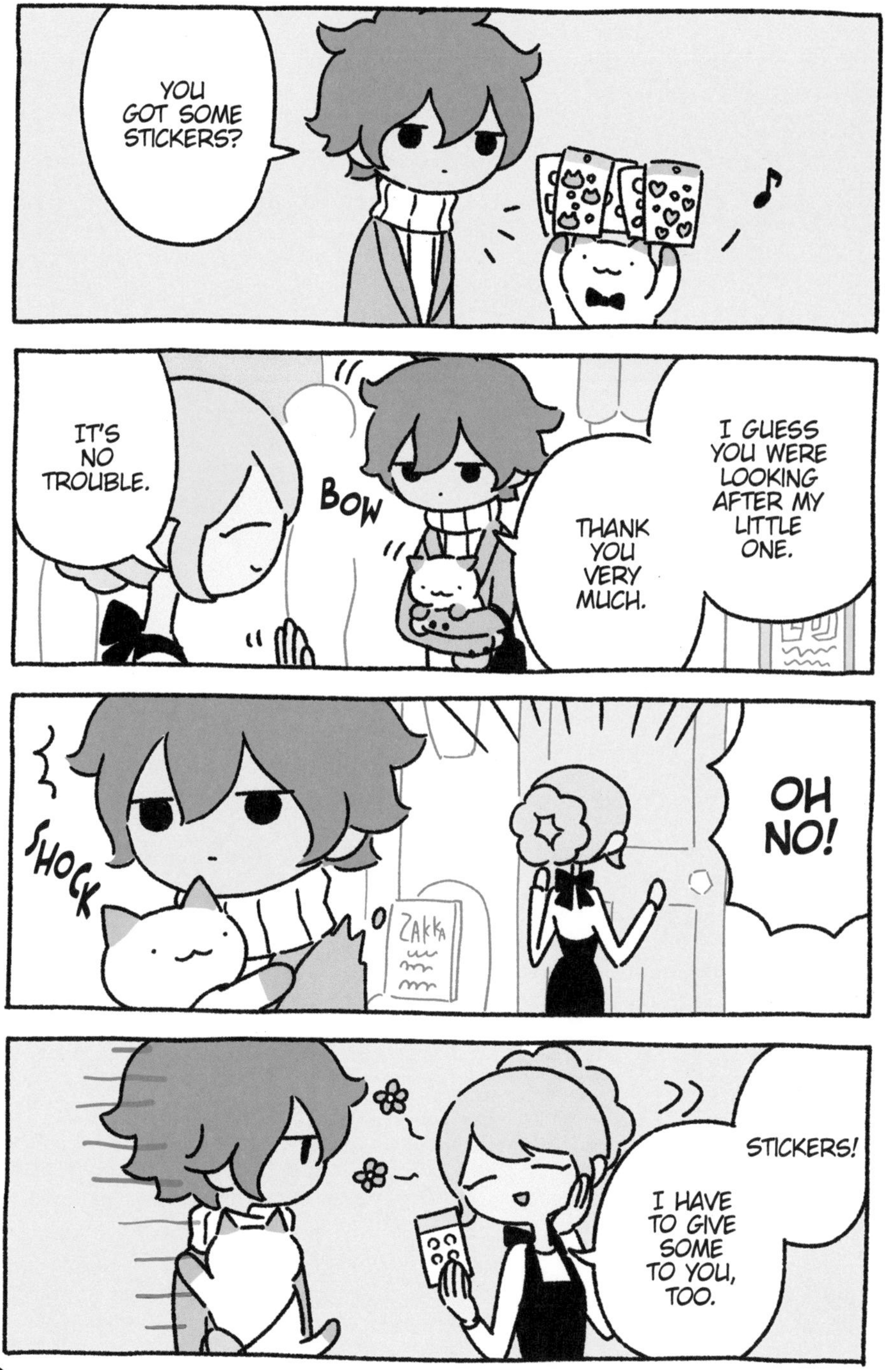
YOU GOT SOME STICKERS?
I GUESS YOU WERE LOOKING AFTER MY LITTLE ONE.
THANK YOU VERY MUCH.
BOW
IT'S NO TROUBLE.
OH NO!
ZAKKA
SHOCK
STICKERS!
I HAVE TO GIVE SOME TO YOU, TOO.

UNEXPECTED

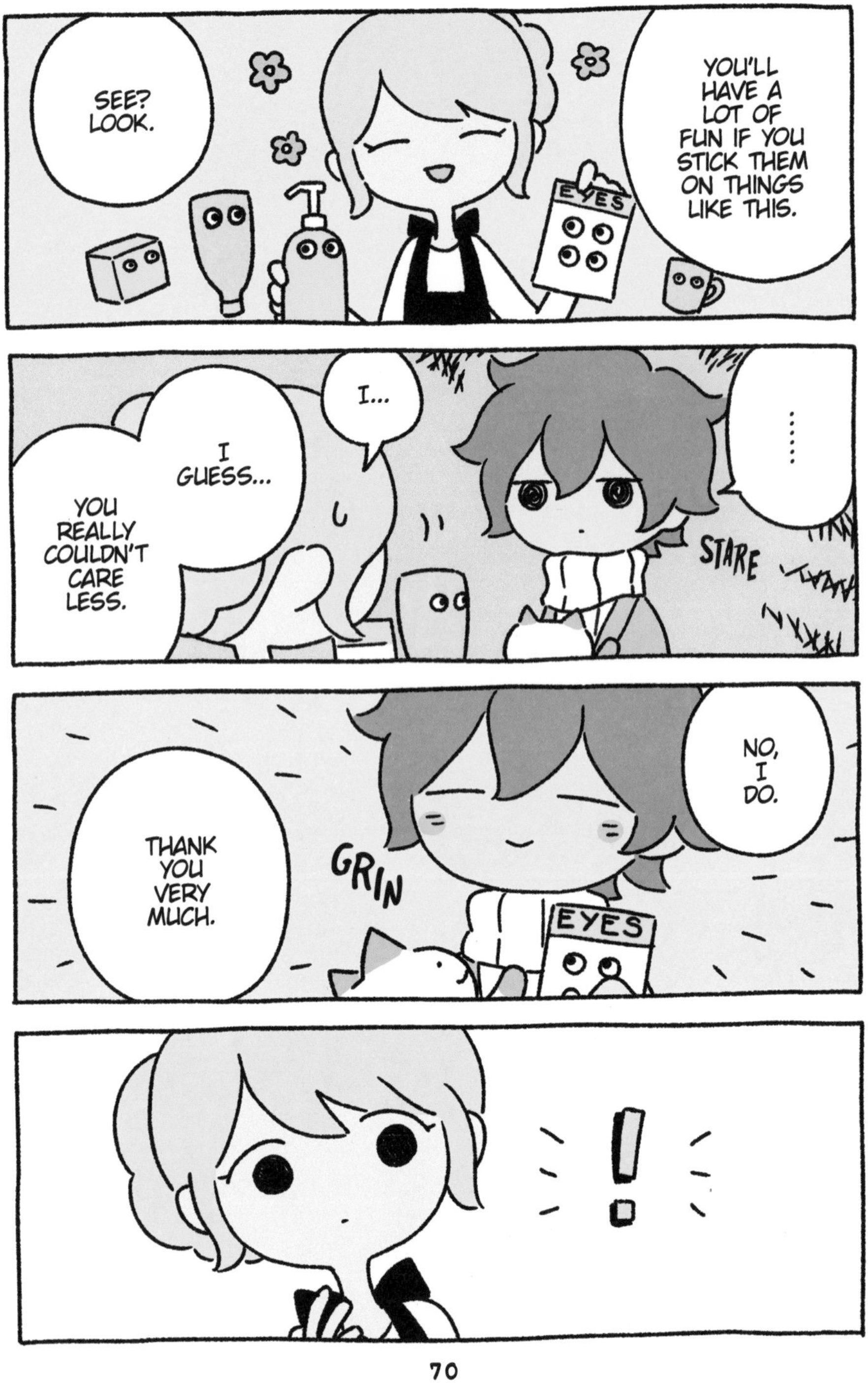
YOU'LL HAVE A LOT OF FUN IF YOU STICK THEM ON THINGS LIKE THIS.
EYES
SEE? LOOK.
......
STARE
I...
I GUESS...
YOU REALLY COULDN'T CARE LESS.
NO, I DO.
EYES
GRIN
THANK YOU VERY MUCH.
!

THE REASON WHY

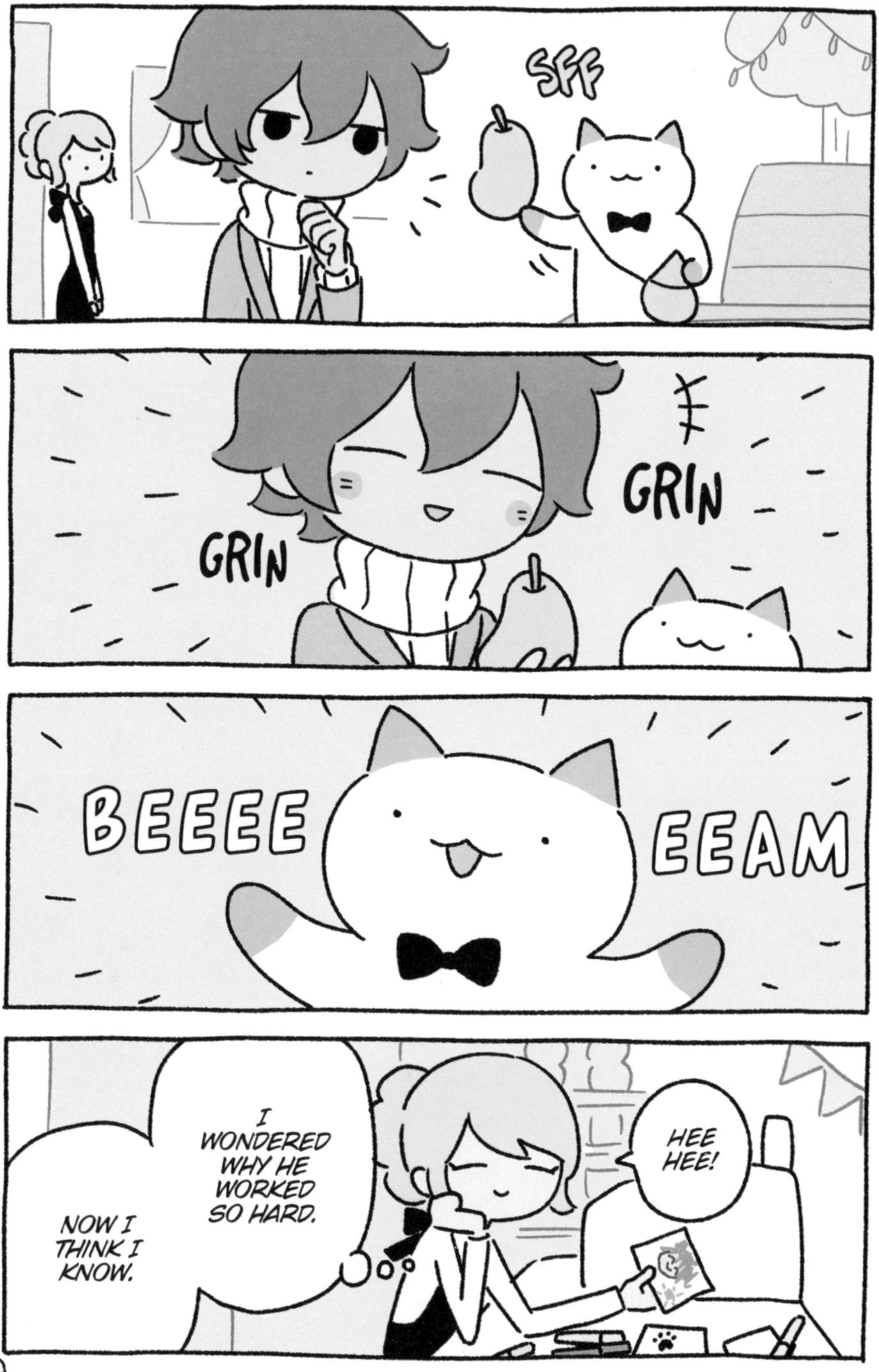
SFF
GRIN
GRIN
BEEEE
EEAM
HEE HEE!
I WONDERED WHY HE WORKED SO HARD.
NOW I THINK I KNOW.

NIGHT OF A FULL MOON

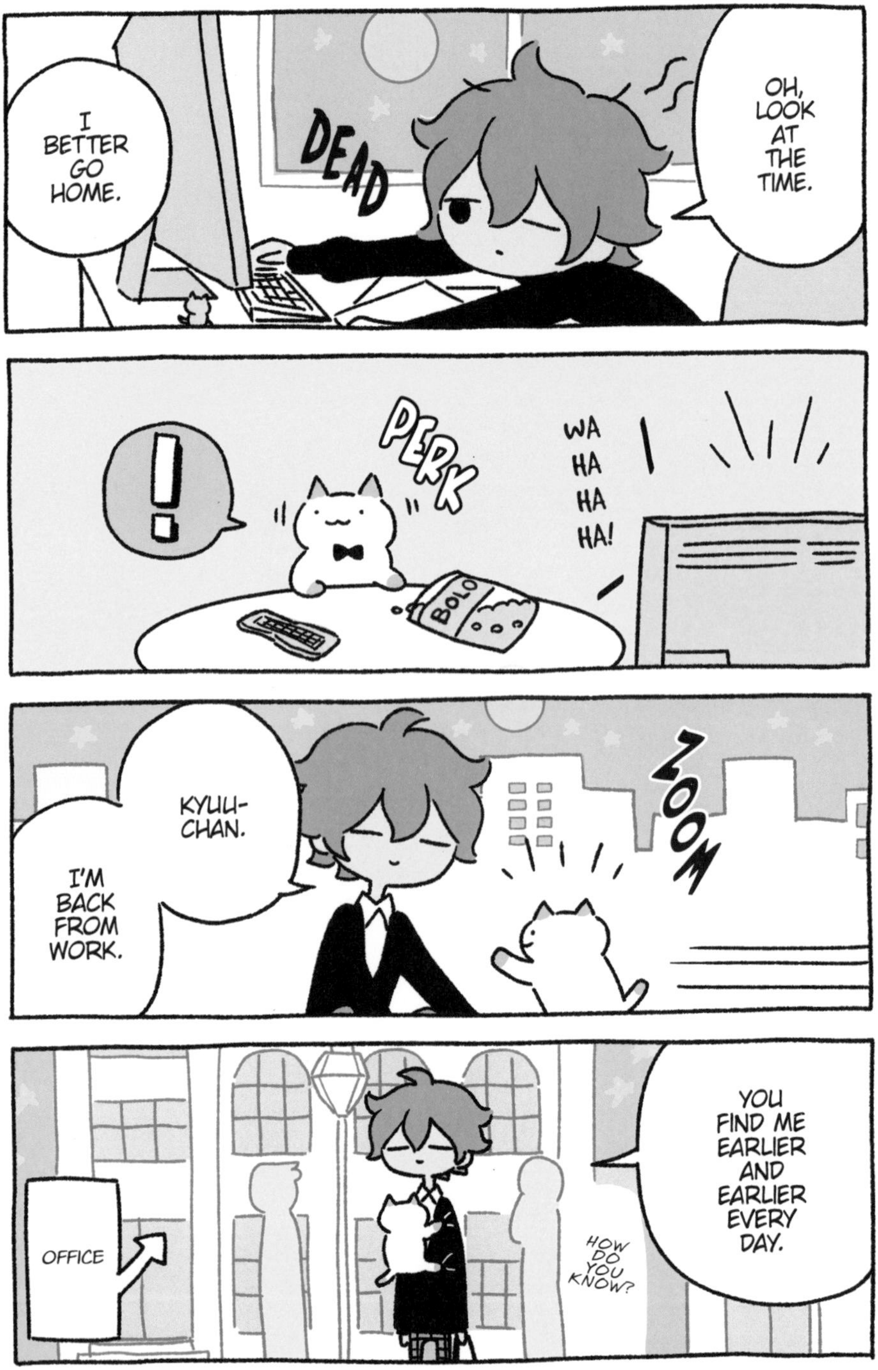
OH, LOOK AT THE TIME.
DEAD
I BETTER GO HOME.
WA HA HA HA!
PERK
!
BOLO
ZOOM
KYUU-CHAN.
I'M BACK FROM WORK.
YOU FIND ME EARLIER AND EARLIER EVERY DAY.
HOW DO YOU KNOW?
OFFICE

CURRY BUN

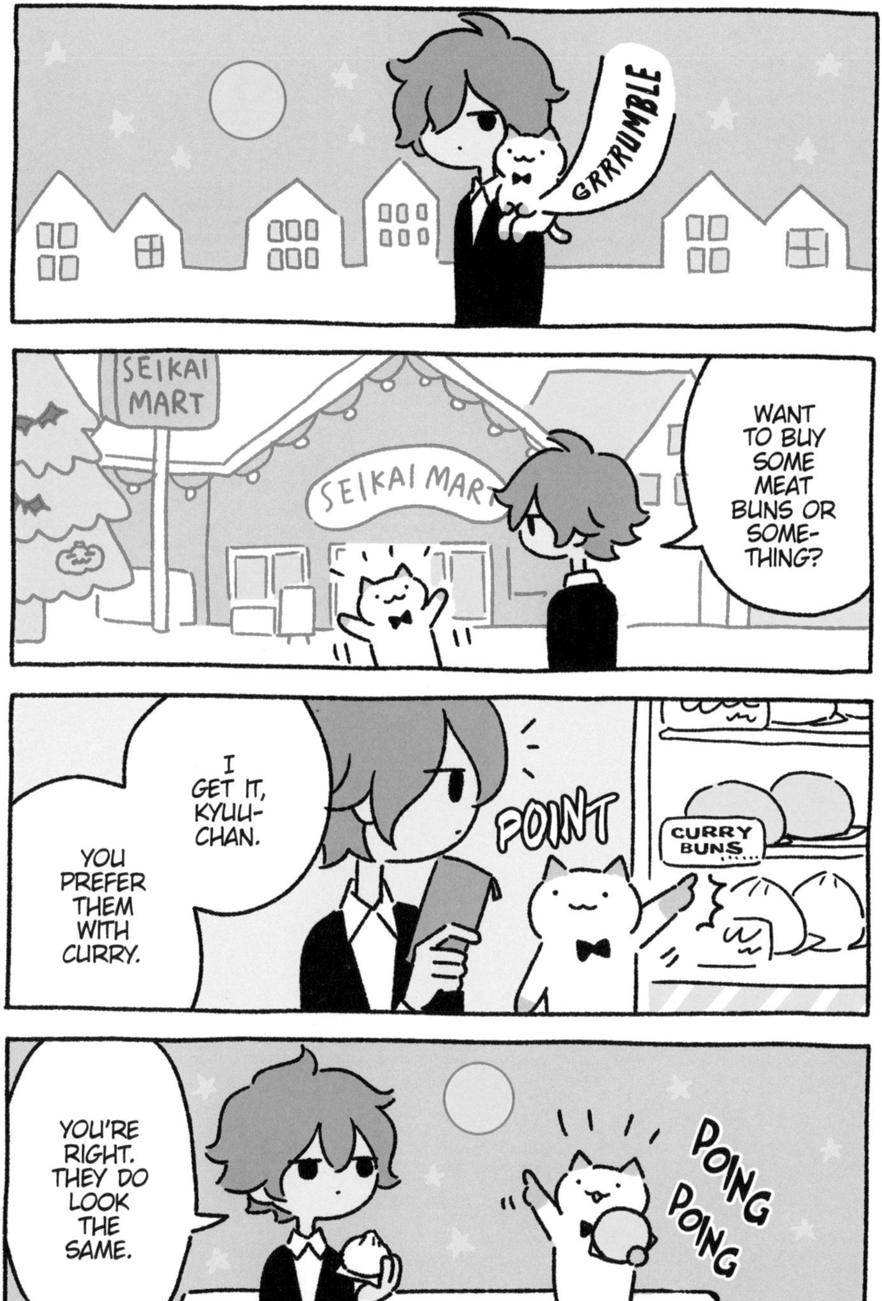
GRRRUMBLE
SEIKAI MART
SEIKAI MART
WANT TO BUY SOME MEAT BUNS OR SOME-THING?
POINT
CURRY BUNS
I GET IT, KYUU-CHAN.
YOU PREFER THEM WITH CURRY.
POING POING
YOU'RE RIGHT. THEY DO LOOK THE SAME.

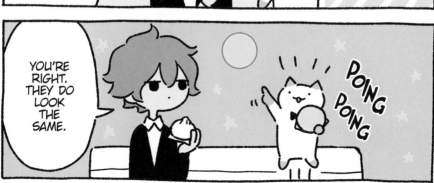

FATIGUE

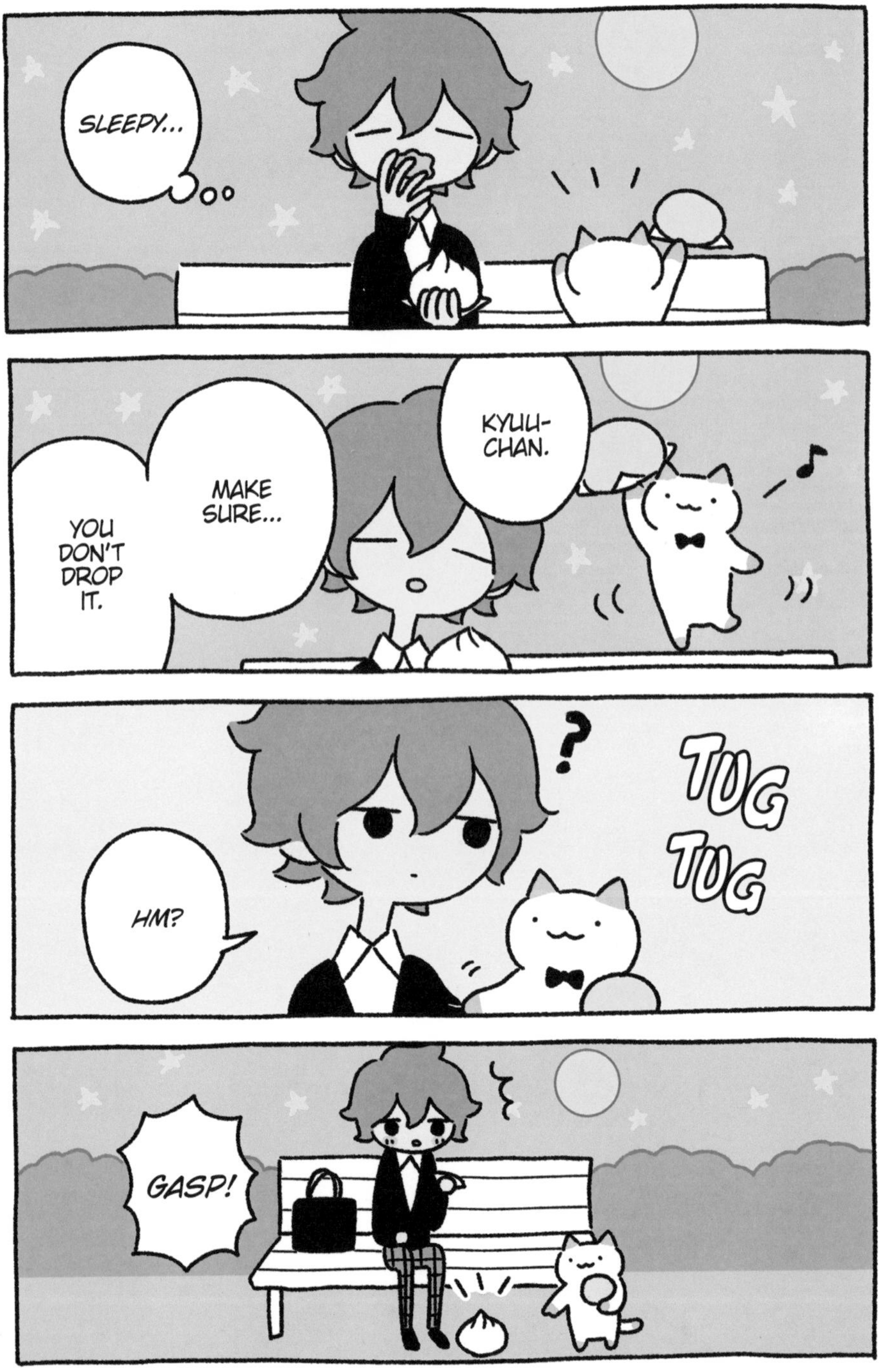
SLEEPY...
KYUU-CHAN.
MAKE SURE...
YOU DON'T DROP IT.
TUG TUG
HM?
GASP!

HALFSIES

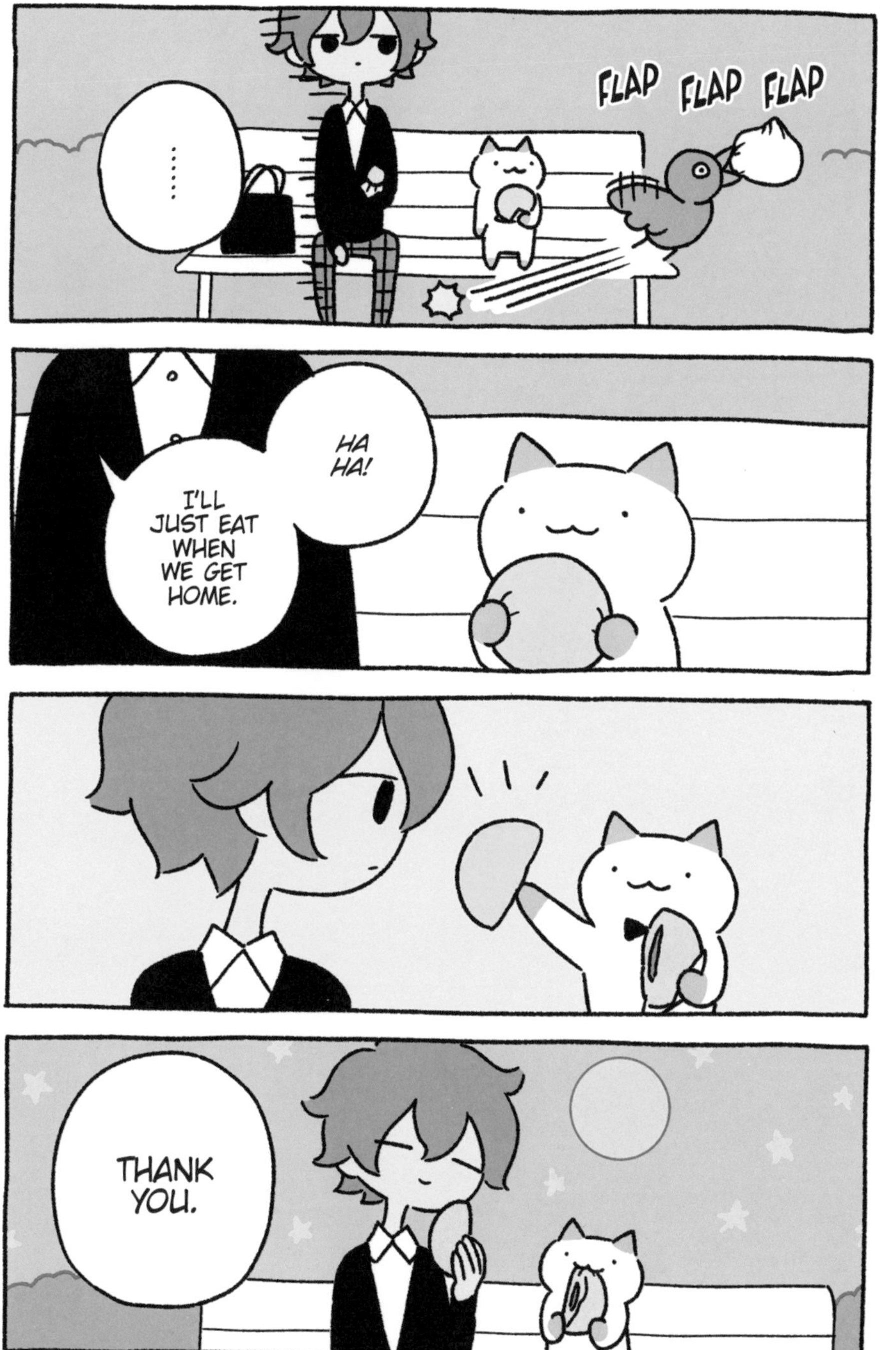
......
FLAP FLAP FLAP
HA HA!
I'LL JUST EAT WHEN WE GET HOME.
THANK YOU.

NIGHT OF A HALF MOON

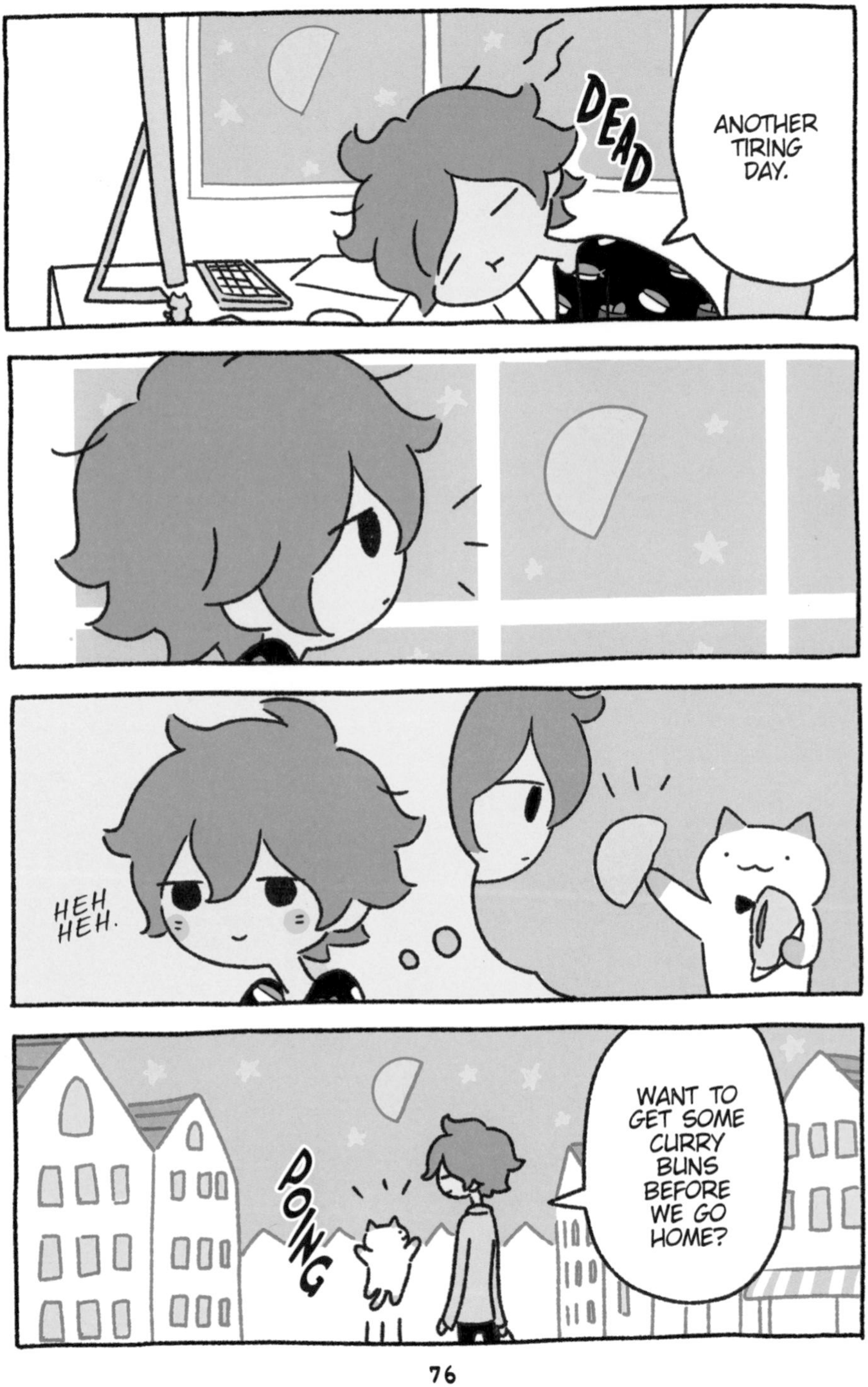
ANOTHER TIRING DAY.
DEAD
HEH HEH.
WANT TO GET SOME CURRY BUNS BEFORE WE GO HOME?
POING

CHEEKS

IT'S SO GOOD, I THINK MY CHEEKS ARE GOING TO FALL OFF.
SFF
GLUE
IT'S A FIGURE OF SPEECH.
JUST A FIGURE OF SPEECH.

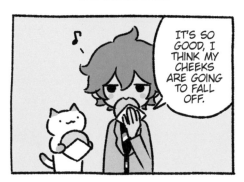

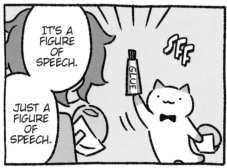

Wonder Cat
Kyuu-chan

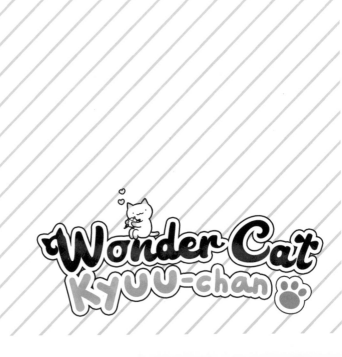

THE FACE OF OBSESSION

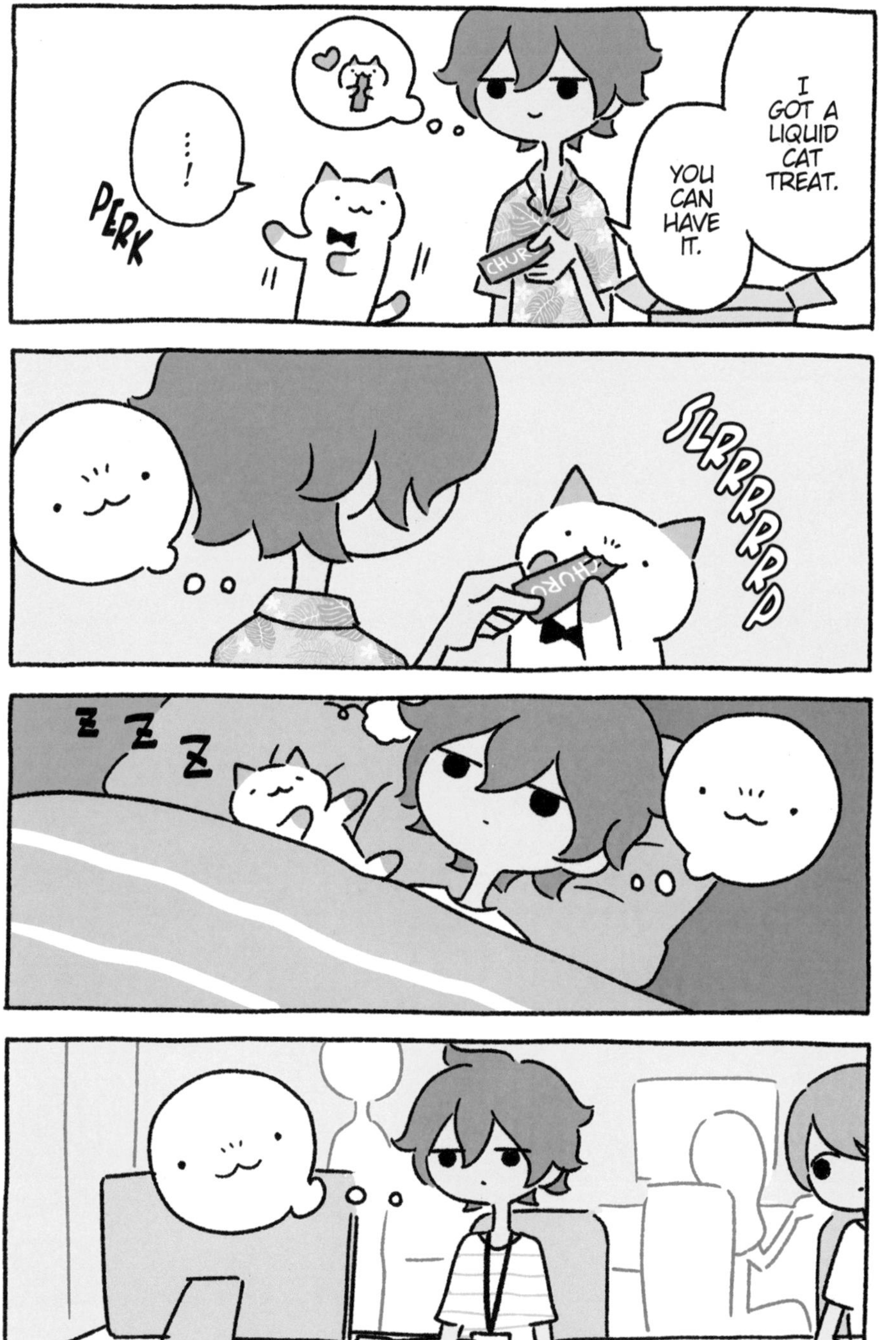
I GOT A LIQUID CAT TREAT.
YOU CAN HAVE IT.
...!
PERK
SLRRRRRP
CHURU
Z Z Z

ELIZABETHAN COLLAR

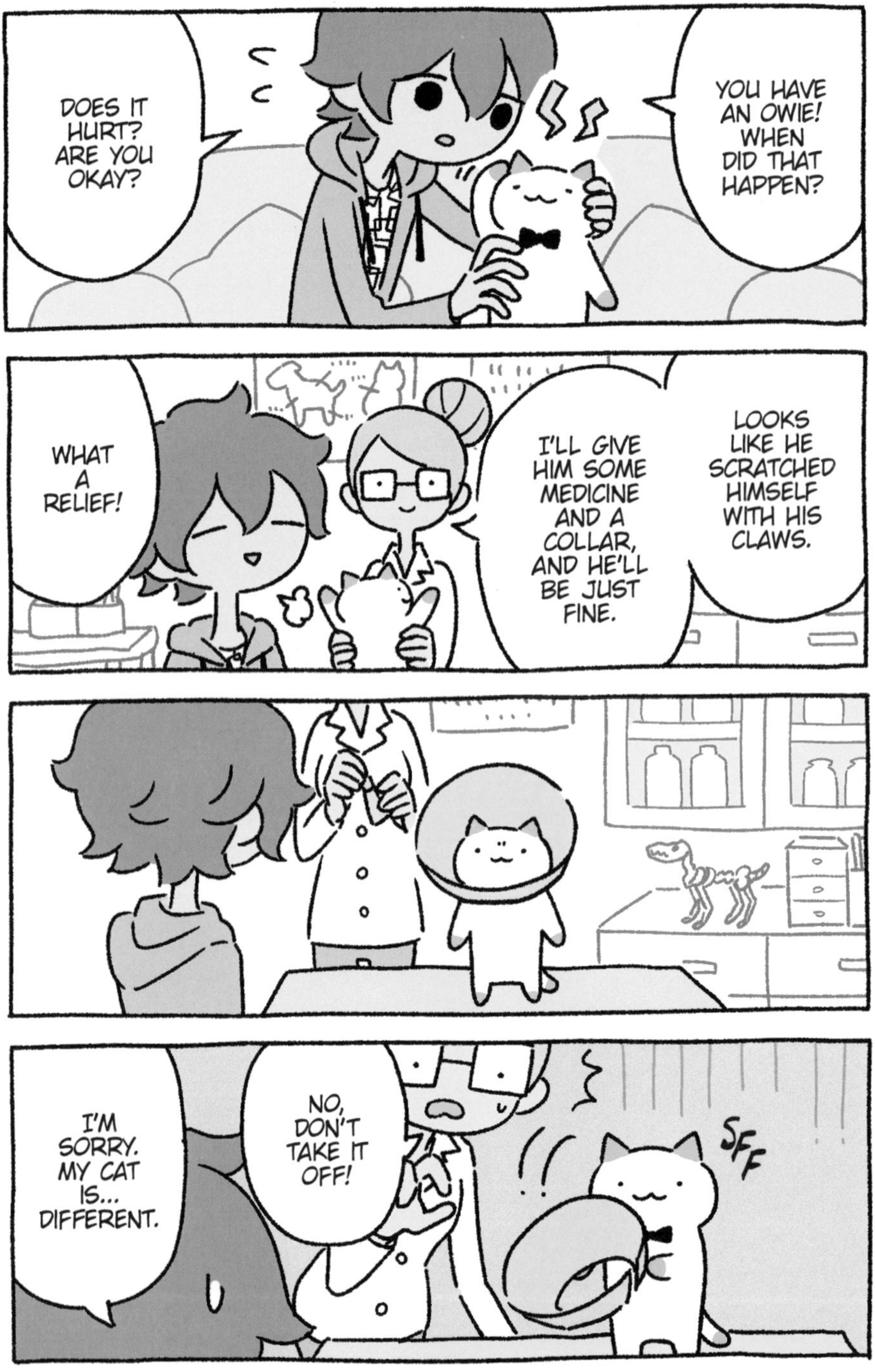
YOU HAVE AN OWIE! WHEN DID THAT HAPPEN?
DOES IT HURT? ARE YOU OKAY?
LOOKS LIKE HE SCRATCHED HIMSELF WITH HIS CLAWS.
I'LL GIVE HIM SOME MEDICINE AND A COLLAR, AND HE'LL BE JUST FINE.
WHAT A RELIEF!
SFF
NO, DON'T TAKE IT OFF!
I'M SORRY. MY CAT IS... DIFFERENT.

PAIN

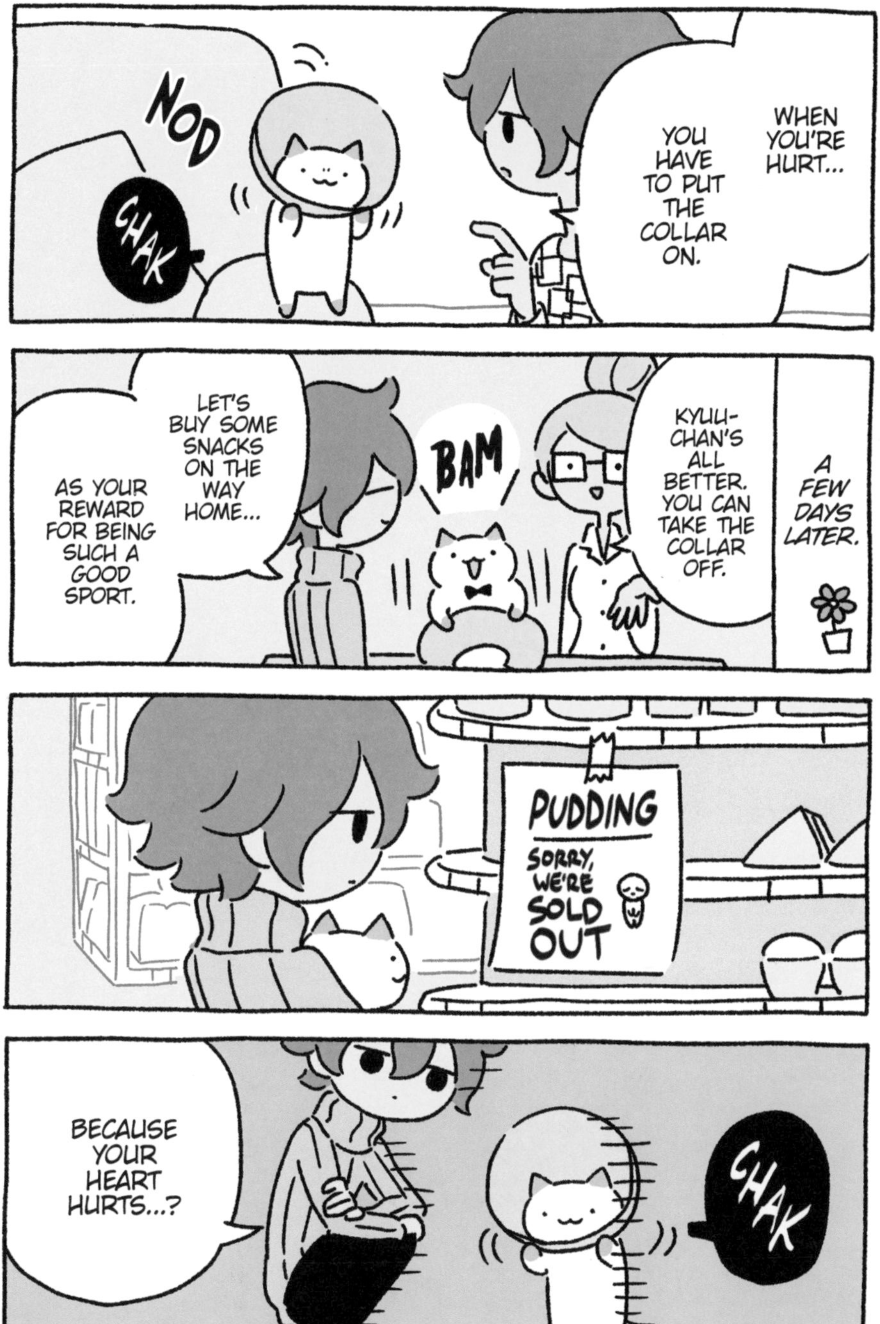

WHEN YOU'RE HURT...
YOU HAVE TO PUT THE COLLAR ON.
NOD
CHAK
A FEW DAYS LATER.
KYUU-CHAN'S ALL BETTER. YOU CAN TAKE THE COLLAR OFF.
BAM
LET'S BUY SOME SNACKS ON THE WAY HOME...
AS YOUR REWARD FOR BEING SUCH A GOOD SPORT.
PUDDING
SORRY, WE'RE SOLD OUT
CHAK
BECAUSE YOUR HEART HURTS...?

FEELING MISCHIEVOUS

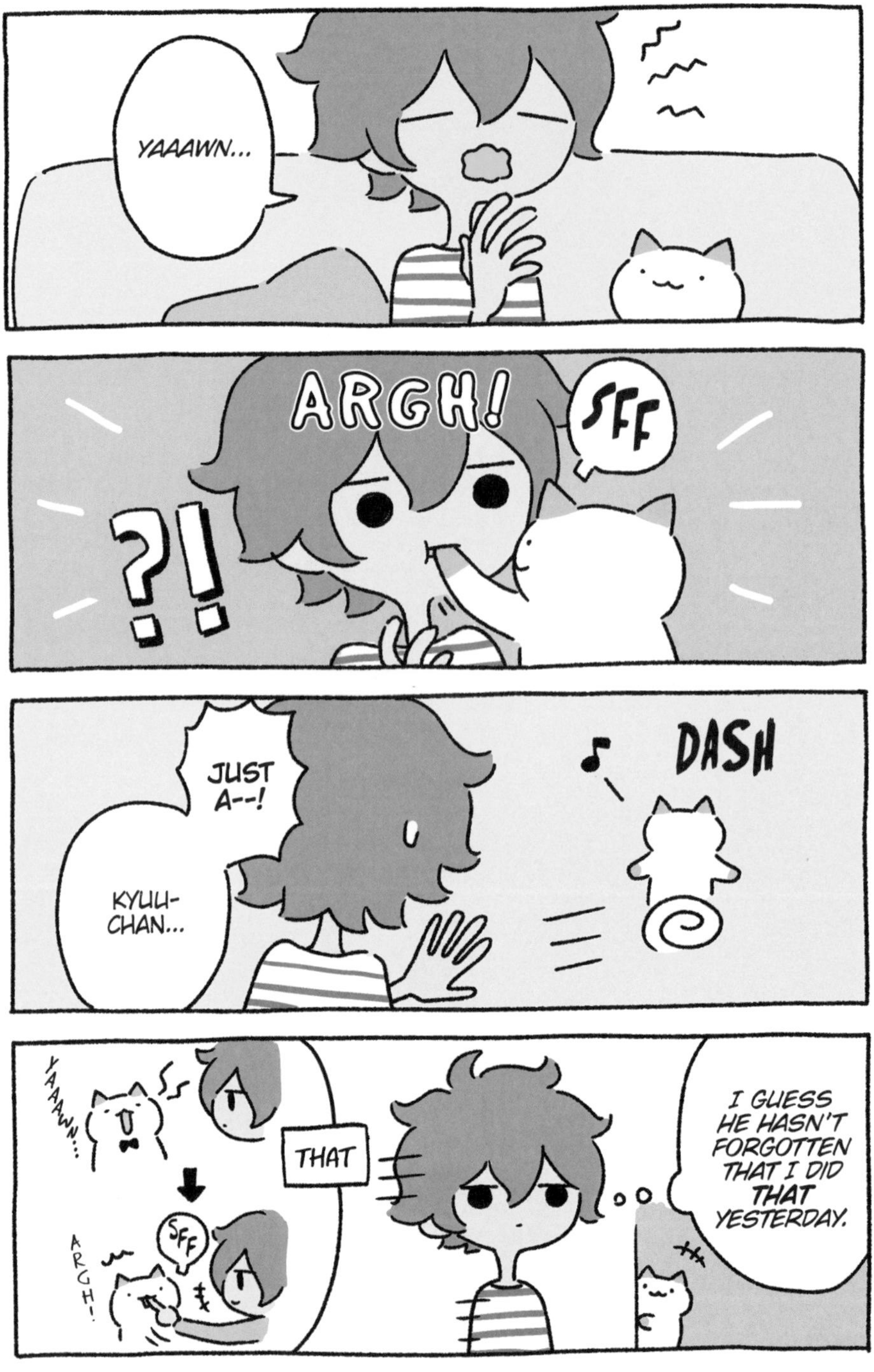
YAAAWN...
SFF
ARGH!
?!
DASH
JUST A--!
KYUU-CHAN...
I GUESS HE HASN'T FORGOTTEN THAT I DID **THAT** YESTERDAY.
THAT
YAAAWN...
SFF
ARGH!

IMPORTANT PAPERWORK

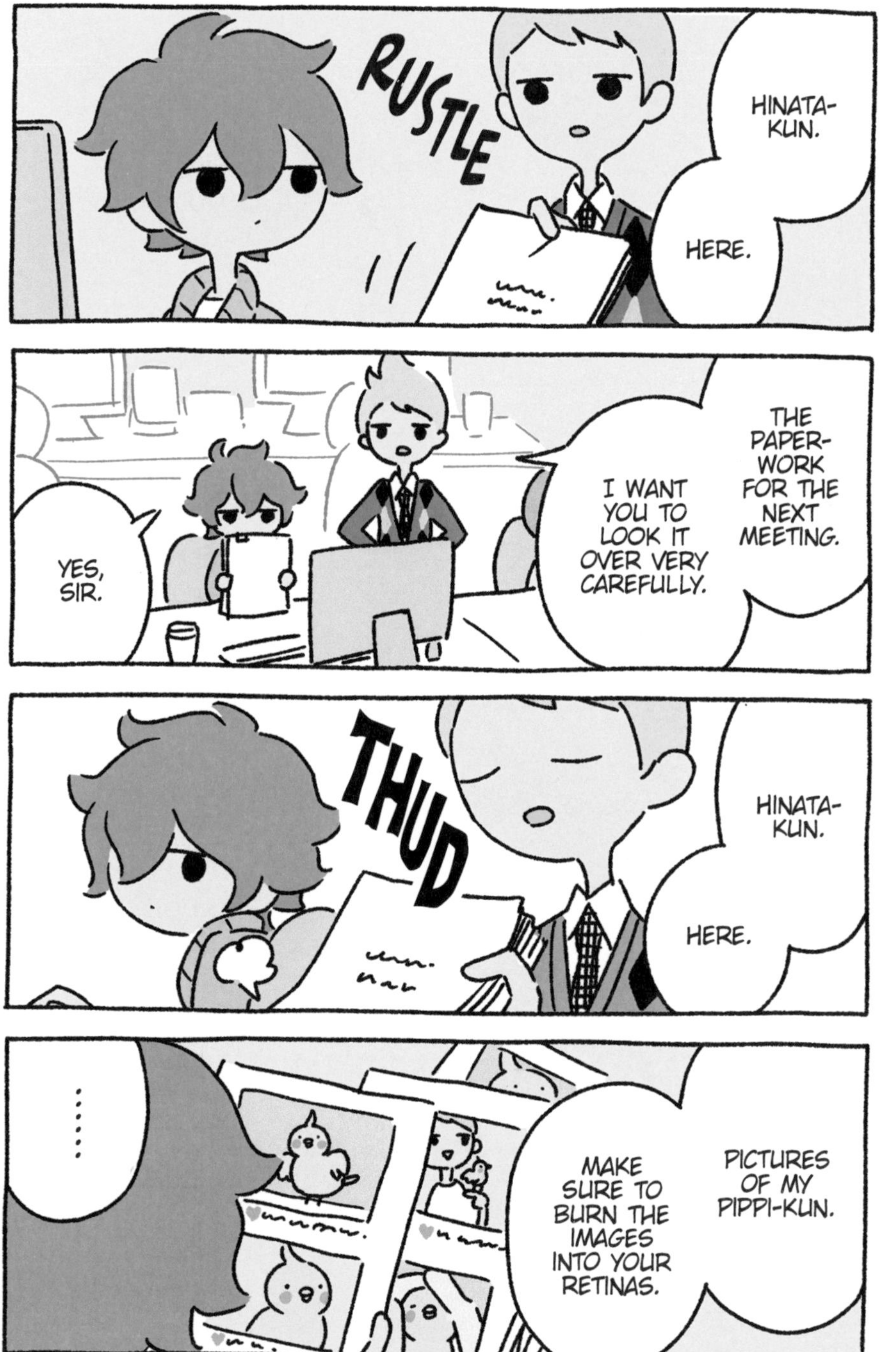
HINATA-KUN. HERE.
RUSTLE
THE PAPERWORK FOR THE NEXT MEETING. I WANT YOU TO LOOK IT OVER VERY CAREFULLY.
YES, SIR.
HINATA-KUN. HERE.
THUD
PICTURES OF MY PIPPI-KUN. MAKE SURE TO BURN THE IMAGES INTO YOUR RETINAS.
......

SMOOTH

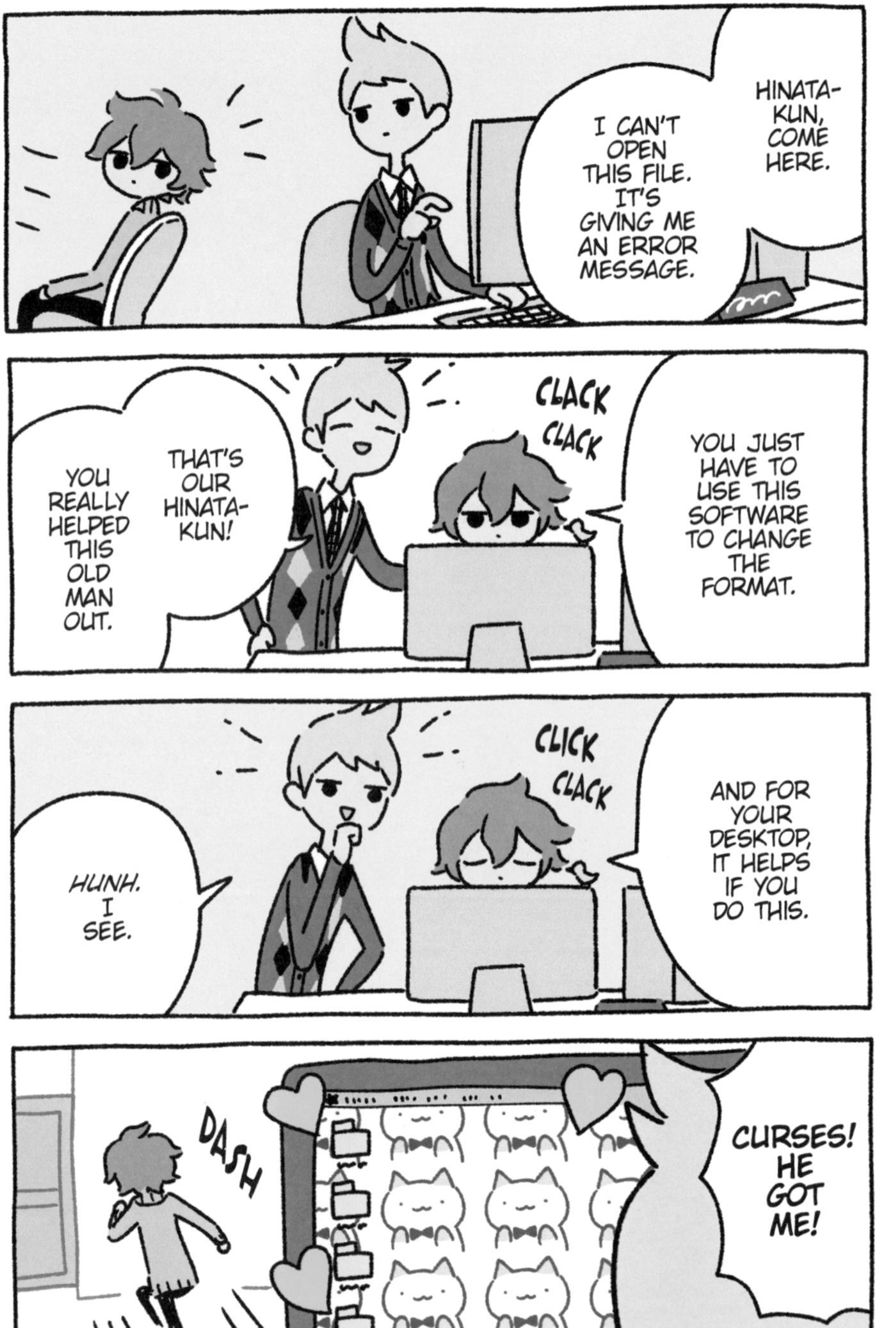

HINATA-KUN, COME HERE.
I CAN'T OPEN THIS FILE. IT'S GIVING ME AN ERROR MESSAGE.
YOU JUST HAVE TO USE THIS SOFTWARE TO CHANGE THE FORMAT.
CLACK CLACK
THAT'S OUR HINATA-KUN!
YOU REALLY HELPED THIS OLD MAN OUT.
AND FOR YOUR DESKTOP, IT HELPS IF YOU DO THIS.
CLICK CLACK
HUNH. I SEE.
CURSES! HE GOT ME!
DASH

TAKE A LOOK

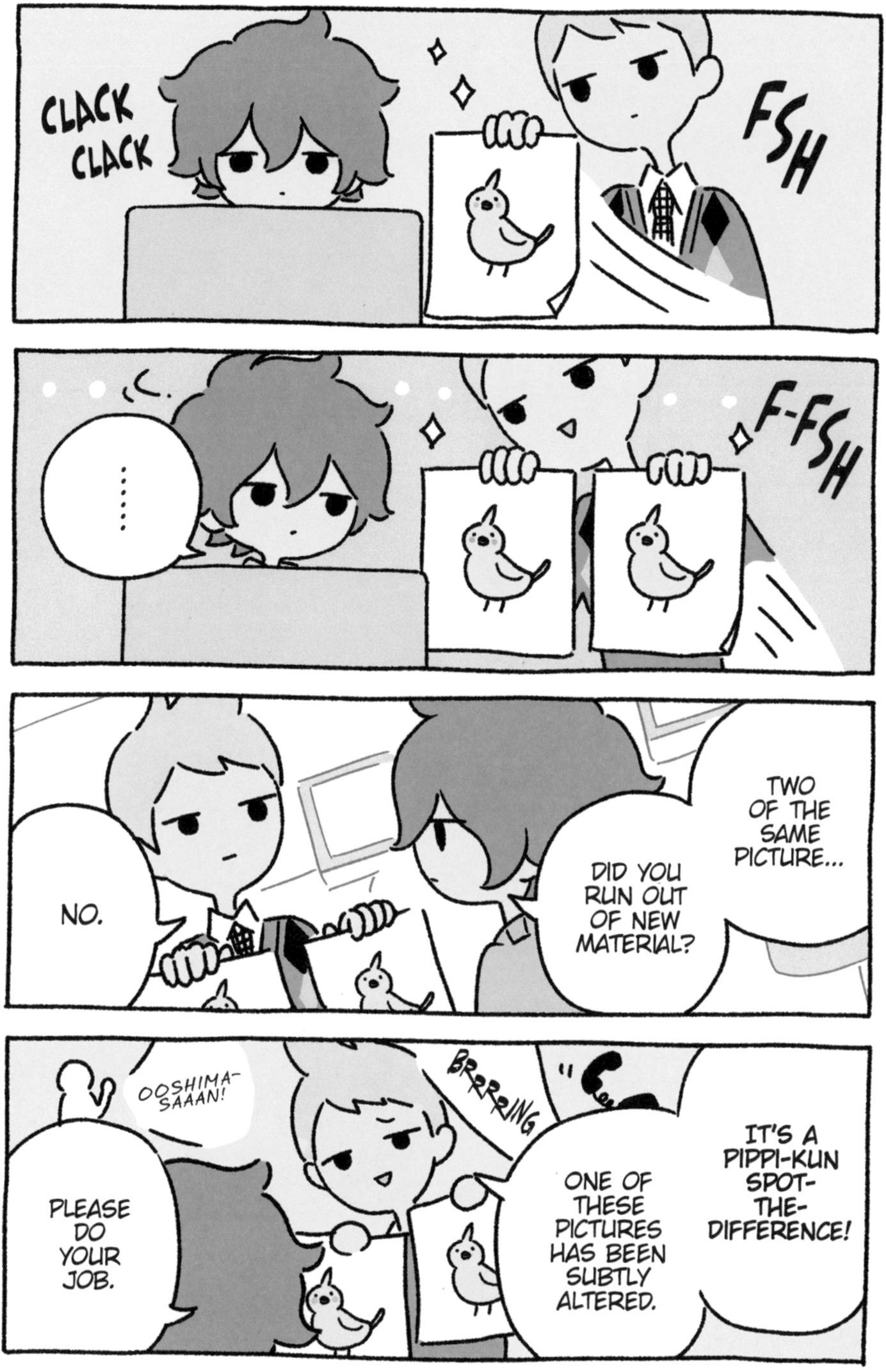
FSH
CLACK CLACK
F-FSH
......
TWO OF THE SAME PICTURE...
DID YOU RUN OUT OF NEW MATERIAL?
NO.
BRRRRING
IT'S A PIPPI-KUN SPOT-THE-DIFFERENCE!
ONE OF THESE PICTURES HAS BEEN SUBTLY ALTERED.
OOSHIMA-SAAAN!
PLEASE DO YOUR JOB.

ACORNS

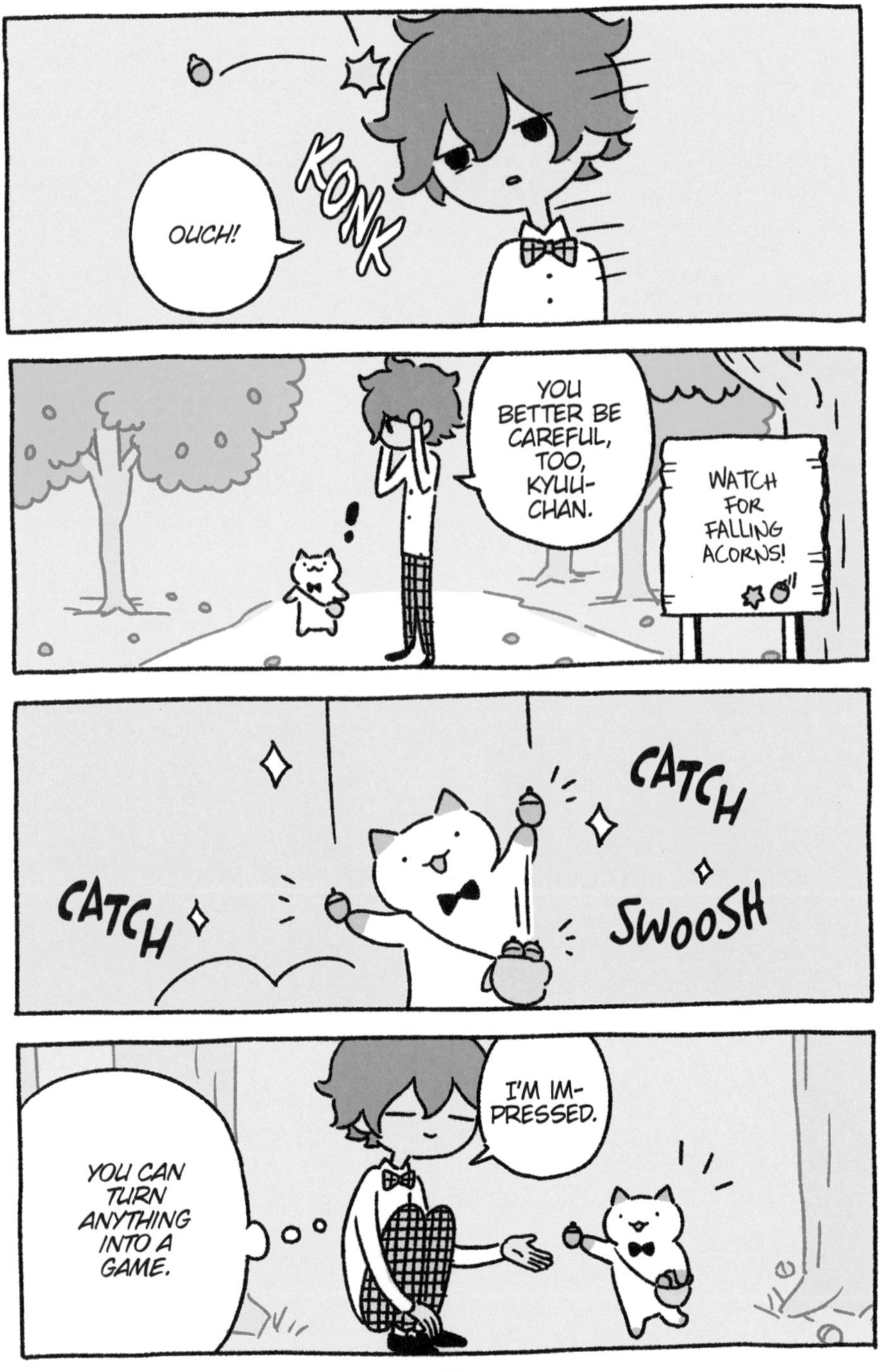

KONK
OUCH!
WATCH FOR FALLING ACORNS!
YOU BETTER BE CAREFUL, TOO, KYUU-CHAN.
CATCH
SWOOSH
CATCH
I'M IM-PRESSED.
YOU CAN TURN ANYTHING INTO A GAME.

BRUSHING

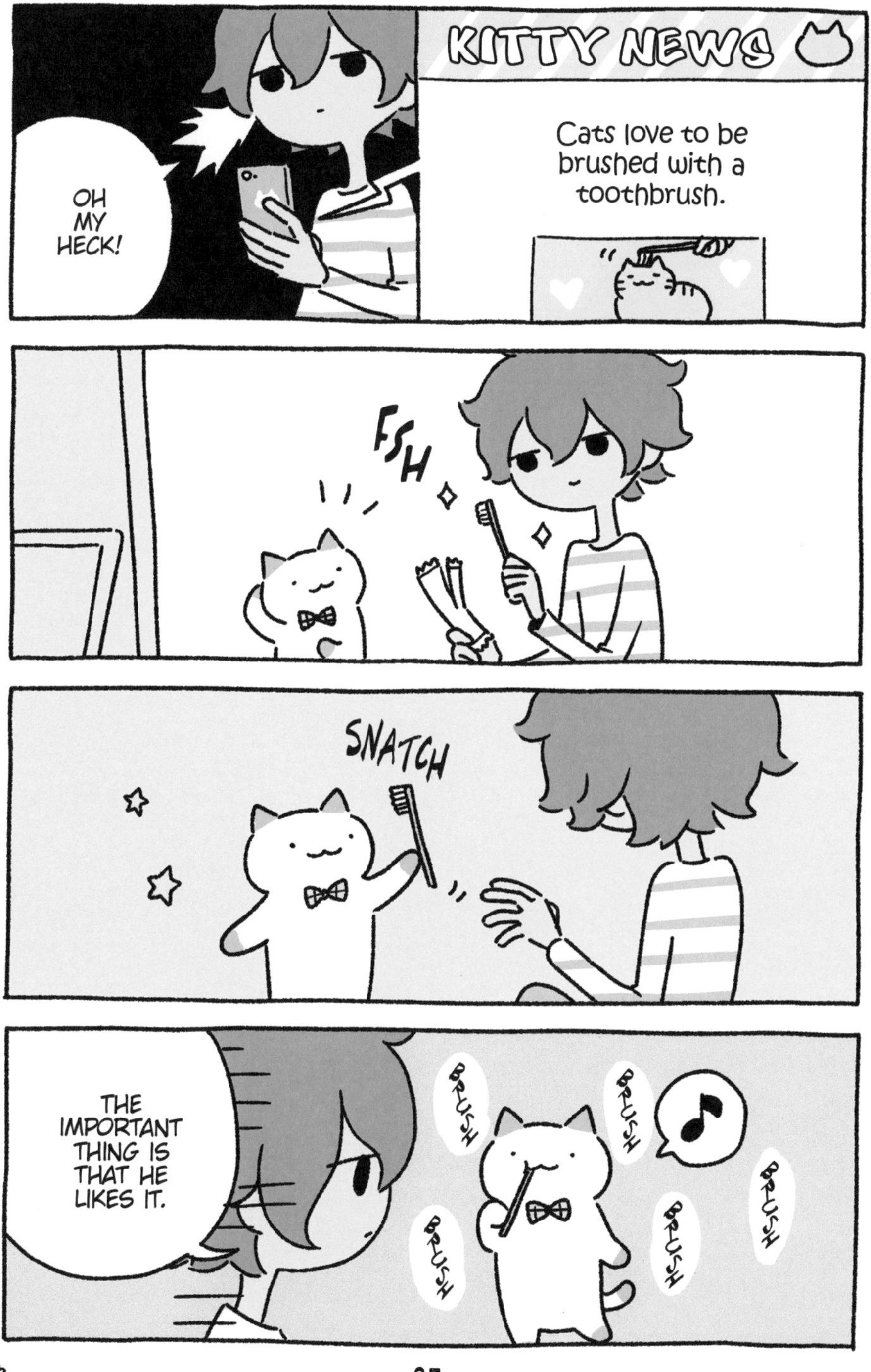

KITTY NEWS
Cats love to be brushed with a toothbrush.
OH MY HECK!
FSH
SNATCH
BRUSH
BRUSH
BRUSH
BRUSH
BRUSH
THE IMPORTANT THING IS THAT HE LIKES IT.

METICULOUS

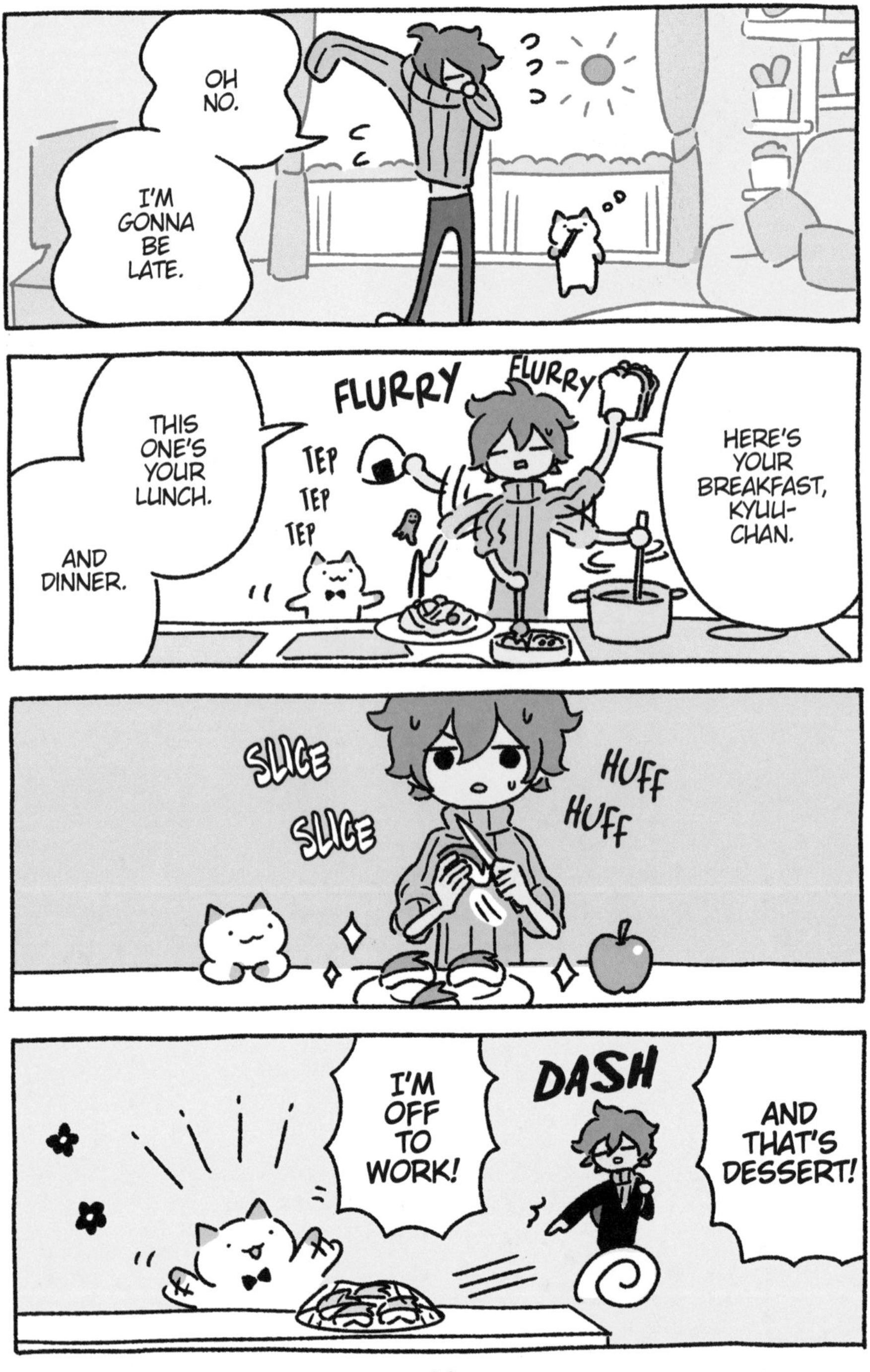

OH NO.
I'M GONNA BE LATE.
HERE'S YOUR BREAKFAST, KYUU-CHAN.
FLURRY
FLURRY
THIS ONE'S YOUR LUNCH.
TEP
TEP
TEP
AND DINNER.
HUFF
HUFF
SLICE
SLICE
AND THAT'S DESSERT!
DASH
I'M OFF TO WORK!

IMPORTANT MISSION ①

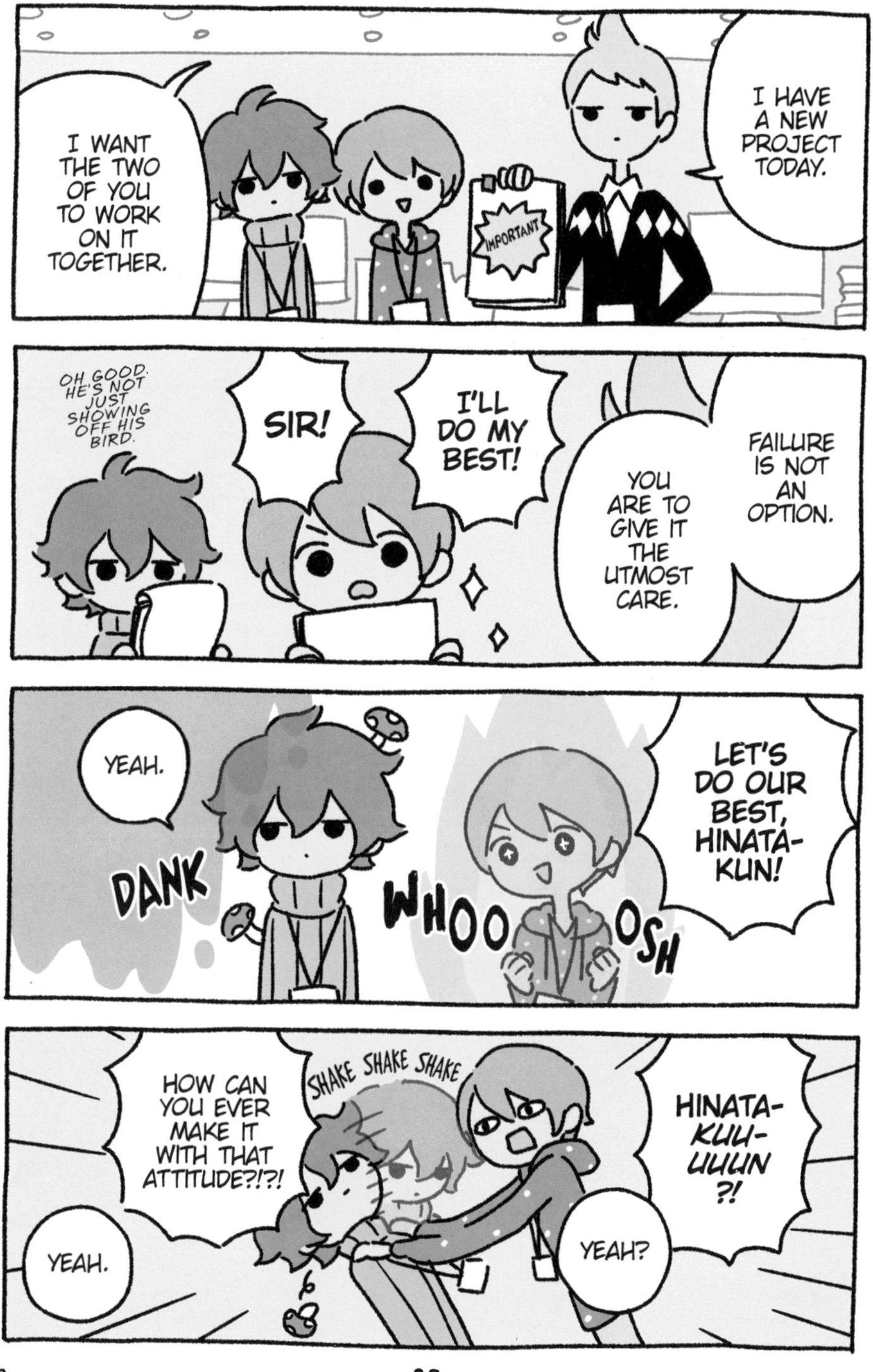

I HAVE A NEW PROJECT TODAY.
IMPORTANT
I WANT THE TWO OF YOU TO WORK ON IT TOGETHER.
FAILURE IS NOT AN OPTION.
YOU ARE TO GIVE IT THE UTMOST CARE.
I'LL DO MY BEST!
SIR!
OH GOOD. HE'S NOT JUST SHOWING OFF HIS BIRD.
LET'S DO OUR BEST, HINATA-KUN!
WHOOOSH
YEAH.
DANK
HINATA-KUUUUUN?!
SHAKE SHAKE SHAKE
HOW CAN YOU EVER MAKE IT WITH THAT ATTITUDE?!?!
YEAH?
YEAH.

IMPORTANT MISSION ②

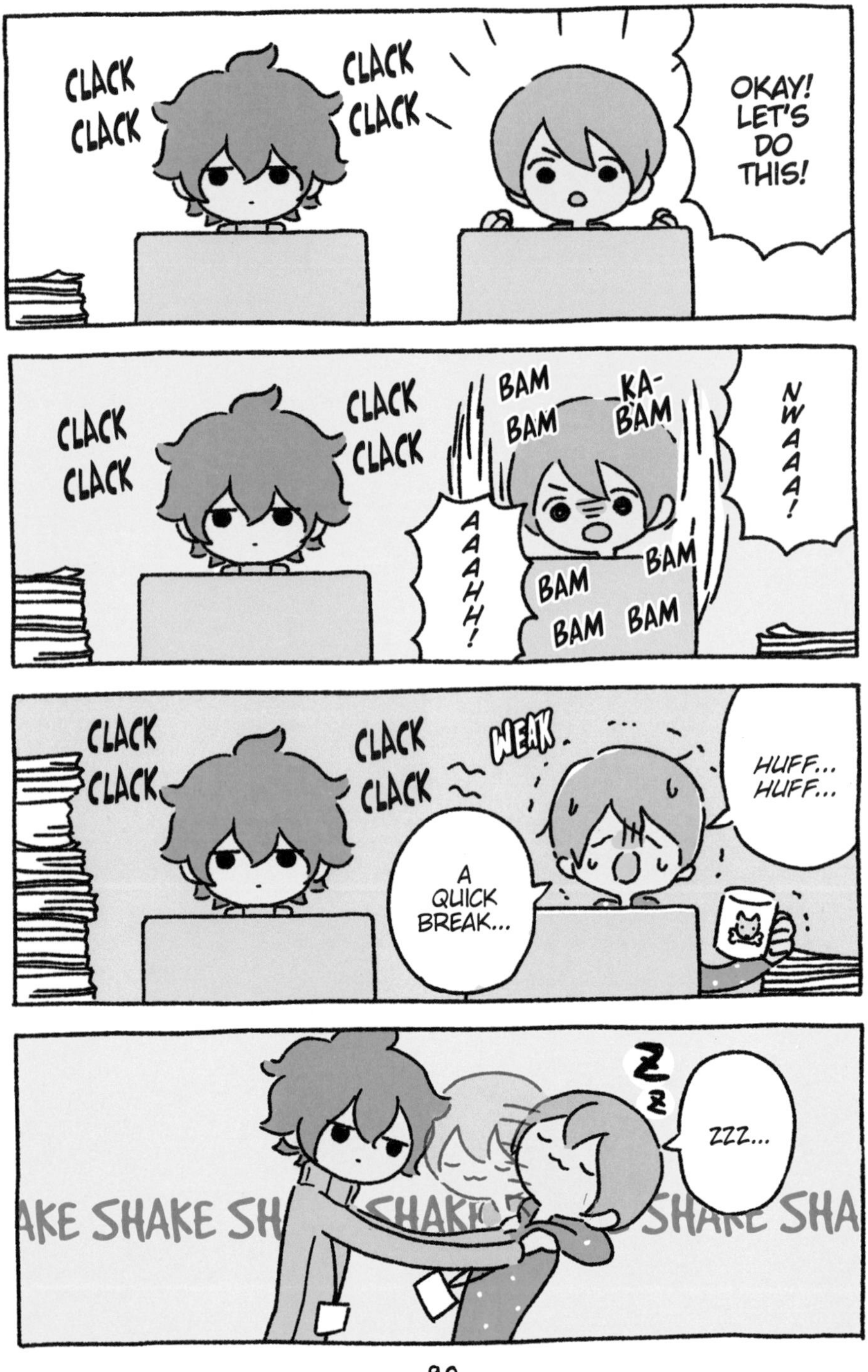

OKAY! LET'S DO THIS!
CLACK CLACK
CLACK CLACK
NWAAAA!
KA-BAM
BAM BAM
CLACK CLACK
CLACK CLACK
BAM
BAM BAM BAM
AAAAHH!
HUFF... HUFF...
WEAK
CLACK CLACK
A QUICK BREAK...
CLACK CLACK
ZZZ...
Z Z
SHAKE

OUT FOR DRINKS

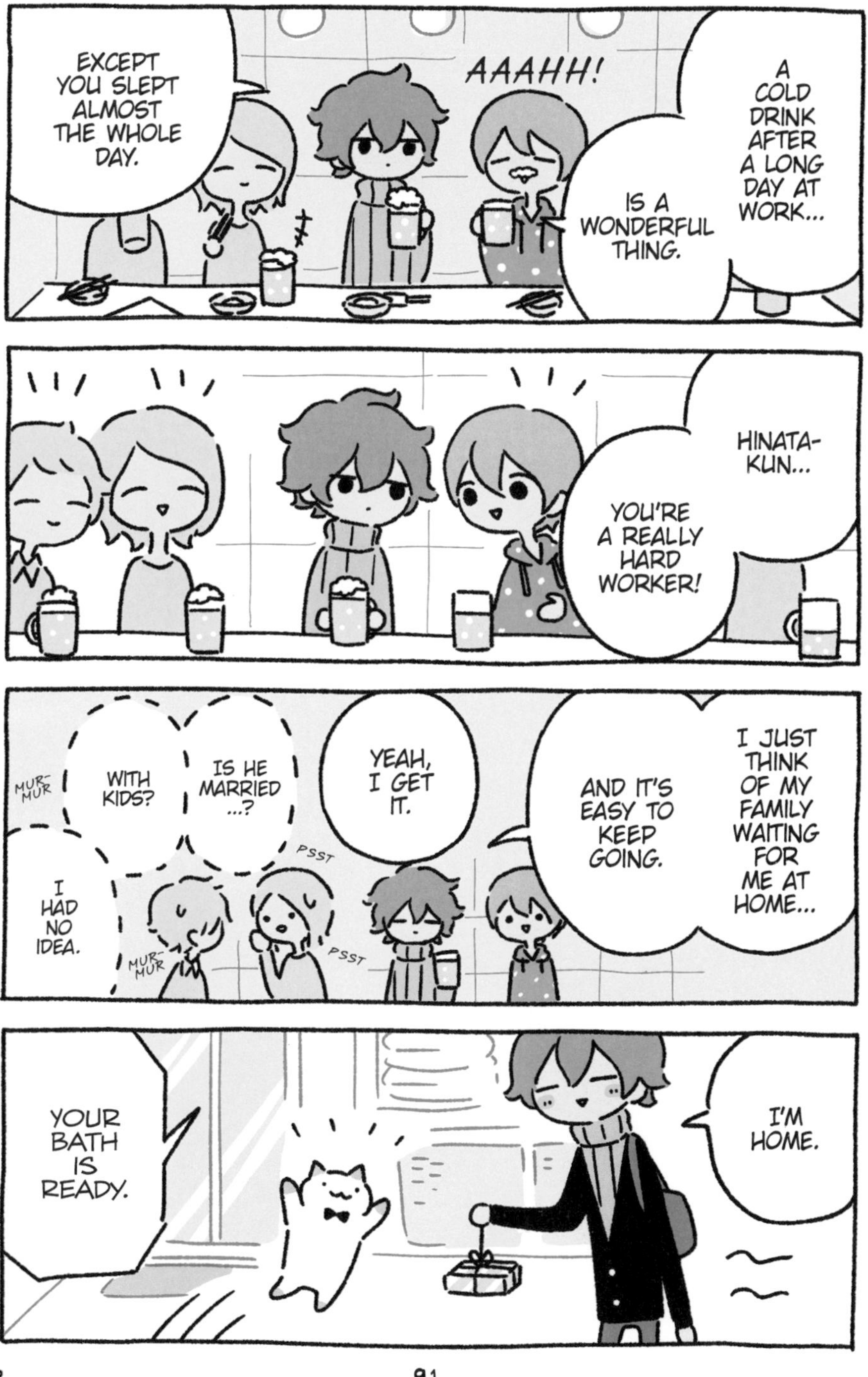
A COLD DRINK AFTER A LONG DAY AT WORK...
IS A WONDERFUL THING.
AAAHH!
EXCEPT YOU SLEPT ALMOST THE WHOLE DAY.
HINATA-KUN...
YOU'RE A REALLY HARD WORKER!
I JUST THINK OF MY FAMILY WAITING FOR ME AT HOME...
AND IT'S EASY TO KEEP GOING.
YEAH, I GET IT.
IS HE MARRIED ...?
PSST
WITH KIDS?
MUR-MUR
I HAD NO IDEA.
PSST
MUR-MUR
I'M HOME.
YOUR BATH IS READY.

THE DELIVERYMAN

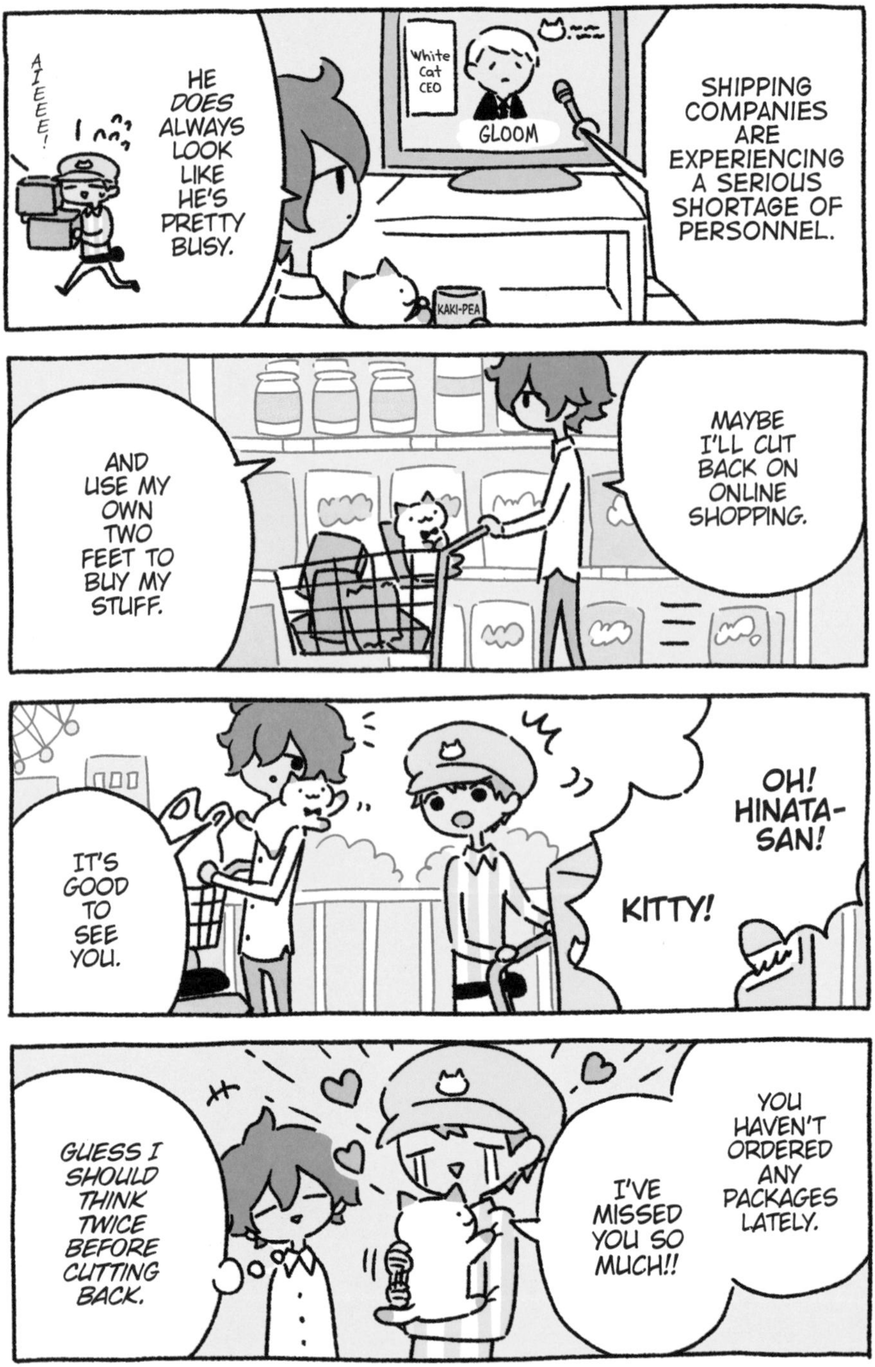
SHIPPING COMPANIES ARE EXPERIENCING A SERIOUS SHORTAGE OF PERSONNEL.
White Cat CEO
GLOOM
HE DOES ALWAYS LOOK LIKE HE'S PRETTY BUSY.
AIEEEE!
KAKI-PEA
MAYBE I'LL CUT BACK ON ONLINE SHOPPING.
AND USE MY OWN TWO FEET TO BUY MY STUFF.
OH! HINATA-SAN!
KITTY!
IT'S GOOD TO SEE YOU.
YOU HAVEN'T ORDERED ANY PACKAGES LATELY.
I'VE MISSED YOU SO MUCH!!
GUESS I SHOULD THINK TWICE BEFORE CUTTING BACK.

TELEPATHY

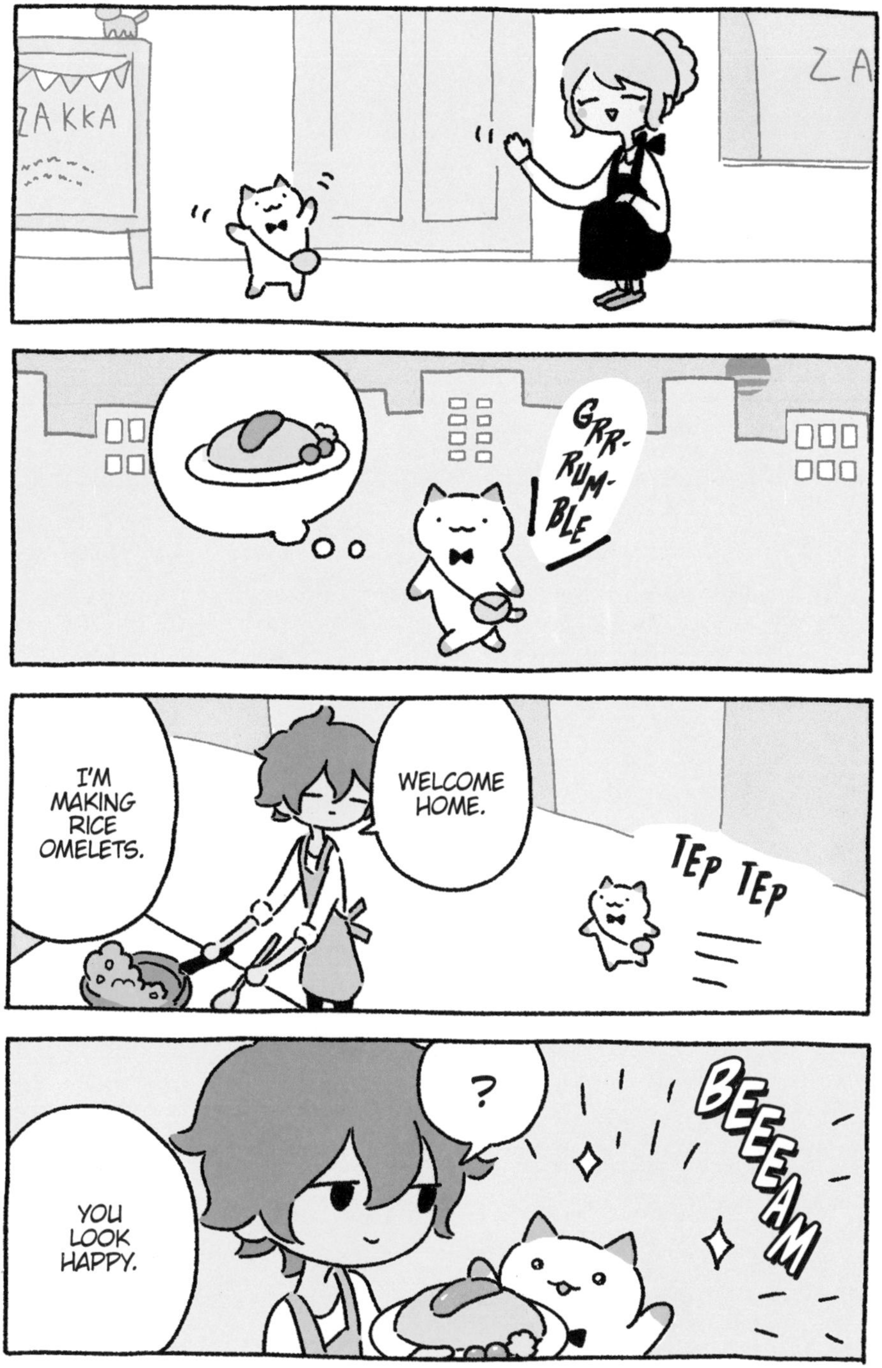
ZA
ZAKKA
GRR-RUM-BLE
WELCOME HOME.
TEP TEP
I'M MAKING RICE OMELETS.
BEEEAM
?
YOU LOOK HAPPY.

EFFICIENT STORAGE

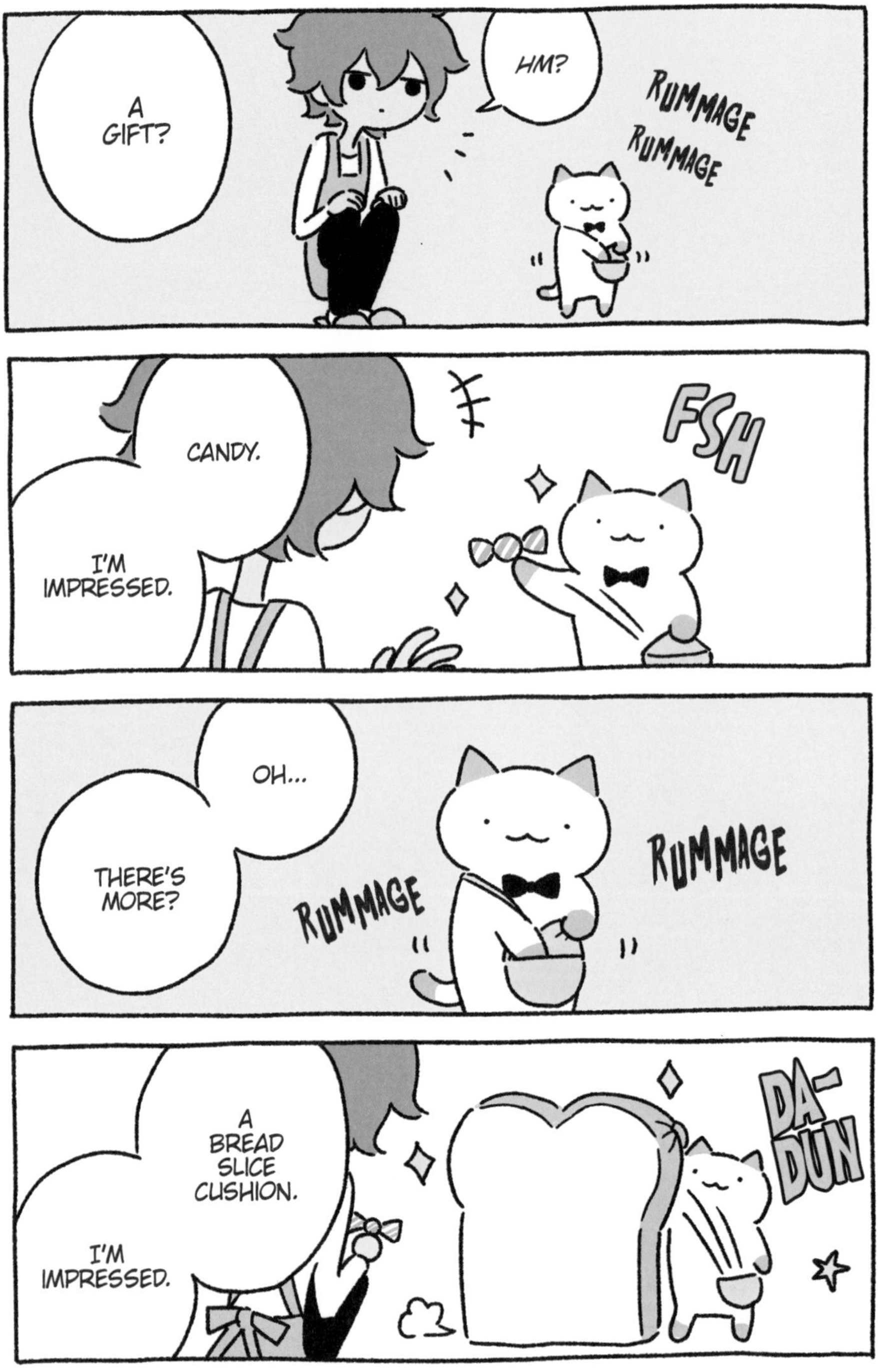
RUMMAGE RUMMAGE
HM?
A GIFT?
FSH
CANDY. I'M IMPRESSED.
RUMMAGE
RUMMAGE
OH... THERE'S MORE?
DA-DUN
A BREAD SLICE CUSHION. I'M IMPRESSED.

SOOTHING CUSHION

PET PET
IT'S SO SOFT.
MWOFF
MWOFF
AND SQUISHY.
BWOFF
...
KYUU-CHAN...
CAN YOU BREATHE?
Z Z Z

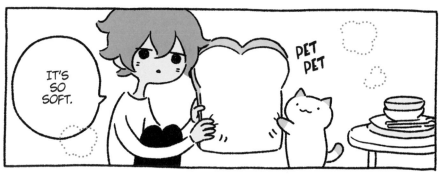

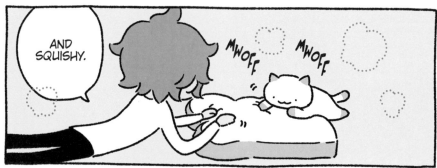

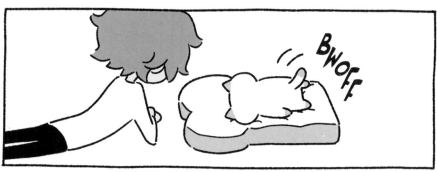

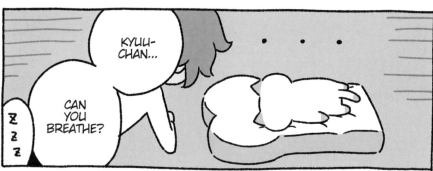

DEPARTMENT STORE

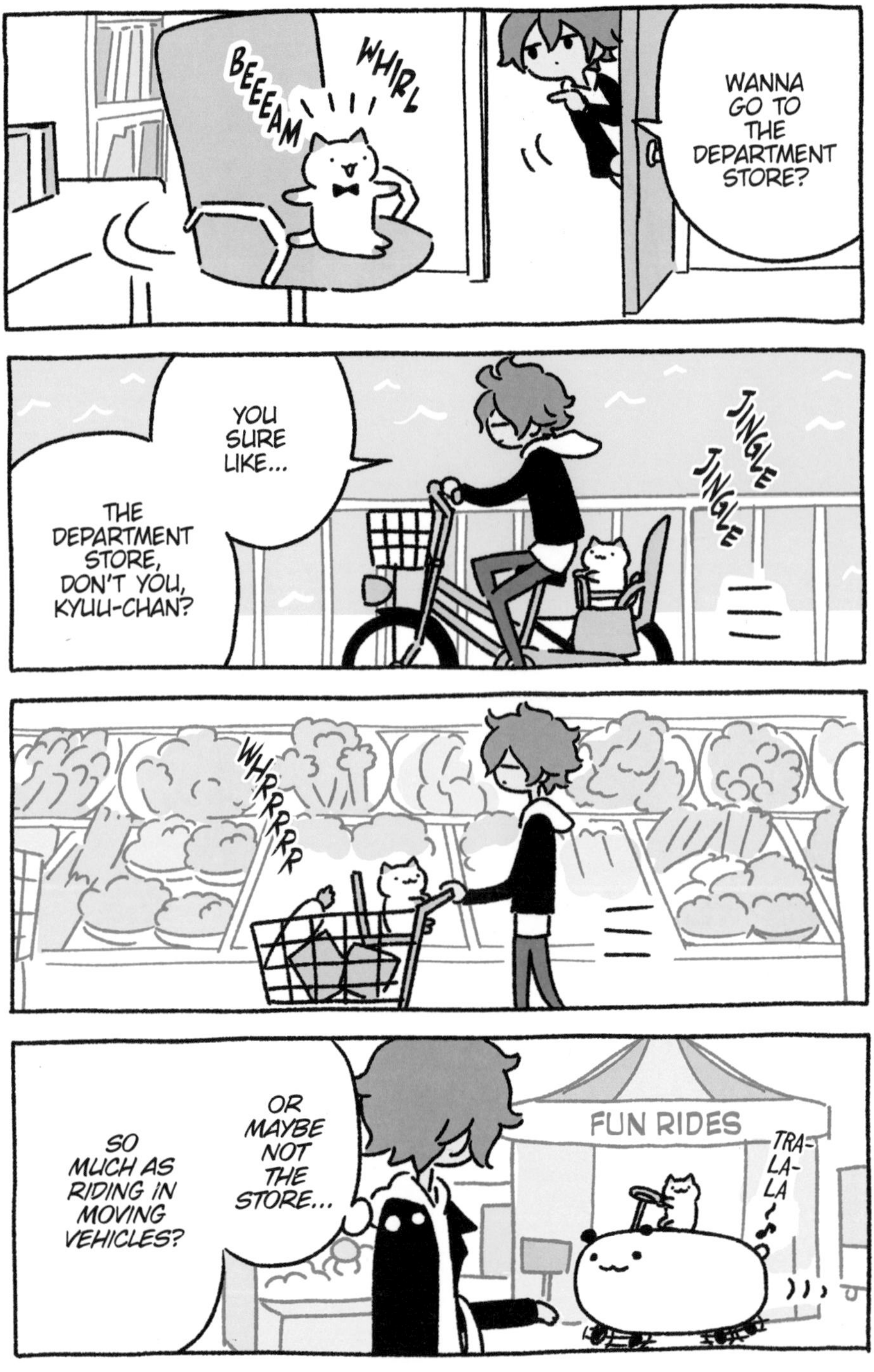
WANNA GO TO THE DEPARTMENT STORE?
WHIRL
BEEEEAM
JINGLE
JINGLE
YOU SURE LIKE...
THE DEPARTMENT STORE, DON'T YOU, KYUU-CHAN?
WHRRRRR
TRA-LA-LA♪
FUN RIDES
OR MAYBE NOT THE STORE...
SO MUCH AS RIDING IN MOVING VEHICLES?

ROBOT VACUUM

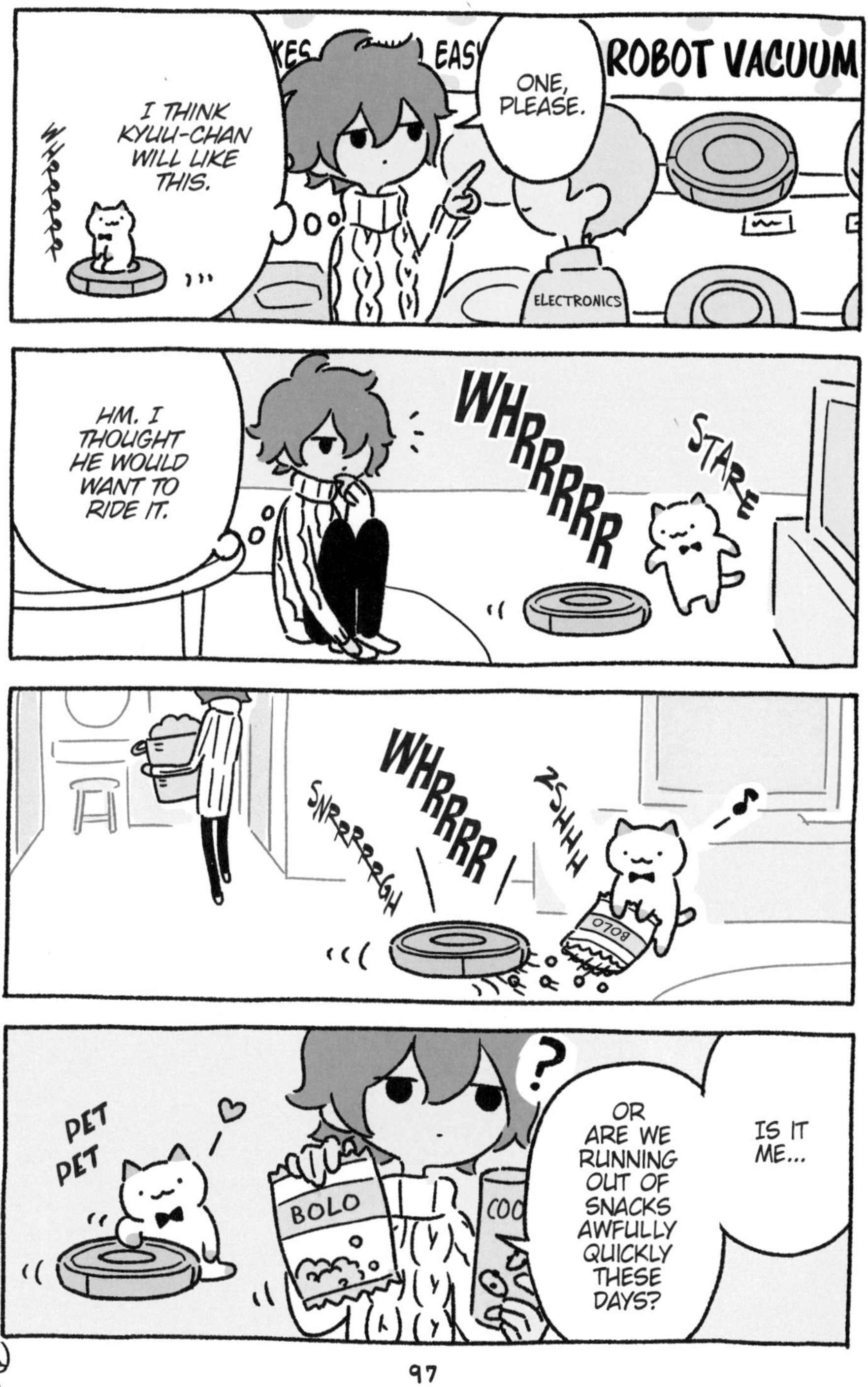
ROBOT VACUUM
ONE, PLEASE.
I THINK KYUU-CHAN WILL LIKE THIS.
WHRRRRR
ELECTRONICS
STARE
WHRRRRRR
HM. I THOUGHT HE WOULD WANT TO RIDE IT.
ZSHHH
WHRRRRR
SNRRRRRGH
BOLO
IS IT ME...
OR ARE WE RUNNING OUT OF SNACKS AWFULLY QUICKLY THESE DAYS?
BOLO
PET PET

SLEEPING BABY ART

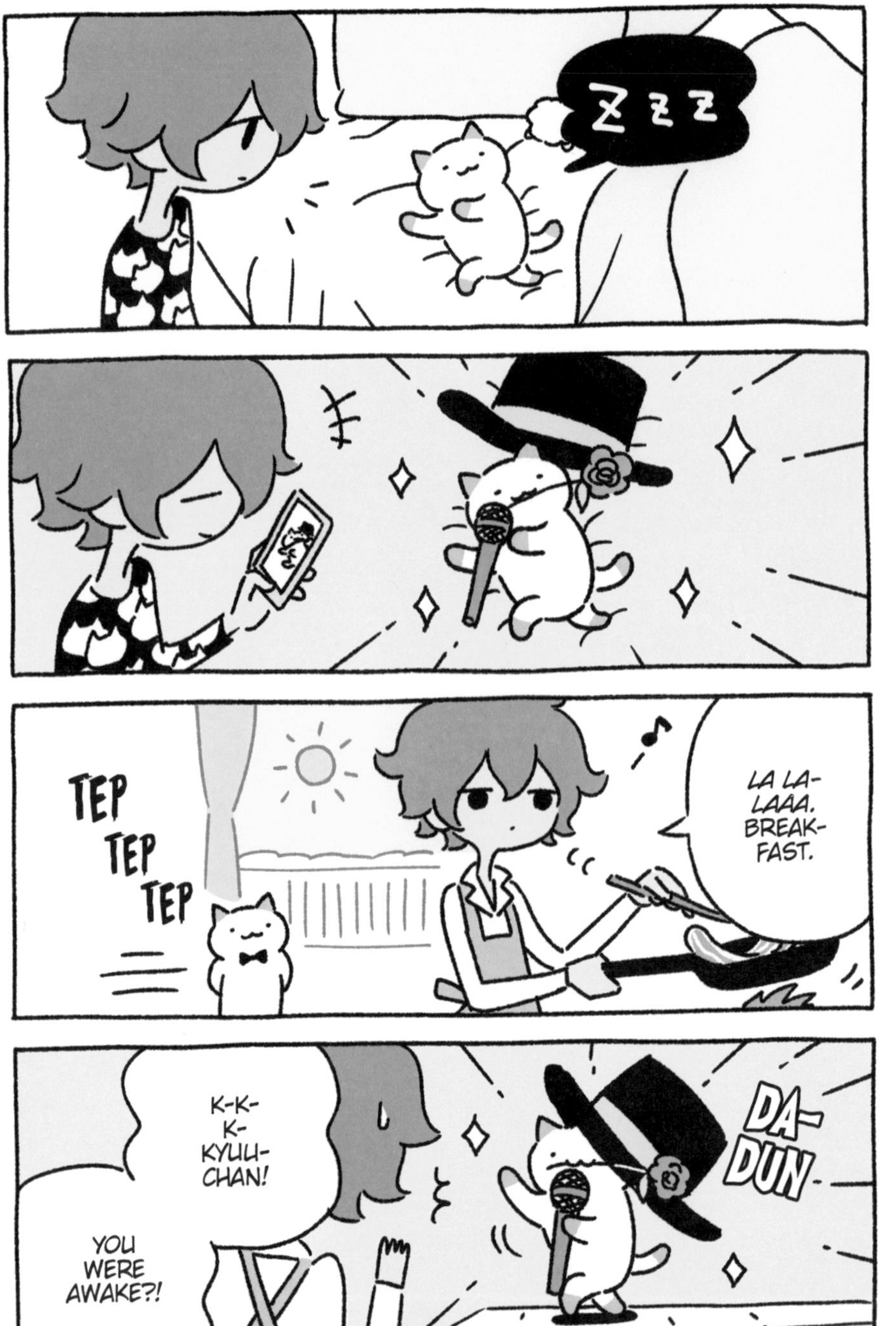
Z Z Z
LA LA-LAAA. BREAK-FAST.
TEP TEP TEP
DA-DUN
K-K-K-KYUU-CHAN!
YOU WERE AWAKE?!

BALL OF FUR

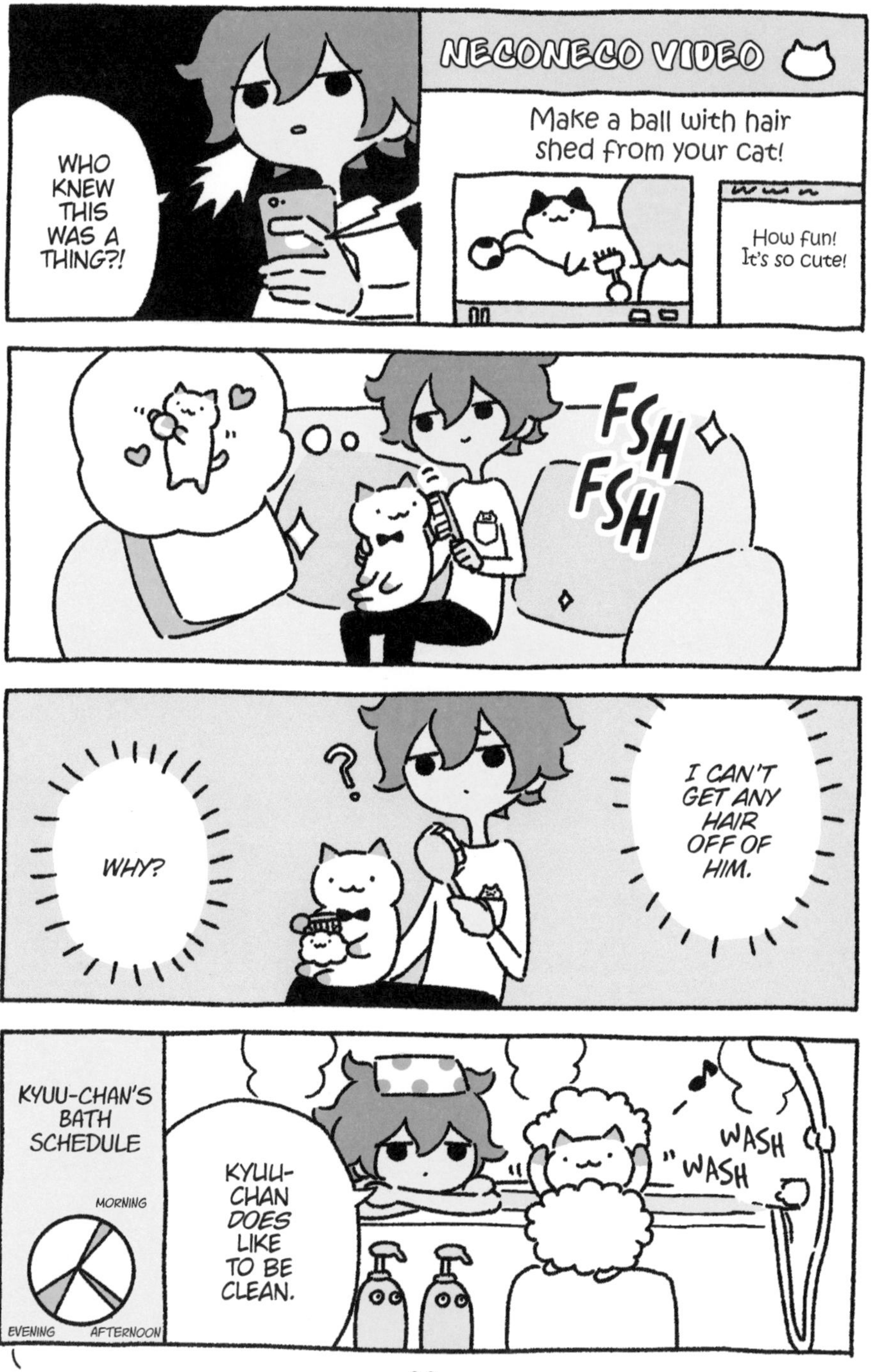
NECONECO VIDEO
Make a ball with hair shed from your cat!
How fun! It's so cute!
WHO KNEW THIS WAS A THING?!
FSH FSH
I CAN'T GET ANY HAIR OFF OF HIM.
WHY?
WASH WASH
KYUU-CHAN DOES LIKE TO BE CLEAN.
KYUU-CHAN'S BATH SCHEDULE
MORNING
EVENING
AFTERNOON

BIRD LOVER

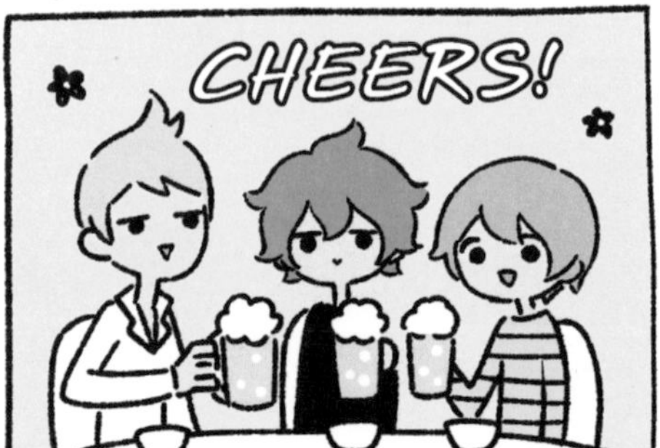
CHEERS!

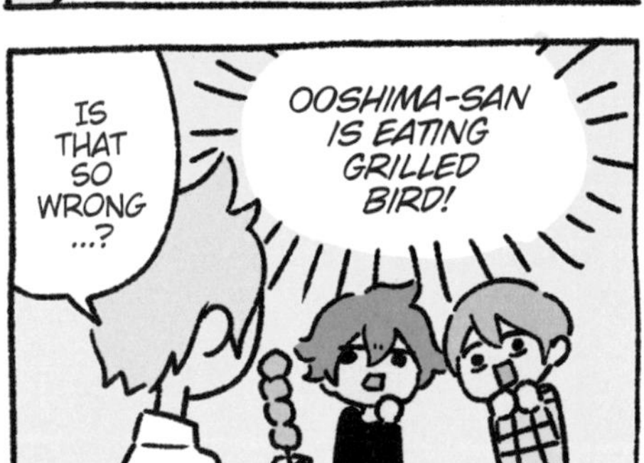
OOSHIMA-SAN IS EATING GRILLED BIRD!
IS THAT SO WRONG ...?

QUESTIONABLY HALLOWEEN

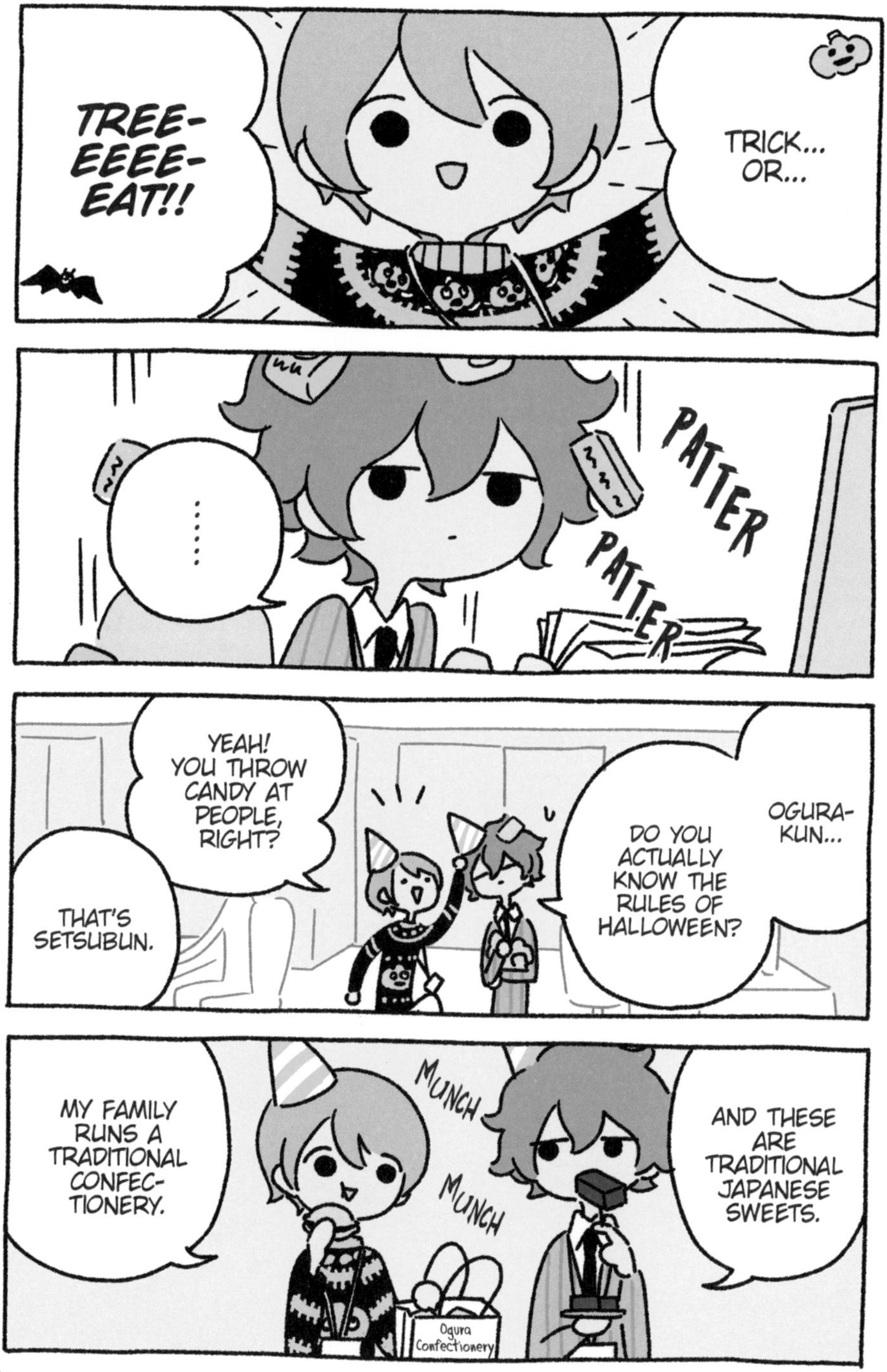
TRICK... OR...
TREE-EEEE-EAT!!
PATTER
PATTER
......
OGURA-KUN...
DO YOU ACTUALLY KNOW THE RULES OF HALLOWEEN?
YEAH! YOU THROW CANDY AT PEOPLE, RIGHT?
THAT'S SETSUBUN.
AND THESE ARE TRADITIONAL JAPANESE SWEETS.
MUNCH
MUNCH
MY FAMILY RUNS A TRADITIONAL CONFECTIONERY.
Ogura Confectionery

MISTAKEN IDENTITY

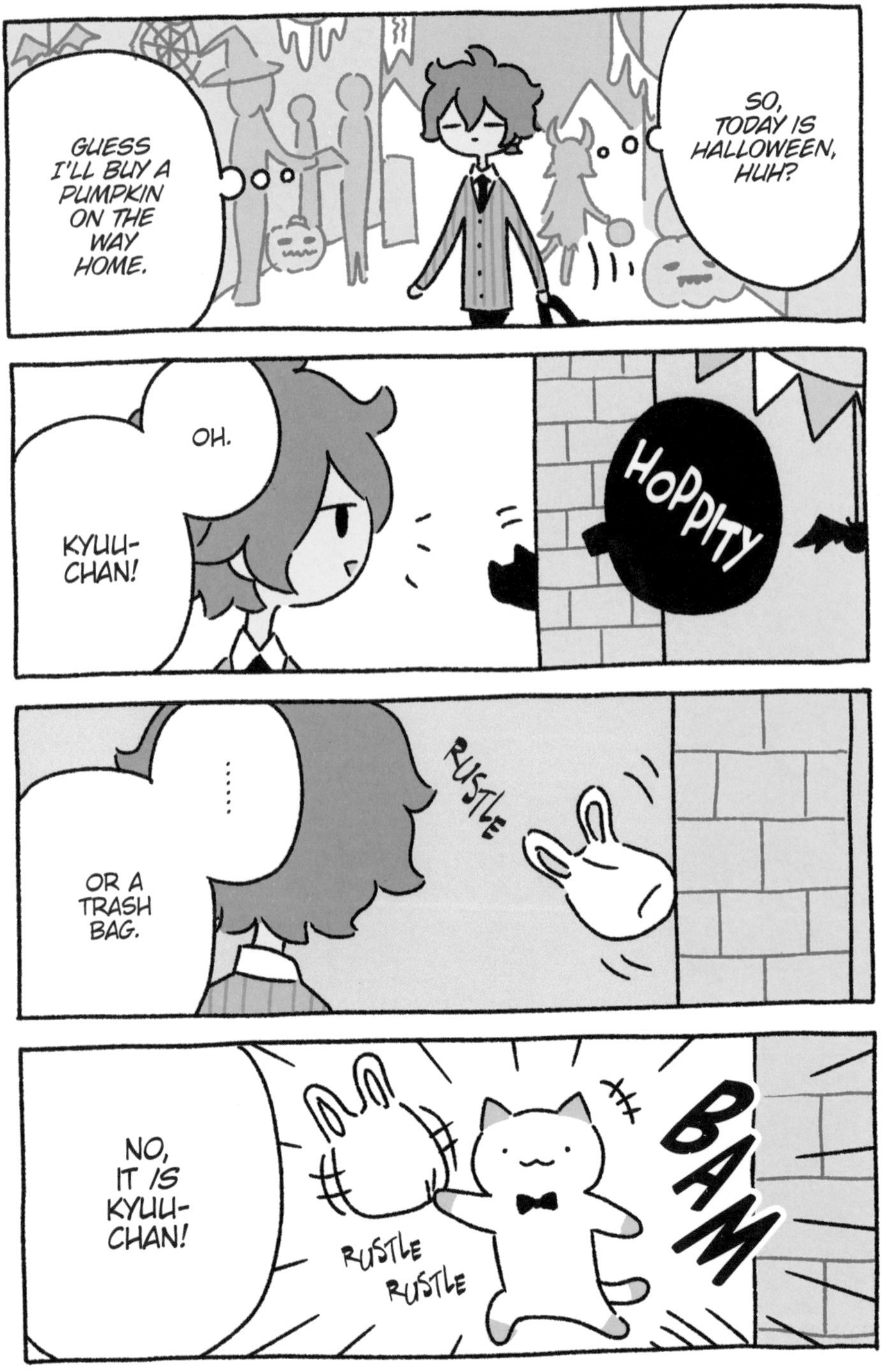
SO, TODAY IS HALLOWEEN, HUH?
GUESS I'LL BUY A PUMPKIN ON THE WAY HOME.
HOPPITY
OH.
KYUU-CHAN!
RUSTLE
......
OR A TRASH BAG.
BAM
NO, IT IS KYUU-CHAN!
RUSTLE RUSTLE

LET'S PLAY

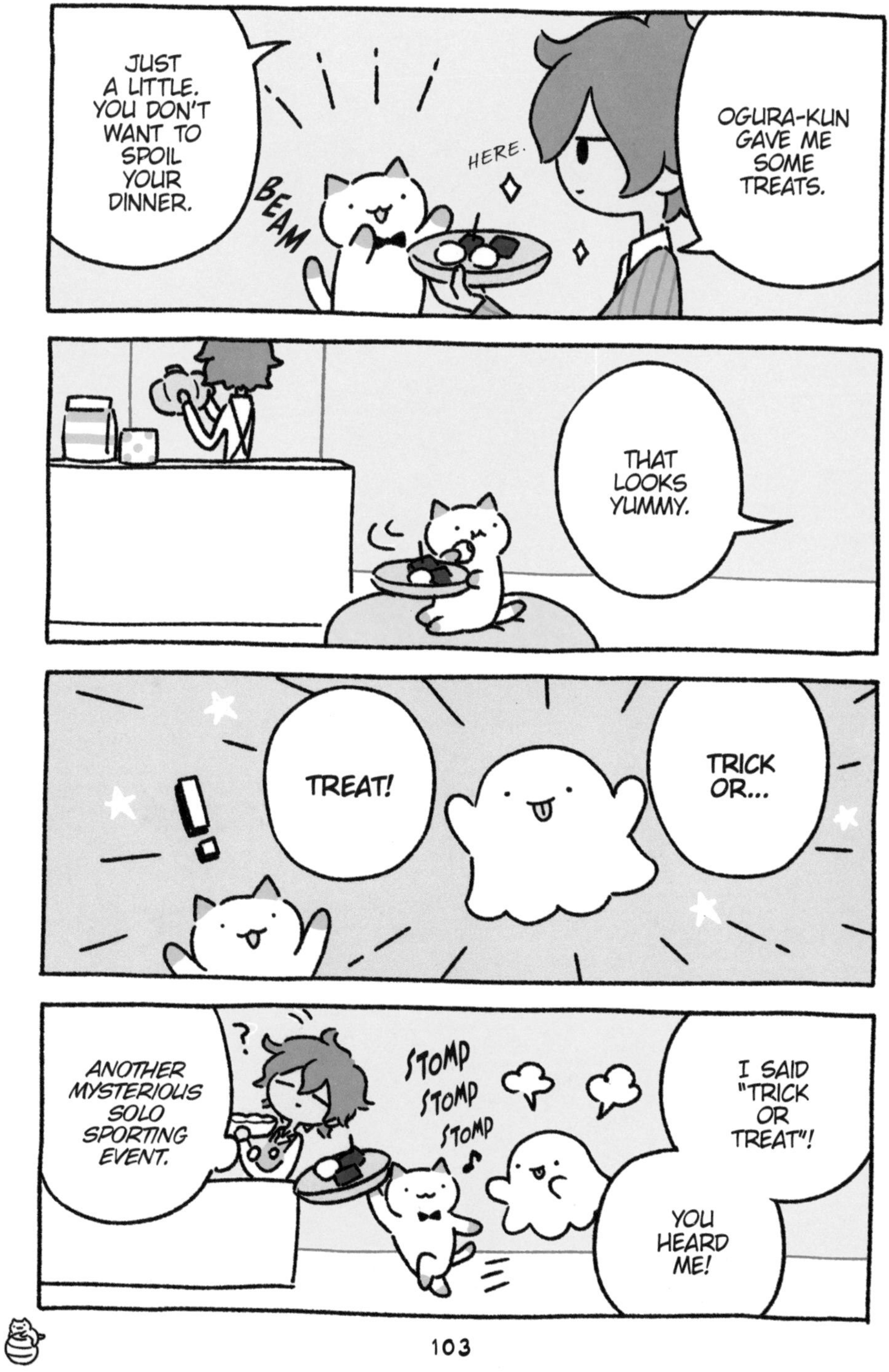
OGURA-KUN GAVE ME SOME TREATS.
HERE.
BEAM
JUST A LITTLE. YOU DON'T WANT TO SPOIL YOUR DINNER.
THAT LOOKS YUMMY.
TRICK OR...
TREAT!
I SAID "TRICK OR TREAT"!
YOU HEARD ME!
STOMP
STOMP
STOMP
ANOTHER MYSTERIOUS SOLO SPORTING EVENT.

LEAVE IT TO ME

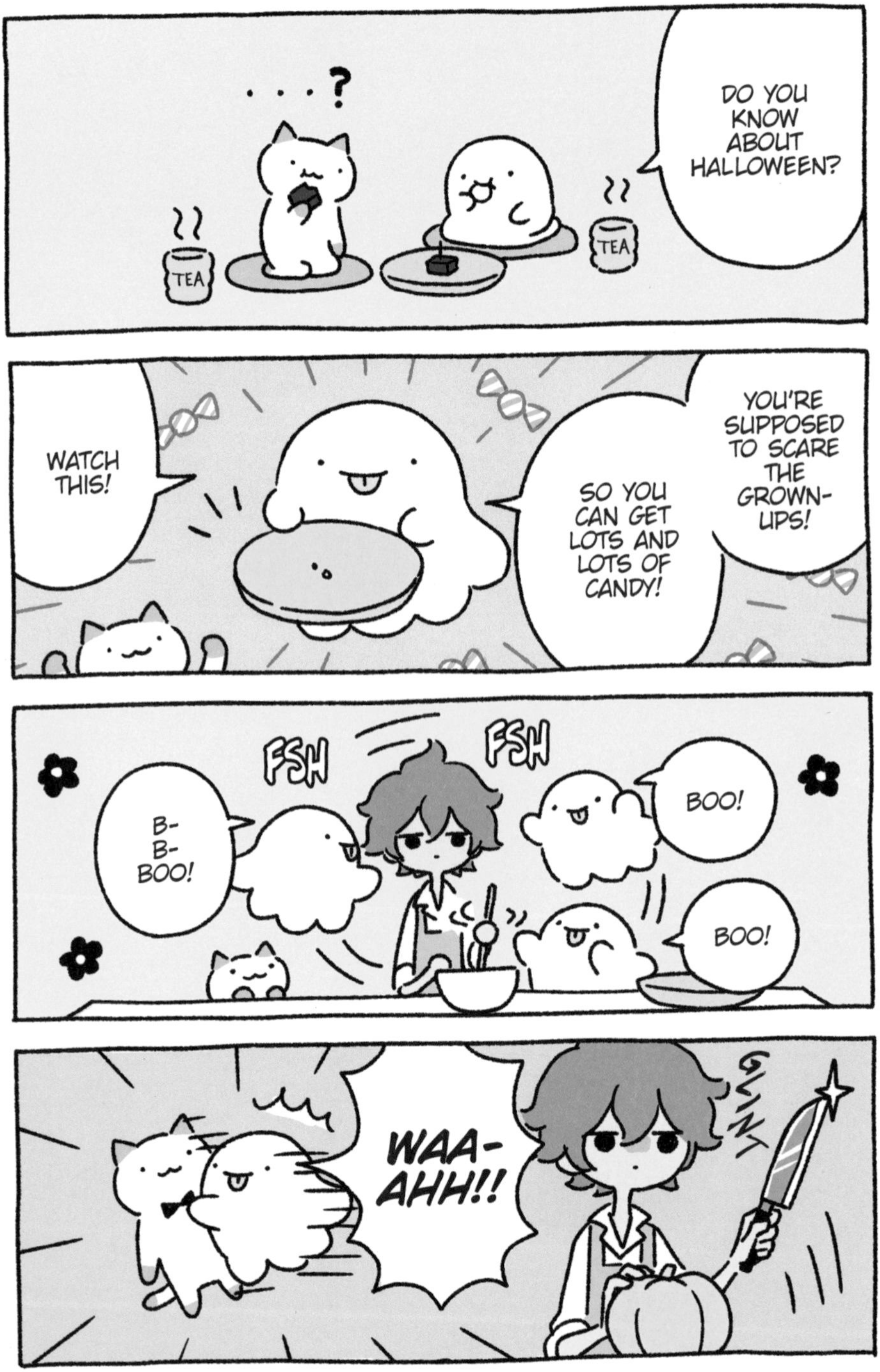
DO YOU KNOW ABOUT HALLOWEEN?
. . . ?
TEA
TEA
YOU'RE SUPPOSED TO SCARE THE GROWN-UPS!
SO YOU CAN GET LOTS AND LOTS OF CANDY!
WATCH THIS!
FSH
BOO!
BOO!
FSH
B- B- BOO!
GLINT
WAA-AHH!!

HEADLINER

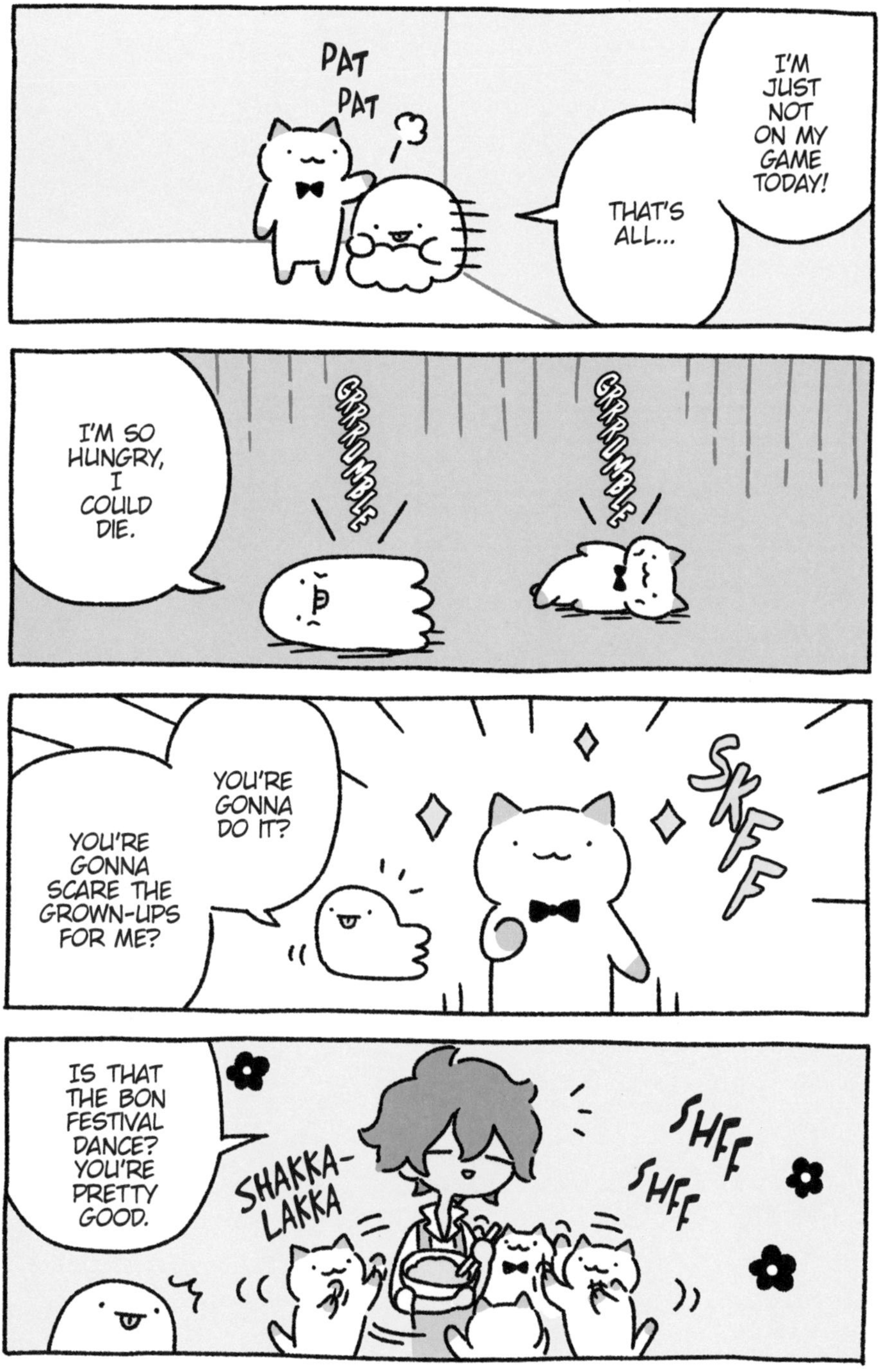
I'M JUST NOT ON MY GAME TODAY!
PAT PAT
THAT'S ALL...
GRRRUMBLE
GRRRUMBLE
I'M SO HUNGRY, I COULD DIE.
SKFF
YOU'RE GONNA DO IT?
YOU'RE GONNA SCARE THE GROWN-UPS FOR ME?
SHFF SHFF
SHAKKA-LAKKA
IS THAT THE BON FESTIVAL DANCE? YOU'RE PRETTY GOOD.

COSTUMES

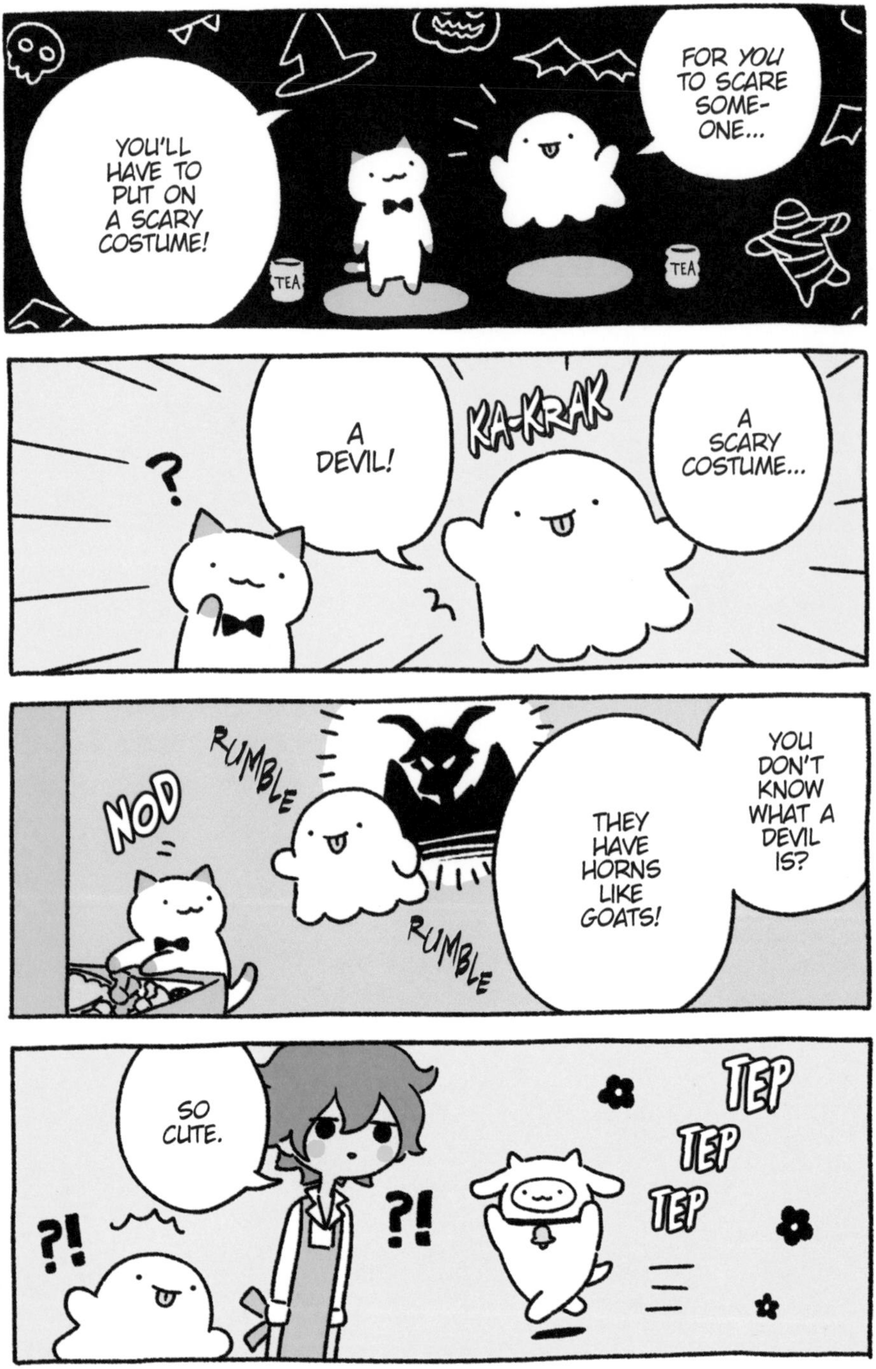
FOR YOU TO SCARE SOME-ONE...
YOU'LL HAVE TO PUT ON A SCARY COSTUME!
TEA
TEA
A SCARY COSTUME...
KA-KRAK
A DEVIL!
?
YOU DON'T KNOW WHAT A DEVIL IS?
THEY HAVE HORNS LIKE GOATS!
RUMBLE
RUMBLE
NOD
TEP
TEP
TEP
?!
SO CUTE.
?!

I CAN'T HAVE ANY?

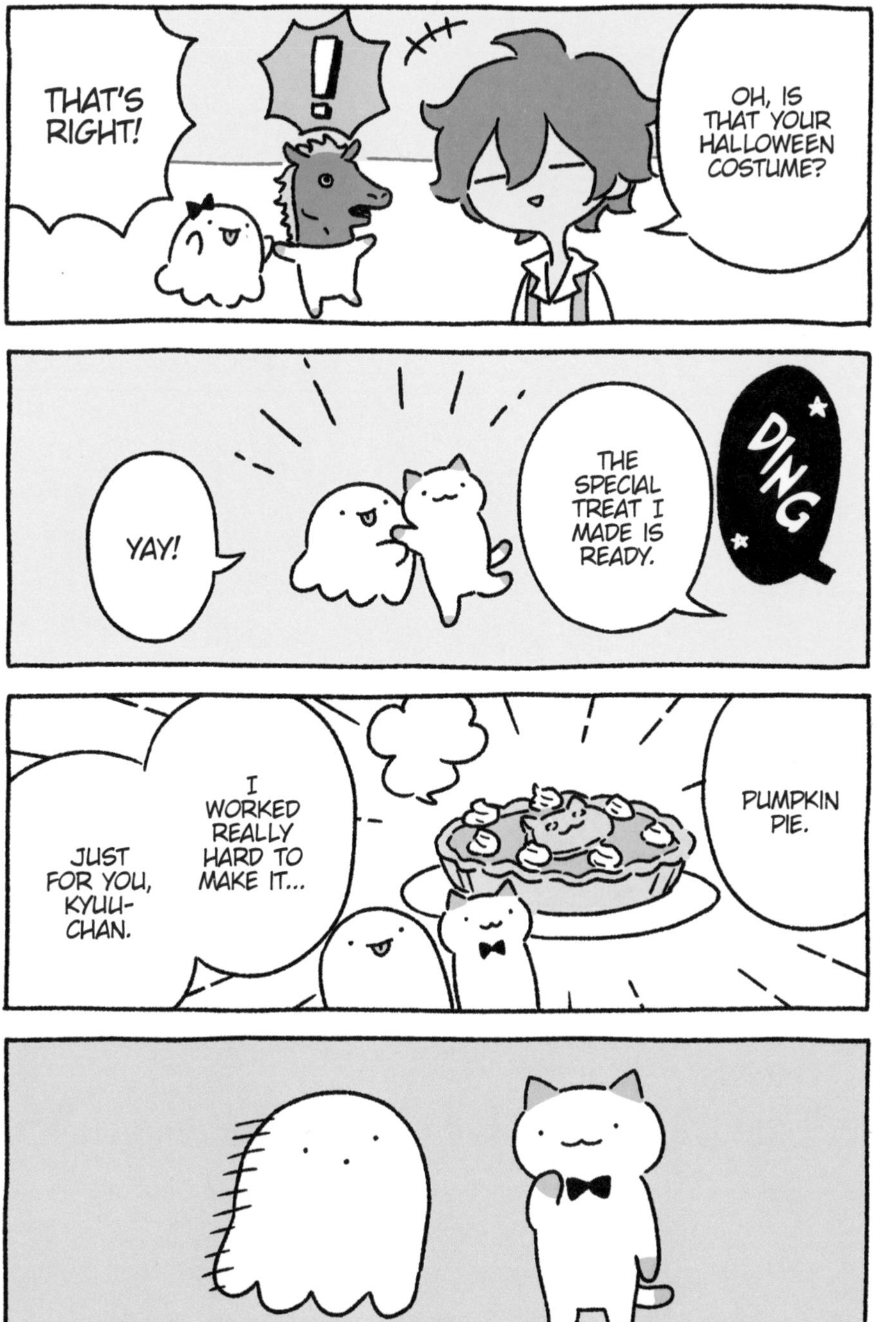
OH, IS THAT YOUR HALLOWEEN COSTUME?
THAT'S RIGHT!
DING
THE SPECIAL TREAT I MADE IS READY.
YAY!
PUMPKIN PIE.
I WORKED REALLY HARD TO MAKE IT...
JUST FOR YOU, KYUU-CHAN.

PARTY

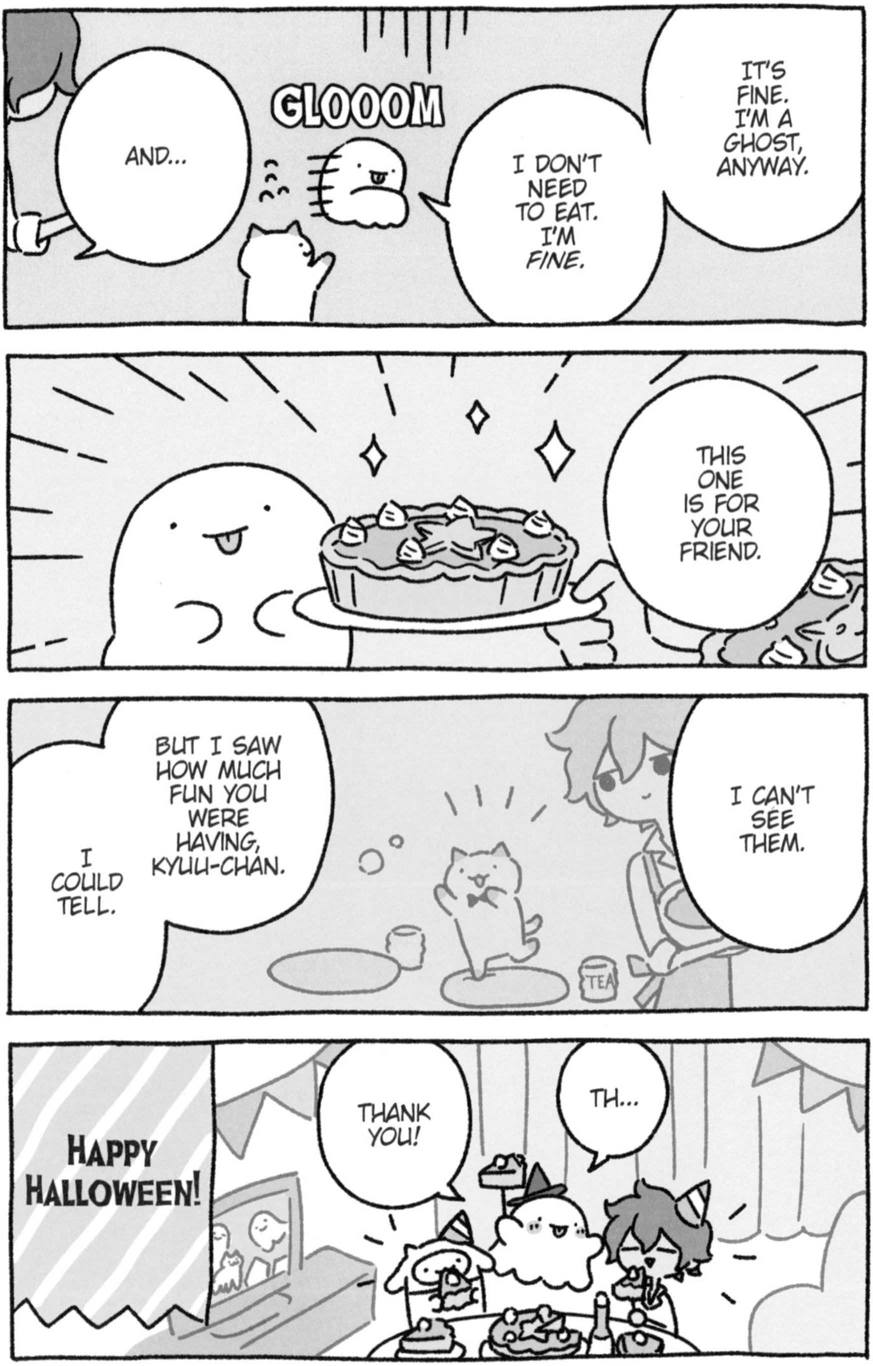
IT'S FINE. I'M A GHOST, ANYWAY.
I DON'T NEED TO EAT. I'M *FINE.*
GLOOOM
AND...
THIS ONE IS FOR YOUR FRIEND.
I CAN'T SEE THEM.
BUT I SAW HOW MUCH FUN YOU WERE HAVING, KYUU-CHAN.
I COULD TELL.
TH...
THANK YOU!
HAPPY HALLOWEEN!
TEA

NEZUMI-KUN

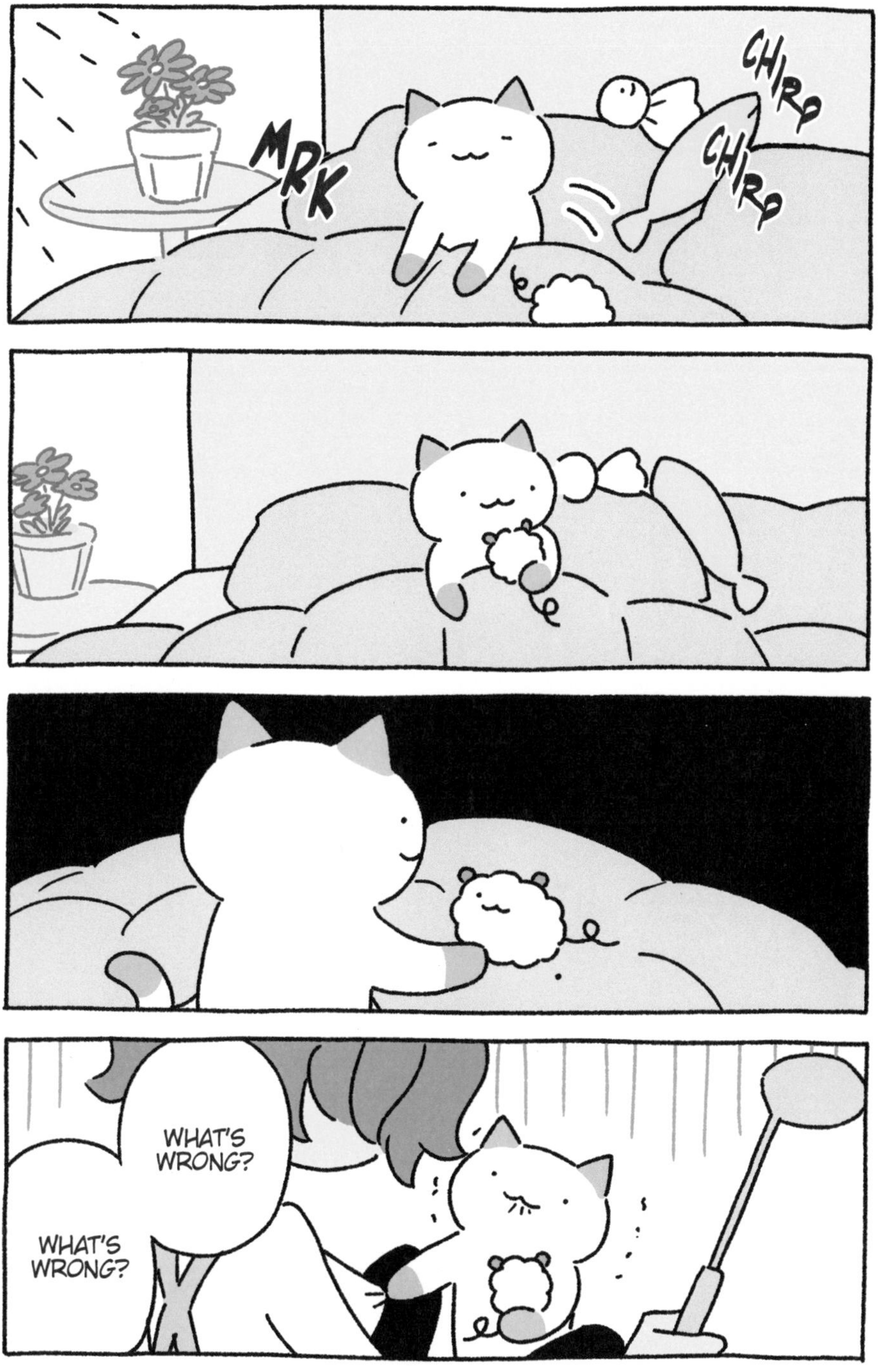
CHIRP
CHIRP
MRK
WHAT'S WRONG?
WHAT'S WRONG?

THE DOCTOR

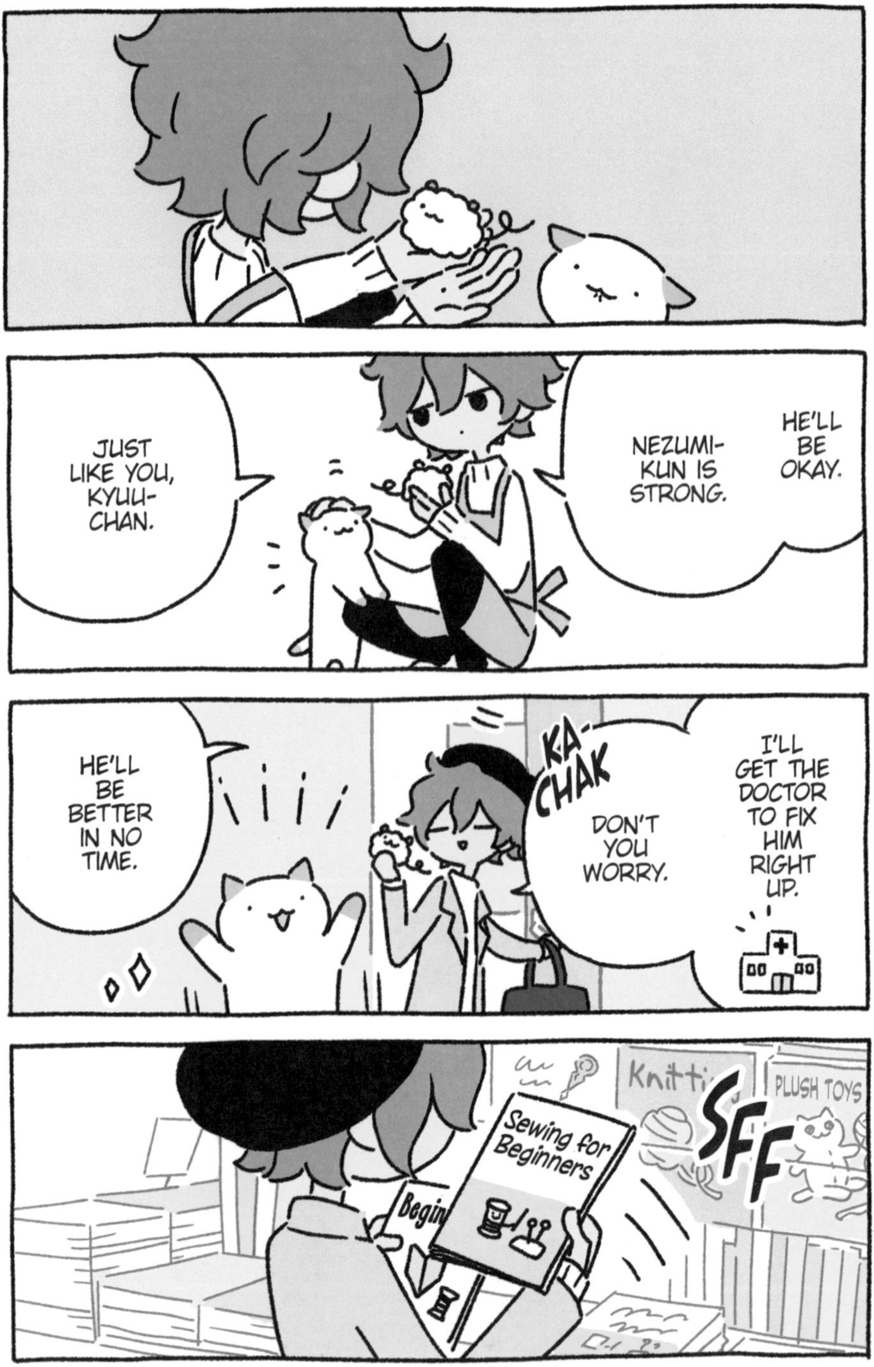
HE'LL BE OKAY.
NEZUMI-KUN IS STRONG.
JUST LIKE YOU, KYUU-CHAN.
I'LL GET THE DOCTOR TO FIX HIM RIGHT UP.
DON'T YOU WORRY.
KA-CHAK
HE'LL BE BETTER IN NO TIME.
PLUSH TOYS
SFF
Sewing for Beginners

SURGERY

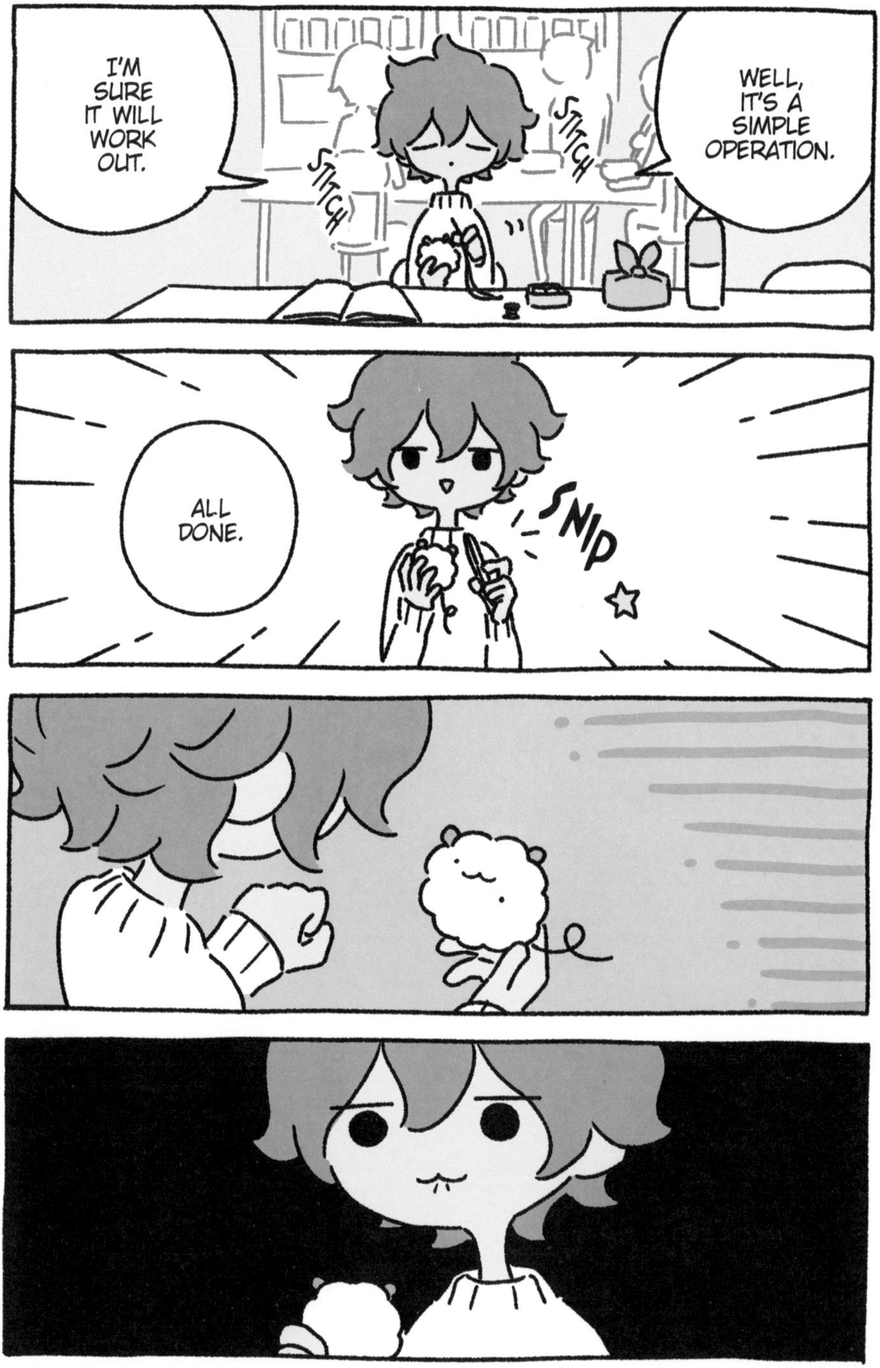
WELL, IT'S A SIMPLE OPERATION.
STITCH
STITCH
I'M SURE IT WILL WORK OUT.
SNIP
ALL DONE.

IN FRONT OF THE OFFICE

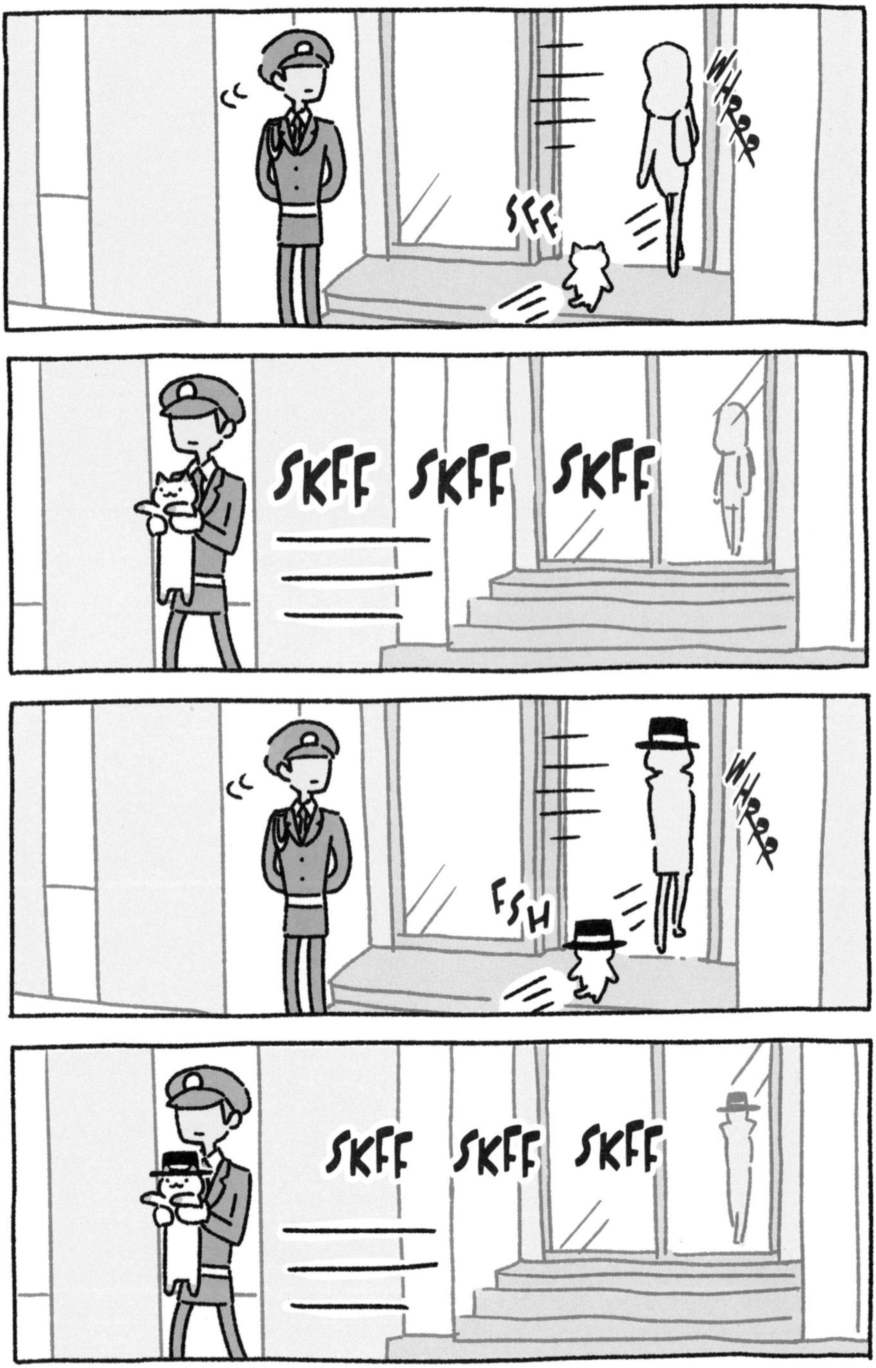
WHRRR
SFF
SKFF SKFF SKFF
WHRRR
FSH
SKFF SKFF SKFF

JEALOUS

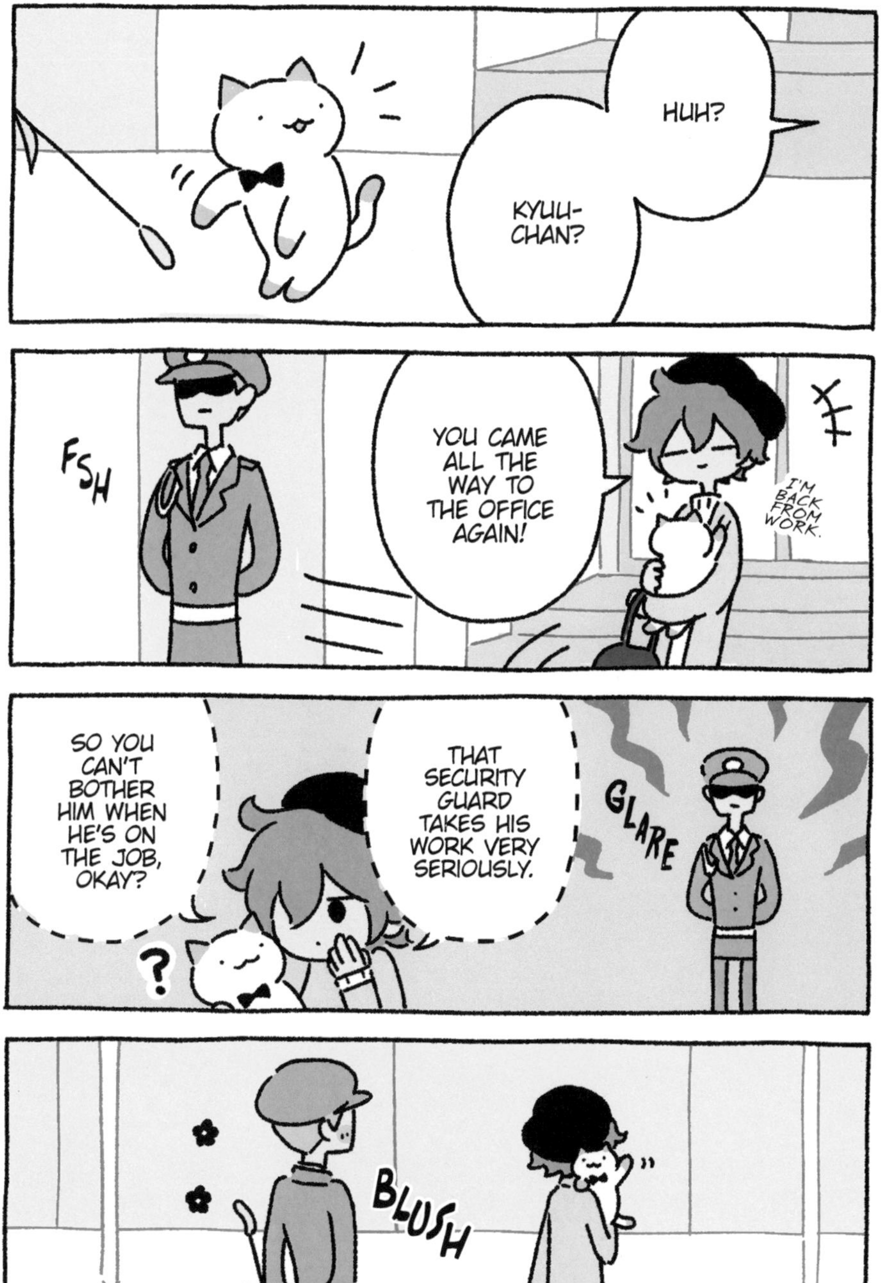
HUH?
KYUU-CHAN?
I'M BACK FROM WORK.
YOU CAME ALL THE WAY TO THE OFFICE AGAIN!
FSH
GLARE
THAT SECURITY GUARD TAKES HIS WORK VERY SERIOUSLY.
SO YOU CAN'T BOTHER HIM WHEN HE'S ON THE JOB, OKAY?
?
BLUSH

HUG x2

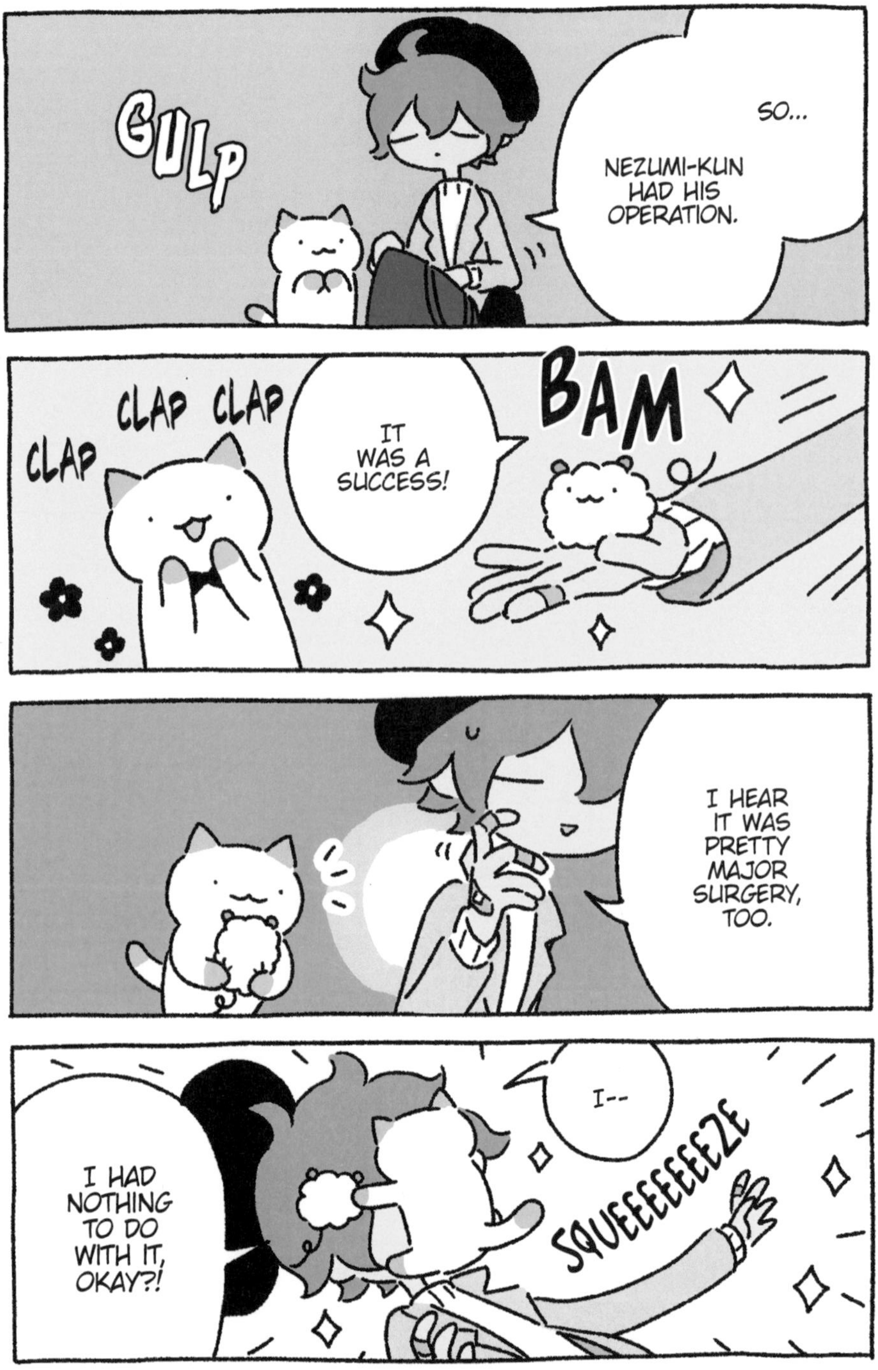
SO...
NEZUMI-KUN HAD HIS OPERATION.
GULP
BAM
IT WAS A SUCCESS!
CLAP CLAP
CLAP
I HEAR IT WAS PRETTY MAJOR SURGERY, TOO.
I--
SQUEEEEEEEEZE
I HAD NOTHING TO DO WITH IT, OKAY?!

BEATING THE COLD

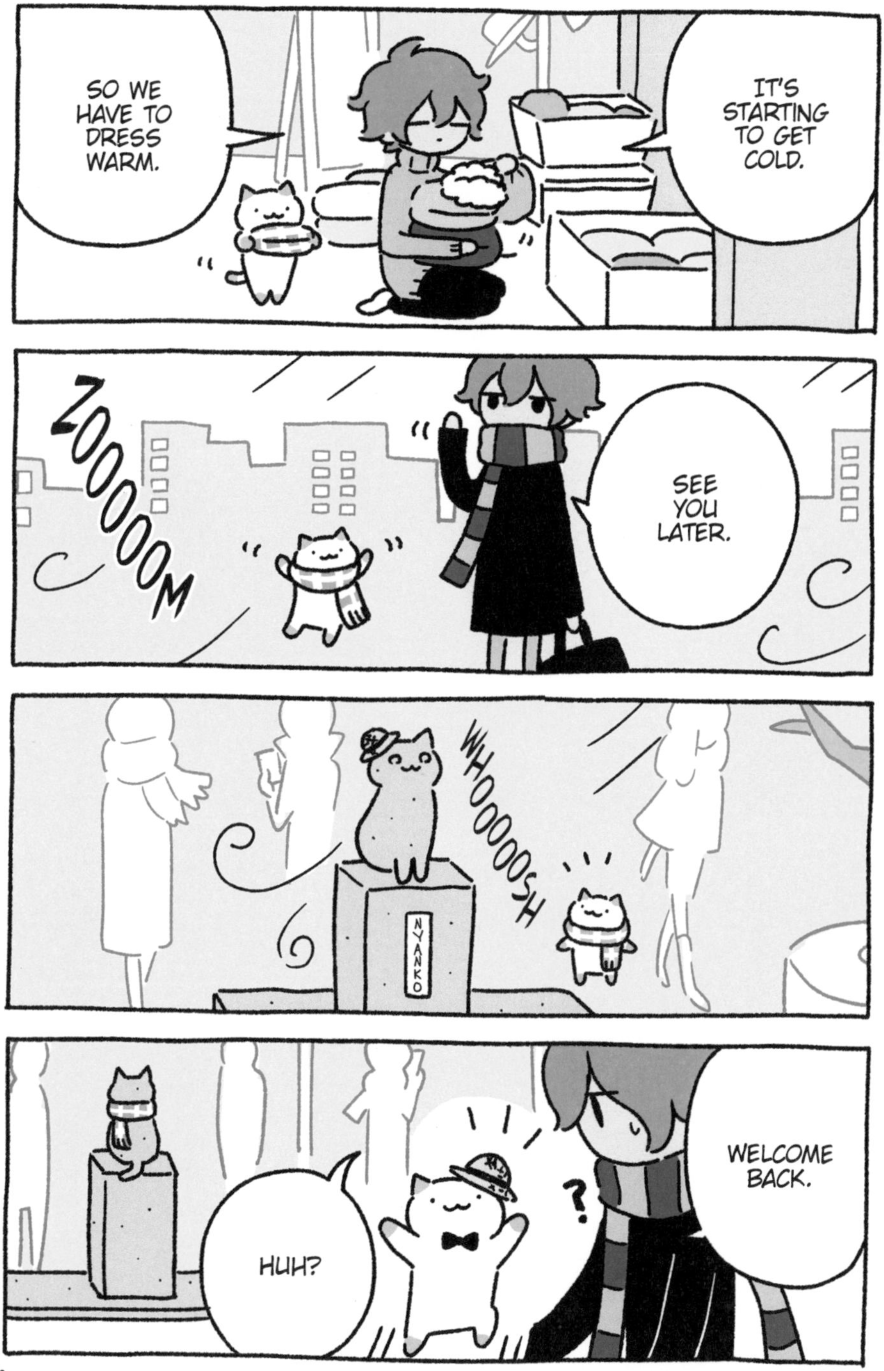
IT'S STARTING TO GET COLD.
SO WE HAVE TO DRESS WARM.
SEE YOU LATER.
ZOOOOOM
WHOOOOOSH
NYANKO
WELCOME BACK.
?
HUH?

FIRST SNOW

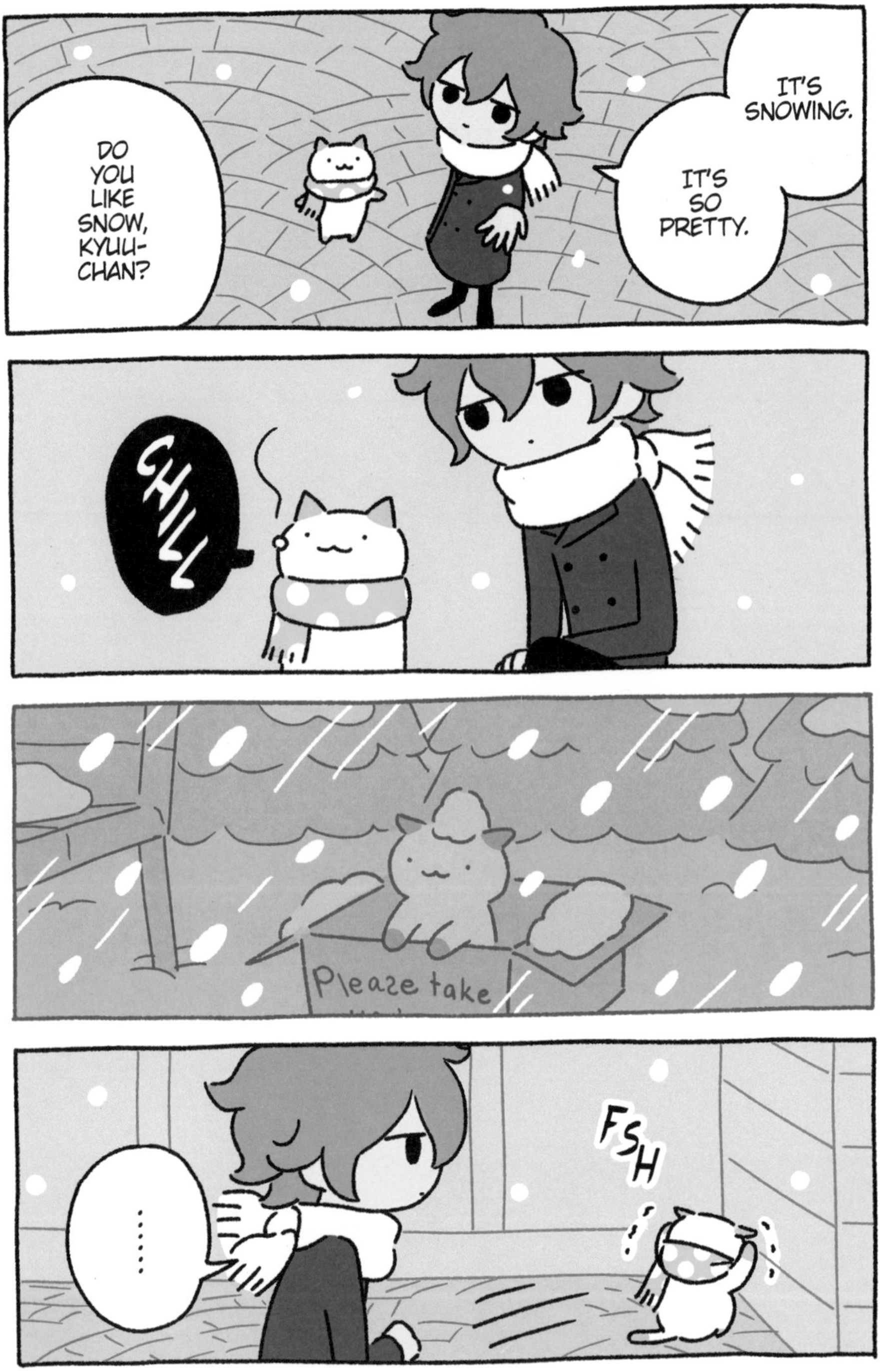
IT'S SNOWING.
IT'S SO PRETTY.
DO YOU LIKE SNOW, KYUU-CHAN?
CHILL
Please take
FSH
......

TOGETHER

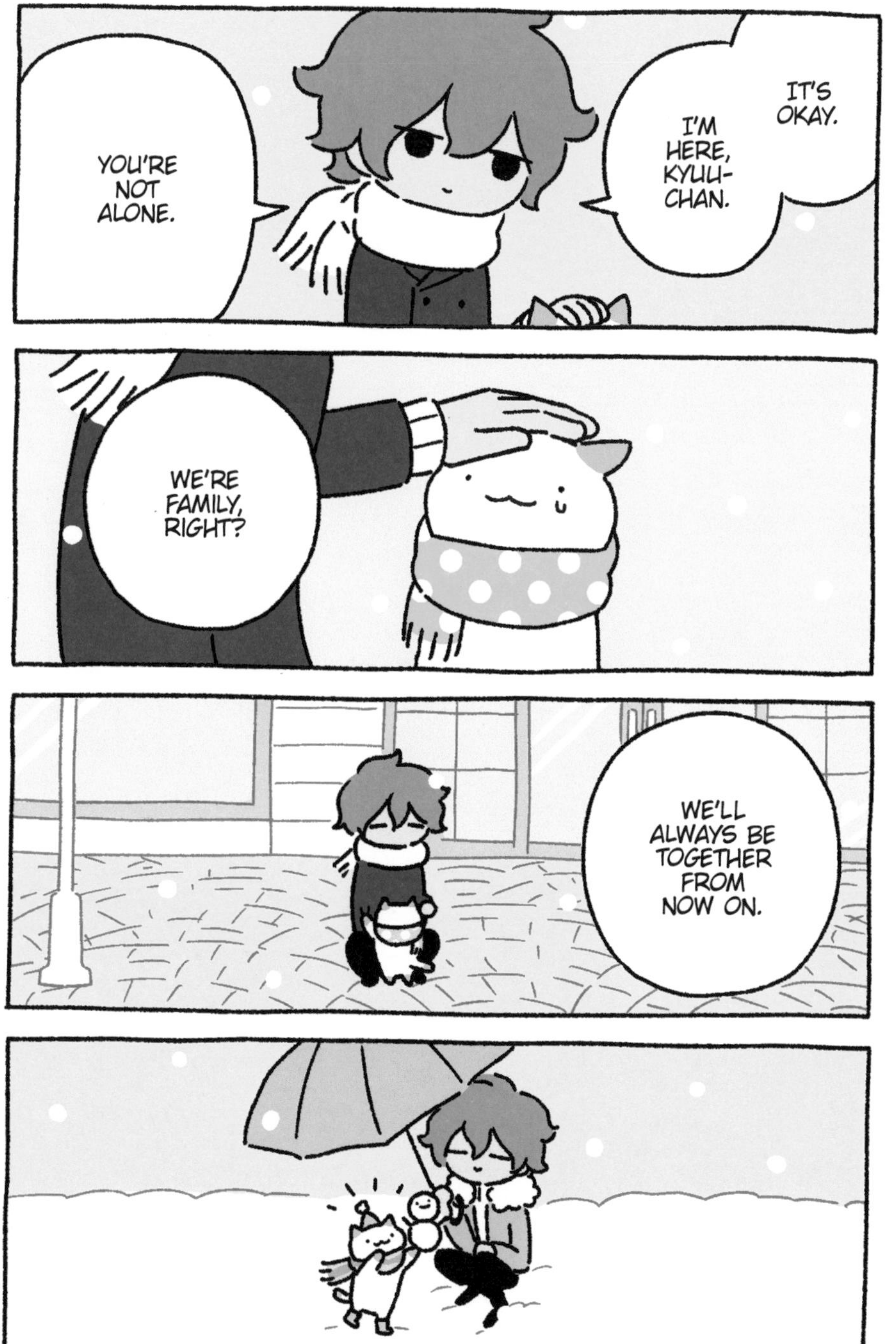
IT'S OKAY.
I'M HERE, KYUU-CHAN.
YOU'RE NOT ALONE.
WE'RE FAMILY, RIGHT?
WE'LL ALWAYS BE TOGETHER FROM NOW ON.

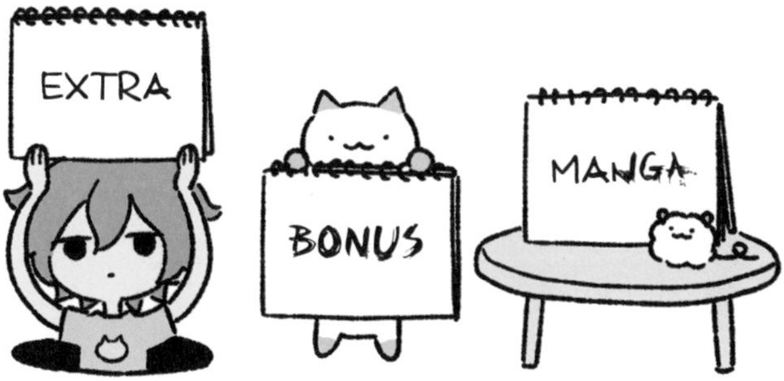
EXTRA
BONUS
MANGA

THE NIGHT BEFORE

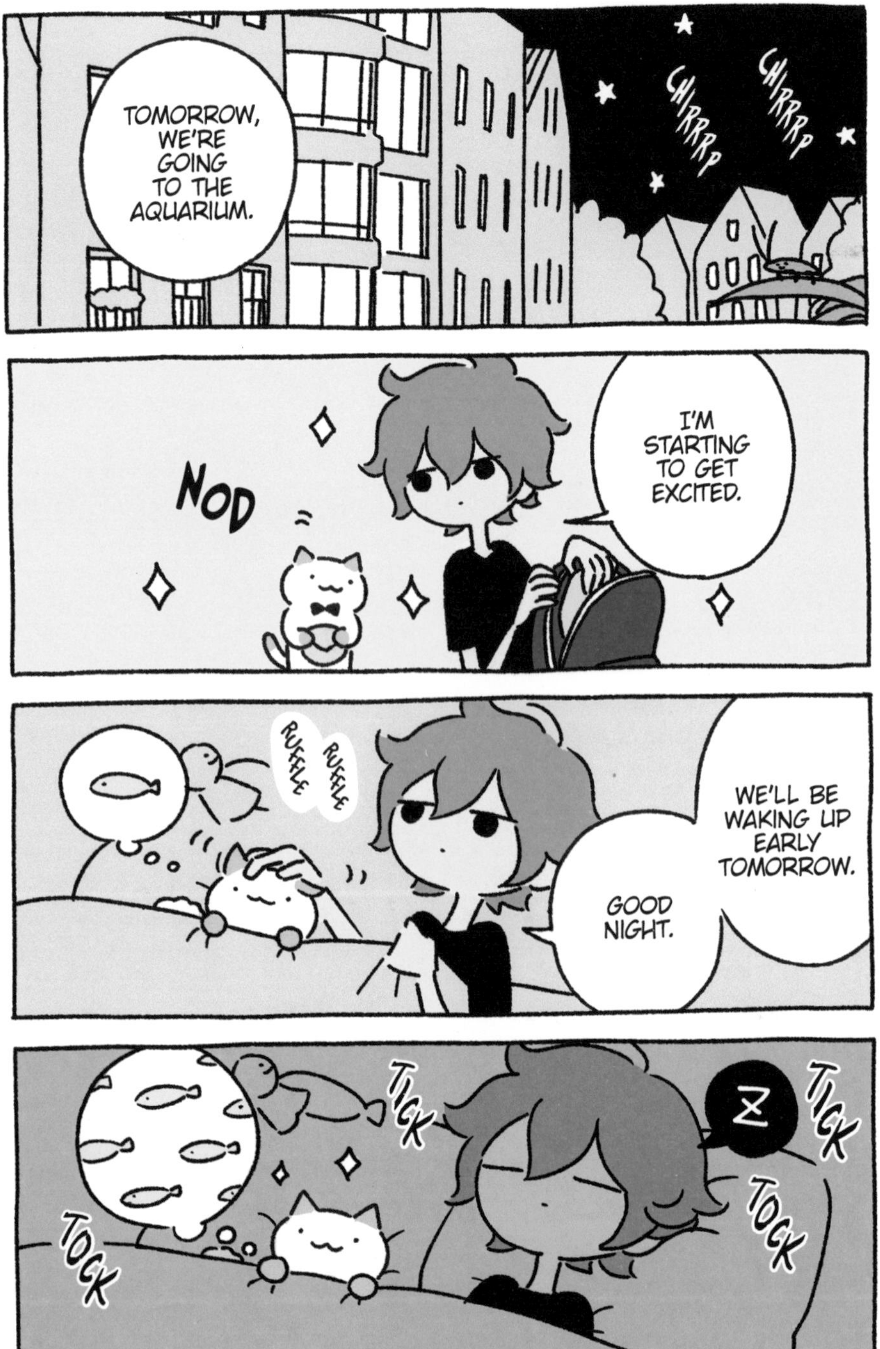
CHIRRRP
CHIRRRP
TOMORROW, WE'RE GOING TO THE AQUARIUM.
I'M STARTING TO GET EXCITED.
NOD
WE'LL BE WAKING UP EARLY TOMORROW.
GOOD NIGHT.
RUFFLE
RUFFLE
TICK
Z
TOCK
TICK
TOCK

NOT ASLEEP

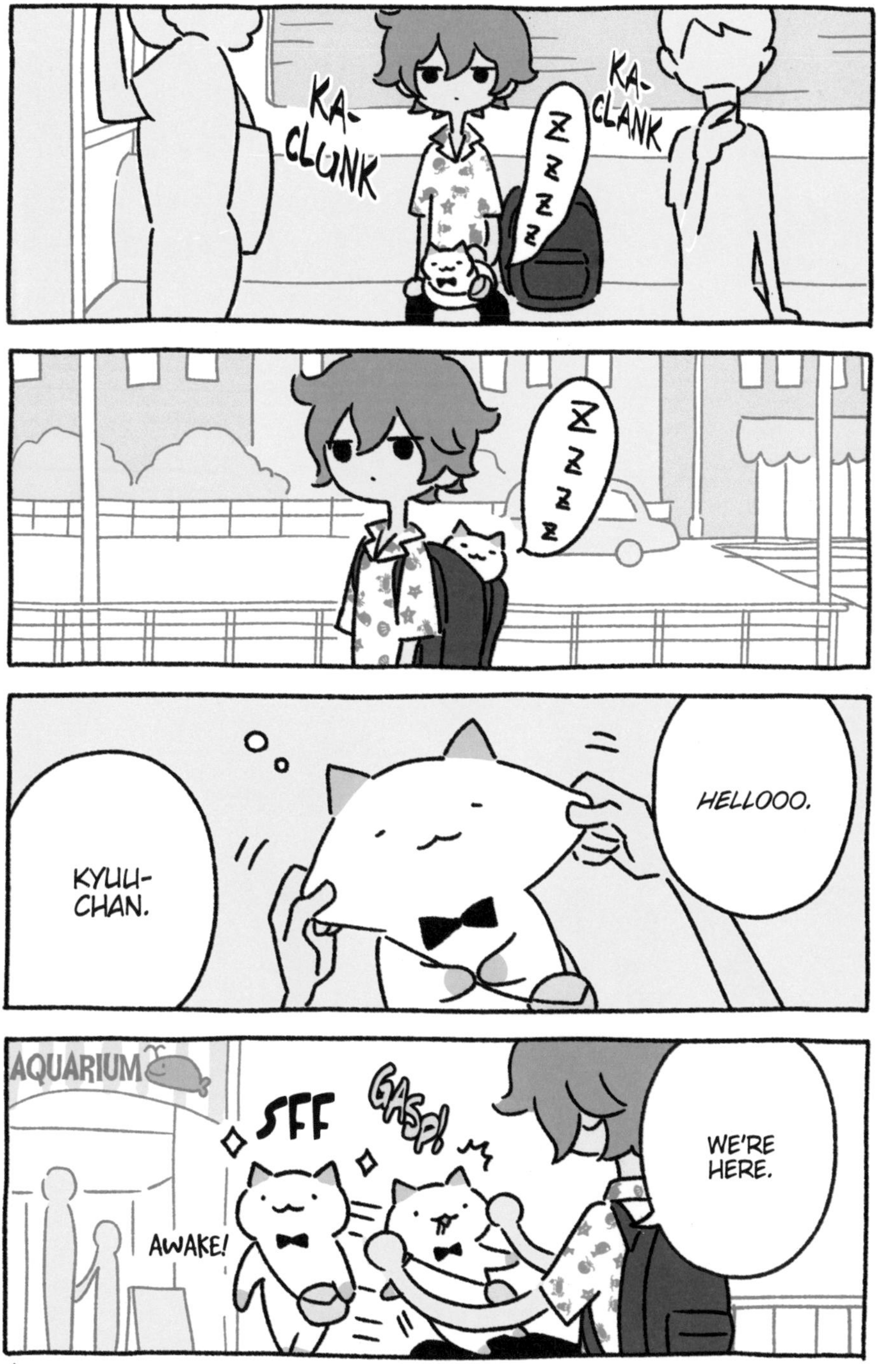
KA-CLANK
ZZZZZ
KA-CLUNK
ZZZZZ
HELLOOO.
KYUU-CHAN.
WE'RE HERE.
GASP!
AQUARIUM
SFF
AWAKE!

WHERE'S THE FISH?

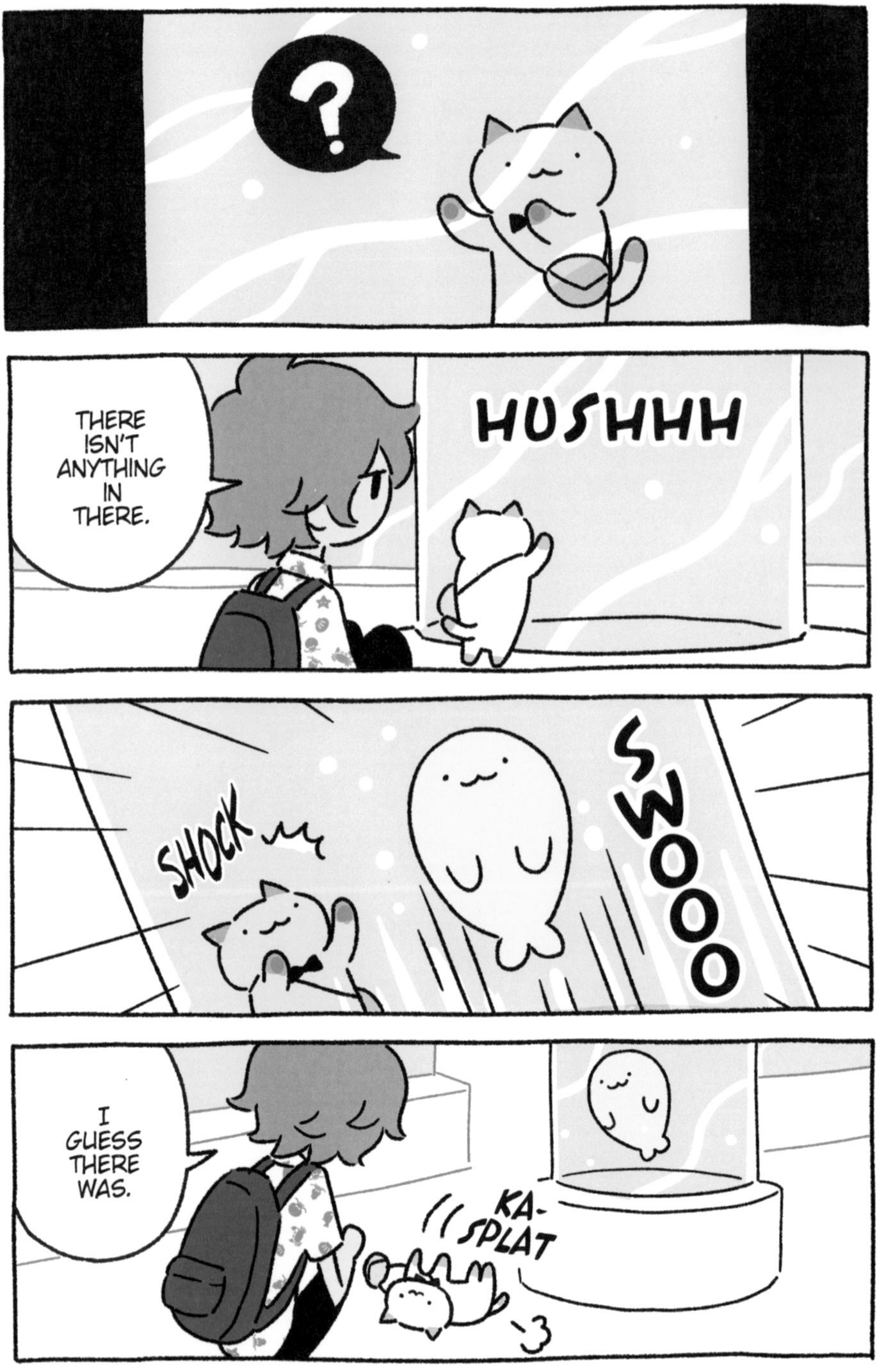
?
HUSHHH
THERE ISN'T ANYTHING IN THERE.
SWOOO
SHOCK
KA-SPLAT
I GUESS THERE WAS.

JAW DROPPING

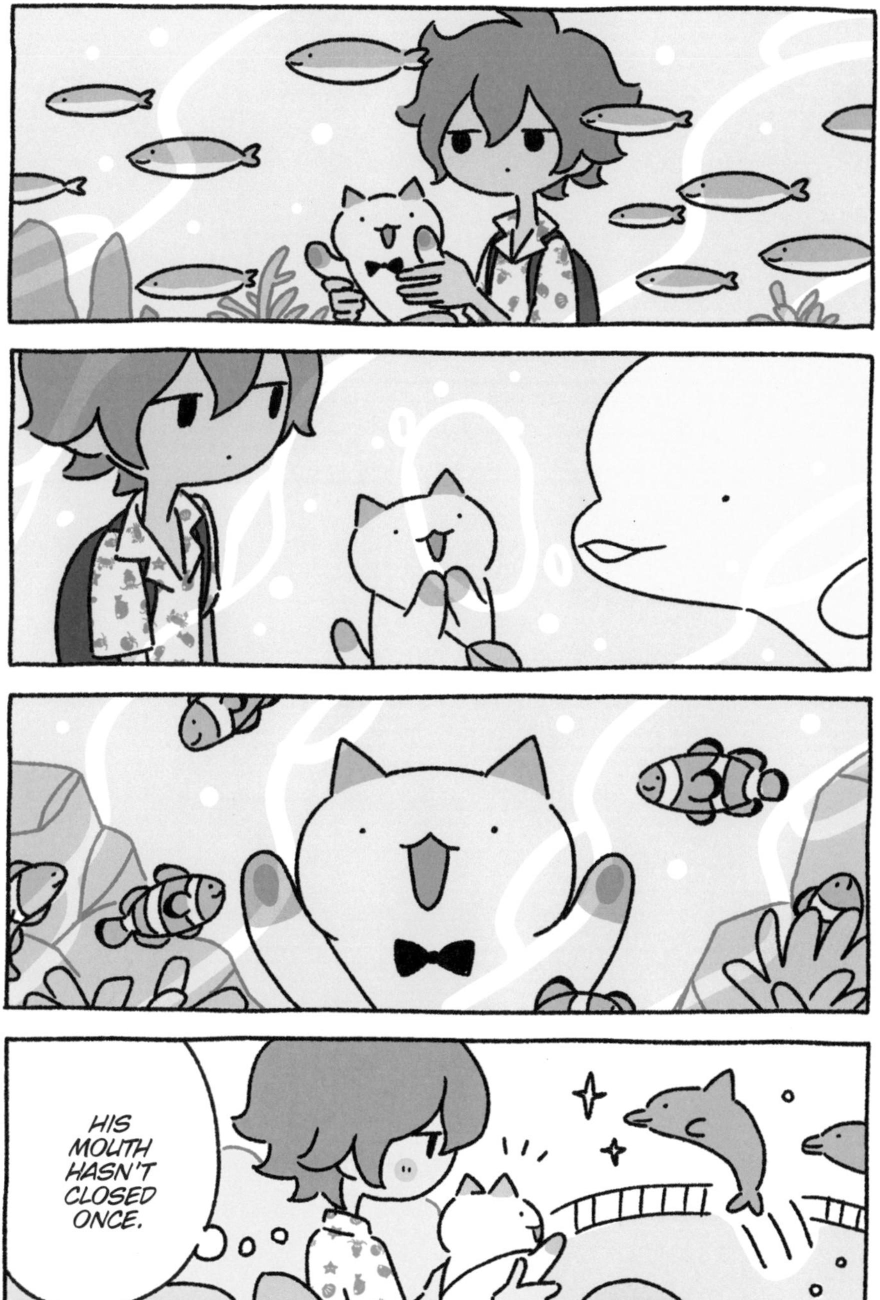
HIS MOUTH HASN'T CLOSED ONCE.

NUMBER ONE

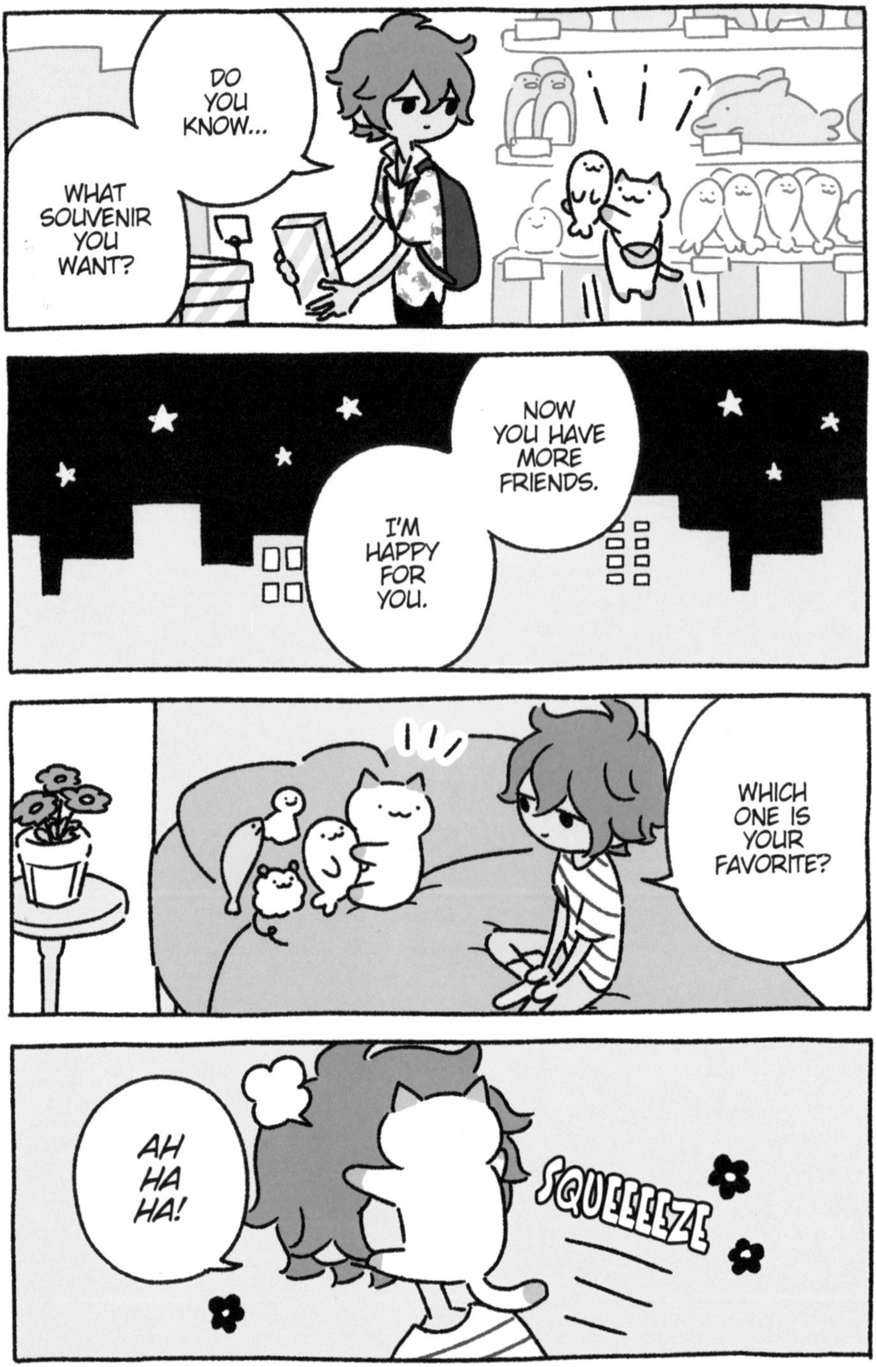
DO YOU KNOW...
WHAT SOUVENIR YOU WANT?
NOW YOU HAVE MORE FRIENDS.
I'M HAPPY FOR YOU.
WHICH ONE IS YOUR FAVORITE?
SQUEEEEEZE
AH HA HA!

SOUVENIR STORY

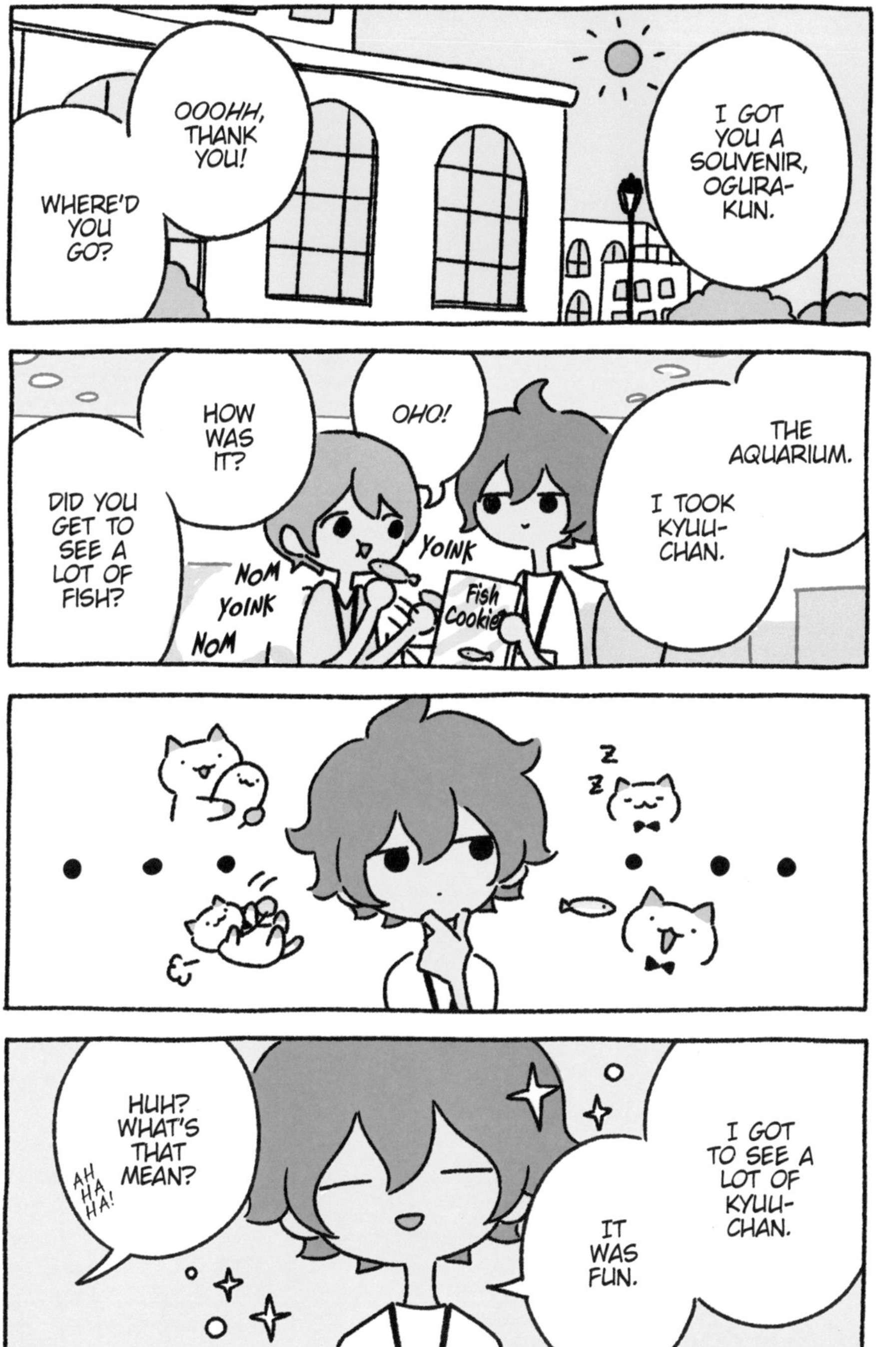

I GOT YOU A SOUVENIR, OGURA-KUN.
OOOHH, THANK YOU!
WHERE'D YOU GO?
THE AQUARIUM.
I TOOK KYUU-CHAN.
OHO!
HOW WAS IT?
YOINK
Fish Cookie
NOM
YOINK
NOM
DID YOU GET TO SEE A LOT OF FISH?
I GOT TO SEE A LOT OF KYUU-CHAN.
IT WAS FUN.
HUH? WHAT'S THAT MEAN?
AH HA HA!

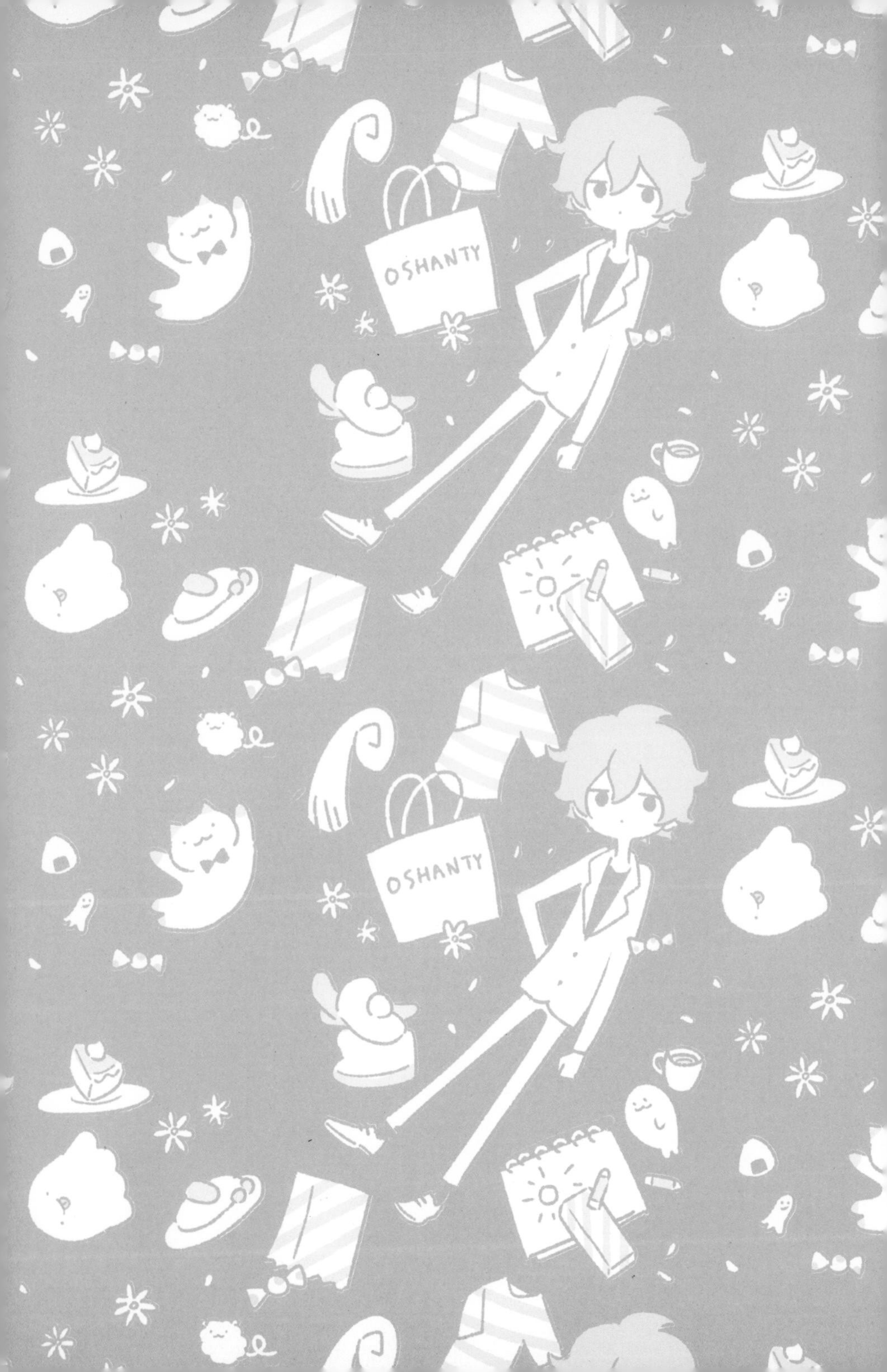
OSHANTY
OSHANTY